The
Judgment Line

David E. Weisenborn

ISBN-10: 0615716369
EAN-13: 9780615716367
Library of Congress Control Number: 2012919655
CreateSpace Independent Publishing Platform
North Charleston, South Carolina

The
Judgment Line

*This novel is dedicated to Janet,
my wife for the last 51 years. She worked
tirelessly to eliminate my numerous grammatical
and spelling errors as well as assuming the role
of first editor. If this book succeeds, it will be in
large part to her efforts. I love her.*

David E. Weisenborn was born in Ohio but has lived in Georgia for many years. He is a retired professor of Agricultural Economics, and has authored or co-authored a wide variety of technical articles. He also served overseas with the Agency for International Development, working in the agricultural sectors of Bolivia, El Salvador, and West Africa. He ended his teaching career at Georgia Southern University. He is married to Janet, and they have two children and four grandchildren. This is his first novel.

one

It was late Wednesday morning July 30, 2015. I was just leaving the Carter County Courthouse after checking on a piece of property I hoped to purchase for my latest housing development project. Nodding to Buck Ingram, the Chairman of the County Commission, I walked out the door onto the portico and paused to adjust to the sweltering South Georgia summer heat. The secretary from the title office came out and smiled at me and said, "It's another hot one, Jack."

I smiled, reflecting on how hot she looked that morning, pun intended. Linda was about 25 and was dressed in a lightweight, sleeveless flowered blouse and thin white slacks. Her peaches and cream skin, natural blond hair, and drop-dead figure made every trip to the courthouse a memorable experience.

Dutifully remembering the wife and kids, I shifted my gaze to the sky and said lamely, "Sure is. Weatherman says we might get some rain this afternoon, though."

"Hope so. We sure need it." She smiled again, floated down the front steps and headed down the street past Chamber's Pharmacy and the First Carter Bank toward Burton's restaurant on the corner. A hint of her bikini panties showed through the thin material of her slacks, distracting me again.

Musing about how fine she looked, and slapping aimlessly at the swarm of gnats that had joined me, I started down the steps myself. I was about halfway down when my foot caught on something and I lurched forward. There was a handicapped ramp with a rail along that side of the steps and as I fell, I swerved toward a rail post and managed to grab it with my left hand to slow my fall. But fall I did, banging both knees and my right elbow on the steps and slamming my head on the lower rail on the ramp. I managed to get myself into a sitting position on the bottom step just as Linda, seeing my fall, rushed back to help.

"Are you all right?"

"Just some bumps and bruises," I lied, shaking my head in an attempt to clear the fuzziness. Not only did I hurt all over, but I also felt pretty stupid sitting there in the heat being nursed by that gorgeous young thing who no doubt thought I was a real klutz. So much for my sexy image.

She retrieved the file I had dropped and said, "I keep telling Buck that someone is going to get killed on these steps one day, but nobody ever listens. Sure you're OK?"

I stood up, smiled through the pain, and assured her that I was as fine as ever and maybe even a little better. She laughed, turned and headed back in the direction of the restaurant.

I leaned against the rail, brushed myself off, and looked back to see why I had tripped. She was right about the old steps. I could see uneven places, worn spots, and even a chunk of concrete that had broken off the front of one of the steps on the other side. The odd thing was that the place where I had tripped was about the only section that had been repaired. It was smooth and clear. Yet I distinctly remembered feeling something catch my foot and pitch me forward. There was just nothing there now.

Hudson Raines, my best friend, my lawyer and sometimes my partner in one venture or another ambled up and said, "Saw you from across the street. If you want to practice high diving you need to go to the pool at the club. Softer landing there. You OK?"

"Hilarious, Hud. You should be on TV." I was still internally grimacing at the pain in my left knee but wouldn't admit it to him.

"At least you have a lawyer for a witness," he grinned. "Of course, I will need to describe to Maggie the little encounter on the courthouse steps between you and Linda. Good nurse, is she?"

I let him ramble on, and limped around testing the knee. Bennie Jackson, our realtor, came strolling up and joined in the festivities.

"What happened, Jack? Practicing your downhill technique?" Hud and Bennie had a real laugh.

Hud managed to regain his composure long enough to say, "Buy you lunch, Jack?" Pointing toward Burton's, he added, "I believe Linda went that way."

"You're a real riot today. I hate to miss the opportunity to hear more of your routine, but I promised to meet Maggie at the club after her tennis match. I'll see y'all tonight at Brad and Mona's party. You're going, aren't you Bennie?"

"Marie and I will be there for sure," said Bennie referring to his current flame. "I'll take you up on that free lunch, Hud."

Hud agreed and they walked toward the restaurant.

I stood and watched them for a moment and noticed that the thermometer on the First Carter Bank showed 96 degrees and it was barely noon. I headed slowly toward the parking lot feeling dizzy from the fall. It was still over a block away and the heat was so oppressive, I was already sweating profusely. And the gnats were thick and aggressive. Not even a breath of air to keep the little bastards at bay. The thought of the air conditioner in the Lincoln caused me to quicken my pace.

Lucky me. The Lincoln was boiling inside since there was no shade in the new parking lot. There had been several large live oaks we used to park under on the site but they went the way of progress. I guess that let them get two or three extra spaces. I got in the car, rolled all the windows down and put the AC on max. As I pulled out of the parking lot, I checked my watch and saw that it was 12:20, just enough time to get to the club by 12:30. I pulled out into the heavy noon traffic and turned onto Anderson Road that would take me to Country Club Road. I found myself thinking again about my fall on the courthouse steps.

For some strange reason my thoughts skipped back to our family farm in Ohio where I grew up. One of my jobs was to catch a chicken whenever my mother wanted to have a chicken dinner. In those days, you know, some chickens weren't raised in factories and didn't have special diets, so they actually tasted like chicken. They had the run of the farmyard at our place and had to be chased down and caught. We had a gizmo designed to make this task easier. It was a stiff piece of heavy wire about 3 feet long bent into a V shape on the end forming a hook which could be used to snag a chicken by the leg. It had a wooden handle on the other end. I could swear something similar had caused my fall today, but the steps had been clear. And there hadn't been a soul close to me. But still there was that vague sensation of something—a hand maybe—on my foot and ankle.

My name, by the way, is John Anderson Warner, known to the world as Jack. I'm 36 years old and have been married to Maggie for nearly 17 years. We have two kids. Laurie is two weeks from being 14-going-on-21, and Mark just turned 11. We live in Clarksboro, a smallish-sized town of about 30,000 people, some 35 miles west of Savannah. In spite of the fact that it was a 40 minute drive to downtown Savannah, our town was becoming a part of the Savannah metropolitan area, and was growing rapidly. Although there was a lot of opposition to this growth from the old time Clarksboro residents, I was content since that's how I made my living, building and selling houses to the commuters.

As I tried to avoid the usual knot of lunch-hour traffic at the new post office by winding my way through side streets, I made a right turn onto Toler Road that had just last week been declared one-way. Falling right into today's apparent plans for me, I was now going the wrong way. A quick u-turn in front of a car load of laughing teen-aged girls made my face burn, and I had a momentary feeling of kinship with the natives even though I was a newcomer, having lived in Clarksboro for only 10 years.

Like any smallish town, we were having labor pains dealing with the birth of this new population. And the situation was made worse by aging and conservative city commissioners who weren't sure exactly how progress should look, arguing with our young, progressive, inexperienced city planner. There was so much foot-dragging and political wrangling regarding new roads and new routes that traffic was beginning to get irritating. I spent the first part of my life not having to deal with traffic at all. Why should I enjoy it now?

Maggie and I grew up in North Central Ohio about 30 miles from each other. But we didn't meet until we were at college. Our farm was near Wooster, Ohio, and I lived there with my family for the first 18 years of my life. I enjoyed those early childhood years. I always had a cow or a lamb which I could call my own, and in spite of daily chores, always enjoyed being home. I did notice that most of my friends at school had few responsibilities at home and knew a lot more about what was on TV than I did. It wasn't until I began to drive that I realized there was a big, unexplored world beyond the farm. It was always assumed that I would become partners with my Dad when I graduated from high school, but I had other plans. I had that itch to be off the farm and to 'see the world' as the old saying goes. Football made that possible. I was just fair-sized for a football player–6'2" and 190 lbs.–but I was blessed with great speed. So Ohio State recruited me and gave me a free four-year ride to study Criminal Justice.

Maggie and I met when we were both in our first year of college at Ohio State in 1997. She was the all-American girl and had graduated at the top of her high school class. She played basketball and ran track and was the prom queen her senior year. She won an academic scholarship to study nursing at Ohio State.

We actually met on the football field at the University of Indiana. Our team had arrived Friday afternoon for a game on Saturday and after a short workout, some of us went out on the field to watch the cheerleaders practice. The band was there too. I was standing on the sidelines as the band members were marching through a routine called Script Ohio when Maggie materialized right in front of me, she and her video camera, taping the rehearsal for a friend in the band.

It was a warm September day so she was in shorts and a halter top. The band director chose the exact moment she was in front of me to stop the routine and chew out the tuba players, and while that was going on, I asked Maggie for a date. She finally agreed to have dinner with me at the hotel where they were staying. When I saw her that evening, I knew she would be the one I would marry. She was tall and full-figured with blue eyes and brown hair. She had a smile that was devastating and a good sense of humor. She smelled so good I was lightheaded most of the evening. I nearly proposed that night. Back at Ohio State we dated for our entire freshman year. My family fell in love with Maggie right away and Maggie's father began to be civil to me. We were engaged in May of 1998 and were married that August.

Maggie and I had lived in the Washington, D.C. area for 4 years prior to moving to Clarksboro in 2005. We had moved there in late 2001 following the birth of Laurie and our graduation from Ohio State in August 2001. We had both secured jobs pretty quickly, Maggie with a major hospital in the Virginia suburb of Falls Church and me as trainee with the FBI. I went through the training program shortly after we arrived, and following that, was given full agent status. I got drug duty, as most new agents did for their first assignment.

Maggie and I had few conflicts in spite of the fact that we held very different views on many things. Maggie was a city girl although from a fairly small town. I was straight off the farm. She was a Democrat interested in animal rights, pollution control, and conservation. I was a hunter and fisherman interested in large, fast cars that burned lots of gas. She was genuinely interested in people, and at a party or in any social situation, Maggie made friends instantly. I was more of a loner type. I hated the commuting and hated the bureaucracy and the crime and the violence that had become a part of life in the D.C. area. Drug use was at epidemic levels and an agent's life was on a tightrope. Maggie, on the other hand, loved being a trauma center nurse and tolerated the commuting and crime resulting in a minor conflict in our relationship. After nearly three years in D.C. I was ready to leave. I wanted to move south and get out of law enforcement and start my own business. But Maggie was dragging her heels.

After Mark was born in July 2004, Maggie announced that she was becoming a stay-at-home for awhile and took an indefinite leave from her job. Such leaves were nearly impossible to wangle but, after nearly three very successful years, Maggie practically ran the place and got whatever she wanted.

I immediately began anew my campaign to move to the Southeast to a small community where Maggie could work at a rural hospital and I could go into business for myself. Above all, our kids could grow up without fearing for their lives every time they left the house.

Maggie continued to resist until one day in January 2005. She and Mark had gone to pre-school to pick up Laurie. When they arrived, they saw several police cars in the parking lot, blue lights flashing. A group of confused people was milling around the front entrance. Terrified, Maggie grabbed Mark and ran toward the building. She was stopped by a police-woman who asked who she was and what she wanted. Almost hysterical by now, Maggie explained that Laurie was in there. The policewoman said that there had been a kidnapping of a little girl about an hour earlier by someone posing as a relative. They weren't releasing the name of the girl so Maggie had to wait an interminable ten minutes while the police rounded up Laurie, who was fine. Later that night we saw on the news that the body of the little girl was found in a dumpster about five miles from the school. We started town-hunting the following morning.

I already had copies of several of the standard town rating books and over the next several weeks accumulated several more. We both wanted a town with a population of 25-50,000 that had growth potential and was fairly near a decent sized city. We had both spent time in the Southeast as children and liked it in spite of the heat and humidity. So we narrowed our search to three cities: Gadsden, Alabama; Newberry, South Carolina; and Clarksboro, Georgia. We used my June vacation to visit all three and Clarksboro won.

When we returned to D.C., I gave the FBI notice that I would be leaving on August 15. Maggie did the same at the hospital where she had returned to work part-time in March. As you might expect, my last weeks as an FBI agent were hell. My unit had a major drug ring under surveillance, and in mid-July, we moved in. It didn't go well and we took a lot of flack. It was also the hottest July on record in the D.C. area that made everyone grumpy and generally miserable. August 15 finally did arrive and we loaded the kids, the dogs, and all of our belongings into a big U-Haul truck and our mini-van and moved to Georgia without ever looking back.

two

I turned into the club entrance at 12:29 and parked. A blast of Georgia heat hit me square in the face as I got out. It had to be approaching the 100 degree mark. And I couldn't see much either. Damn sunglasses fog over every time you take them out of the AC. I crossed the lot and walked gingerly up to the front entrance. The knee was stiffening up considerably by this time. I was greeted by a delicious gush of cool air as the door opened. Gil Benson, the State Farm man, was on his way out. We exchanged a comment or two and he tried again to sell me a new policy, right there on the top step. I could see Maggie waiting for me at the back of the foyer talking to Hud's wife, Jenny, a petite, blue-eyed blond beauty from a small town near Savannah. I seem to have a thing for blondes. I need to analyze that some day.

I excused myself from Gil,, who promised to call me later. As I limped over to the ladies, they both smiled and Maggie said, "What happened to you?"

"Little fall on the courthouse steps. Banged up my knee."

"We've all warned you about drinking before noon," said Jenny. "Now you see why." Maggie laughed and said she thought it was probably just old age.

"Too bad I didn't break my leg. That would have given y'all a real laugh. Maybe you could join Hud and Bennie on the TV comedy hour. They were at the courthouse and did a sweet little routine for me, too."

Maggie patted my cheek and said, "Now, now, baby, we're only kidding. Let's get some lunch. I'm famished. Join us, Jenny?"

"No, I've got to pick up the kids at the library. I promised them a trip to McDonald's. How's that for excitement? But we'll see you at the party tonight."

Maggie and I went into the dining room. It was a large and airy room with high ceilings and four large crystal chandeliers. One wall was entirely windows looking out over the patio and the golf course. The walls were covered with some sort of a print with flowers and birds. It was a little feminine for my tastes, but I suppose it was easier on the digestion than eating surrounded by dogs, horses, deer, guns and men in Day-Glo vests. The place was about half full so we got a table with no difficulty. It was next to the window and we could see one of the beautiful lakes off to our left. I never really enjoyed playing the game, but appreciated the beauty of a well-kept golf course.

The waiter brought us some sweet tea and took our orders. When he had gone, Maggie began to talk about the decorator who had been to the house yesterday. I was preoccupied, though, thinking about the fall and about everything I had to do that afternoon. I was halfway through my tuna salad before I even realized I was eating. Exasperated, Maggie finally said, "Hello? Did you damage your head in the fall?"

"Sorry. I am trying to decide what to do about the Johnson property. I wasn't paying attention, was I?"

"That's putting it mildly. Isn't that the piece we looked at with Bennie last month out on Old River Road near Brannen's mill?"

"Yeah, that's it. Turns out the mill is actually part of the property. Fred Johnson bought it in 1954 when Brannen's widow died. I think it's prime for a high income housing development, but Hud isn't so sure. He's afraid that the new development in Middletown will have the market saturated before we can move on it. He may be right, but the Johnson tract is much nicer than Middletown. I think it could be really popular."

"I think so, too. There aren't very many pieces of property in this part of Georgia where there's enough slope for a split level. Doesn't the Alahasa River run through a piece of it?"

"It borders on it. The mill is actually on Arrowhead Creek, giving us waterfront lots on two sides of the property. I'm going out there once more after lunch to have a last look around. Bennie said he would try to break away from the office and meet me there at 2:30. I should be home by 6."

Maggie nodded and reminded me of the party. I got up and limped out. Did I finish my lunch?

three

Hud's objections were on my mind as I drove to the Johnson property. He's one of those annoying people who is rarely wrong but at least he hadn't totally shot down the idea of buying the land just yet.

Hud is 37 and has been in Clarksboro for about 12 years. He and Jenny have been our close friends and neighbors for the last 10 years. He's originally from a small town in rural North Carolina. His parents were missionaries so Hud spent three years in Kenya. He was 15 when they came back to North Carolina. He was all-state in football and threw the shot and discus in track. I believe he still holds the North Carolina discus record. That's what he tells me at least once a week, anyhow. When he finished high school he joined the Marines for a four-year hitch. He took special forces training but two days before he completed training, he was washed out when he severely damaged his knee. Disappointed, he turned his attention to working on a BS Degree in Economics at a college near the base. By the time his four years were up, he had the degree.

Still only 22, Hud applied to several law schools and was accepted at the University of Georgia. That first fall he met Jenny, a senior biology major. She had grown up on a dairy farm near Savannah. At her rural high school, she won every academic and athletic honor they had to offer, was a cheerleader and homecoming queen, and had the lead in the school play her senior year.

Hud proposed after they had dated for six months. And Jenny turned him down. He was devastated when she told him her daddy didn't approve of Yankees. Hud reminded her that he was from North Carolina. She said her Daddy told her anybody from north of Augusta was a Yankee. She finally quit pulling his leg and told him she didn't feel they knew each other well enough to get engaged, but that she was moving in with him and he could ask her again in three months. He did and they were married three weeks after Jenny graduated in June of 2000.

Jenny worked as a lab assistant in the School of Pharmacy while Hud went to law school. He finished in June of 2003 and they moved to Clarksboro, where he passed the bar and opened his own office.

He was immediately successful, partly because he is big easy-going guy who people like instantly. I can walk into a bar with him and within two or three minutes he will be surrounded by people he never saw before asking him about where to fish or which stock to buy. It is remarkable. Women's reactions are the same but he's really all talk with them. He's too afraid of Jenny, I think, which is ridiculous since she is small, about 5' 3", and 105 pounds soaking wet. Hud is at least 6' 3" and about 220 pounds. They look pretty funny walking down the street together.

The first week I was in Clarksboro, I met Hud through my realtor, Bennie. On Bennie's recommendation, I asked him to close on the house Bennie sold us. It turned out to be three doors down from his and Jenny's. They gave us a housewarming party and we have been very close friends every since.

four

When I arrived at the Johnson property it was about 2:10 and hot as hell. Since I was early, I decided to go through the old house again. It was basically a Pennsylvania Dutch-style farmhouse, really out of place in rural antebellum Carter County, Georgia. This imposing two-story brick had a large porch plus an upstairs balcony, both overlooking the river. The house had been vacant for six years while Mr. Johnson died slowly of some sort of cancer in a nursing home in Savannah. His son, Jerry, had used it for awhile as a place to take his mistresses, but once his daddy was dead, he abandoned his wife and kids and left for California. He was selling the property to raise money for his new lifestyle. And child support. And alimony.

The old house was in a pretty sorry state. The roof leaked and the interior was damp and mildewed. A section of the first floor ceiling had fallen in and lay in chunks in what had once been the dining room. The floor was about the only thing that was OK since it was heart pine, virtually indestructible. But it would take major dollars to bring this place back. Hud favored tearing it down, but I was holding out for a B & B.

I went inside and made my way up to the balcony. As I gazed out over the river off to my right and the hardwood slopes to the left, I could picture restoring the place and living in it myself. It was as pretty a setting for a home as I had seen since visiting the mountains of Virginia.

I was turning to leave the balcony when I heard a loud crack. Like a slow motion movie, the balcony began to collapse under me. There was a big oak tree off to the left near the corner but it was too far to reach. I remember how powerless I felt and how angry I was that I was going to die so young when the balcony hit the porch roof and pitched me off. I flew through the air and landed on my back in a huge cluster of pampas grass. It was a minor miracle that I fell where I did since there were flagstones and concrete tables and benches all around the area. The grass cushioned my fall and left me out of breath and considerably scratched up, but otherwise I seemed OK.

I didn't even know anyone was around until Bennie and Hud peered down at me sprawled in the grass.

"My God, Jack, are you OK?" Hud asked anxiously.

I struggled to sit up, wincing as I realized that my earlier inventory had missed a badly strained back muscle.

"Hell, no, I'm not OK. But I don't think anything's broken."

"What in the hell happened?"

"I don't know. I heard a loud crack and down it went. I don't have a clue."

"Probably one of the main supports gave out while your weight was on it," Hud said. He began to nose around the fallen balcony.

"I don't think so," I said. "It was louder than an old beam splitting".

Bennie extended a hand and I managed to pull myself up. I hurt all over, especially my back. I was shaking like a leaf and limp as a rag doll. I limped over to where Hud was standing and sat down on one of the benches. He was squatted down intently examining a piece of one of the broken boards.

"You may be right, Jack. Those two main beams are shattered, not broken. And not because of the fall. Something caused them to shatter."

I moved in for a closer look. Hearing some distant thunder, Hud said, "Was it lightning from the storm?"

"No way. I would have seen the flash, and there just wasn't one. Just a loud crack."

"It's almost like there were explosive devices attached to those beams. Maybe some jealous husband set them to get Jerry," Hud observed with a grin.

"Could be," I said, grinning back. "But if you look closely at these fractures, there's no explosion pattern. It's more like they were ripped or maybe twisted apart. I saw something like this in houses leveled in that earthquake in L.A. a couple of years ago. But there was no quake today."

"Very bizarre," observed Bennie. He was so laid back he rarely got excited enough to respond to anything. "Something clearly happened, but there's no reasonable explanation for it. Well, in any event, you are a lucky man, Jack."

Hud turned to Bennie, "Let me use your cell phone to get the Sheriff. I want an official record of this in case Jack wants to sue Jerry Johnson. You've had quite a day, Jack. First, the suit I'm preparing for you against Carter County over the courthouse steps and now this. I can't wait to see what happens at the party tonight."

"Neither can I. Think I'll just go home and go to bed. Alone."

The deputy arrived about 4:00, listened to my story, and scribbled three pages of notes. He looked at the balcony at length but had little to add. We left without reaching any firm conclusions. When the official police report came out the next day, the conclusion was that it was a lightning strike. Hud was incensed but I wouldn't let him take any action other than to take a photographer and a construction engineer to the scene for pictures and an analysis of the damage. The engineer was as puzzled as we were. His report read "cause of collapse undetermined".

I did go to the party, but it turned out to be an ordeal. I hurt in every joint and muscle and I was having spasms in my back causing me to walk sideways like a crab. Hud and Bennie told everyone about my accidents. Everybody had a good laugh and had several really original comments to make. A talent scout for a comedy show would have had a field day in Clarksboro that night. We stayed long enough for Maggie to stir up all the local men and then she graciously agreed to leave early and I put the body to bed without further incident.

five

Thursday passed quietly. I spent the afternoon catching up on my paperwork. Since I felt some better, I pronounced myself fit enough to return to work on Friday. Thursday evening I had decided it was time to make a move on the Johnson property, so I planned a trip to Savannah to visit several construction supply firms to get bids for materials for the first four houses. Although I was prepared to buy the property myself if necessary, I really wanted Hud to come in on the deal. I needed to spread my risk a little bit.

I left about 7:00 Friday morning and was there until nearly 6:30 that evening making the rounds. The whole day went so much better than I expected that I left for home feeling pretty cocky. I was hungry and stopped at a Wendy's for a burger. On the spur of the moment, I decided to take an alternate route home on some back roads that would take me past Cedar Creek, our current subdivision project. I wanted to see if the new house slab had been poured. Supposed to have been done last Tuesday, but that's the construction business, you know.

I was cruising along Highpoint, a deserted rural road that didn't have a high point as far as I knew when the fries and double cheeseburger began to take their toll. I was sleepy as all get out. I stopped the Lincoln at a shady pullover, got out and milled around. The sun was low in the west and it was a beautiful evening although still hot as hell. I had left the car running and as I turned to go back to it, I heard a loud crack coming from under the Lincoln. I looked around and underneath but couldn't see anything. I shrugged it off, got in and started back down the road. I had just set the cruise control on 60 when I heard it again. It didn't take me long to realize that I had lost the steering. Completely.

I experienced that unreal slow motion again as I began to methodically evaluate my alternatives. A big log truck was approaching from the opposite direction and I was beginning to drift left. That would put me right in the dead center of his grill, I figured, in about three seconds. The second and only other alternative I could see was to stand on the brakes and hope for the best. I did, and the Lincoln pulled to the right. This solved the immediate problem of the log truck, but now I was skidding directly toward the mother of all live oak trees. It sat right along the edge of the road in a field of young, planted pines about six or seven feet tall. There was no real ditch on the side of the road so I was making a straight line for that tree with nothing in my path to block for me.

The car lurched unexpectedly to the left, missing the big tree by inches, and plowing instead into the 6-foot pine trees in the field. The air bag inflated and the car ground to a stop after bowling over about 15 of the smallish trees.

I sat there unharmed but stunned. I don't know how much time had passed when I saw an anxious face peer into the side window. It turned out to be the truck driver.

"You OK, buddy?"

I told him I thought I was, and then tried to open the door. It was jammed, so he grabbed the handle, I put my shoulder to it, and our combined efforts broke it loose. I climbed out but didn't go too far before my legs buckled. I had to grab the Lincoln to keep from falling.

"Are you sure you're all right? I'm gonna call an ambulance."

"I'm OK, I think. Just weak in the legs and got the shakes."

"I'll call 911 and get the sheriff and a tow out here for ya'." He turned to go and added, "Watch out for snakes."

I waved and thought to myself that a snake wouldn't add signifi-cantly to my difficulties. As I emerged from the pine trees and got a bit closer to the road, I saw a yellow Cadillac flash by. It had to be Bennie's. Couldn't be two like his in the whole state. I ran forward and waved my arms like a madman, but he didn't see me and disappeared into the distance. I eased over to the big live oak tree and sat down on the ground in the shade to wait for the tow truck. I was miserable.

Mike Andrews. the sheriff, arrived first. I was surprised to see him out of his office. He's usually glued to that computer screen.

"Evening, Jack," he said. "What's happened?"

"No clue, Mike. I lost the steering and had to hit the brakes. Fortunately, the car swerved right and just missed this big live oak tree or I'd have been killed, airbag or not."

"Let me have a look," he said and wandered off.

The tow truck arrived and the driver and I joined Mike, still there on hands and knees looking under the front end.

He stood up just as we arrived and said, "Connector to the steer-ing sector is completely sheared off. Never seen anything like it. Take a look, Freddie."

Freddie mashed his fat torso under the front end. "Damnedest thing I ever seen. There ain't nothing left of that connector. You hit something before this happened, Mr. Warner?"

"I think I'd have felt it if I had. Probably another lightning strike, don't you think, Mike?"

"Very funny, Jack." He pulled me aside out of earshot of Freddie. "Your little series of unexplained accidents is the reason I came out myself. I don't know what's going on in general and I don't know what caused this break in your steering connector. And lighting strike my ass. I told that dumbass insurance investigator that it couldn't have been lightning, so lay off the insinuations, Jack." He turned back to the car. "What caused it Freddie?"

"Damned if I know. A hit could've caused it but a hit that hard would've damaged the suspension parts. They're all OK, near as I can tell."

Mike persisted, "What should I put on the official report as the cause of accident?"

"I guess the damn connector was cracked and just picked this time to give out. Probably somethin' they missed at the factory. Some of the shit they put out now it's a wonder we all don't get killed. I remember a Teeota that had a broken–"

"Save it Freddie. Jack, that's probably what I'll put, but I really don't believe it."

"What do you believe, Mike?"

"It looks like sabotage to me. We'll never know for sure without the part itself. But our chances of finding it are pretty damn remote. I'll send Jason Matthews out here tomorrow with a metal detector and let him have a go at it. Since his girlfriend left him to go to Vegas and become a hooker, he's not worth a shit for anything else anyway. Let's give Freddie a hand and I'll give you a ride home."

It was nearly dark by the time Freddie got the Lincoln winched aboard. Once he cleared the field, I got into the Sheriff's car and we shot forward toward Clarksboro.

After we got up to speed, about 85 mph for Mike, he turned to me and asked, "Pissed anyone off lately, Jack? Screwing anyone's wife?"

"Do you really think someone's out to get me?"

"Looks that way to me, but I can't for the life of me think of any way they could have caused those balcony supports to be torn apart. And how did they know it'd be you who would be the one to go out on the balcony? Maybe Jason will find that connector tomorrow. I don't know how to tell you to act, but you'd better be careful the next few days while I try to get to the bottom of this."

He pulled into my driveway. I got out and thanked him for the ride and he promised to let me know something tomorrow. As I walked up to the door I remembered that in all the excitement, I had forgotten to call Maggie. And it was nearly 9:30. She met me at the door. Worried was not an adequate description. Pissed off would be better, but even that doesn't do it justice.

"Is this your idea of 7:00 or 7:30?" she hissed. Then, seeing the sheriff's car sitting out on the driveway she said, "What happened, Jack? Where's your car?"

"Small accident. Had to have it towed in for repair."

"My God, Jack. What kind of accident? Are you OK?"

"I'm OK. Just another set of bruises and contusions," I said wincing as she poked at a spot on my forehead I hadn't even realized was part of the trauma.

"What happened?"

I explained the accident to her, judiciously leaving out only the part about Mike's sabotage theory. It didn't really matter, though, because she cut right to the heart of the situation.

"Someboy's out to get you, Jack."

I didn't marry an airhead.

"That's what Mike thinks, too. Seems pretty farfetched to me. Who would have a motive? I don't have an enemy in the world in my present or my past unless it's some drug runner from D. C.

"I don't know, Jack, but I'm worried."

"Me too. But right now I need a drink. Join me?"

I moved over to the bar and began to fix two margaritas. Maggie followed me.

"Do you want some supper or something?"

"I had a burger on the way home but the 'or something' sounds good. What do you have in mind?"

"I thought your body was so sprained, broken and bruised that you could hardly move. But take a shower and a good soak in the hot tub and we'll see."

"That's the best offer I've had all day," I said, taking her in my arms and rubbing her ass. She wriggled free and fled toward the bedroom. I heard her take the cover off the hot tub and wandered that way, undressing as I walked.

"Where are the kids?"

"Next door. Melanie Foster turned 12 today and Anna is throwing her a neighborhood party. They'll be home pretty soon."

"I guess until we get some answers we'd better tell them to be especially careful about where they go and who they talk to. These 'accidents' may spread. Have you noticed anything unusual or out of the ordinary in the last few days?"

She thought for a moment and said, "No, but I'll ask the kids when they get home and warn them to be careful. Do you really think someone is responsible? How could they have tripped you on the courthouse steps or know you would be on that balcony? And the Lincoln part probably was defective. You can get Hud to sue Ford Motor and forget the whole thing."

"You're probably right," I said as I shucked the remainder of my clothing and headed for the hot tub. "We may know more tomorrow. Mike's checking things out."

The front door bell rang and Maggie said, "That must be the kids now. I don't know why we gave Laurie her own key. She never remembers it. I'll go talk to them while you soak."

"Try not to scare them."

I had just turned on the shower and was about halfway in when I heard Maggie scream. I came out of that shower like a shot, ran through the bedroom, stopping long enough to grab my shotgun, and headed for the living room. Buck naked, of course. Maggie and another woman were leading someone over to the chair by the fireplace. It was Jenny and Hud. Blood was pouring from his scalp, and was already covering most of his face and shirt.

"What the hell?" I shouted. "Is he all right?"

All eyes turned to me. There I stood dressed in my 12-gauge.

"I think he's OK. We just need to stop the bleeding. You know how scalp wounds are. We could use a big towel, Jack. Might want to get one for yourself, too."

Jenny smiled and said, "Now, Maggie, no need to hurry. He looks kind of cute."

I beat a hasty retreat to the bedroom, pulled on a pair of shorts and grabbed two old towels. I raced back to the living room and went over to look at Hud's head. He had a nasty gash just above his left ear. Maggie pressed a clean towel on the wound.

"When the bleeding slows we'll clean it up and decide if it needs stitches or not," she said. "Sorry I screamed, Jack. I guess I'm a little on edge from your accidents."

"What happened here, Jenny?" I asked.

"We were out walking when we saw the sheriff's car sitting in your driveway. Hud was curious, so we went back to the house to tell the kids where we were going and headed back over here. Mike had just pulled out of the driveway and started down the street. When we walked under that big streetlight right out front, it just exploded. Glass went everywhere. A chunk of it hit Hud on the head."

"You're stealing my act, Hud," I said. "This your first incident?"

"What do you mean 'incident'? That old street light could have blown at any time. We just happened to be under it when it went. What are you driving at?"

I proceeded to tell him about the Lincoln and about Mike's theory that these acts were deliberate. I also pointed out to him that when street lights 'blow', they don't normally explode like that.

Hud was quiet for several seconds and then said, "You know, I never thought much about it until just now, but the other day, I was out at Cedar Creek checking on the lot the Morgans want to buy. As I walked into that wooded area at the back, this huge German Shepherd appeared out of nowhere and lunged at me. I froze, and at the last minute he veered to the side and missed me. Instead of attacking again, he ran back into the woods and disappeared. I just put it out of my mind. Thinking back on it now, though, I don't know how he missed me. It was like something just shoved him aside."

"Same feeling I had when the car sort of jumped to one side to miss the big live oak tree. Anything else, Hud? Jenny?"

Jenny couldn't think of anything unusual. Maggie said she was going to warn our children to be careful and said that Jenny should do the same for their two boys, Jimmy and Wayne, aged 14 and 11.

"Probably a good idea," said Hud. "I want to think this over some more and then talk about it again tomorrow when my head is clearer. Maybe it's someone we pissed off on a house deal, Jack."

"I can't think of anyone offhand who would be that mad." We give a pretty high-quality product and rarely have even a complaint much less this kind of reaction.

"Let's get some sleep. Tomorrow's Saturday. How about coming over to our house for breakfast about 9:00?" said Jenny. Maggie agreed. She and Jenny checked Hud's wound and decided he didn't need stitches. About that time the kids arrived so Maggie went to their rooms to talk with them and I resumed my well-deserved soak.

I soon got sleepy. I didn't stay long.

six

The night passed without further incident and 9:00 the next morning found us walking down the street to Hud and Jenny's. When we arrived, all was calm. Hud was still in bed. Jenny went to rouse him and shortly we all were enjoying one of her western omelets. Hud looked bad, and complained about sleeping poorly.

An idea had popped into my head in the wee hours of the morning, and I brought it up for consideration. "Hud, was Bennie around when you had your incidents?"

Hud thought awhile and said, "Well, as a matter of fact, he brought the Morgans to meet me at the lot in Cedar Creek. They pulled up right after the dog took off. Why?"

"I don't know. It just occurred to me that Bennie was around every time I had trouble. I forgot to tell you that he went by in his Cadillac right after the accident last night." "I don't remember seeing him last night near the streetlight. Think he might have something to do with this?"

"I don't know. It's a possibility. I can't think of a motive, though. We make him a lot of money every year."

"You're way off base, Jack. He's acted a little strange since Martha died in that auto accident a couple of years ago, but he's not crazy. No way is he involved in this. I've known him for 12 years now and there's just not a chance. I consider him a good friend."

"All I'm saying is that these are strange coincidences. What other explanation do we have up to this point?"

We all brainstormed a bit about two or three other people and agreed that they were unlikely candidates. After an hour of wrangling we went back home. I mowed the lawn and washed the Windstar, grabbed some lunch, and then took a long nap. I had some bizarre dreams involving dust storms, extreme thirst, and fights with something I couldn't identify. Someday I'm going to write these dreams down and try to sell them. No time now, though.

That evening Maggie and I were supposed to help chaperon a party being given by the Thompson's 14-year-old daughter, Penny, at the neighborhood pool and clubhouse. We had supper and about 7:30 we were getting ready to leave when Maggie had a dizzy spell and almost passed out before we got her to a chair. She said she felt feverish. I told her to take some aspirin and lie down and if she felt better later to come on down. She agreed, and the kids and I left for the party. As we walked down the driveway, Bennie passed by in his Cadillac, honked and waved.

By the time we got to the clubhouse, Bennie had parked the car and was busy at the snack table. Evidently he was a chaperon, too. He was dressed in bright red swimming trunks and a blue, yellow and red flowered Hawaiian shirt. Not a pretty sight.

I walked up, shook his hand and said, "How's it goin'?"

"OK. Where's the wife?"

"She wasn't feeling real good. Probably be here later. Who else is coming?"

"Just Hud and Jenny. When Hud comes, let's talk about the Johnson property."

"Sounds good," I said. Just about then Hud and Jenny's boys came in and I asked Jimmy about his mom and dad.

"Mom's coming soon," he said. "But Dad felt sick. He's staying home."

A group of girls near the pool kept Jimmy from making any lasting eye contact with me. "Have fun," I said.

He grinned and walked over to talk to the girls.

A half-hour later the phone in the clubhouse bar rang. Mary Sue Thompson came over and said it was for me. I was surprised but figured it was Maggie. I was surprised again when I heard Jenny's voice.

"Jack, come over here right away."

"What's the matter?"

"Just hurry," she said and hung up.

On my way out, I ran into Bennie, who was also leaving, and told him I was going to check on Maggie. He gave me a strange look, and then said it was a good idea. He said that Mary Sue had asked him to run up to the corner market for some ice.

"How about a ride?" he asked.

I debated and decided that I'd get there quicker by car than on foot. Besides that, riding with Bennie would make this look more on the up-and-up to the nosy neighbors. He dropped me off at the corner and roared off. I hurried back to the Raines, fearing another accident. When I rang the bell, Jenny appeared at the door dressed in a pink, knee-length terrycloth robe.

"Come on in, Jack."

"Is everything all right?" I asked. "Where's Hud?"

"Everything is not all right."

Jenny was clearly agitated and was pacing back and forth. Now I could see she had been crying.

She turned to me and said, "I'm so mad I can't think straight. I don't know where Hud is now, but about 20 minutes ago he was fucking your wife."

"Sure he was," I said grinning.

"I'm not joking, Jack. We were just leaving to come to the party when Hud got dizzy and was feeling feverish. He decided to stay home. He insisted that I go on, and practically pushed me out the door. He was acting so weird that when I left, I walked into the garage and just stood there for awhile. About five minutes later, he came out and turned toward your house. We knew Maggie had stayed home because she called to say she was sick. I followed at a distance and saw him go into your house. I stood around for about 10 minutes and then went up on your porch. I started to ring the bell and then decided to look in the window instead. There was Hud on top of Maggie on the couch."

"Jesus, Jenny. This isn't funny. Tell me you're kidding"

"You want to walk down there and look for yourself?" Tears welled up in her eyes.

"What did you do?"

"I came back here and called you. I didn't know what else to do. I guess I should have walked in and asked them what the hell they thought they were doing but instead I turned and ran home."

I didn't say anything for a moment. I had been stunned at first but now the anger overtook it. I didn't understand how Maggie could do such a thing. Or Hud.

"I'm going down there and see what the hell's going on. Do you want to come?"

"I don't know. I guess so. But I'm going to kill that son of a bitch soon as I see him."

At that point the doorbell rang. Jenny gave me a quizzical look and I moved over to answer it. It was Bennie.

"Oh, you're over here, Jack. I just stopped by your house on my way back from getting ice to see how Maggie was, but there was no answer when I rang the bell."

I saw no reason to tell Bennie anything.

"She's in bed. You can't hear the damn thing ring very well in the bedroom. I just dropped by to check on Hud. Jimmy told me he was feeling bad, too. He's running a fever and Jenny put him to bed."

"Probably a flu bug."

We didn't invite Bennie in. I wished he would leave.

Jenny moved into view behind me and when he saw her he said, "I hope Hud feels better soon, Jenny."

"Thanks. I'm sorry we're missing the party."

"Don't worry about it. There's plenty of help. But I better get back with that ice before they send out a posse."

Before he turned to leave he stared straight into Jenny's eyes for several seconds. He must have noticed that she had been crying. Then he shifted his gaze to me.

I was uncomfortable and said, "I'll be back down at the party in a few minutes."

"Don't hurry, Jack." He smiled, turned and left.

I shut the door and turned to Jenny, huddled into a corner of the couch. "There's something about Bennie that bothers me, but I just can't put my finger on it."

Jenny didn't respond to this. Instead, she looked at me with smoldering eyes and stood up unsteadily, almost drunkenly. She untied the robe and it dropped to the floor. There was nothing under it but Jenny.

"Come over here, Jack."

I was stunned and was trying to stammer something to the effect that this was no solution to the problem when a wave of passion surged through me and I was really aroused. By the time I got to the couch, a trail of my clothes marked the path. She fell into my arms. I laid her on the couch, spread her legs and entered her. I remember thinking that I had always wondered if she was a natural blond. She was. Our passion was so intense that we were quickly finished. Exhausted, I lifted myself off of her and sat up on the couch. The intensity level, the passion, the drugged feeling were now gone and guilt began to set in.

"I'm sorry. I don't know what got into me. Hud and I have been married for 15 years and I've never even looked at another man. Must have been a reaction to seeing Hud with Maggie."

"I don't know what to say, Jenny. I started to explain to you that while I had always found you desirable, I was a one-woman man. Then it hit me. Wild horses couldn't have kept me off of you. I guess I still don't want to believe Hud and Maggie did the same thing."

I was pulling on my shorts when Hud walked in.

He stood there for a moment seeing Jenny nude and me in only my shirt, which I had not had time to remove, and said, "What in the hell is going on here? Can't a man take a walk around the neighborhood without someone tapping his wife?"

I was at a loss for words. Jenny wasn't.

"You son of a bitch," she said jumping up, and not bothering to cover up. "Walk around the neighborhood my ass. I saw you fucking

Maggie through the front window. Perhaps you'd better explain that before you start on us."

Hud didn't answer but instead slumped into a chair and stared at Jenny. She began yelling and hitting and slapping him. He covered his head with his arms and waited for her anger to subside. It didn't last long. Soon Jenny began to cry and, grabbing her robe, fled upstairs.

Hud avoided looking at me, but said, "She seems a little upset, Jack. Maybe you'd better go on home."

"Good idea," I agreed. I got up and pulled on my pants and shoes and headed for the door.

"Don't be too hard on Maggie. I've got to think some more about this, but something weird happened. I'm not sure either of us had any control. It was like...like a wave of passion."

That stopped me in my tracks.

I looked at him and said, "Jenny and I had the same feelings exactly. I swear I never had any idea something like this could happen. Hud, we all need to talk when we calm down." I moved out onto the front porch. I debated about going on back to the party but knew I would have to face Maggie sooner or later so I headed home.

I guess it was easier for me because I already knew about her and Hud but she didn't know that. Nor did she know about Jenny and me. When I walked in she was sitting on the couch with a magazine.

"How's the dizziness?"

"Much better. Party over?"

"No, I just came home to talk to you."

I was uncomfortable and just wanted to get it over with.

"Hud just walked in on Jenny and me right after we finished making love on their couch."

"What? What did you say?" Maggie exploded. The magazine sailed across the room.

"You heard me. Jenny called me at the pool because she saw you and Hud through the window."

Maggie sagged and began to cry. I didn't know exactly what to do so I did the obvious. I walked over, sat down beside her, and took her in my arms.

She cried softly for awhile and then said, "I'm sorry, Jack. I lost control. Hud called and said he wanted to talk for a few minutes and I told him to come on over. I had this wave of desire so strong that I thought I would pass out. When Hud walked in the door, we started doing it without saying a word to each other. We weren't even undressed at first."

She sniffled again and said, "I was going to tell you all about–."

"Enough," I said. "I want you to just listen a minute. Jenny and I just had a similar experience. I like Jenny, even love her in a neighborly way, but I never really planned or had an overwhelming urge to screw her."

"That's exactly how I felt about, Hud," Maggie said. "I never seriously thought of him as a potential lover before today. I really can't explain how it happened. Jack, what is going on here? I'm really scared now."

"I don't know. I just don't know. We'll talk more later. Right now I'm going back to the club to help them wind up the party and bring the kids home. It's almost 9:30. It's hard to believe how much can happen in less than two hours. Do you want to go?"

"No, I'll stay here. I can't even think straight," she said.

The rest of the evening went without incident. The kids and I got home at 10:15 and they went straight to bed. I went to our bedroom and Maggie and I talked for hours and finally fell asleep physically exhausted and mentally drained.

seven

Getting the Savannah newspaper is always a thrill in our neighborhood. Jeff Thomas has the route. Although he's only 15, he must drink heavily in the morning because the paper might wind up anywhere within a 100 yard radius. I have found it behind shrubbery, under the car, in the neighbor's yard, twice up on the roof and most original of all, on a branch of our dogwood tree. When it's not raining, he plastic bags it and when it does rain, he doesn't. Today it was actually on the sidewalk in front of the steps. It was bagged, however, so I knew without looking that the sun was shining. I unwrapped it and looked at the headlines. There were riots in the Philippines, floods in Bangladesh, a drought in West Africa, and a typhoon in the Pacific. Four people had been murdered in the Savannah area Saturday night and six more injured in various incidents. I looked at the names and Hud's was not there, so I guess Jenny didn't kill him. I wandered back in the house, fixed some coffee and sat down to read the paper.

I couldn't concentrate. My mind kept drifting back to last night's activities. I wondered if Maggie had really been aroused to a point beyond her control, or if she had just said so to get a free romp in the hay with Hud. Then, feeling guilty for doubting her, I reexamined my own encounter. Was I really out of control? As I let my mind

35

wander, I got a mental picture of Jenny standing there with the robe at her feet, and the way she looked as I laid her back on the couch, and was aroused all over again. Then guilt took the picture away. I brought up a picture of Hud with Maggie and anger surged up again at both of them. I shook my head to clear it and got up to fix more coffee. Just as I sat back down and started reading the paper, the phone rang. It was Hud.

"Jack. Sorry to call so early but can you and Maggie come over for a while? I think we need to talk."

"I'm surprised to hear your voice. I expected Jenny to finish you off after I left," I said, deciding to use the casual approach.

Hud chuckled and said, "She considered it, but reason prevailed. She finally quit trying to hit me this morning. Now she's alternating between crying and calling me a son of a bitch, so it's getting better. When can y'all come?"

"Maggie's still in bed. Let's say about an hour. OK?"

"See you then."

I woke Maggie and told her we were expected at the Raines house in one hour. She didn't seem thrilled.

"I'll never go over there again. I couldn't face Hud and I would probably attack Jenny."

"Now, now. Where's that old 'love thy neighbor' spirit?"

She gave a halfhearted grin. "We really did 'love' our neighbors, didn't we?"

"We did. Now drag the body out of bed and let's go try to work through this thing."

"I'll die of embarrassment."

"People don't die of embarrassment. Besides we all four did the same thing so you won't be any different than the rest of us. Bounce up and hit the shower."

She did but reluctantly, and after a light breakfast, we wrote the kids a note and left for the Raines'. We walked slowly so it was nearly 9:45 before we arrived. When Hud opened the door, Maggie turned crimson. This caused him to blush too and we all stood there looking at each other.

Finally I said, "Can we come in?"

"Sure, come on in." Hud moved toward the kitchen. "Coffee?"

We both accepted and he went off to get it. Jenny walked in from the back, both of her cheeks flushed. Maggie said hello, I chimed in, and the ice was broken.

"We're all embarrassed about what happened last night," Hud said, setting a tray on the coffee table. "It's unfortunate, but it happened, and it's over. We can't change it or wish it away. I suppose it's a good thing, in a way that we all four did the same thing. It's hard for me to fault Jenny or be mad at Jack when I remember what I did. So what we need to do is examine this objectively and try to determine why it happened."

"Eloquent summation, counselor," I said lamely trying to inject a little humor into the situation. "Seriously, I think Hud's on target. We've been friends and business associates for nine years now. We have partied together, raised kids together, shared good and bad times, and even hugged and kissed each other. I think we probably love each other, but before last night did any of you have a strong urge to carry it that far? I'm sure it crossed all of our minds at one point or another, but speaking for myself I wouldn't have done it and jeopardized my relationship with Maggie or with you two for anything in the world."

I looked around and everyone was nodding agreement.

"You're right." Jenny said.

She got up and walked over to Maggie who was sitting on the couch. They hugged each other and started crying. I looked at Hud and he was blinking rapidly. I was too.

After a few moments Hud said, "Actually, Jack, I had a strong urge to sleep with you. But I was afraid people would talk."

Maggie and Jenny both giggled and I said, "You're not my type, Hud. You don't wear an earring. Now let's be serious. Do any of you feel like you were manipulated by something beyond your control? I felt like I had just been given a dose of Spanish Fly, if there really is such a substance. I was completely out of control. As charming as Jenny is, I performed at a level way beyond my normal abilities. Something or someone caused this thing to occur."

Jenny said, "And I thought it was me that had you so excited, Jack. Seriously, I had the same feeling. I felt like I could do it forever."

Hud and Maggie both confessed to having similar feelings. Maggie surprised me by being quite open about the whole incident. Hud said, "All right. We're in agreement that we were not our normal selves. It seems likely that we were somehow put under the influence of some drug or something that caused our arousal. The questions now are how and when and by whom?"

"Assuming that a substance like that would work on the system fairly quickly, it probably would have to have been administered at or about supper time," added Maggie. "I suppose I left the kitchen long enough for someone to come in but the kids ate what we did and had no reaction. My God, I hope they didn't."

"I made a pizza and salad and all four of us ate the same thing last night, too," said Jenny. "Also remember that Hud and Maggie had a different timeline than Jack and I. If it was something we ate, Hud and I would have reacted at the same time."

"True. It doesn't seem likely that it was a substance simply due to the timing and logistics involved, but if not a substance, then what?" Hud asked.

Nobody had a clue.

"I think I may know," I said. "I hate to bring this up again but check me if I'm wrong. The kids and I leave for the party at 7:30. Bennie Jackson passes by in his Cadillac while we are in the driveway. Maggie has just experienced a dizzy spell. At about the same time, Hud has similar feelings. Jenny leaves and hides in the garage at about 7:40. Hud leaves for our house at 7:45. Jenny follows and sees Hud and Maggie at about 7:50 or 7:55. Jenny goes home and calls me at about 8:05. I arrive at 8:15. Jenny and I are talking about Hud and Maggie when, get this, Bennie appears at the door."

"I didn't know about that," Hud said.

"Neither did I," added Maggie.

"My fault," I continued. "Anyway, Bennie is telling us he stopped to ask about Maggie and rang the bell but got no answer. I don't think he stopped at all. Do either of you remember the bell ringing?"

They didn't.

I continued, "I didn't think our problems were any of his business so I told him Maggie was in bed and that Jenny had just put Hud to bed. He said he had to go and hoped they both felt better soon. He turned and stared directly at Jenny for several seconds and then he turned back to me and did the same. I finally made some remark about seeing him back at the party. He smiled and said 'don't hurry' and left. Bennie did this. I just know he did. He no more than got down the driveway until Jenny and I had the dizziness and flushed feelings."

"I wondered why he stared at me like that," said Jenny. "That son of a bitch."

Hud looked thoughtful for a moment and finally said, "It seems pretty damn farfetched to me but I have to admit, Jack, that he appears to be the only common denominator for all of these weird events. At least he's taken over my role as the son of a bitch. How's he doing it?"

"I don't know. But it does appear that he has to be in the general area where the event takes place."

"Should we confront him and see what he says?" Jenny said.

Before anyone could answer, the doorbell rang.

Hud got up and started for the door. "I wonder who that could be?"

I heard him open the door and speak to someone but I couldn't make out what they were saying. I heard the door close. He reappeared with an incredibly old lady in tow.

He said, "This is Mrs. Angelo. She wanted to come in."

We looked at each other.

Then Jenny bounced up and said, "Come in, Mrs. Angelo. Won't you sit down and have some coffee with us?"

As Mrs. Angelo turned toward a chair, Jenny gave us a quizzical shrug of her shoulders and went for coffee.

I'm not sure just how to relate the next part of this story. I'm not even sure that it happened at all. Perhaps it is just a nightmare or a temporary mental breakdown. In any event, I'll try to tell it just as I believe it happened. You can judge for yourself.

eight

As I said before, Mrs. Angelo was old, really old. Unbelievably old. She had long gray hair combed straight and pinned back in a bun, and was wearing a brightly colored flower print dress with white low-cut shoes. She carried an ancient white purse. Her face was a mass of wrinkles but still hinted at the beauty she had undoubtedly been. She radiated such a strong inner strength that I immediately experienced a feeling of calm and well being. I sat back in the chair. Mrs. Angelo finished her coffee.

"That was wonderful coffee, my dear," she said to Jenny.

"Thank you. Would you like more?"

"Oh, no, thank you. One is my limit."

Hud had been fidgeting around and finally said, "What can we do for you, Mrs. Angelo?"

"Dear me, young man. The question really should be what can we do for each other."

"Who are you?", I blurted out.

"This is going to be a little difficult," she said. "I'm sort of an undercover agent for God. I suppose for want of a better term you could call me an angel. I've come to explain what is happening to you and why. Is that clear?"

"Oh, perfectly clear, ma'am," I said in that tone one might use with a demented person. "We're so glad you came. Can we call someone to pick you up?"

"Don't use that tone with me, young man. I am not a candidate for a mental ward and I am not senile. Dear me, it's always this way. I suppose I'll have to offer you proof. Did anyone note the time when I came in?"

"I did," Maggie said. "I was wondering if the kids were up yet. It was 10:35." She looked at her watch and frowned and said, "No. That must be wrong. It's 10:35 now. I could have sworn—."

"You were right Maggie," said Jenny. "I happened to check my watch, too, because I wanted to put the lunch casserole in the oven at 11:00. It was 10:35 when the doorbell rang. And my watch still reads 10:35."

"That's because when you're with an angel or when you are off-planet, I can cause Earth time to stop for you," explained Mrs. Angelo. "When I leave, you take up right where you left off."

Hud and I must not have done very well covering our skepticism because she sighed and said, "I can see I need more proof."

She stood up and said, "This is how I go to my home."

The old woman mumbled a few words and disappeared. My mouth dropped open. Just as I started to say something she reappeared.

I don't know if I was convinced as to whether or not she was an angel, but I was smart enough to realize we had someone unique here with us.

Hud managed to stammer, "So you're the one responsible for the unexplained things happening to us."

"Dear me, no," she said. "But I am here to explain what's going on. And to solicit your help."

She then proceeded to relate the following story.

"God has dominion not only over this planet but several hundred other planets in this part of our galaxy. Other Gods exist and rule in this and other galaxies and universes but the being you call the devil is a local phenomenon and at present, operates only on Earth. The actual conflict between this God and this devil began in Earth's Biblical eras. Over time, the devil has won his share of souls and Hell has become a lively place but he has never become strong enough to challenge God's rule. Now, however, that may be changing.

"God has grown discouraged with the people on Earth. They have not responded in the way She had hoped. Because She also has problems on other worlds, She hasn't decided how much more effort to expend here.

"You see, Earth is somewhat of an experiment in that Her predecessors accelerated the development of intelligent life. They wanted to see how an evolution process would react to outside intervention. Later, She was selected to be God for the Earth in order to oversee this process. Most of the other worlds She rules were already fully established and had intelligent life when She took over.

"When intelligent life finally evolved on your Earth, She arranged for certain revelations to be made to these beings to encourage the kind of lifestyles She was trying to achieve. This was the basis of the experiment, and resulted in writings such as the Christian Bible and the Koran, and in religions' casts of characters, such as Jesus, Muhammad, and Buddha. All have a similar central theme: If you want to get to heaven you must lead a 'good life'. This 'good life' is presented in many different forms such as your Ten Commandments. But again, all religions which worship Her must include the provision that you must be kind to your fellow man. You must not do anything which will hurt someone else.

"She understands that people as they evolve will make mistakes and therefore provides for repentance and forgiveness for some of these mistakes you call sins. Be assured, however, that no one religion has a lock on heaven. An animist sun worshiper in West Africa who leads a good life without harming others will get to heaven more quickly than a good Christian who knowingly sells defective merchandise to his neighbors. She makes the final determination.

"The devil was an unexpected addition to the experiment. Even She was not sure precisely where he came from. I've never been told exactly how it happened, but he just appeared on the scene and began a campaign against Her commandments. She was very annoyed, but for some reason continued to tolerate him. He was stronger than he first appeared and She probably allocated too few resources to this new problem. Anyway, in time, She realized the cost of ousting him exceeded what She would gain so She met with him and set the Customs. There were many of these Customs negotiated at that meeting but I am only going to cover the most important ones for you.

"She agreed to make no attempt to dislodge him unless he broke the Customs and he agreed to make no direct or indirect move to harm Her. She insisted that there be a way to verify his actions and movements but he refused to allow angels in Hell. They compromised by his agreement to allow mortals to enter but reserved the right to punish them if caught. He wanted similar privileges in Heaven but She refused. Keep in mind that She could destroy him at any time if She wanted to pull resources from other worlds. He finally agreed. He actually didn't give up much. She always speaks the truth and keeps Her word.

"They agreed that his designated top demons, limited to ten at a time, could enter Earth at will. If She identifies and captures these demons, She can banish them forever. This is a hardship to the devil, not because he cares about the demons, but because it takes years to train one to be able to integrate into Earth's society. I must point out that we recently learned how to identify them without their knowledge. But it has often proven more useful to leave them alone for awhile to see what they are up to and then to banish them.

"She agreed to limit the number of angels to ten at a time on Earth as well and these could be the top ranking angels such as myself. It somewhat provides a balance of power except an angel is significantly stronger than a demon.

"Finally, they both agreed to limit themselves to existing communications on Earth. If beams came in from Heaven or Hell, Earth would intercept them. They can't be shielded to prevent this and it would confuse the mortals even if in code. Also on Earth, communications were limited to Earth's existing system."

At this point, Mrs. Angelo sat back, sighed and said, "This is the last Custom I want to cover right now. But I do need to give you some other background information.

"Now, Earth religions generally prohibit more activities on the part of their followers than She does. She, as I already told you, decides your fate on the basis of whether or not you have harmed another being. This sounds easy but is really quite difficult. Let me give you an example. Some religions allow multiple spouses. But a Christian cannot have more than one spouse. This is even civil law in many Christian countries. Now if a Christian takes a second spouse, this could cause severe harm to the first spouse and could be cause for denial to heaven. This would also break the Christian commandment against adultery. But in another religion, the taking of a second spouse would violate neither rule and would cause no hurt to the first spouse. It can really get complicated. Another example. In certain tribal groups in Africa, young boys and girls must go through ceremonies to prepare them to become men and women. They undergo mental and physical trauma, are crudely circumcised, and are given a pattern of tribal scars on their bodies. If a Christian family did this to their children, it would certainly be defined as harmful and the child would be severely traumatized. In those parts of Africa where it is the normal practice, however, it would cause hurt only if it were denied to the child. `

"These examples help explain why there can be no "master list" of sins. She and only She decides each case. So you go to Hell or not based on Her decision, not on the devil's. He tries to convince you to lead a lifestyle that under Her rules won't let you into Heaven and he succeeds all too often. Occasionally, a human specimen comes along who is so 'bad' that he doesn't even measure up to Hell's standards. This includes serial killers, child molesters, hired killers, Nazi death camp officers, and so on. She reserves the right to deny them an afterlife even in Hell and instead sends them to Terminus, a section of Heaven where they are terminated and their souls are utterly destroyed.

"How about children? There are no children in Hell. If they are under 18 and die and can't qualify for Heaven because they are 'bad', they go to an intermediate world where they are kept in a fairly comfortable environment and attend rehabilitation sessions until age 18 and then a decision is made.

"So, with the Customs established, evolution proceeded with a friendly competition for souls between Her and the devil. She actually saw some benefit in his actions as it tested the peoples' commitment to Her principles. However, the influence and strength of the devil slowed the process of acceptance of Her principles. What She thought would take a few hundred years has dragged along for thousands.

"In fact, Her influence peaked in the late 1800's and has been on a downturn ever since. In other words, the devil's influence is beginning to prevail. She contemplated abandoning Earth about the time of Hitler, who was an agent of the devil. But She brought the U.S. into the battle and good prevailed. I worked on that one, and let me tell you, it was rough. She thought this incident would deter the devil but he soon resurfaced stronger than ever and has been instrumental in creating more decades of stress and conflict. Now She is discouraged. She is involved in too much on other worlds, even for one with Her powers. As a result, She pays less and less attention to Earth and the devil gains ground.

"Under his influence, people on Earth have become less respectful of the rights of others than at any time in history. They have abandoned their religions in large numbers. There are increases in child abuse, spouse abuse, torture, slavery, wars, murders, rapes, property crimes of all types, and She is really becoming discouraged. The devil, on the other hand, feels that he is winning.

"I am very much afraid She will abandon Earth, even though that would be unlike Her. If She does, She will not leave Earth to the devil but rather will destroy all life and thus end the experiment. The devil knows this, and he is preparing to mount a serious campaign, not just to win, but to preserve Earth for his own benefit. To do this, he must actually defeat Her in such a way that he can bargain for Earth's survival. He has never been strong enough to attempt this and I can't see that he is now, but it appears that he is preparing to make that attempt.

"You are probably wondering about my role. It is extremely unusual for an angel to appear to humans and, in my case, even rarer since I am the Leader of the Angels and second only to Her with respect to Earth. I died in Earth year 617 AD and joined the angels shortly thereafter. I took the leadership about 500 years ago. Since my origins are on Earth, I have a special spot for it and I am fighting for its survival. Yes, I do share Her discouragement but unlike Her, I still believe that there is hope. I am afraid that this hope, however, is contingent upon the devil either suffering a severe setback or being destroyed. And this is where you four come into the picture."

nine

We were all mesmerized. Mrs. Angelo sighed again and continued.

"You four, you see, have been the victims of an agent of the devil. My counterpart, the head demon, is on Earth in the persona of Bennie Jackson."

I gave a start. "Do you mean Bennie has been possessed?"

"Bennie Jackson died in the same car accident as his wife, but the demon known as Karg took his place so no one ever knew he was dead. Why Bennie? We don't know yet. There may or may not be something significant about the choice. I actually began watching Karg several months ago, but he has begun to suspect something and has been very careful. I think he's confused because he knows that our usual policy has been instant banishment upon detection of a demon on Earth.

"Karg somehow discovered last week that I had been looking for mortal agents and that you four were on my short list. He then made his attempts to disable some of you. He didn't give it his best effort, of course, because he knows that on Earth he can't kill you while you are under my 'wing of protection'. But he could and did disrupt your lives. To your credit, you had just about zeroed in on him as the perpetrator of the incidents. Since he must be physically close to anyone he is attempting to harm or influence, your suspicions were aroused once the four of you put your heads together.

"In any event, I nudged Jack toward the rail at the courthouse to break his fall. I shoved him over to the pampas grass when the balcony collapsed. I pushed his car to the left to miss the big live oak tree. And in Hud's case, I shoved the dog aside and chased it away. I must admit that I let that one piece of glass cut you, Hud, because I had to be sure you would be serious about what was happening.

"The sexual encounters occurred without my interference simply because my 'warning light' did not go on until it was almost over. I am 'warned' based on the degree of potential harm the action may involve. It is a mind link, which I establish with you without your knowledge. When your mind signals the threat, I drop back in time and go to the scene to take the necessary action. The warning is pretty much limited to life threatening or serious injury situations. Karg hoped the sex incidents would create stress and split you up, but it didn't. You four have been so close for the last nine years that you have shared everything except a sexual encounter, so I let it go. Now it will be a factor in our favor.

"You can quit worrying about your children, and I know you are, because use of children is against the Customs. Karg will never violate this Custom because he knows that would be the end of the game. She would immediately turn all of Her powers against him and the devil and none of them would survive. It would not be a simple banishment for Karg. He would be destroyed. She would follow with the devil. This would cost Her a lot since destroying the devil would require a large expenditure of Her powers. But She would still do it. So neither Karg nor any other demon would dare violate this particular Custom. They have been very carefully instructed by the devil in this area.

"I have so much to tell you and so little time. As I said earlier, the devil is moving rapidly to increase his control and must be stopped soon. Why am I trying to enlist you four? First, you know more about Bennie than anyone else I could enlist and I want to grill you in some depth about his activities. Also it will be easier to convince you of the truth and importance of what I say since he has already used off-Earth powers on all of you.

"Second, someone has to actually go to Hell, and if you will recall, it can't be any other angel or me since Custom forbids it. It has to be a mortal. The advantage there is that you can be taught to blend in and would stand a good chance of not being detected. While Karg is on Earth, the Customs forbid him from communicating with Hell. So only Karg would be able to identify you, and I plan to keep him plenty busy here on Earth.

"The residents of Hell look just like they did in real life except that no one wears clothing. In fact, clothing is an invention of Earth. No other world I know of uses it, and neither Heaven nor Hell adheres to this unique and curious Earth custom. While in Hell, you may meet someone you knew who died and is there, but they will just assume that you died, too. By the way, the real Bennie is in Heaven, so there should be no confusion if Karg should get back to Hell.

"The final reason we selected you can't be revealed to you right now except to say that all four of you possess the set of character-istics we believe will make you ideal agents in our battle with the devil. We need to take some of the pressure off of Ruth, you know. And we need to start figuring out a screening system so that we can rid earth of evil and maybe have a clean slate to work with.

"There is no reward I can promise you if you succeed except the knowledge that Earth may be saved for at least a while. Oh, I can give you a monetary reward and will, but I can't promise guaranteed access to heaven or angel status or anything like that.

"Should you agree to go on this mission to Hell, you lose my protection at the gate and are on your own. If the demons catch you, you will appear before the devil. He can do anything he wants to you, including taking your life. He usually banishes mortals from Hell and deports them to Earth because if he takes your life you will likely go to Heaven. If he sends you back, he has a good shot at get-ting you later. But there are no guarantees as to what he might do.

"Now let's talk about what I want you to do while you are in Hell. Ideally, we would just destroy the devil for all his latest transgres-sions, solving our problem permanently. But his power has become extremely strong. He can now sense when a mortal is planning to kill him. We have proven this many times by sending mortals against him. The last to try was a famous aviatrix in 1958. She simulated a plane crash to explain her absence. The plan was to have her 'found' after her mission was complete. She is still in detention in Hell. You don't want to hear what her life is like.

"We have also tried sending mortals to merely get near him. This has been more successful. We have been able to get a young woman into his domestic service who sees him every day. This woman may be key to your success or failure.

"Apparently, the devil cannot or does not easily detect mortals who have no fatal plans for him. We have told the young woman only to observe and report on his activities, and we believe that she has not been detected. While your proposed action would not be fatal to the devil, it would cause him permanent harm. So you cannot get too close to him or he will sense your intentions. That will be the job of the young woman I mentioned. The key is to get her to carry out the mission for you without her knowing that it is harmful.

"This is the plan that we have in mind. God's scientific corps has developed a drug that it believes will divert the devil from his quest to take over Earth. It works in part by inducing a mild state of indifference to everything going on and in part by rendering the person impotent. He prides himself on his sexuality. Few women arrive in Hell without a long session or two with the devil. It truly guides his life and he would be devastated if he couldn't perform. We believe that administering this drug to him would give us the edge we seek in reducing his power and preventing him from taking Earth. And the effect is permanent unless counteracted by an antidote he won't have access to in Hell."

She paused and then continued, "Before I describe life in Hell and your strategy, are there any questions?"

We looked at each other. It was pretty hard to formulate a coherent question at this point.

Hud finally asked, "Why us? Why not four young, athletic, military-trained recruits?"

"I can't tell you exactly why because it might affect your performance. Suffice it to say that no computer search was ever more exhaustive in a selection process. A team of you four represents the best chance for success."

"How did this 'computer' rate our chances?" I asked.

"Approximately 5 to 1 against," she said calmly.

"What about our children? How many days would we be gone?" asked Jenny. "We can't just leave them."

Mrs. Angelo responded, "You don't have to worry because you won't be gone. Remember that time does not pass on Earth when you are with an angel. It's still 10:35, isn't it?"

Then she dropped a bombshell. "It shouldn't take more than eight or nine months in Hell. You will actually age those eight or nine months and may weigh more or less when you get back but you will come back at the same instant you left."

"If we come back at all," Maggie muttered under her breath. Mrs. Angelo may have looked old but there was nothing wrong with her hearing.

She looked at Maggie and said, "You're right, my dear. Fifty to one against you coming back at the same time. Even worse, you might wind up like the aviatrix."

The room was silent. We could hear the hum of the ceiling fan.

Finally Hud said, "How do we know all this is true? For all we know, you may be the agent of the devil and Bennie might be the angel. What proof do you have?"

Jenny said, "Really, Hud–"

"That's all right, dear," Mrs. Angelo interrupted. "It's a fair question. Hud, I don't have a membership card which says 'Member of the Angel Corps'. So no matter what I tell you, there will always be the possibility that I am lying or misleading you. You will just have to go on faith for a while. I will give you proof before we leave for Hell."

Maggie stood up and paced around the living room and said, "This is too much to absorb. We need time to think about this. It's not an everyday occurrence that someone comes to talk to us as an angel."

"I understand, but we don't have long. Time is running out and I will need at least two weeks to give you physical training and to teach you the Customs. Shall I be back tomorrow at noon?"

"Why not just hold time constant for the training?" Jenny asked.

"No, dear, it doesn't work that way. I can remove you from your own space-time and reinsert you at the same time here, but off-world time goes on. I have been with you here for about three hours now and it is still 10:35. But be assured that three hours have passed in Heaven and Hell and that we have all aged 3 hours."

"OK." I agreed. "We'll try to decide by tomorrow at noon."

Mrs. Angelo stood up and then simply disappeared.

ten

Hud finally broke the long silence. "I don't know about y'all but I'm taking the first plane to Australia. That's the craziest story I ever heard. Now explain why I believe her."

Maggie said, "I don't have an answer for you, but my watch is working again. It says 10:37."

"Under the circumstances, I don't think it's too early for a drink or four. Hud, how about a triple scotch on the rocks?"

"Good idea. Ladies?"

Both ordered Cokes. After Hud got our drinks, we once again sat in the living room, perplexed about our next move.

"What are we going to do?" asked Jenny. "I'm afraid, but she makes me want to help her in any way I can. Of course, she apparently has the power to make me feel that way. Do you think we're being manipulated? Or am I having one of those realistic dreams?"

Maggie said, "I liked her. I think we can trust her. She did say she would give us proof before we went to Hell. Oh, that sounds funny. We're going to Hell!"

We all laughed, which helped ease the tension. We were back to serious all too soon.

Hud said, "What about the kids? I know they won't know we're gone, but what if one of us never comes back? And how would you ladies feel about several years of the devil doing despicable things to your bodies?"

Maggie had a quick answer to that one. "You did despicable things to my body yesterday. If I can survive that I won't have any trouble with the devil. Seriously, I haven't really thought about the problem of the kids."

"It would be an experience few people will ever get. And it's probably not as dangerous as it was to be a soldier or nurse in Vietnam," added Jenny. "Besides, if Mrs. Angelo can be believed, it may be more dangerous not to go. If God really intends to destroy the world, we all die. Kids and all."

"Good point, Jenny," I noted. "And if we believe Mrs. Angelo, if we should die in action, at least we now know that there is an after-life. And if we're fighting for God and the angels, we probably have a lock on going to Heaven."

Hud had begun to pace around the room, something he does when he's trying to make a decision.

He ran his hand through his hair and said, "Sounds like you three are basically in favor of going. I'm still skeptical, but guess I agree. I just hope the devil is a strong heterosexual if he catches me. How about it, Jack?"

Everybody laughed, which along with the scotch helped relieve more of my tension. After making plans to meet later, Maggie and I went home.

The kids were up, so we fixed and ate a big lunch together. I felt a twinge of emotion at what very well could be one of our final meals together as a family of four. I finished reading the paper and repaired a faucet in Laurie's bathroom. About mid-afternoon, the kids left for the swimming pool and Maggie suggested a nap. That seemed like a good idea since Mrs. Angelo had managed to add about three hours to our day. We both slept like we were dead.

That evening; still tired, Maggie and I discussed the proposed trip to Hell. The whole idea was so preposterous that I had trouble once again taking it seriously. You may have noticed that all four of us had swung wildly that morning from being serious to being silly. But solemnity finally won out and we came to the decision that there really was no alternative if Mrs. Angelo was telling us the truth. We decided we had to go.

I slept poorly that night, not out of fear, but because the old "sense-of-exhilaration-in-the-face-of-the-unknown" took hold. I finally got up feeling like I had just put in a full day's work. I made a few phone calls to get the workweek started and arranged to be out all day. Hud called to make sure we hadn't changed our minds, and we agreed to meet at their house at about 11:30. The kids were all to be sent to the club with money for lunch and an afternoon at the pool.

At 11:15 Maggie and I walked to the Raines' house.

Jenny had lunch ready, but we all just picked around it.

"Do you think she'll show?" I asked. "Was it all a dream?"

"That's exactly what Hud said earlier today," said Jenny. "Honestly, you men don't have a tight grip on reality."

Maybe we had too tight a grip, I thought.

Maggie laughed and said, "Jack kept me awake half the night tossing and turning."

"I don't think Hud even made it to the bedroom."

"I slept very well on the couch, thank you," Hud said defensively. "Besides I was more worried about missing today's appointments than I was about our mission. I keep forgetting that time stands still when she's around."

At exactly noon, Mrs. Angelo appeared just as she had promised.

She seated herself in one of the wingback chairs and said, "Good morning, my dears. Have you had a chance to talk it through? Can I explain anything to you?"

Hud answered for us, and the lawyer in him made it sound like a contract.

"We have decided to accept your offer on the condition that before we go, we receive both a complete briefing and the proof you promised."

"Excellent. And all conditions will be met. You do realize that you can change your minds up to the last minute, don't you? We don't want you to go on a mission unwillingly.

"So let's set up a schedule. Your time on Earth will go on as before, so continue with your normal activities. I will need about four hours a day for training for the next two weeks. I would like to take more, but you'll be working an extra four hours in 24 and you'll be too tired if we do more.

"Let's have two sessions a day, one at 7:00 in the morning and one at 7:00 in the evening. Each session will be one hour of lecture and one of physical training. We'll begin tomorrow, but today I want to describe Hell and the most important Customs to you. Any questions before we begin?"

I was tired just thinking about it.

eleven

I had always pictured Hell as a series of super-hot underground caverns somewhere in the bowels of the Earth. In my Hell, the residents worked 24 hours a day shoveling rock or coal or something hot and red and flowing, and were beaten by overseers with big whips. All in all, a pretty grim place to spend forever.

Mrs. Angelo had a good laugh over that one. It seems that Hell is not on Earth at all. It's on a previously unoccupied planet that the devil took over when he first came to this sector of the galaxy. Most of the planet has a climate about like Gila Bend, Arizona. Hot. Dry. The extreme polar regions are considerably cooler and the northern polar cap even has a small ice field. The devil maintains his headquarters in the Southern polar region.

"Assume that you die and are sent to Hell," she began. "When you arrive you are assigned to a demon to get you installed into your new society. What you call your soul will receive a new body exactly like the original, and all bodily functions are retained. Your new body will also be age-adjusted to about 35 years so that you can be a productive worker. Since all sickness and disease is easily prevented or cured, there is no need for sick leave.

"Yes, I mentioned work. Hell, you see, is a commercial enterprise. The reason the devil came there originally was that he could attract people away from Heaven and have a free captive labor force. The work is all agricultural hand labor, believe it or not, and is very demanding. On Hell, they raise a plant called tchadbe that thrives in that hot, arid climate. The tchadbe seeds are planted by hand and cultivated by hand, and the entire plant is eventually harvested and baled by hand for shipment.

"The devil has an exclusive contract with a supplier who ships the bales to some seven thousand planets. This dried tchadbe is then processed to make a powerful sex-enhancing drug used by beings on many other worlds. On Earth, however, this drug contains a substance fatal to Earth humans. It has something to do with a mineral in Earth's soil which bonds with the drug and alters it chemically."

"Now let me explain how the economy of Hell operates. It really quite simple. All food is imported and controlled by the demons. It is served cafeteria-style in huge halls with hundreds of tables. You can eat all you like as long as you have worked. Attached to these food halls are huge barracks with showers, bathing pools, restrooms, and sleeping quarters that you can use free of charge if you so choose. You can also build your own house and tap into the central water and sanitary facility, or carry water and have an outhouse if you prefer the really rural areas.

"Also attached to this main building is a huge recreation area where you can get a drink, listen to or dance to music, and watch videos. Gambling machines are there too. You must work to enter this facility, too.

"Basically, you can do anything you want free except for eating and using the recreation hall. It's these two activities which guarantee that you will work because you can't go without food and you can't buy consumer goods for entertainment because there are none. There are no goods of any kind to buy. Period. No clothes, no transport, no telephones, no TV's, no golf clubs, nothing. Part of the reason is that there are no metals allowed on the planet. If you are energetic enough, of course, you can use rock, wood, and clay free of charge to make anything you want like a house or dishes or even a swimming pool. But most residents don't have that much energy.

"It takes three work-days a week to feed one person. All other work beyond those three days earns credit for recreation. You can recreate one night for one day's work. This gives you up to five free drinks and 2000 units of gambling credit. If you win at gambling you can keep your winnings, but can use them only for more gambling or for vacation activities. But you can't win at gambling and use the winnings to eat or to buy drinks. This guarantees that you will work. These complexes are spread around Hell, and residents are free to move from one to another at will. People aren't classified and regimented like they are on Earth. They have no addresses, no social security numbers, no licenses.

"Transport is by foot, with one exception. All food is delivered from the South Polar Region in huge convoys of carts pulled by teams of large, ox-like animals from Gherlyn, which thrive on the local vegetation. On the return trip to the South, the carts haul the tchadbe bales. If there happens to be a light load in either direction, residents can catch a free ride. But since the centers are only about 20 miles apart, most residents walk.

"Finally, you can save up days of work and gambling winnings for a vacation to the capital at the southern polar region. There are huge hotels and casinos located on the southern sea, and a wide variety of other recreational opportunities, so most residents work hard in order to go there. It takes the average person about a year of working six days a week to save enough for a two-week vacation.

"Are you wondering why you have to eat if you're dead? And if you can be killed again? The latter is easy. If you are killed or injured, you are sent to a repair facility and returned to work in short order. To discourage killing, however, the killer must work six days a week to be eligible to eat. This is double the normal amount of work needed to get food and goes on for one year. Murders are rare in Hell.

"You have to eat because the body functions just as it did on Earth. Food is essential. But if you are already dead can you starve to death? Yes, but if you suicide by any method you are repaired and put back into the system. If you refuse to work or eat or try to suicide again, you get a lobotomy and join a special work force closely monitored by demons. There is no escape and no way out and every-one works.

"Sex is the one form of recreation that is free. Anything goes as long as both or all parties agree. Those who take sex by force are given the same penalty as one who kills. Rape is as rare as murder in Hell.

"Finally, why don't some people simply steal food credit from others and thereby avoid work? As part of the initial processing you are given an injection of a substance that guarantees you will tell the truth. When you enter the food hall each Sunday you must pass through a portal where a machine asks you if you worked three days last week. If you answer yes, you can't be lying so you are given credit to buy a week's worth of meals. A similar procedure is used for recreation."

Mrs. Angelo paused and asked if we wanted a break. She had been talking for about an hour. Everybody was hungry so Jenny got some chips and dip and some cokes. Mrs. Angelo resumed her explanation.

"It is possible for an angel to introduce still-living mortals like you into the Society of Hell. God's technology is more advanced than that of the devil and that makes this type of transition possible. For example, She has an injection that overrides the food and rec-reation machines so that the mortals need not work. She also has an injection that provides immunity to all sickness and disease. You could be killed in Hell but if you were, you would be sent routinely to the repair shop. You would be repaired but the demons would know then that you had been a mortal when you were killed. That can't be disguised. So after repair you would have to appear before the devil. If you were injured, the results would be the same. But She has a potent salve we will send with you which heals all but the most severe wounds overnight. The chances of you having to submit to a repair shop are very slim.

"One problem is that even a small tin of salve will be difficult to carry since no one has any goods in their possession. But there is one item that is general issue when a person first arrives in Hell, and that is a water container to take with you on the job. You will have one just like the real workers. It is leather and has a strap so you can wear it over your shoulder. You can hide small items in our version of this water bag because we included a specially made inner pocket. The salve is all you really need except for the drug we have for the devil. Each of you will carry a packet of this drug. I'm sure I don't need to tell you what the consequences would be if these two items were to be found on you.

"You will have to integrate yourselves into the society. I will be placing you down near the North Pole but off the ice cap and below the northern sea. This is the only place where you can enter unannounced. I will drop you there in the morning when the temperature will be about 50 degrees fahrenheit, so you will have to move south quickly. By nightfall you will be in a slightly warmer zone. Expect a low of about 55 degrees. If you sleep together with some foliage over you, you'll be OK. It won't be too many days until you beg for a cool night.

"To reach the devil, you must travel clear to the South polar region. You will have to travel on foot for the first 200 miles in order to reach the first agricultural complex. There is nothing but native vegetation in that 200 mile stretch all the way around the globe. It is hilly, rocky, and too cool and wet for the tchadbe to grow. It is off-limits to residents of Hell but is never patrolled because there is no food for anyone who enters. You will have no difficulty crossing it without detection but you must do it quickly because you can only arrive with a limited amount of food and water. A week should be sufficient. When you reach that first settlement you will wait until nightfall and go to the barracks. This will be your first contact with the people of Hell. I will brief you in more detail over the next two weeks. Do you have any questions so far?"

"I'm not sure I could walk 200 miles in a month, especially on bare feet," said Maggie.

"Leave that to me, my dear. We have a few tricks to enhance your physical abilities and some techniques to prevent sun damage and to toughen feet. You'll be ready."

"What about a broken bone?" Hud wanted to know. "Does that mean an automatic trip to the repair station and the devil?"

"I should have covered that. We have ampoules that you can inject after the bone is set that will heal minor breaks in hours and major ones in about 48 hours. You inject it near the break. We'll make sure you have some of them in your water jug along with the salve and the devil's special. Maggie is capable of setting bones and dealing with wounds and Hud had medical training in the Marines, so you should be covered in about any medical emergency.

"One more thing. There is always a certain amount of uncertainty when it comes to dealing with the devil. For example, somehow Bennie found out about our plans for you four. Since by Custom he can't communicate with the devil from Earth, it will not matter since I don't intend to let him leave Earth, but in learning of my plans to recruit you four, they did do something we didn't think they had learned how do. We are still reasonably certain that you won't be identified in Hell unless you make a mistake or some unexpected thing occurs to cause your death but one can never be 100 percent sure. Now let's quit for today and start tomorrow morning at 7:00. Where would you be comfortable meeting to leave for your training? We need a private place from which we can leave without being seen."

"How about our hot tub room?" Maggie offered. "The only way in is through our master bath and the only windows are skylights."

"Perfect. I'll see you there at 7:00 tomorrow morning."

And after a moment, she was gone.

It had been a mentally exhausting three or four hours. Of course, it was still noon by regular time, whatever that was. We ate the lunch that Jenny had fixed earlier–it was as fresh as though she had just set it out– and Hud and I both left to see what had happened with our respective businesses. Monday mornings are always bad, but this one takes the cake.

twelve

I let Hud and Jenny in at about 6:45 the next morning, and we all went right to the hot tub room. What a fashion statement we made! Hud was dressed in old marine fatigues and Maggie and Jenny in loose fitting karate type outfits. I had on old jeans and a tee shirt. Hud said, "You'd better change, Jack. It'll be hard to work out in those jeans."

"Unless I miss my guess our choice of clothing it isn't going to make much difference."

Before I could explain, Mrs. Angelo arrived.

"Good morning, all. I hope you slept well. I must confess to a small transgression on my part. Mrs. Angelo was created to give you a sense of calm and well being. She served her purpose. My real name is Deena and I look like this."

Mrs. Angelo was gone. A naked woman about 25 years old stood in her place. She was a knockout, to say the least. I stared at her without even thinking about how rude I was being. A quick glance around showed me that everyone else was doing the same.

Deena said, "I told you no one wears clothing in Heaven or Hell. You'll get used to it and then you'll really enjoy it. Off with your clothes. Time to go."

I gave Hud an 'I told you so' look and started to undress. Maggie and Jenny had turned their backs to us and were peeling down.

I believe I was the only one who had thought about this aspect of our training coming this morning.

When everyone was finally naked and blushing, Deena said, "We are going to what you would call a space station. It is one of about 20 around the Earth, all much further out than the Earth space voyages have gone. We will get there by process known as REGEN which is very similar to that used in your old TV series, Star Trek. We will be disassembled here and reassembled there on Noah's Ark, the name we have given to our particular station. Now come over here and press your hands against me. You must be touching me in order to be taken along."

We moved over close to her and sort of stood there. I mean where do you touch a naked angel? She reached out and grabbed my hands and placed them on her shoulder and then did the same with Hud on the other side.

Maggie and Jenny moved in and touched her. She mumbled a few words in a language I didn't recognize and suddenly, we were standing in a small well-lighted room somewhere else. To say it was disconcerting would be an understatement.

I let go of her shoulder and she said, "First order of business is physical exams and minor body repair. Come this way."

We walked out into the corridor and proceeded to the right. Deena said, "The main purpose of the stations is to process Earth's dead before they go to Her. When an Earthling dies, their soul is sent here, and it is fitted with a new body. The new body is identical to the old at this point, but all disease and physical defects are removed. From here you board the transport line to Heaven where you are judged by Her. If you get to stay in Heaven, you are given a chance to age-adjust your birth date to any age you desire. As you can see, I chose 25. If you go to hell, they will automatically peg you at about 35. Well, here we are."

She turned right into a large sterile-looking room.

A gray haired woman of about 50 came forward. Deena introduced us. "This is Charity. She is a doctor of sorts, and will give you your physicals and make your repairs."

We all nodded and mumbled greetings and she said, "This way," and moved over to one side of the room. "I can only do two of you at a time. Ladies first?"

Maggie and Jenny, neither looking particularly happy, moved forward.

Charity continued, "Now don't be alarmed. These two chambers are the diagnosis and repair units. They were developed on an advanced world in another universe. They can detect the smallest abnormality in your bodies and if it is minor, repair it on the spot."

The units she referred to looked like large mummy cases. They were completely transparent and sat upright. You simply walked in, turned around, and waited for someone to attach a number of straps to you. Charity finished strapping Maggie and Jenny and announced that she was about ready to start the machines.

"Now just relax and enjoy. It will all be over in about 20 minutes."

She closed both doors and started the units. It was an amazing sight. An assortment of laser rays passed over their bodies in rapid succession. There was a readout screen on the side of each machine, and Charity was watching both Maggie's and Jenny's during the scanning process.

"Jenny, you have a few cancer cells in your right breast. They are being removed. And, let's see, your vision is being corrected. And no more PMS. Otherwise you are healthy.

"Maggie, those hemorrhoids are history. Let's just correct this nearsightedness. And the scar tissue from a burn on your left thigh has been removed. Looks like you had a broken ankle sometime in the past. It was set incorrectly and must cause you some occasional pain. It will take about two hours in the repair unit to fix that. We'll schedule it for tomorrow."

Maggie and Jenny were flushed with a green liquid and after a short drying cycle the unit hummed to a stop. Both emerged, grinning and looking radiant. Maybe even glowing.

Charity looked around and said, "Your turn gentlemen. Let me change the settings." She strapped us in and turned the units on. There was no pain and no sense of discomfort.

A moment or two passed and then I heard Charity say, "You are a mess, Jack. You have a mild blockage of the right coronary artery, three very small ulcers, and a prostate infection. In addition, you have an amazing assortment of bruises and contusions. Maggie mad at you?"

Thanks to the hum of the unit, she didn't hear my answer.

"Hud, you have some minor lung damage from smoking in the past. You are also a carrier of Hepatitis B virus, and show some calcium deposits in your right shoulder. You also have a severely damaged left knee. This is all going to require a 12-hour repair cycle which I'll schedule for tomorrow."

The unit flushed the green liquid as if it were a giant toilet and after drying we emerged. I felt renewed and my skin tingled all over.

Charity said, "That green liquid was a skin treatment to protect you against sun damage. You will tan but you won't burn or suffer any skin damage. I am going to paint your feet now to increase their toughness."

We went across the room and each in turn sat on a small stool while Charity sprayed the bottom and low sides of our feet with a skin colored liquid.

"We'll do that three more times this week and then you'll be able to walk on broken glass or over a hot bed of coals. Now let's go over and get your injections."

We crossed the room and Charity picked up an injector device.

"I'm going to give you each three injections. One will protect you from all known diseases and conditions on Earth and in Hell. This includes everything from dandruff to cancer. It will also render you sterile. That injection lasts about a year. The second one is a physical fitness enhancer. It will assist in your training and will allow you to about double the things you could do when you were in top condition. You could easily win any Olympic event you chose to enter after two weeks of workouts. Finally, the third injection is to counteract the food and recreation-vacation machines. When you are asked if you worked 3 days last week, you can say that you did and that answer will be accepted. These last two are good for about a year as well."

She turned to Maggie, told her to turn around and laid the injector against her left buttock and fired away. We each took our turn. Deena came back and gathered us up. We thanked Charity and went on down the hall.

"This next room is a Hell simulator. This is where you'll complete your physical training."

We entered a large room that was, excuse the expression, hot as hell. Deena explained that the temperature was kept at 105 Fahrenheit. She then proceeded to lead us in the toughest 30 minute workout I have ever been through. Hud said later that she made a Marine DI look like a sissy. Interestingly enough, the injection was already working, because even though I was winded, I actually felt stronger and extremely energized. After the 30 minutes we hit the treadmills. They alternated from a fast walk to a fast run and had inclines to add to the fun. They also had rough treads to toughen our feet. At the end of 30 minutes I'll admit I was ready to quit.

Deena said, "Great first day, troops. Maggie, here are some extra exercises you can do to strengthen those chest muscles. You'll tighten up."

I had noticed during the running that Maggie, who is well endowed, was really bouncing up and down. Jenny, who is small breasted, had no real problem.

Deena said, "Time to go, dears."

We had no more than touched her when we were back in the hot tub room. Deena said, "See you at 7 tonight," and disappeared.

Maggie walked over to the hot tub. "I never thought this would look so good." she said as she gingerly climbed in and motioned for us to join her. We all had a good soak.

Hud finally said, "Well, group, it's 7:30 and I have an 8:30 court appearance. I'm out of here".

Jenny got out, too, and they dressed and left.

I turned to Maggie and touched her breasts. "Do they hurt?"

"Not much. I'll be OK. Are you sorry we got into this?"

"I probably will be when we get to Hell, but right now I feel 16 again. I'm going to take better care of myself when this is over."

"Me too." She moved around and lay back against me and added, "If it's ever over."

She gave a little shiver and I held her close for awhile. We finally agreed we had to get up, so we showered and dressed.

After all that exercise we were both ravenous and ate a huge breakfast. I needed to make a move on the Johnson property but couldn't bring myself to call Bennie. I did call Hud after lunch and to my surprise, he said to go ahead, count him in. I asked him what changed his mind and he said he had a new lease on life and was going to be more of a risk-taker.

I drove by Bennie's office to see if he was there. He wasn't, or at least, the Caddy wasn't, so I took a chance and went in. Earl Ray Butts, the office owner and broker was there, so I told him Hud and I wanted the property, so they could set up the closing. He said that it was a shame I had missed Bennie. I agreed and left.

thirteen

We all gathered again in the hot tub room waiting for 7:00. Jenny said, "Why don't we undress and be ready when she comes. I'm starting to like the nudist lifestyle."

Deena arrived precisely at 7:00. We touched her and were gone.

At the station, Deena said, "Charity has scheduled Maggie's ankle repair for the two hours following our session tomorrow morning if you don't think you'll be too tired."

"That should be fine," Maggie said.

"Hud, I notice that you're limping from this morning's exercise. We need to schedule you to start at the same time as our second hour while the others exercise. It's going to make for a long day, but you can go to bed at 7:00 when you get home. OK?"

Hud nodded agreement.

"Good. Tonight I want to show you a video we made of Hell."

It wasn't much different than a video shot of our desert southwest. There was a sea and a small polar icecap in the northern hemisphere and we were shown the likely landing spots. The 200 mile stretch of wasteland we would be crossing looked even more foreboding than I expected. The settlements were clear as a bell as the camera zoomed in for some amazingly clear close-ups considering they were taken from 200 miles out, the Custom limit for angels. I could clearly see the residents of Hell around the huge settlement buildings and see the workers and the demon overseers in the planted fields of tchadbe. Over to one side of the complex was a small building that Deena said was the demon barracks. They ate and recreated in the human halls but their personal habits caused problems when they were housed with the humans.

The camera switched to the South polar region. Once again there was a polar sea with an island which contained the South Pole. It was on the seashores of this island that the devil had his complex. The vacation area was also on this sea, but opposite the island. The devil had a seawater buffer zone of at least 20 miles all the way around the island except for one area where a small peninsula jutted out to within about a mile of the island coast. This potential access point was about 20 miles from the devil's residence. Deena noted that it was quite closely guarded. The South Polar Region also had roughly a 200-mile strip of unusable land stretching from the polar sea inland. This strip, while not guarded, was always being crossed by vacationers and wouldn't make a good entry point for us.

Close-ups of the devil's complex revealed three main structures. The first was obviously the residence. It was a huge gray stone building with spires that reminded me of an old castle that I had seen on a visit to Germany some years back. It had a large interior courtyard that was bustling with activity. Deena said these beings were the domestics and the craftsmen working on daily chores. The second building was for the human domestics, and contained the already familiar complex with food, barracks, and recreation areas. The third structure was a complex for the upper-level demons who had direct access to the devil. Bennie would be housed and fed and recreated there.

Hud observed that there seemed to be very few defensive precautions taken. Deena explained that few are needed since no one really had access and, if someone did get in, the devil at close range could sense potential harm and was easily able to defend himself with a demon corps stationed in the palace itself. She also said that since our intentions were not fatal, if we approached from the right direction, we could actually be inside the human complex and remain undetected. But approaching the palace directly would result in almost certain detection and capture by the demon corps.

The hour was up and we moved to Hell for our physical exercise hour minus Hud. Seemed much cooler today–maybe only 104.

The remaining two weeks consisted of more briefings and more exercise and more sweating and some self-defense tactics thrown in for good measure. This was interesting to me, with my background, because it was not self-defense against humans. We were too strong already for that to be necessary. It was self-defense against demons, the topic of one of Deena's daily lectures.

"Apparently, the demons come from a world only the devil knows about," she explained. "We haven't yet found their origin. He imports them as he needs them, but we understand that they are extremely costly. He would rather use many human workers because they are quite inexpensive. Now, the demons he brings in are of two classes: worker-guard and elite. The worker-guard are of about average intelligence and are dedicated and diligent in their duties.

"The elite are highly intelligent and possess powers that workers don't have. For example, they can change their form, like Karg did with Bennie. They can teleport themselves for short distances, up to about 50 feet. They can exert a crude form of mind control and can disable or destroy matter with their mind on a limited scale. For example, Bennie is the top demon, yet he was strained to the limit to break the steering part in your Lincoln, Jack. Both workers and elite are strong enough to handle two humans in a fight. They average about six and a half feet tall and weigh roughly 275 pounds.

"Their bodies resemble humans but their facial features appear rather beaver-like, particularly the protruding upper teeth. This is another caution: they bite when they fight. They are also a little humpbacked, and when they walk, they look like they are going to fall forward. There are both males and females but they have been sterilized so no children are possible. We aren't sure why but it's probably to keep inbreeding out of the picture."

Deena told us that demons fight for keeps, and if we had to fight one, all four of us would need to jump in and kill it quickly. "You don't have to feel remorse because a dead demon goes to repair and gets a new body anyway. The same is true if you kill a human resident of Hell. All that will happen is that the demon in charge will change the food machine to require that you work six days a week in order to eat. No big problem. All you have to do is say yes to any of the queries on the machines and you will pass.

"The last thing I will mention is weapons. There are no metals in Hell, either native or imported. This is by decree of the devil. No one is one hundred percent sure why, but one likely reason is that without metals it is difficult to make weapons. Another is that the devil doesn't want anything to detract from the production of tchadbe that, you remember, must be cultivated by hand. Having no factories producing consumer goods frees more workers for tchadbe production."

So we go in weaponless. We argued for small guns to hide in the water bags but Deena said that there was a detection field spread across the planet that would instantly expose us, so guns were out. Apparently, there are stones to throw and wood to make clubs and some rubber trees to supply rubber for the cart tires which could be used to fashion a slingshot or a crude bow and arrow but essentially, we would be weaponless. If we had a bow and arrow we would stand out like a sore thumb anyway.

Finally, we were ready. At our last training session we shifted the order of business, did the physical stuff first hour and used the last hour for final briefing. Deena gave us our water bottles and showed us the inner pouch in the upper part, positioned so we wouldn't have to dump any water in order to have access to the various items secreted there.

"I'm proud of the progress you have made in just two weeks. You are truly ready. But now is the time to make that final decision. Before you do, remember that I promised to give you proof that I have been telling the truth. Here it is now."

The lights in the room dimmed. The wall in front of us began to brighten and in front of it just becoming visible was a large chair on a raised platform. In the chair was a figure. All I could tell was that it appeared to be a woman. As she became more visible the lights became brighter so that no matter how hard I tried, I couldn't see her face clearly.

After a moment, she spoke. "I am God. Deena told me of your mission and I want to assure you that it is vital to the future of Earth. We are very grateful to you and will support you all the way. I will see all of you again soon. Bless you and good luck."

And She was gone.

I can think of numerous ways a good movie company could have rigged that scene but I had no doubt in my mind that I had just met God. It was a powerful and moving experience and one I will never forget.

"She is so busy. I told Her that coming here was not necessary, that it could be done by video, but She insisted," Deena said.

"I've never seen Her do that before, so it probably means that She has decided to make the attempt to save the Earth, and that She feels that She has the right team on board for the job. That would be you four. Things are still deteriorating, I hear. Three more elite demons are on Earth with other personas and we are desperately trying to figure out what the devil has planned for them. What is unusual is that the demons are acting as if they are aware that we know about them and are daring Her to ban them from earth, Her right under Custom. And if we know about four, there are probably six more we haven't found. Some of our analysts feel that the devil may violate the Custom and send more than ten. Anyway, this information shouldn't affect your mission. But it does make your mission even more urgent."

Deena continued, "Remember that the lady who is the devil's domestic is named Ella. She was told when she was sent in there that she should expect someone to ask her for help, so she won't be surprised to see you. But she thinks we are only observing the devil's personal habits, which she is diligently coding into a little notebook kept in her water jug. She will have to be the one to take the drug to him but you will have to come up with a clever reason to give her so that she believes it will not cause harm to the devil. If Ella knows your true purpose, he will spot the deception instantly. Talking to her about her routine and contacts with the devil and about his habits may help her think that you are only interested in observations.

"I'll come for you in the morning at 7:00 as usual. Now let's get you home."

We grabbed her and were home. We took the kids to the Pizza Hut for supper and I had to bite my tongue several times to keep from telling them to be careful while we were gone. When we got home, they went to finish homework and I paced, sat, paced, sat and finally went out for a walk. It was a nice night for mid-August and after half an hour I felt a bit more relaxed. I went back in, told the kids goodnight, and joined Maggie, who was reading in bed. I wasn't really present, though, and she knew it.

"This is all so unreal, Jack. I can't believe the four of us are just accepting all this as though it were an everyday occurance. You do seem uptight tonight. Are you all right?"

"Fine. I'm just a little tense."

"Well, hurry up and get in bed and we'll take care of that tension."

I hurried.

fourteen

The next morning we met at the usual time and place. Deena took us to Noah's Ark. We went to a room we had not seen before for the REGEN process, our transport to Hell. Everything was ready. We were ready. Deena had some last minute instruction.

"Remember that the presence of the REGEN will alert Hell that you or someone is coming. However, as I told you, we started sending REGEN beams in several days ago with no one in them to mislead the demons. At the same instant you are sent, the other 19 stations will simultaneously send beams to different areas of the polar region. They are somewhat used to this process and shrug it off figuring that sooner or later they will catch the mortal or mortals involved.

"You know the routine. Implanted behind your left ear is a REGEN alert device made entirely of non-metallic components. To activate, press the device with a finger on the left hand and the same spot on the right side with a finger on the right hand. This will send a signal and we will attempt to lock on and pull you out. You must use this only if your mission becomes hopeless or upon completion of your mission or if you are captured by the devil and your sentence is death or detention. If you are sentenced to detention, try to get the lady flyer out with you. She only has to be touching you when REGEN occurs, so that should be relatively easy. Any questions?"

"You mentioned briefing us in the field. Anything new?" Hud asked.

"I'm glad you asked. If it becomes imperative that we reach you we will send a message by REGEN. It will appear beside you while you are walking between settlements or are outside a settlement and are isolated. We will send 20 beams at once to confuse them, but once you have the capsule, change location quickly. The capsule will open only to your fingerprints."

"Anything else?" Deena continued. "No? Well, I guess it's time. Good luck and vaya con Dios."

She kissed each of us and moved back. The beam came on.

The next few moments turned into a nightmare. As we materialized and were beginning to move in our unfamiliar surroundings, two demons hit us from behind.

Jenny screamed, "Jack and I take the female."

There was no doubt about which one was the female. We met her charge full on. I ploughed my head into her midsection driving her back and Jenny jumped and got her around the neck. I caught a quick glance at Maggie and Hud and saw that she had the male by the balls and Hud was on his back trying to take him down. Our female went down and I jumped on top of her. During the fall Jenny's neck hold was broken, which allowed the female to twist over on her stomach. As we hit the ground, she bit Jenny on the left shoulder. I was pounding the back of her head and shoulders when she twisted again, leaned up and bit me on the arm. I jerked loose and she squirmed free and was starting to get up when Jenny hit her on the head with a fairish-sized rock. She went down instantly, but Jenny hit her a few more times to be sure.

Jenny screamed again, "Jack, help Hud."

I looked over and saw that Maggie was out of the battle. Hud was on the ground and the demon was on top pummeling him. I made a flying tackle and knocked him off of Hud. We rolled over and I came up on top and kneed him. He screamed and sat up, and Hud, who had recovered, got him from behind and snapped his neck.

It lasted about two minutes. I jumped up to check on Maggie. Jenny was with her and had a thumb pressed on the arterial pressure point of her inner thigh. Maggie had a gaping wound below that point and had lost a lot of blood.

Jenny said, "Jack, the tube of salve, quickly. Hud, watch our ass."

I found a water jug and retrieved the salve and quickly went over to Maggie.

"Hold out your finger."

Jenny stuck out the index finger on her free hand and I put a generous portion of salve on it. Then I bent down and gently moved the flesh around until I had the wound closed. I held it that way and Jenny applied the salve. A wound this size with an artery puncture had to be held for about 5-10 minutes until the initial knitting took place. Jenny and I planned to stay 10 minutes to be sure.

After about 5 minutes Hud came over to check on us.

"How is she?"

Jenny said, "We don't know yet. What did you find?"

"I did a quick scan, and everything appears to be clear for at least a hundred yards in every direction. It's hard to be sure with all these plants and trees."

I should mention to you that the surrounding vegetation was about 10 to 15 feet tall here since the rainfall in the extreme north was higher than on the rest of the planet.

Hud continued, "I found their camp, such as it is. They have several water jugs and some food stores but nothing to keep warm with."

I hadn't noticed in all the excitement that I was slowly freezing to death. It was the coldest 50 degrees I ever felt.

Jenny said, "Maggie lost a lot of blood. I'm not the medical expert but I recall Charity telling us that if we push fluids, the injection for disease would allow blood to be replaced at a rate of a pint every two hours."

Hud agreed. "That's right." He came over and looked at the pool of blood. "She probably lost about three pints, so that'll be six hours minimum."

"It looks more like five or six pints to me," Jenny said, shifting uncomfortably.

"Trust me. It always looks like more than it really is."

"OK. But she's got to be in shock by now. We're going to have to warm her up soon. Let's ease up on the pressure, Jack."

I looked at the wound and was surprised to see that it was already beginning to knit together. We slowly eased off and everything held. And Maggie was already beginning to stir. We checked her vital signs, looked for other wounds, and found a torn spot on the back of her shoulder. We salved it. She moaned and relaxed again. Hud was bleeding from a bite on his arm, so Jenny applied some salve to that, too.

She finished her nursing duties, stood up, looked around and said, "We need some bedding, guys."

"How about these?" Hud held up some primitive fern-looking things with six-foot fronds tightly covered with leaves.

"Should work." I struggled up to help him gather more.

"Just a minute, Jack. Let me see that arm."

"It's nothing," I said holding it out to Jenny.

Now that she had mentioned it, it began to hurt like hell. She smeared some salve on it and on a banged up knee I had picked up sometime during the fracas.

Then I remembered the bite on Jenny's shoulder. I told her to turn around. It was nasty. Ugly red tooth punctures ran between the top of the shoulder and the shoulder blade. I put salve on it and two or three other minor cuts and left to help Hud. I realized that it was not even daylight yet, which meant we had been in Hell less than half an hour. I was really looking forward to the next few days. Yeah.

Hud had walked over and was looking at the two bodies.

"We'd better drag those off somewhere. They're really starting to stink."

"Good idea. Let's cover them with some of this long grass here, too." I started ripping off big bunches of the stuff, and realized that they smelled nice, like ripe cantaloupes. "This just might fool some-one for awhile."

We dragged each of the bodies about 100 yards from where we were going to camp and covered them with the grass. Then we went back and began to gather the fronds in earnest. We found a spot under one of the giant ferns near Maggie that was thick and soft with years of dropped foliage. We put more fronds over this until the base was about a foot thick. Then we carried Maggie over and laid her down. We went for the rest of the fronds, enough to make a blanket about a foot thick and laid them beside Maggie. Jenny ran off to pee, and when she came back, forced another pint of water into Maggie. That made three in all, which should speed along the healing process even more, according to some of Deena's instructions. It was nearly daylight by this time, probably about 9:00 or so, and it looked like rain.

"We need to move on, but we'd better not chance it with Maggie until early afternoon," Jenny said. "Let's get some rest and try to stay warm."

We laid down, Jenny and I on either side of Maggie, and each put one leg on top of her. Hud piled on the fronds, then squirmed under next to Jenny. I gradually started to warm up, at least my front side. We were all unusually quiet. What was there to say?

About an hour later, Maggie sat up abruptly. "What in the hell's going on? Is this one of those orgies I heard about?"

I was glad to have her back.

I gave her a hug and Jenny said, "Everything's fine. You lost some blood in that little spat. While we were waiting for you to recover, we were trying to keep warm."

Maggie gave a shiver that had nothing to do with cold and said, "Is everyone else OK?"

"Except for a few minor bites here and there," I answered. "Drink some more water and try to rest."

We all quieted down again and I think I slept about two hours. When I woke up, it was full daylight. Felt like about noon, but I had no way of knowing for sure. I looked around. Hud was gone and Jenny was awake. Maggie was apparently still asleep.

"Where's Hud?"

"We woke up about half an hour ago. Hud heard something so he went to look."

Just then he ducked under the fronds and said, "Afternoon, all. Lunch?"

He had apparently visited the demon camp and had taken their water and food.

"Did you see anything?" I asked.

"Just a big lizard passing through."

In evolutionary terms, Hell was barely in the reptile stage, and these were smallish and primitive. The seas had fish and on land were the lizards, snakes, turtles, and some crocodiles. There were no birds or mammals.

"What kind of food did you find?" Jenny asked.

"Some dried fish, dried beans, and this bread. It's pretty much like Deena described. I tried it. Not too bad."

As we munched bread, we evaluated our situation. We knew it was just a matter of time before someone came to check on the demons. Hud could find no communication device of any kind on them or at their camp, so a roving team probably came around to check on them on a periodic basis. The devil is notoriously slack in security matters mainly because he faces virtually no opposition internally and very little external other than the occasional mortal spy. Having these demons on guard proves that Deena was right about something big happening on Earth. It also meant that he knew that God was sending a team to Hell. We hoped the reason for the team was unknown to him.

I started the conversation with a general philosophical observation. I seem to do that a lot.

"This is a helluva situation. How did we get involved in this? We're just typical suburbanites trying to make a living and raise our kids and here we are fighting demons in Hell. If the devil knows we're coming, he probably knows why. If so, we're in deep trouble."

Nobody disagreed.

Jenny said, "You're right, Jack, but we really have little choice but to go on and wait to hear from Deena. I think we may be special, though, Jack. I don't think She would pick 'typical' people to recruit for a mission like this. Think of all the effort that's been spent getting us prepared."

She was right, of course. There were a few more moments of silence.

"Of course, we assume that Deena knows something is wrong," said Hud.

"If her cameras were on us as they should have been, she already knows about the demon fight," observed Maggie.

Everyone chewed on that for a minute and I said, "That's the least of our problems. We really need to get away from here as quickly as possible. How soon can Maggie travel?"

"Now," Maggie said struggling to sit up.

Jenny looked at the sky and said, "Back down, girl. Not yet. It's too cloudy to see the sun's position, but I think we need to try to figure on two more hours. We need to keep Maggie warm but also need to stay warm and flexible ourselves. I propose that one of us stay with Maggie and the other two move about and scout the area as well as guard our site."

I agreed. "I also want to bring up something Deena said this morning. She told us we really need a leader but that we shouldn't decide on who it should be until we had action in the field. I had always assumed it would be Hud because of his military background, but I believe that during the last six hours, one of us really stands out. I nominate Jenny."

"That's crazy," Jenny exploded. "I'm just a housewife."

"Second the nomination," Hud said. "You were just a housewife but now are a leader. You've made every important decision since we hit this place and you've been right every time."

"Agreed," said Maggie. "No choice, Jenny. You're selected."

"I think y'all are crazy. I have never led anything in my life," said Jenny.

No one responded.

Finally she jumped up and said, "Hud, you stay with Maggie first. I want you to get right up close to her to keep her warm." She grinned and added, "But not too close. You saw what I did to that demoness?"

"Yes, dear. I will add no internal warmth."

"Jack, let's scout around a bit."

I grudgingly got out from under the fronds and immediately started to shiver. Somewhere in the deep recesses of my mind, I recall hearing that bodies adjust to changes in temperature and altitude pretty quickly as long as the changes are not too severe. We'd just have to see about Hell.

I handed Hud a new water bottle for Maggie and joined Jenny as she moved out of camp. To add to our fun and games a light cold rain had started to fall. Needles of water pricked my skin and I was truly miserable.

We moved toward the demon camp first. It was easy to find because it was under the tallest tree in the area. Probably made them easier to locate by the roving teams. Of course, the team probably had detectors of some kind, so maybe it was just for comfort.

Anyway, it served its purpose. Jenny proposed we use it as a starting point, move out about 500 yards and then split up and make a circle around the tree with one of us walking in zigzag fashion just outside the circle and the other doing the same just inside, staying about 10-20 yards apart. If either of us encountered demons, we would try to avoid detection and head for our partner as quickly and quietly as possible.

I took the outside portion since I could cover more ground in the same amount of time than Jenny. As I worked my way through the bush, I wondered for the hundredth time what I was doing here. I was mildly uneasy about Jenny's decision to leave Hud with Maggie, but I knew she had done it on purpose, no doubt to break down any old barriers and habits which might affect our performance. I understood this but I was still uncomfortable. I also felt guilty because I still had a reaction every time I looked at Jenny nude. I couldn't keep from sneaking peeks at that little tuft of blond hair. It wasn't so much a desire to sleep with her again, although I admit I would, but rather a reaction to running around with a naked woman who was not my wife.

Back to business. I looked around. The vegetation was fairly lush with those big ferns dominating the flora. There were a few real trees of some type I didn't recognize. These were the tallest of all the vegetation. There were a lot of low, 3 to 4 foot shrubs, many of them spike-leafed with sharp tips. Thank heavens—pardon the pun—for Deena's salve.

About halfway around, a relatively exciting thing happened. I almost stepped on a fair-sized snake. Jenny was close enough to see me so I motioned her over for a look. As it turned out, she was deathly afraid of snakes and I almost had to carry her away. We moved out of the sight of the thing and sat for a few moments under a fern out of the light rain.

"I can take demons, cold, rain, and the devil but I hate snakes. I really hate those sneaky bastards."

"Relax. That snake wasn't poisonous. It was a constrictor type. Don't you remember that Deena said only one variety was even slightly poisonous? And she said the salve would take care of any bites."

"I know. I know all that. After all my major was biology. I still hate the little fuckers."

"Have you seen anything?" I asked changing the subject.

"Not a sign of anything out of place. You?"

"Nothing at all. Boring."

After a pause Jenny said, "Jack?"

"What, Jenny?"

"How do you feel about Hud staying alone with Maggie?"

"I don't know exactly. I guess it bothers me some. Why?"

"I did it that way on purpose to try to break down our old hang-ups. Poor Jack. You're the first to suffer but we'll all get our turn."

"Aren't you even a little bit concerned?

"I guess so. But I'm trying to get over it. I love you and Maggie. If she and Hud should decide to have sex again, I think I could live with it, assuming of course it was not for keeps and Hud kept coming home."

"I don't know if I'm quite that understanding, but I agree with you. In fact, I admit that I find the prospect of another romp with you pretty exciting. But I have no intention of leaving Maggie if it ever happens."

"Really, Jack. Is that a proposition?" Jenny said with a grin.

I grinned back and said, "Could be. I'll let you know."

We were shivering uncontrollably by then. We jumped up and Jenny said, "Back to work."

Then she reached up, threw both arms around my neck and kissed me hard, rubbing her small body against mine. I had an instant reaction and, when she let go and backed off, it was pretty obvious.

She reached out and gave it a pat and said, "Poor Jack. All dressed up and no place to go."

She grinned and disappeared into the bush.

Shaken but much warmer, I resumed my zigzag course. When we had made full circle, we rejoined, neither of us having seen anything.

When we arrived back at the camp, Hud said that Maggie was asleep again but had taken more water and seemed to be fine.

Jenny said, "It's nearly mid-afternoon. I'm getting nervous about being in this area. Somebody's bound to check on those missing guards. Let's check Maggie's leg and think about getting out of here."

We removed the fronds and looked at the leg. It was truly amazing. There was only scar tissue and a little redness along the tear lines. The healing was 90 percent complete.

"Does it feel OK, Maggie?" Jenny inquired, probing around on the wounded area.

"A little sore and stiff but I think OK. Let me stand up and try it out."

Jenny glanced at me and I nodded yes.

She said, "OK. Take my hand."

Maggie pulled herself up and walked gingerly around testing the leg.

"Feels OK. I think I can use it without trouble."

"Good. Let's get out of here. Guys, get those two full water jugs the demons had. We'll just borrow those in addition to our four. I'll take Maggie's and mine. You each take two and the two empties we'll fill with the demon's food and take them along."

We still had our four bags of food concentrates from Deena to carry, so in the end, the three of us had four bags each to carry, leaving Maggie with none for the present. We got everything loaded and Jenny led us out.

She headed north, which got an immediate reaction from Hud.

"If they come to investigate this site," she explained, "I think they'll come from one of the three other directions. We'll go north about a half a mile, turn west for about the same distance, and then go south. We'll be especially careful crossing the east-west line but then we can move pretty rapidly south-south west toward the settlement. We just don't want to be enough off line to be obvious. Since the settlement is due south, that would be the most logical place for them to expect us. We just won't go that way."

Jenny's precautions paid off as we neared the east-west line. We had stopped to listen and we heard movement ahead. Staying low behind a large clump of ferns we soon saw a demon edging through the bush toward the east.

He had a communication device across his back and Hud whispered to Jenny, "We'd better take him."

Jenny agreed, "Maggie, stay back. Hud and Jack, take him down from behind and I'll part his hair with this rock."

We nodded agreement and waited for him to pass. He made it easier by veering toward us and passing close. As soon as he passed, Hud and I charged. He never had a chance. We had him before he turned around and Jenny did her job quickly. It was over in seconds.

As we got up Hud whispered, "Quiet now. There may be a trailer coming along. I'll go scout."

"Go ahead. But be quick," Jenny said. "I want us out of here soon."

Hud left and Maggie walked over to have a look. I bent over the demon and turned him over to check out his communication device. As nearly as we could tell, it was turned off, so until his regular check-in time, we were OK. I dragged his body into the area under a giant fern and covered it with fronds. Then I carefully policed the area to remove as many signs of activity as I could. Hud returned without seeing any other demons, so we picked up our packs and headed out.

We alternated between walking and jogging for the next two hours and Jenny called a halt. If Deena had been with us, I would have kissed her on the spot. Because of our training sessions with her, I was holding up well. Maggie sat down and began rubbing her thigh but insisted that it was fine, just a little stiff. Since it was getting close to evening and still raining, the temperature was dropping rapidly.

We shivered and shook and Jenny said, "Let's eat some bread and drink some water and go on for a while. We need to go farther than they think we can tonight."

Everyone agreed.

We were too cold to really rest so we ate quickly, drank some water and left. We went hard for another four hours or so, with stops only for water and nature calls. It had gotten dark during the last couple of hours and the cold had really set in. Deena's plan called for us to be several miles further south by nightfall but our long delay messed up the plan. It felt like it was below freezing but was probably about 50 when we finally stopped.

We camped near a huge clump of the giant ferns, several of the plants massed together. I pushed my way between the base of two of them and entered an area that was totally covered and relatively dry. It was just big enough for four and the floor was thick with the old fronds. I backed out and told the Maggie and Jenny to get in and get settled. Hud and I went over to some other plants and began removing some of their lower and dryer fronds. We carried several bundles over to our little hotel room, shoved them through the thicket to Maggie, then pushed our way in.

They had more bread ready plus some of the dried fish. We wolfed down the meal, then laid down and pulled the fronds over us. Maggie and Jenny were in the middle and I was next to Maggie and Hud to Jenny. We shivered for awhile but gradually our body heat and the insulating effect of the fronds made it almost cozy. Hud was up once during the night, and said that it was really cold, probably near or even below 40 degrees. We survived it, though, so once again, our physical training was serving us well.

Jenny had us up and eating at dawn and ready to leave after toilet stops. We moved out rapidly, easy to do since it was cold. It was a pleasure to jog, so we made great time in the first few hours. By then, the sun had warmed things up nicely, so we took a break, snacked, and discussed our situation. We estimated that we had gone about 20 miles yesterday and probably 12 more already this morning. We had originally planned to do about 30 miles a day, and now agreed we could handle more. We also discussed whether or not we had been detected. The consensus was that we had not, given the lack of sophistication in the tools the demons were searching with. They apparently didn't even have helicopters, due no doubt to that ridiculous ban on anything metallic. We decided that if there were no more surprises, and if we moved rapidly, we could reach the settlement unmolested.

"What's to keep them from just setting up a watch and waiting for us at the settlement?" Hud asked.

"Good question," I said. "Maybe we ought to divert to another settlement."

"If memory serves," Maggie said, "there is one about 50 miles southwest of our original target. They are farther apart this far north."

"It makes sense to me," Jenny said. "We're still west of where we should be anyway, so we'll stay over here and head more southerly at the appropriate time."

This decided, we struck out again. That night, we estimated that we had managed to put in a 50-mile day.

We were in much warmer country now, with the temperature probably about 60. The next day, Thursday I think, passed without incident except that it got noticeably and progressively hotter. Not being too fond of hot weather, I was not a totally happy camper. But, you know me. Never a complaint to the masses.

Our new settlement target was called Ceras 2, and was one of a whole tier or ring of Ceras settlements running east and west, along the latitude lines. These Ceras settlements were the northernmost ring or tier. Ceras 1 had been our original target. Ceras 2 was west of Ceras 1 and an estimated 220 to 230 miles from our touchdown point. We had covered about 120, leaving us about three more days. Our water and food would hold out but only because we had that extra stuff from the demons. Without that, we couldn't have reached the alternate site. Poor planning on someone's part.

The next day, Friday, we traveled about 35 miles, then stopped for a late afternoon rest. The bush was even lower now, barely reaching the tops of our heads, which meant we were traveling exposed to any surveillance in the area. The terrain was becoming more desert-like as we made our way south. The prodigious ferns were gone, replaced with a gray-green shrub resembling the creosote plant in Arizona.

Over the next two days, the brush would continue to diminish to no more than knee high. And it was considerably thinner. I could see now why the major agricultural area was in this latitude—the sparse native vegetation left room for the tchadbe plants to grow. They were actually planted right in among the native bushes and grasses so that the young tchadbe was shaded from the brutal sun.

At the end of our rest stop, I stretched and started to stand up when I caught movement out of the corner of my eye. I ducked back down and motioned the others to stay low. I crawled toward the movement and came to a fairly tall shrub that would shield me from view. I slowly raised up and looked across the bush. There was a demon riding on one of the large draft animals. He was headed almost due north and was going to miss us on the east side. I motioned to the others and they moved over cautiously. One by one, they had a look. Hud observed that he looked like he was wearing a communication device similar to the one worn by the demon we killed several days ago. What worried us was that there shouldn't have been a demon this far west unless it was on a special mission of some kind. I hoped we weren't that mission.

After he passed from sight we resumed our journey and did another 25 miles, not stopping until nearly midnight. Seeing that demon convinced us that we needed to arrive at our destination and integrate with the locals as quickly as possible. It was still about 60 miles away, but we could make it tomorrow if we started early.

Jenny had us up before dawn, bless her demented little soul, but we were all so stiff and sore we weren't too eager to start out again. We limped around a bit, complained about how old we all felt, and tried to loosen up. As I watched my colleagues, I noticed a remarkable and almost overnight change. Everyone was a deep bronze color. Maggie had lost several pounds and looked marvelous. Her breasts rode high again and she was firm all over. Jenny was even trimmer than before, and looked solid as a rock. She looked good in all the right places. Hud had probably lost 20 pounds and was clearly more muscular. He looked like he could go 15 rounds with a heavyweight champ. As for me, I realized that I felt like an 18-year-old. I wondered if it would carry over into my sex life. No, 'wondered' is the wrong word. Hoped.

fifteen

We left for the settlement after agreeing that we would have to slow down as we neared the fields. Four people not working but rushing somewhere together would be sure to attract the wrong attention, you know. We decided that as soon as we could see any tchadbe workers, we would stop and wait until dark to move in. We knew from our briefings that we would hit these fields about two or three miles out of this settlement on the north side. And because we no longer had the luxury of the head-high vegetation to shield us, we would have to use the crouch-and-run technique to make our final approach, going from brush area to brush area one at a time, using one of us as a forward scout.

With evening fast approaching, we finally stopped. Hud, our navigator, said we were somewhere between four or five miles out and needed to begin our scouting maneuvers. He volunteered and off he went. We found what shade we could and settled in to rest. I can promise you that I'm going to be good for the rest of my life because I want to go to Heaven. It's hot in Hell. It was easily 105 degrees that afternoon. And I had nothing but my gritty grimy hand to wipe away the sweat pouring down my face.

Hud returned about an hour later and reported finding the workers about a mile ahead. We walked upright for awhile and then went to a crawl alternating with a duck-walk until we reached a point near the fields. The workers were mostly gone, but two of them were still there, talking to a demon overseer. About five minutes later they all left. We waited about 15 minutes and then cautiously moved forward. About two miles later we came upon a crudely built house. It was a really primitive adobe with one narrow window opening and a larger hole for a door. A resident of Hell had obviously constructed it by hand. We saw no sign of life, but still gave it a wide berth and continued on until we saw the settlement buildings in the distance. I have to admit to a twinge of homesickness, realizing that my own home and my own kids were not waiting up ahead for me. Exactly what was waiting up ahead? Once again, I had to focus on pushing those vague fears and doubts out of the old brain.

At dusk, Jenny asked me to go into the area near the settlement to find out whether or not any new arrivals had come in on the food caravan that day. It was Saturday, and we needed access to the food machine. Since credit was normally given on Sunday, we needed a plausible reason for passing by the machine. I left feeling naked and alone. Of course, I was both. As I neared the settlement, I saw people walking in from all directions toward the food hall. Others were coming out of the barracks. I picked a man walking alone from the barracks toward the food hall and joined him on the path.

"Evening," I said casually.

"Evening," he returned.

"Do you know if the food cart from Acton 2 came in today?" Acton 2 was a settlement in the second ring.

"I don't know about Acton 2, but I came in on one from Ceras 1 about an hour ago."

Ceras 1 was the settlement we had originally targeted.

"Did a lot of people arrive with you?"

"About fifty, I reckon. Why?"

"No reason. Just curious. I'm expecting a friend but he should come from Acton 2. Who can tell as erratic as the schedules are these days."

"You got that right," he said and moved slowly on.

"Thanks," I called to his disappearing back. So far I seem to be saying the right things.

He waved a hand and went on.

I returned to my group and reported. This was better than we could have hoped for since we had been thoroughly briefed on Ceras 1. We moved on toward the food hall and entered the door used to receive credit from the machine. The room was large and was divided by ropes and stanchions into lanes for crowd control on Sundays. The credit line was deserted now, so we moved on over to an entry point. Maggie went first.

She pushed the button and the machine said, "What is your reason for coming on Saturday?"

"I just arrived from Ceras 1 this evening."

"Are you alone?"

Maggie looked around nervously and said, "Yes."

"No food credit is being granted without an interview by the commander. Record your hand prints and report to the commander's office immediately. Failure to do so will result in punishment."

Maggie backed out quietly and we moved quickly toward the door.

"Record your hand prints now. You are required to record your hand prints now," the machine droned.

We had cleared the door and were moving toward the path to the fields when the sirens started. Jenny had us pause and look around like everyone else was doing and then move slowly onto the path to the fields. If the building had been equipped with better lights we would have been caught but we were able to fade quickly into the darkness and run rapidly away.

Again, Hell's lack of expenditure for security came to our rescue. Lacking vehicles or helicopters, they were limited in their ability to pursue. We could run faster and for longer distances than a demon and almost as fast as one of the ox-like beasts with a demon aboard. They also didn't know which direction we had taken, and they probably were looking for a lone female, anyhow. In truth, we didn't know which direction we were going either. We just ran and ran together.

After about three miles at a fast run, Jenny called a halt. We took stock. We each had our water bottles but had abandoned our food bottles and the demons' bottles so we wouldn't be conspicuous. Our bottles were each about a third full, enough for a full day's trek in the heat. Hud said we were headed east or maybe a little southeast. We decided to continue in that direction for awhile to lose any remaining pursuit and then make a decision about what to do next.

In the next two hours we covered an estimated 10 miles and were beginning to feel it. Jenny stopped us and we all dropped to the ground. I knew I was thirsty and hungry, but I was too tired to care right at that moment.

"It's nearly midnight. We've got to decide what to do," she said. "It won't do us any good to go to Ceras 1 because they were expecting us there. In fact, all the perimeter settlements are likely to have a block on the food machines. I think we're going to have to go to one of the Actons in the second tier of settlements. What do you think? Hud?"

"There are three within reach. We just left Ceras 2 and are already about 15 miles southeast. From here if we head southwest for 60 miles, we reach Acton 1. Directly south of here, about 45 miles away, is Acton 2. And some 35 miles southeast of here is Acton 3. There is a fourth option. If we go south-southeast, we'll pass between Acton 2 and 3 and arrive at Nikor 5, which is in the third tier. It's a good 80 miles away and we won't have enough water for 2 days."

Maggie sat up and said, "Since they know we were in Ceras 2, the logical thing for them to assume is that we will try to make one of the Actons. They will program those machines too."

I agreed. "She's right. We need to shoot for Nikor 5."

"Out of the question," Jenny responded. "We have just enough water for about 30 miles in this heat. Be reasonable, Jack."

"I am. The solution is simple. We travel at night while it it's cool. We can cover 35 miles by the time it gets hot tomorrow. We can cover the rest Sunday night."

Hud said, "We'll still run out of water sometime Sunday night. And remember, we have no food."

"We'll be dehydrated and half-starved but we'll be in the third tier and have a chance," I countered.

"How about this?" Maggie offered. "We head for Nikor 5 and do the 35 miles tonight. Then we rest all day and take stock at that point. We either try for Nikor 5 or abort. We should only be about 20 miles from Acton 3 by then. Right Hud?"

"Closer to 15. We'll actually be going a little east of south-southeast." Hud somehow managed to keep track of where we were thanks both to the skills he learned in the military, at a two-hour session on Noah's Ark, and to the small non-metallic compass he kept in his water pouch. Although he had no way of being sure, he could usually tell how far we had gone or had to go.

Jenny said, "I think that's our best plan. Let's go."

"Wait 'til I pee," Hud groaned as he struggled to get up.

We all followed Hud's lead and then were off. It was a long and tedious night. We alternated running and walking and took occasional ten minute breaks. Seven o'clock found us about 35 miles closer to Nikor 5 with about 45 miles to go. We had used about half of our water so we were thirsty all the time now. We broke off some shrubs, built a thick shelter from the sun and stretched out in our shady nest to sleep. It was really hot by noon making sleep almost impossible. We still managed a few hours each. About 4:00 that afternoon everyone was wide-awake. It had to be 110 degrees. We were thirsty and hungry. And beyond dirty.

Maggie said, "Anyone for sex?"

This elicited a few chuckles but nothing firm came up. Pardon the pun.

"Well, gang, how do we want to proceed?" asked Jenny.

"Do we have a choice?" Hud asked.

Maggie said, "I vote for Nikor 5. If we go to Acton 3 and can't get food, we'd have to wait until next Sunday, a week from today. We could live on water that long but what if the machine is set to question anyone new? Then we'd have to abort the entire mission and go for recall. We've come too far for that, in my opinion."

"That may happen to us at Nikor 5, too, but at least we have a better chance there," I added. "And, like Maggie says, we can always abort and activate recall if it turns out we can't make Nikor 5 tonight."

Jenny and Hud agreed, so as dark approached we struck out for Nikor 5. About midnight we stopped to rest. We were all beginning to feel dehydrated. Hud said we had done about 20 miles.

"We can't keep up this pace all night," Jenny panted, "but we have about 7 hours to make about 25 more miles so that we get there during breakfast hours. I think I can make it."

"I feel like I can, too," Maggie said. "But I'm worried about Hud and Jack."

We both protested but she went on. "Seriously. You both have covered the same distance on the same amount of water with a much larger body mass. You both show the classic signs of dehydration. Neither of you went on our last pee stop, did you?"

She had been very observant.

"What do you think we should do?" Jenny asked.

"I think we should give each of them a good drink now and split the rest four ways for the rest of the night."

Hud and I protested vehemently. And lost. No surprise there. And I'll have to admit, it did help. I could feel life come back into my limbs. Maggie and Jenny each took a small sip and we pushed on.

The rest of this journey was, again, nightmarish. Hud fell and cut his arm on a palmetto-type plant. The damn thing must have been poisonous because his arm began to swell almost immediately. The injection should have stopped it, but it didn't. We tried the salve and after about 20 minutes it started to go down. Nevertheless, it slowed him down considerably. We took our last drink on that stop. It was no more than a few tablespoons each. The remaining two hours were really hell. We had reached the fields and at least had a path to fol-low, but Hud kept falling and I fell several times myself. Maggie and Jenny were staggering and almost delirious by the time we sighted the settlement.

It was still the breakfast hour and people were leaving the bar-racks to go to the food hall. I saw the water-fill spigot over near the barracks' entrance. Some asshole had it turned on wide open, presumably to make it cooler, and the ground 10 feet around it was slick and cool and deliciously wet. I was on my way before I even started to say "I'll go over and fill a jug and bring it back."

Nobody protested so I continued on all fours. We were over on the side of the barracks but I wanted to approach from behind and appear as though I had come in from a private home. The demons' barracks would also be blocked from view if I approached from that direction. I got on line and moved in to the barracks and around to the front. There were three people in line ahead of me for water. I sauntered over and became the fourth. Just in front of me was a saucy redhead (yes, a natural redhead) who chose to be friendly.

She looked me over and said, "Rough night?"

I tried to grin. "It was. Had a fight with the little woman and had to sleep outside."

She laughed and said, "From the looks of your face, she must have clouted you several times."

I just grinned. It was her turn for water and the sound of it was slowly driving me mad.

"See you later," she said with a smile. "Maybe we can get together when you get cleaned up some. Interested?"

"Could be," I said, and politely listened to her give me her name and particulars as I started to fill my jug. I leaned over and moved the jug and took a small drink. It tasted like Heaven. Then I finished filling it and slowly moved back to the side of the barracks. Once at the back, I went toward the bush and found the others. I handed the jug to Jenny. She hand fed some to Hud and then gave it to Maggie. Maggie had a short pull and returned it to Jenny. We made the rounds about four times before everyone took a break.

"Let's move into the barracks for showers," I said. "We're going to attract attention the way we look now. Trust me. I speak from experience." Nobody even asked me for details. Very disappointing. I wanted to brag about how the redhead had practically propositioned me on the spot, dirt and all.

We ambled toward the barracks entrance, casually chatting among ourselves. We hadn't showered since we hit Hell, and we were a pretty gamey group, to put it mildly. Our body sweat had dried until we literally had white salt deposits on our skin mixed in with gray and brown and red dirt. And of course lots of sand.

Fortunately, the breakfast hour was in full swing and the barracks were practically deserted. As we approached the door a couple came out and stared at us but went on, shaking their heads. We went on in like we belonged there. The place was really impressive, much bigger than we expected. There were long rows of cubicles on either side with a wide center aisle. The cubicles were stacked three high, with ladders providing access to the upper levels. The building must have been about 300 feet long and would probably hold around 800-1000 people. Some inner ring settlements near the equator had up to 10 of these buildings. Ours here in the outer ring settlement had just two.

Looking down the aisle, we could see that about every 15 cubicles there was a huge room on the left with toilets and another on the right with showers. They were, of course, unisex. Wasn't hard to tell as we watched people moving in and out of the rooms and the cubicles.

We sauntered down the aisle to get a closer look at the barracks. The cubicles were not all the same size. Most were for two persons but a few would accommodate four and a few more up to six. The ceilings were about seven feet high with a central light. There were no doors, so there was no real privacy. The walls were painted a pale peach-pink, and both the floor and ceiling were a darker shade of the same color. They didn't really have beds but instead had shelves about the size of twin beds, covered with a blanket-type of material. Some people had placed the shelves side by side to make a double while others used both sides of the cubicle to make twins. These shelves were apparently not made of a super-hard material because they did give a little to the touch, but they weren't what you would call luxury-quality either. Triple-extra firm might cover it. Yes, I did try out one of them in an empty cubicle. Nobody would be mad over that, I decided.

We moved on to the first set of showers and went inside. Along one wall was a long row of shower heads about three feet apart, each with a drain, none with any privacy. The other wall had lavatories, each with a mirror above and, on the left of the mirror, some sort of shaving-hair cutting device, electrically powered but made of a non-metallic material I couldn't identify.

"I can't wait to get undressed," said Jenny. She took off her water jug and placed it on a lavatory.

We all did the same and moved to the showers. I wondered why there was only one faucet. I soon found out. There was only one water temperature–cold. But at this point, it didn't matter.

I moved into a shower next to Maggie, who was dancing around in the cold.

I pumped the soap dispenser and offered to wash her back.

"Just be sure that's all you try to wash, you dirty old man."

She turned around, I soaped her back thoroughly and then reached around and grabbed both of her boobs.

She laughed and said, "Later, you pervert. Now turn around and I'll do your back."

I can't remember a better shower.

We finished and walked towards the lavatories. As we approached, a drying fan was automatically activated for each of us. You simply raised your arms, turned around, and rubbed the wettest spots until you were dry. Then we used the razor machines. And let me tell you, that was a weird experience. The devices were reminiscent of those dog-grooming machines you see advertised on TV in the wee hours of the morning. They each had a vacuum tube to suck away the hair as you cut it off. I shaved close, leaving no stubble at all, and on the spur of the moment, cut my hair very close in what seemed to be the latest Hell style. Maggie and Jenny also had adopted the very short haircut and shaved armpits and legs. This seemed to be an optional grooming routine on Hell, though. Some women did and some didn't.

When we finally felt human again, we went into the Hall and moved to the far end where there was a sitting area for those who wanted to socialize or play games and cards. It was deserted at this hour. We went to a table for four in the far corner and held a strategy session.

"The first priority has to be food," Jenny said. "Let's assume we get in OK."

"I think we had better scout around and try to determine first whether or not they are checking. If we try and fail we'll have to run again," I said.

"I think Jack's right," Hud said. "What do we do if they are checking?"

It was quiet for awhile and then Jenny said, "We have three choices. We can wait until Sunday and hope they don't check then. Or we can take today's cart to another settlement one more ring in. Finally, we can abort and do recall."

Maggie said, "None of those has much appeal but I think if we have to choose we should move in one ring. That would put us much closer to our objective plus each ring in reduces the chance that we will be checked. I don't think I can go until Sunday without food."

Jenny responded, "Sounds reasonable to me. Let's fan out as the breakfast crowds leave and see what we can learn. Meet at the water fill in 30 minutes."

We went out into the yard and separated. I moved over near the food machine entrance and sat on a bench nearby. I hit pay dirt almost immediately.

A man and a woman were heading for the entrance, the man saying, "This is too much. I got in at noon yesterday and haven't eaten since. What is this bullshit about having to interview the commandant before passing the food machine? Those stupid damned demons always have some dumbass new rule."

They entered the door and I went toward the water fill nodding to Jenny and Maggie as I went by them. I didn't see Hud. They sauntered over and I told them the bad news. We stood around chatting casually, and finally Hud arrived. He had heard the same story, and had gone on to check on food convoys for the day. One was leaving in about 30 minutes, for Echal 2 on the next ring. He had watched them loading the tchadbe and loading some people making the trip and saw that the demons weren't checking anybody.

"I guess we'd better try it," said Jenny. "We can't walk it without food."

Everyone agreed, so we went to the warehouse area next to the food court to load up. This particular convoy was three carts long and had 10 of the big draft animals just being hooked up. The last cart had very little cargo. This is where the passengers were loading. To one side of the cart there was a stack of seating pads made out of the same material as the mattresses. We each took one and boarded. I didn't even see a demon look our way. They were preoccupied with loading the tchadbe bales. Within minutes the driver got aboard and we left 10 minutes early.

We had not slept all night and were totally exhausted, so the first hours of the journey were a blur. We had hoped some lunch would be provided but no such luck. The sun was low when we sighted Echal 2 and thirty minutes later we were there.

No one met the cart and we immediately went to the food machine area to see how the new arrivals made out. Several of our fellow travelers got in line and we fell in at the back. They passed through without incident and it was Maggie's turn.

"Why are you here on Monday?" queried the machine.

"Newly arrived from Nikor 5"

"Did you work three days last week?"

"Yes"

"Press your hand on the screen."

Maggie did.

"Credit granted until Sunday. Move on. Next."

We all passed.

The dining hall opened at 6:00 and the wait was interminable. We waited until about 6:30 and then went in. The machine took our hand prints without incident and we had our first meal in days. I ate like a starved man and was so full I could hardly walk. Later we took a walk and then went to the barracks. Maggie and I selected an upper level cubicle that felt more private than the lower ones. After "settling in", we took showers. We made love for the first time since we arrived in Hell and then slept like the dead.

sixteen

The next morning, Tuesday, we rejoined Hud and Jenny and went to breakfast. It was bland but adequate and again I ate too much. After breakfast we held a council of war in the barracks sitting area, pretending to play a rousing game of poker. It was still about 4000 miles to the southern polar regions and at the normal cart rate of about 80 miles per day it would take 50 days to cover it if we traveled everyday. That would be hard, however, since the average resident who was headed to the South Pole for vacation traveled three days a week and worked four. This kept them in food and built up a day of recreation each week that could be used for vacation or recreation at a settlement. Deena said we should adapt ourselves to a similar schedule. If we traveled four days per week it would take about 13 weeks or more than three months. Add to that the fact that some settlements did not have a daily cart automatically going in the direction you wanted to go. So more delay—maybe another month or two.

We reviewed and refined all of our options. Hud had a schedule of cart departures that we studied and restudied. The next cart of interest to us left Sunday morning going south to Fugim 3, in ring 5 and then on to Mento 5 in the 6th ring, a total distance of about 90 miles. We decided to take this one. We continued to talk and at

9:00 the cleaning warning sounded. That meant that in 10 minutes the entire barracks would be pressure-washed for the day. This was an automatic process, and struck me as a pretty good idea in the circumstances.

We went outside and took a walk in the bush. There were people milling around all over–those choosing to take a day off–so we were not conspicuous. After lunch we went back to the barracks, showered and took a nap. After the evening meal, we went to the recreation hall. The inside was gaudy and loud and crowded. Music blared out of a huge set of speakers and a few were dancing. We found a table and ordered drinks.

Jenny wanted to dance so Hud obliged. Maggie and I talked awhile and then joined them on the dance floor. After awhile we switched partners and danced some more. Fortunately they were all fast songs and didn't involve much body contact.

We had another drink and then Maggie said, "Let's go play the slots awhile. Maybe we'll win a free trip to the South Pole."

We took our drinks and wandered into the gambling area. To play the slots you put your hand on the screen and your credit balance was transferred to the machine. To quit, you did the same.

Maggie picked her machine and started. In about five minutes, she hit a jackpot large enough to keep her in gambling money for a month, at least.

"I've always been lucky at slots," Maggie said happily. "How are y'all doing?"

"Don't ask," Jenny said. "I'm jealous."

"The winner buys our plane tickets," Hud quipped.

"First class, of course," Maggie replied.

I had my usual good luck and lost most of my allotted credit. Hud ran out early and was hanging around the bar area when we came up to leave. We gathered him up and went outside.

It was a rather pleasant night, cool and dry as usual.

We were walking toward the barracks when Hud, who had been unusually quiet, said, "Let's move away from the buildings. I have something to tell you."

We sauntered over to one side and he continued, "After I lost my credit allotment I went to the bar and struck up a conversation with a guy drinking alone. We talked awhile and he finally asked me what I thought about the mortal spy rumors. I told him I had just arrived, and pleaded ignorance, so he told me what he had heard about it. The demon overseer at his field was kind of matey and often told them things she shouldn't have. This evening after dinner he ran into her walking across the yard. She said word had just come in that there were four spies from Earth loose and they thought they might be here. They are going to wait until tomorrow after breakfast and then run everybody through blood tests to determine mortality. They hope to identify them at breakfast and avoid the hassle."

"Those sons of bitches," Jenny exploded. "Why don't they leave us alone?"

"Now, Jenny. Don't get excited," Hud said. "We've got to figure out a plan. I've been thinking about it. We're OK for the night and morning until we approach the food machine. Then they will be able to tell we're new arrivals and we will be questioned. So we get out before breakfast."

"Get out where?" Jenny said. "I don't relish walking to the South Pole, but you are right, Hud. Should we leave now or at breakfast hour?"

"If we have to make another foodless trek," I said, "I think we should chance it tonight and get some rest and then leave at daybreak. Like Hud pointed out, the immediate danger for us is the food machines. They've got our hand prints but can't identify us as people until we use the machine again."

"Maggie?" Jenny asked.

"I would prefer to sleep first, if it's safe to wait."

"So would I," Jenny said. "And who knows what's safe anymore? Let's go to bed and see what the morning brings."

They took Maggie and Hud out right in front of me. We were all up early, ready to leave. As we started out of the barracks door, Jenny said she had to go to the bathroom. We told her that we would mill around outside while we waited. I decided to look behind the barracks to be sure that route blocked the view from the demons' barracks like it had on Nikor 5. Satisfied that it did, I started back around when I saw a squad of six demons taking Hud and Maggie toward the demons' barracks. They appeared to have given up without a fight, a smart decision with six demons to contend with. I quickly edged my way up to the front and saw that their water bags had been dropped in the capture and were still there. I strolled casually over, retrieved them, and turned back to the front door of the barracks just as Jenny emerged.

"Where are Hud and Maggie?"

I moved up close to her and said in a low voice, "Captured. Come with me quickly."

"What do you mean captured? Where were you?"

I explained briefly and then as we were about to leave the back of the building and enter the bush said, "Let's get below the level of the foliage and move out of here."

"But we can't just leave them."

"We have to. Think about it. What good are we for them if we're caught, too?"

"Yeah, OK, you're right. Let's move."

It took a while to get out of sight of the settlement. We were crossing fallow fields and no one was working as far as we could tell. I got out Hud's compass, checked our course, and saw that we were headed Northeast. I turned to say something to Jenny and saw that she was sitting on the ground, crying softly. I squatted down and said, "Hey, fearless leader. What's our next move?"

"I don't know," she sniffed. "All I know is that those sons of bitches have my Hud and Maggie and if they hurt them I'm going to spend the rest of my life trying to kill every fucking one of them."

I guess I must have smiled a little, because she puffed up and said, "I mean it, Jack. I'm already fed up with this bullshit mission and those fucking demons."

"Me too. Now listen. We probably need to circle the fields of Echal 2 over to the east and then turn to the south toward Fugim 3 and Mento 5. We've got to have food. Luckily, we've both got the two jugs of water Maggie and Hud left behind for us to find. The demons won't have a clue about what we're going to do, so if we move, we can stay ahead of them. Now follow me on this one. The cart train to Mento 5 has got to be the one that they'll put Hud and

Maggie on to get them south. We'll have to figure out a way to rescue them from that cart."

"Let's go," she said.

We broke into a fast jog and moved out. I didn't ask any questions, but I knew she already had formulated a scheme.

I seem to remember that the world record for the 26+ mile marathon was a few minutes over two hours. We didn't try to match that pace in 115 degree heat even though we were physically fit, but we really came close. Early in the afternoon, some 40 miles later, we spotted the workers of Fugim 3. We circled around the workers and entered the settlement from the north. Once again, we were able to come up behind the barracks and arrive undetected. We filled our jugs at the water spigot and went into the barracks. We could hear someone in the shower but no one else was around. We moved down to the lounging area and sat down on a sofa-like piece of furniture to wait. We hoped the cart train with Hud and Maggie aboard would arrive soon. We could see the loading area through the glass at the end of the building so we just sat and feigned some flirty chatting.

After a bit, Jenny dozed off. I was nodding myself when a cart pulled in. I nudged Jenny and got up to look out the window. She moved up beside me and said, "See 'em?"

"I don't know. This is going to be tough with all those people getting off. I would guess they'll give them a coach to themselves and let others wait for later carts. Let's go out and get a closer look."

"Is it safe?"

"If Hud and Maggie aren't there, it is. There's no direct communication between settlements so we shouldn't be known here. I don't think anybody will be looking for us yet."

As we were passing the food hall, a man walked by us, and I said casually, "Where'd that convoy come in from?"

"Mento 5, I think," he said.

"Thanks." I turned to Jenny and said, "I hope your sister is on it this time."

"Don't mention it." He moved on.

"Jenny, let's get in the food line."

She agreed. We breezed right through, had a snack, and then walked slowly back to the barracks. I really hate snacks, because they leave me still famished but teased about the food to come. But it was only 5:00. No meal for at least an hour. So we went into the barracks to shower before the workers arrived and filled the place up.

I thought I was used to nudity. But Jenny was really nude in that shower. She knew it and danced around obviously for my benefit.

Finally, she said, "Trade you a backwash."

"OK. Turn around."

I pumped my hand full of soap and began to wash her back. I could feel myself becoming aroused, but I couldn't control it. Fortunately, no one else was around. I don't know why that mattered since at our last shower a couple did it right in front of us. But it did. Traces of the old puritanical upbringing, I guess.

Jenny said, "Now you." And she turned around.

She looked down and said, "Poor Jack. I'm glad you find me stimulating. Now turn around so I can wash your back."

She scrubbed a while then turned me around and looked again and said, "I thought cold showers were supposed to take care of that problem."

"Very funny."

"I'm bad to tease you, Jack." She reached out and took me in her hand and said, "Just let me know when you're ready. I think Hud and Maggie would understand."

Then she turned and went to the dryer.

I stood there long enough for the shower to do its work and then moved to the dryer. Jenny was shaving and I went over to do the same.

We killed time until 6:00 and then went to the food hall. We ate a huge meal in case it was our last for a while. As we were leaving the food hall another convoy pulled in, this one from Echal 2. We saw them unload Hud and Maggie. They had on some sort of rope handcuffs and a leather collar with a leash, but there weren't any signs of abuse. We stepped into the waning sunlight and then shrank back into the shadows when I knew for sure that Hud had seen us. We slowly walked back toward the barracks.

"You know we can't stay here tonight. The commander is getting a report on us as we speak. Let's get our water bags and go."

"What about Hud and Maggie?"

"We'll try to intercept the convoy tomorrow between here and Mento 5. They were the only ones on board besides a guard and the driver. Surely we can handle two demons even though you are really undersized."

She grinned and said, "I swing a mean rock."

We got the water bags and left. It was still daylight so we did the "around to the back of the barracks" trick and headed to the east and then south. We paralleled the main trail to Mento 5 and looked for a good ambush spot. It soon became dark but Hell's moon was brighter than Earth's and, lucky for us, it was full tonight. The terrain, which had been unrelentingly flat and boring as an empty kitchen table since we arrived, was now gently undulating. Spread out ahead of us were actually some recognizable valleys and small hills. When we were about 10 miles out and moving slowly in the cool night, the trail entered one of these small valleys. About a half a mile down was a sandy stretch which the carts had obviously had trouble negotiating. There were several separate trails off to the left and the right of the main road, showing that there had been various attempts made to find a better way. Alongside the most used of the trails was a particularly thick stand of vegetation four to five feet high and unusually dense all the way from the ground up.

"This spot was made for us, Jenny. We'll crouch behind this clump of thick shrubbery, and when they slow to go through this sand, we'll take 'em. The driver won't see us coming, so you part his hair with your rock, then come over and help me. The guard is sure to see me come into the cart and will fight like a tiger. Hud and Maggie might be able to help some but we can't count on it."

"OK, sounds fairly straightforward to me."

"Let's find a place to sleep near the trail in case they try to make a night run." We wandered over to a large rock outcropping and down at the base, sure enough, there was a small area just big enough for a cozy two-some under a jutted-out piece of rock. I gathered some foliage to lie on and to cover with. It still got down into the low 60's at night, which is chilly even for a tough country guy like myself. We drank some water and settled down under the rock. Jenny started shivering and I turned over and laid against her spoon fashion. I again felt myself becoming aroused. I was angry with myself for thinking of making love to Jenny while Maggie was trussed up in some demon jail. I resolved not to do it.

Jenny felt me growing and squirmed back tighter against me. I knew that I was going to lose.

"Jenny."

"What, Jack?"

"I'm ready if you are."

She didn't answer but turned onto her back and grasped me in her hand. I moved my hand between her legs and gently caressed her. After a few moments, I moved on top and entered her. There was none of the frantic haste of that first time on the couch. She moaned softly and said, "That's it. Nice and easy. We've got all night."

Jenny was a talker.

"Oh, God, Jack. It feels so good. I'm getting close. Oh, God. Yes. Yes. Yes."

Totally spent, I rolled off of her. An hour had probably passed.

"That was wonderful, Jenny."

"Mm-hmm. Sure was."

I lay there thinking for a while.

Then I said, "This is pretty profound for the middle of a desert in Hell, but I think I am beginning to understand the difference between sex and love. I love Maggie and sex is one of ways we express that love. People also have sex sometimes without much love and involvement. I had several teenage flings when it was strictly a physical thing. Maybe you did, too. And that's what happened to us the day Bennie first got involved. Don't get me wrong. I enjoyed it. But except for the guilt afterward, it wasn't very emotional for me and I don't think it was for you either. I was fond of you, but not in love with you. I had thought about what it would be like to have sex with you. Any normal man would. But I had never thought about what it would be like to make love to you, or in other words to have sex because I loved you.

"Sometime during the last couple of weeks, Jenny, I fell in love with you. I think it was a result of the Bennie affair and our close interaction during the training sessions but I really don't know. I just remember thinking one day that I wanted to be around you permanently. I don't think I fell out of love with Maggie one little bit. In fact, I have had to resist the desire to tell her about it so far. I have this fantasy that she will be pleased and say something like 'That's wonderful, Jack. I love her too. She's welcome in our household and our bed.' I didn't know it was possible to love two women at the same time. But I do. Loving you in no way takes away from my continued love for Maggie." I paused. "Jenny, this seemed so simple a moment ago. But it's not. It's damned complicated. And it's going to take some sorting out once we get back to our real lives."

"I know, Jack. I fell in love with you over a year ago at the Fourth of July picnic. It was not any one thing that caused it to happen that particular day. I just looked at you and realized that I loved you. It's a feeling so deep inside that it hurts. Hud knows. I told him and I also told him it didn't mean I wanted casual sex with you and he believed me. I still haven't lied to him. Tonight, though, was different. This was not casual sex. Still, I'll have to tell him. I think he can handle it because I think he's got strong feelings about Maggie and understands my problem."

"Maggie's hard to read. I know she really likes Hud but she won't tell me how she really feels. Maybe when I tell her about this, she'll open up. Or perhaps she will hire Hud to handle the divorce. I don't know."

"It will sort itself out."

We were both quiet for a while.

"Jack?"

"Umm."

"What are we going to do assuming we are successful tomorrow in freeing them?"

"I think I'll wait a few days before I tell Maggie."

She smacked me on the arm and said, "Not about that, silly. About the mission."

"I don't know. You're the leader."

"Thanks a lot. Seriously, when that convoy doesn't arrive at Mento 5, we had better be a long way off. And I have a feeling we are going to get mighty hungry since all the food machines in Hell will be programmed to question newcomers."

"I agree. I also think the devil will cough up the credits needed to put in better communication between settlements in the next few weeks. We don't have a snowball's chance in Hell of getting to the South Pole."

"Agreed. Deena based our potential odds for success on the backwardness of Hell allowing us to move about undetected. We have to consider aborting, don't we?"

"Let's wait until morning and see what happens. This conversation could be academic if you miss that driver's hairline."

"All right. But I'm not going to miss."

She wriggled around and somehow managed to get even closer to me. Inevitably I began to react again. She didn't say anything, just turned over and began to stroke me. A long time later, we drifted off to sleep.

seventeen

We awoke early the next morning, performed our morning ablutions and began brainstorming about the day ahead. The most likely scenario was for the cart to arrive at our location around mid-morning. They only had about 10 miles to cover to get this far, and the usual departure of these carts had been about 8:30. Of course this was not a usual departure. Everyone on the planet had to know about our presence by now, and would be on maximum alert.

We decided that a weapon would be in order for me for when I jumped into the cart with the demon. I let Jenny know how disappointed I was that she doubted my newly discovered machismo, but a grin was as close as I got to an apology from her. We scouted around the area, and I found a straight, solid tree trunk about four feet long with the diameter of a heavy shovel handle. It apparently came from one of the few stunted trees that still grew this far south and I was lucky to find one that large. I broke it at ground level, and it broke in such a way that a point was already partially formed. I found a rock and used it to fine-tune that point and wound up with a pretty serviceable spear. Maybe I could skewer the demon guard before he got to me. Feeling pretty smug with my new equalizer, I practiced my best thrusting technique but again received only a grin as payment. Women!

We worked to improve our hiding place a little bit, designing and arranging so that someone would actually have to stumble right on it to know that it was there. Jenny had found the rock she wanted to use and took it in with her. Actually, I think she took it in to brag. It was a fine obsidian-looking boulder the size of a man's fist. Her hand settled down over it like a glove, thanks to four shallow grooves set parallel to each other on one smooth surface. The opposite surface was a mass of sharply broken points some of them quite long–a really nasty looking weapon. We settled in to wait.

We heard them before we saw them. They were at least an hour early. I gave Jenny a quick kiss for luck and we crouched down ready for the ambush. Jenny was going first since I had to know that the driver was out of commission before turning my back on him.

The convoy was still out of sight when Jenny whispered, "I'm scared and I have to pee."

"I'm scared, too, but it's too late to move. You'll have to go where you are."

She did. Shortly thereafter the convoy entered the valley. As the driver approached the sandy area he slowed and took the most traveled track just like we hoped he would. I gave Jenny's arm a little squeeze and when the driver pulled the cart up even with us, she shot out. He never knew what happened. She hit him as he was leaning forward to whip the animals. As I sprang out, I saw her hit him again and again to be certain. And yes, it was a nasty weapon. His head was not a pretty sight, what with one ear gone, a huge hunk of cheek hanging clear down to his neck, and blood pretty much covering whatever was left of his face. He didn't complain, though. Pretty quiet fellow.

I went up the side and dropped over into the cart. Hud and Maggie were there tethered by their necks on loose leads. To my surprise, there were two demon guards instead of one. Two big males. They both charged and I buried the spear in the chest of the one on the left. He went down without a struggle. The other one, however, never missed a beat, and as I turned to meet him, he slashed my chest open from my left shoulder almost to my navel with a rock similar to Jenny's. I managed to grab his arm as I went down, knocking away the rock. Nevertheless, he fell on top of me and began to pummel me with his gnarled fists. I tried to throw him off but couldn't budge him. Then I saw Hud, stretched out to the limit of his lead, draw back and kick him in the balls. He roared and rolled over, grabbing himself. Hud tried to kick him in the head but he grabbed Hud's leg and shoved him back, twisting the leg violently. You don't forget the sickening sound of breaking bone, so I wasn't at all surprised when Hud screamed in pain. I managed to regain my feet as the guard turned back to me. Maggie jumped forward and with her bound hands dealt him a terrific blow to the back of the neck. It would have killed a human, but this thing just turned and knocked her down. I had seen his rock weapon on the floor of the cart as I got up the last time. I grabbed it and as he turned around I struck and opened a deep gash in his left forearm as he tried to ward off the blow. He bellowed and closed on me again. Just as he grabbed me, Jenny smashed the back of his skull with her rock. Several times. He fell forward on top of me and I hit my head on a bench when we fell. I must have blacked out, because I really don't recall anything more in the cart. I learned later that Jenny had delivered yet another follow-up blow on him, then went to the other one who was still breathing but unconscious, and took him out, too.

I do remember regaining consciousness to find two beautiful women bent over me doing something to my chest. Both of them were crying. I stirred and weakly asked if I was in Heaven.

"Almost, dear," Maggie said. "Now don't move while we try to fix your wound."

Ah, yes. I remembered. Just then a wave of pain washed over me and I went away again. When I faded back in, they were still there apparently holding the wound together while it started to heal.

"Don't move, Jack," Jenny said. "We need you quiet for 10 more minutes."

"What happened to Hud?"

Maggie answered, "Fractured leg and a badly wrenched neck. He fell while he still had the tether on. We'll get to him in a minute. Now shut up and lie still."

I persisted. "And you two?"

Jenny said, "Maggie has a gorgeous black eye. I came through clean as a whistle. Now shut up and lie still."

I sighed and made some comment about lack of respect in today's world before fading out again.

The next time I came around, they were working on Hud. I heard Maggie say, "He's fine. Now, Hud, shut up and be still."

"What does a guy have to do to get any respect around here?" I yelled.

Maggie came over, checked the progress of the healing, and told me not to move for a bit longer. I asked her how bad it had been. She said I hadn't lost any vital parts but had intestines hanging out when they got to me.

"Don't worry," she said. "The salve is working. And we set Hud's leg and injected the ampoule, so we hope his neck will be OK. We rubbed it with salve, so that may help. I don't know, though. Try to rest awhile."

I looked around and could see we were still in the cart with the dead demons. Jenny was in the process of opening the rear gate. Then they moved Hud over closer to me and we held a strategy session.

Jenny started. "We probably have several hours before another convoy passes but we can't be sure. But it doesn't matter because neither of you can move before late afternoon. In Hud's case, it may take until morning. We can carry you over to the next valley in a few hours and hide out there in case someone comes but that doesn't look like a good alternative. Maggie and I could leave and try to somehow sabotage the next convoy that comes by."

I started to protest when the REGEN beam came on right beside the cart. Maggie jumped up and said, "Message." She ran out to retrieve it. The case opened to her touch and she quickly scanned the contents.

"It says, 'Abort repeat abort. Initiate recall immediately. Remember to touch each other. Love, Deena.'"

Maggie and Jenny pulled Hud over beside me until we were touching. They knelt down beside us with their bodies touching each other and us and Maggie said, "Everyone ready?"

She touched behind both ears and we were in Noah's Ark.

It had been our tenth day in Hell.

Deena was standing there smiling and looking as lovely as usual. As Maggie and Jenny got up, Deena came over to us and said, "Jack, I believe you and Hud need to visit Charity's repair chambers. I've ordered two gurneys and some help to move you. Ladies, go to the first door on your left for showers, then take a turn in the chambers. That's a nasty scar on your thigh, Maggie. We need to fix that."

Hud said, "How about telling us what's going on?"

"I have many things to tell you. First, repair. Then food and a short rest. We'll talk after that."

Two huskies with gurneys arrived and loaded us up. If they were angels they were the ugliest ones I had ever seen. They took us to Charity, who was waiting at the chambers, beaming at us.

"Dear me," she said. "Whatever have you two been up to? No. No. Don't tell me. I really don't think I want to know."

They loaded Hud into the capsule first. Charity told him it would take about 4-5 hours. She gave him an injection to make him sleep. I was next. Charity probed my wound that was already healing thanks to the salve.

"I'm sure Maggie did her best but the wound almost certainly has some dirt in it. The machine will probably re-open it so I must sedate you, too. It should take about 3 hours."

She hit me with the injection gun and I went out. Three hours later I walked out a new man. Remarkable.

Maggie was there waiting. "Welcome to the world of the living." She sniffed the air and said, "Why don't you catch a shower while I repair?"

I was clean from the repair machine, of course, but did notice a cloud of disinfectant hanging around me. Probably not a real sexy smell. Charity said Maggie would need a couple of hours for the thigh, so I left to shower. I passed Jenny on the way. She was sitting in a lounging area eating ice cream and generally looking good. Hard to believe this was the same rock-wielding terror I had watched snuff out three demons less than 6 hours ago. I told her I was headed for the shower and she said it was about time. Still no respect.

The best thing about the shower was that there was plenty of hot water. I stayed in until I looked like a pink prune and then walked under the dryer. After shaving, I went back to the lounge to join Jenny.

"How does a person get fed in this place?"

"There's a food machine right over there. Fantastic array of goodies. Just punch in what you want."

While I was at the food machine, Charity called for Jenny. A minute later Maggie and Hud walked in and we all ordered a big meal. It was about 5:00 local time so I guess it was dinner. Whatever it was, it was just what I needed. Jenny came back about 6:00. We were all sitting around talking when Deena walked in.

"Time to update you. Let's go to the briefing room."

The room was relatively small but had comfortable chairs and a small podium with a video screen behind it. We got settled and Deena took a place beside the podium.

"First I want to tell you how well you performed under extreme duress. None of what happened to you was expected, but we now know that the stakes are higher than we thought. And I now know what Bennie is doing. Believe me, it is dynamite. I can't tell you anything about the next 10 days, however, since you have to go live them on Earth. It seems illogical, I know. Let me try to explain.

"On Earth and in Hell, as well as here, 10 days have passed since you left. To keep from disrupting your lives on Earth, She decided to relax the space-time Customs slightly and let you go back when you left. So actually you will relive the same 10 days on Earth that you did in Hell. Now, even though I know what happened to all of you during those days, I am forbidden to tell you because it could alter the future. For example, if you, Hud, got hit by a car and were killed and I knew it, I still couldn't tell you because you might not show up for the accident, which would be altering the future. I can't do anymore until you get back home and catch up with me, time-wise. Space-time relationships can be confusing for some of you, I know, but you'll catch on one day. Now, any questions before you leave?"

"You mean we're going home?" asked Jenny.

"Yes, you are, right after the briefing. Now where was I? The importance of the devil's new strategy with respect to Earth and the need for secrecy has caused him to increase spending on security in Hell. That's probably why you were met by the demons when you arrived. Communication between settlements is still limited to word of mouth using primarily the convoy drivers as messengers, but a new system is being installed now which will link all the settlements digitally, believe it or not.

"Finally, the devil has located a REGEN-type machine. It is very crude and slow but it's the best available to him. He has had to set it up on their moon because it is metal. It will only work on special predetermined sites on Hell, each of which is very costly to set up. He has three so far–one at his residence, one at Tetri 6 in the Southern Hemisphere, and one at Mento 5. Hud and Maggie were to be sent to the residence via REGEN from Mento 5 so freeing them was essential."

"How do you know all of this?" Hud asked.

"For one thing, we have pulled three agents out since you went in. And of course we use satellite video. We were able to follow you at times on your trek."

She flipped a switch. On-screen I saw us land and the two demons attack us. It was remarkably clear. Too clear. Tough to watch yourself get roughed up. She scanned through some of the other footage of us in Hell. Fortunately there was none shown of Jenny and me under the rock. She went on.

"I probably should have pulled you out sooner but there seemed to be a chance that you could break free. Hud and Maggie, when you were captured, I was sick. I hoped you would recall but I knew you wouldn't with Jenny and Jack still there unless and until they were taken to the devil. So that rescue was critical. I compliment Jack and Jenny again on a superior job.

"Now, where are we?" she said. "I want you to agree to continue working with me on this matter. You will be going home to assist me with Bennie and his cohorts first and then it's probably back to Hell."

She saw the way we looked at each other and added, "This time we drop you near the residence. We've learned how to partially shield your arrival by REGEN."

"Why don't you just go into the future on Earth and see what happens?" Jenny asked.

"I can't do that. I wish I could. It's very difficult to explain but let me try. I can enter Earth only on the current or a past timeline. I can't go into the future. Today is Thursday, August 28 both here and on Earth and I can't go past that date.

"Try to follow me now. When you get home it will be Tuesday, August 19. If I come to see you the next day, Wednesday, it will be the 'me' of last week and I won't know what happened after that day. The current 'me' does know what happened in the 10 days coming up for you, but I am strictly forbidden to talk about it to you or anyone except Her."

I'm sure we still looked puzzled. She paused a few moments and then said, "I told you it was confusing. It will clear up as you think about it more, I hope. Perhaps one more example will help. If I go to the past I am also forbidden to make any change which could alter the future. For example, suppose I take you four back to August 19 and kill one of you. That would permanently change what has already happened in the next two weeks. She doesn't want to begin altering the past to change the future.

"In 1956, when we found out how to go into the past, I argued strongly for Her to let me go back and kill Hitler in the early 1930's, but She flatly refused. I do think She has been sorely tempted to go back to when the devil arrived and wipe him out before he got so strong. But She won't. She rarely uses trips to the past and I am the only one She has ever let go there as far as I know. You four are a special case."

She paused and then said, "Enough of this. Questions?"

"Are you going to see us in the next ten days?"

"Time will tell," she said grinning at Jenny. "Now I must get you home. Notice that your suntans are gone thanks to the repair machine classifying suntan as a skin injury. So no one should notice anything different about you except for the weight loss. You can wear loose bulky clothing for a few days and it won't be so noticeable. Stand up and touch me."

We did and were in the little hot tub room at our house.

Deena kissed us all and said, "This 'me' will see you in ten days. If the earlier 'me' comes, remember you must not tell her anything you recall about your trip. Remember, She is placing a lot of trust in you four. Bye." And she was gone.

eighteen

We just looked at each other. Nobody said or did anything for several seconds. It was like we were in a dazed state, unable to move. What was there to say or do?

Then Maggie said, "I've got to get the kids some breakfast so they can go to school."

"Me too," Jenny said.

"Why don't you two come back for coffee after the kids leave. We can discuss our next move, if any."

They agreed and we all dressed and left for our respective chores.

We got the kids off in time to catch the school bus. Laurie told Maggie at breakfast that she looked much younger this morning. Who says kids today aren't observant?

Hud and Jenny came back and we all sat down at the kitchen table. Maggie poured the coffee and started the conversation.

"It seems so strange to be home again and even stranger to have clothes on. I never noticed how constrictive they are."

"Take 'em off if you want to. I don't mind at all," Hud generously offered.

"I'm tempted, but I think we have to get used to them again. When this is over we'll have to join a nudist colony."

Changing the subject, I said, "I want to know about your capture and experience with the demons. How did they know it was us? How did they treat you?"

"They really didn't know it was us," Hud responded. "When you left us to check out the back of the barracks, this squad of demons approached from the direction of the food hall accompanied by two humans. The humans pointed us out but they didn't see you or, of course, Jenny. One of them was the guy I had talked to at the bar. Apparently, I tipped him off somehow. It appears the demons are using human spies."

"I wonder how they pay them off?" Jenny asked.

"Probably with free food or recreation," I said. "What else is there?"

Hud continued. "Anyway, we were grabbed and were obviously over-matched, so we went quietly. Maggie was on the ball when she told me to drop my water jug, figuring you would find them, and it worked. They took us to the commander's offices and, in spite of my attempts to claim a lot of phony legal rights, they gave us a blood test and that was that. We were cuffed and the tethers and collars were put in place and we were dumped into a vacant storage room with the tethers hooked into a wall bracket. It wasn't too bad since the cuffs were in front and the tethers were long enough that we could actually walk around or lie down comfortably. They even threw in some bread and a water jug and an old wooden bucket for bathroom needs.

Later they came and questioned us. They were really amateurs including the commander. They wanted to know where the other two were and we claimed ignorance. They wanted to know why we were here and I said 'for vacation' and earned a clout to the head. They threatened torture but their hearts weren't in it. I feel certain that they had orders to catch us and send us to the South Pole unharmed. They shoved and hit us a few times and then left. About dinnertime, they threw in more bread and another water jug. The next morning they loaded us up and you know the rest."

"Hud makes it sound so easy," Maggie added. "But I was terrified. One big male kept looking at me and stroking himself. I would have rather died than have that happen but I guess they had their orders. I have never been so happy to see two people as you two that next morning." Tears came into her eyes and she got up and headed for the bedroom.

Hud said, "It had to be worse for Maggie. Sorry I couldn't make it easier."

"She'll be OK," I said.

Jenny jumped up and went after her and soon they both came back.

"I'm sorry," Maggie said. "I guess I'm a little stressed out. I just hate those bastards so much. It's kind of interesting that I could build up that much hatred in such a short time and with such limited contact with them."

"What happened to y'all?" Hud asked.

"Jenny came out just after I saw them take you away. We grabbed the water jugs and left. I could see no percentage in us taking on all of the demons at the commander's offices to try to free you. We felt certain you would be taken south, so we went on to Fugim 3 and went in there. We got through the food machine OK and had dinner. Then we saw you arrive, as you already know because Hud saw us. We were pretty sure that there would be a search for us, so we left on the road to Mento 5. About 10 miles out we found an ambush spot. We camped close to the road in case they made a night run and just waited. After that, it was easy. When you arrived, I simply unleashed Jenny, the Rock, onto the demons. The rest is history."

"Very funny, Jack," Jenny said. "Like Maggie, I was scared to death. When I heard the convoy coming in the distance, I wet my pants except luckily I didn't have any pants on. Some leader. I don't relish the prospect of going back to Hell but I know we probably will."

"I can't wait," Maggie added.

"Cheer up you two," Hud said. He grabbed the coffeepot and added, "Here you are home in exciting Clarksboro, Georgia."

He poured coffee all round and we talked awhile longer. Just as we were about to break up, the doorbell rang. I went to answer it and found Mrs. Angelo.

"Dear me, Jack. How are you?"

"I'm fine, Mrs. Angelo. And you?"

"Very well, thank you. May I come in?"

I held the door open and she preceded me to the kitchen. Maggie and Jenny jumped up and hugged her and then she changed to Deena.

"I didn't want to just pop in without an appointment. And I thought I might look conspicuous on your front stoop nude, so I came as Mrs. Angelo."

"We're glad to see you, Deena," Jenny said. "By the way, which Deena are you?"

"I'm the one that saw you off to Hell this morning on Noah's Ark. I know you left and am glad you all came back but I don't know how long you were gone or any details and remember, it must remain that way. Don't tell me anything until we catch up to the other me. OK?"

We all nodded agreement.

"Now that you're back, I can use your help if you're still willing."

She looked at us and again we all nodded agreement. Was there another choice?

"Good. It's Bennie again. We must learn what he's doing. I know he keeps going somewhere out Highpoint Road, maybe about 15 miles from town. I don't know where or why. Jack, I want you and Hud to follow him and try to find out. You were trained to do this in the FBI, weren't you?"

"I guess. But why don't you follow him and pop in like you do here. Isn't that easy for you?"

"It is, but if I do, he'll detect me easily. Because of the powers I possess, I radiate an aura that Bennie could detect at great distance, probably a mile or even more. He has to be near you mortals to detect your presence or to influence your actions. My thought is that you could get close enough to where he's been going to identify it, and then after he has left, we all go in and see what's there. If other elite demons are present, I can detect them before they detect me and we'll adopt some other plan. My detection range is several miles. I have followed about a mile back and know about where he goes, but when he leaves I can't find it."

"So what if he detects you," Jenny said. "You can just have Her banish him."

"True, but if I can learn what he's doing here, it may help us uncover the whole operation. On the other hand, if he identifies me and covers up, his banishment may not be enough to stop what's going on."

"OK," I said. "What kind of schedule is he keeping? Or is he likely to go anytime?"

"He usually goes after lunch. He tries to do his real estate business in the mornings and evenings. He usually eats at Burton's and leaves from his office parking lot. You can pick him up there or someplace on Highpoint Road."

It was just 8:15. In fact, it had been 8:15 for the past 20-30 minutes. I asked Hud if he could break away at noon and he said he could. We agreed to meet for lunch at a truck stop called Ruby's where Highpoint Road turned off of Highway 67. I was planning to take the Lincoln back to the Ford place. It wasn't handling right since they worked on it, so I planned to rent an Explorer to follow Bennie. Deena would be back at 6:00.

Everything went according to plan and I was already sitting at a table at Ruby's when Hud got there.

He walked up and said, "I parked in the back so Bennie won't see my car when he passes by."

"Good. I put the Explorer on the side so we can see him as he turns onto Highpoint. We'll stay way back and try not to alert him. I wish Highpoint Road had more traffic. Sure would make this easier."

"I'll go along with whatever you say. I'm a novice at tailing someone."

We ate a quick sandwich and by 12:30 were sitting in the Explorer waiting. At 12:55 Bennie turned the yellow Caddy onto Highpoint and roared away. We waited until he was well down the road and pulled in to follow. There was a car in between us, which was good until Bennie really poured it on and I had to pass the other car to keep up. About 12 miles out, Bennie turned left onto a dirt road. I kept right on going past the road and saw that Bennie hadn't stopped. We did a quick U-turn, went back and turned right into the road behind him. The pine trees shielded my turn from view.

We hurried to catch up a little and he came into view again, just as he turned on his right turn signal and turned into what had to be a farm driveway. There were heavy pines on the right and then a cleared area. He turned into that clearing. I noticed a small feeder road on the left and quickly turned into it so he would think we lived back there. I stopped the Explorer on the entrance to a logging road, next to a stand of pines.

Hud and I raced back to the intersection and looked to our left. We could see where Bennie had turned but he had quickly passed from view because of the pines on the right. We sprinted across the road and slipped into the pines. We then moved to the left toward the clearing and soon were there.

"There" was the farmyard of a typical small South Georgia chicken farm. There was a modest one-story frame house painted white many years ago and a small barn behind that. Off to the side toward us were three rather new chicken houses. The third one looked almost brand new. They were long narrow buildings, each of them able to hold several thousand chickens at a time. A big semi loaded with chicken crates was backed up to the middle one. The procedure is to wait until dark to load to minimize stress to the chickens. Bennie was trying to maneuver past that truck to put the Caddy in the barn. He finally made it and parked inside. He closed the door and we saw him come in behind the truck and enter the third house in the line.

Hud said, "What the hell is he doing in a chicken house, for God's sake?"

"I don't know. Let's watch a few minutes."

The only thing that happened during the next hour was a guy came out of the third house, went to the cab of the truck, got something out and went back. We got bored and left. We had accomplished what we had set out to do.

I dropped Hud off at Ruby's to get his car and went on my rounds of the construction sites. I was really tired. It had been evening on Noah's Ark and we had been put back here at 7:00 in the morning. I finally got home about 4:30 and told Maggie to wake me a little before 6:00. I woke up feeling even worse, but sloshed cold water on my face and bloodshot eyes, pulled on a black shirt and jeans, and dutifully went to the living room. No rest for the wicked. The doorbell rang and Hud and Jenny came in. We went back to the hot-tub room and then Deena arrived.

"We found out where he's going," I said. "It's a small farm about a mile off Highpoint Road. No clue as to what's going on. We hung around for an hour, but no action."

"We should be able to find out tonight," Deena said. "I think we'll leave the ladies at home this time. There should be little resistance if Bennie isn't there. We need to check on that before we go crashing in."

Deena was dressed in a dark blue jumpsuit and dark shoes, fitting for a night mission. Hud had on dark blue jeans and a dark brown shirt. For some reason, I had put on dark clothes as well. Maybe some esp working there. Anyhow, the three of us got into the Explorer and left. I called Bennie's house on the cell phone, and when Bennie answered, I quickly muttered 'sorry' and hung up. Deena asked me to tell her when we were two miles out and I did. We stopped and she scanned and said Bennie was not there. She couldn't detect any other elite demons either. She said to move closer slowly and she would just continue to scan. At the stand of pines just before the driveway to the farm, she said she noted two humans and four other somethings. We eased the Explorer off the road so it was still in the shelter of the pines.

We eased out, moved into the pines, and again reached a point where we could see the little farm. The pines went back quite a distance and then turned in behind the buildings, forming an 'L'. If we moved around in the shelter of these pines, we would wind up behind the houses with about 50 yards of open land to cross. Moving slowly and staying well back in the trees, we moved around until we were in position to observe all the buildings. It was then about 7:45.

We settled in to wait for darkness. The sun was already down and it didn't take more than about half an hour for the remaining daylight to fade. We waited until 8:30 and moved in slowly. When we reached the back of the third building, it became obvious that this was not your ordinary chicken house, at least not here in the back, because while the side window covers were propped open on all the houses for ventilation, this house had no openings under the window covers. The back door was steel here and wood on the other two. Hud moved forward about 100 feet along the side and came back and said that it was a chicken house at the front.

Deena pulled us over close and whispered, "I'm going to blow the door and go in. I know what the 'somethings' are now. They are worker demons, probably in human form, with no special powers. I'll go in first and deal with them and the two humans. Come in right behind me."

I had a vision of the three of us fighting four demons even in human form and was glad to let her deal with the situation.

Deena concentrated on the door for a moment. There was the sound of a bolt being withdrawn and then the door flew open. She leaped through and froze the demons and the two humans with no problem.

The humans were two men, one tall and fat and the other short and thin. They were both in their 40's, and were dressed in a dark green uniform with "South-by-South Regional Trucking" printed on the back in red script letters. This pair had been packing something in a chicken crate when we arrived.

"Don't try to move until I tell you it's OK," she said to them all. "I want you two humans to walk over to me."

She told us to search them.

They walked over jerkily still under her power and we searched them and found revolvers on both. We removed the guns, and Deena told them that they wouldn't be able to get up after they sat down. She told them to sit down. They did, and sure enough, they were totally immobilized.

Deena turned her attention to the demons. There were two males and two females, all in human form and dressed in industrial-gray multi-pocketed coveralls, so we had to search them pretty thoroughly. One pair had been filling small bottles with a dark colored liquid and the others had been cooking something really rank in what looked like pressure canners. There was a large noisy window-type fan pulling out the fumes. Three stoves and six or seven of the canners were in use.

"When you sit on the floor, you will not be able to move," Deena told the demons. "Sit on the floor."

They did and we began to look around.

The humans had been packing those little bottles in the false floor of a chicken crate, several of which were stacked on one wall. These crates were cleverly fabricated, and would be hard to detect from the real thing once the birds were inside.

Deena asked the male demon what he had been cooking. The demon just glared at her. She reached out an invisible hand and grabbed him by the balls and squeezed. He screamed.

"Answer me," she demanded. "Now." She gave him another tweak.

"Tchadbe," he spat out.

"This is bad," she said to us. "I'd better try to find out as much of the whole story as he knows."

She turned back to the demons and said, "Who's in charge?"

No answer. Another squeeze. "She is," he screamed, indicating the female with whom he had been working.

The female spat at him and called him something in her native tongue. Probably not an endearing term.

He responded, "It wasn't your balls being crushed."

Deena turned to the female and said, "You could be next. You may not have the same equipment, but I am very creative. Tell me the story. Remember, I can detect lies and absolutely will not tolerate them."

I noted a touch of respect in the female's voice. "I will remember, but I don't know much. We were sent here to process the tchadbe for use on Earth. We were taught how in Hell. The liquid tchadbe is so unstable that it must be used within two weeks, so we had to begin processing it right here on Earth. A Tarcan ship by way of shielded REGEN sent us. The tchadbe arrives the same way."

Deena said to us, "The Tarcans are the ones who supply the devil with demons. They have a primitive REGEN that only works at short range, but it can be shielded on some planets. Obviously Earth is one of them."

She turned back to the demoness and said, "Go on."

"There's nothing more to tell."

"Oh, yes, there is. Tchadbe is fatal to humans. Why are you processing it on Earth?"

"I think we're using an additive in cooking that removes the fatal ingredient but leaves the drug intact. It's still just as unstable, though. It must be used quickly or it breaks down and is useless."

"How much has been manufactured and sent out so far?"

"We will have made about 10,000 bottles after tonight. Each bottle holds three ounces. We haven't shipped any yet, though. These bottles were due out tomorrow."

"Where is it being sent?"

"I don't know that."

"How long have you been here?"

"About three weeks?"

"Karg has been here for several months. Why?"

"I don't know. He and a couple others were working on another project when the additive was discovered about two months ago. That's all I know."

"How long are you to stay here?"

"I don't know."

"How long does it take to make 10,000 bottles?"

"About three days if we cook around the clock."

"Who is in charge?"

"Karg."

"Do you know that your being here violates the Customs?"

"I know nothing of Customs."

Deena frowned and turned to the truck drivers. "Who's in charge?"

"Fuck you, lady," the big one said. He was treated to a Deena special squeeze and screamed, "I am. I am."

"That's better. What's your story?"

"We were hired to deliver chickens. That's all." He screamed again and added quickly, "With a special stop in Atlanta. We were told to deliver the special boxes to a warehouse at 345 Tenry Street to a dude named Ernie. That's it until we get called again."

"By Karg?"

"Don't know any Karg. We work for a guy named Bennie. What's the deal with those four assholes over there? Are they from outer space or somethin'? What the hell's goin' on here?"

Deena ignored him, turned back to us and said, "We need a sample of that additive, Jack. Put it in one of their little bottles. Let's also take a bottle of the tchadbe liquid. Hud, check the rest of the buildings. No one alive is in them, and I need to know what other surprises might be in them."

She returned to the female demon. "When is Karg due back?"

"Tomorrow night when we load. These stupid truck drivers came a day early."

"Fuck you too, sister. By God, you're ugly enough to be from outer space," the big one said.

"Enough," said Deena. "How many other labs are there on Earth?"

"I don't know."

"You're lying. You know something. Give."

"All I know is that there were 40 of us in training and in the drop room. We were the third group of four to drop."

"Where were the first two dropped?"

"I really don't know."

Deena sighed. "We might as well leave when Hud gets back. There's little more we can learn from these four." She turned back to the demons and two men and said, "You will not remember that we were here. Do you understand? Each of you must answer 'yes'."

They all did.

"Ten minutes after the back door closes, you will all get up, resume what you were doing, and remember nothing. Is that clear?"

They again responded positively.

Hud arrived with nothing to report, so we left. Deena closed and re-bolted the door with a penetrating stare. We dissolved back into the pines and on to the Explorer.

Once we were on Highpoint Road heading back to town, Deena said, "This is far worse than I imagined. The entire society of Earth is in imminent danger. Forgive me for leaving but I must get to our labs on Noah's Ark immediately. I'll see you tomorrow at Jack's at noon. Will you be free?"

We both nodded, she mumbled something and was gone.

Hud shook his head and said, "She's really a piece of work. That demon will be soaking his balls for the next week and not have a clue as to why they're sore."

"The big guy, too," I said laughing. "What do you think she'll do?"

"I don't know. She seemed really upset."

"She sure was. Now that the devil has openly violated the Customs, can't God do anything She wants?"

"I guess so. I can't see why She couldn't anyway."

I didn't have a response. We turned into our subdivision and went back to my house. Since we had been operating in real time on earth, the time spent with Deena was not suspended, so it was almost 10:30.

As we walked in Jenny said, "I see y'all made it home in one piece."

"Nothing to it. Since we weren't hampered by you two, we finished early."

"We didn't think you could survive without us," Maggie said. "Now give. What happened?"

We told them about the evening's fun and games, and when we finished Jenny said, "The violation of the Customs scares me most. The devil must be very confident of his plan. I wonder what this drug will do to humans?"

Hud said. "I think that's why Deena wanted to get to the lab immediately."

Maggie, looking really worried, said, "If he is willing to violate one Custom, why not another? Remember why we didn't worry about our children?"

"Oh, my God. That's right," said Jenny. "That son of a bitch Bennie is right here in Clarksboro. We need to be careful until Deena arrives tomorrow. I think I'll keep the boys home in the morning."

"Not a bad idea," I said. "What do you think, Maggie?"

"I agree. This is ceasing to be fun."

Once again, none of us even mentioned quitting.

It had been a rather long day and we were all exhausted, so we saw the Raines out, locked the door and went to bed. Maggie and I went to sleep immediately.

nineteen

The next day, Wednesday, Jenny and Hud came over a little before noon with Jimmy and Wayne in tow. We sent them up to Laurie and Mark's rooms to hang out. We had agreed to tell them nothing except that we were worried about their safety at school today and would discuss it with them after lunch. What we really wanted to do was discuss it first with Deena.

Deena arrived right on schedule.

Jenny said, "You'd better dress, Deena. All of our children are here and may come down."

"You keep forgetting that time doesn't pass for you when I am here unless we leave the house. So don't worry. Now, we need to begin. I've got a lot to tell you and not much time."

She was clearly agitated. I didn't like it. She was supposed to be calm and reassuring. She started to sit down but instead began pacing.

"First, I have the lab results on the tchadbe extract and the additive. This additive is a compound that bonds with the fatal element in tchadbe and allows it to pass through the human system without harming the person who took it. That's the good news. The extract itself is not affected by the additive and is as potent as it was before, just not as stable. It will only retain its effectiveness for about two weeks and then it will have no effect on a human system. Now then, I've never told you what it does to users. It is unusual among drugs in that it is a relaxant and a stimulant at the same time. When you take it in the proper dosage, it imparts you with a sense of calm and well being. You don't lose touch with reality, but you are in a dreamlike state and have lost all sense of responsibility. This state lasts for nearly six hours and is powerfully addictive. The other effect is worse. It has a very strong aphrodisiac effect. Sexual performance is greatly enhanced. It doesn't drive people to rape and perform violent acts on others unless they were already predisposed to such actions, but it can be harmful as one tries to perform more often and with more intensity than their equipment is designed to handle.

"That's still the good news. Now the bad. After about two months of use, addicts will have burned up their immune systems and will have a weakened resistance to most fatal diseases. Antibiotics and other medicines won't work. Our repair stations will, but there aren't enough of them in existence to handle even a small portion of those who will become addicted. Children will be neglected or addicted themselves, and the parents under the 'cause harm to others' rule will go to Hell. It's a nightmare scenario for Earth but the devil envisions acquiring literally millions of new workers as the people of Earth die and go to Hell for their harmful acts. From his standpoint, it's a brilliant and foolproof plan. I can see him rubbing his hands together and counting his potential new tchadbe profits from the increased acreage he will be able to bring into production."

She paused and asked for questions.

I asked her how much of the compound it took for a 6 hour dose. I was thinking of those 10,000 three-ounce bottles we saw at the chicken farm.

"A three-ounce bottle cut to the proper dosage level and combined with inert ingredients to form pills will supply about a 1,000 pills. Remember, Bennie had 10,000 bottles ready. That's 10 million doses. Since 40 demons were trained and sent to Earth in teams of four, we are assuming at least 10 labs just like Bennie's. That means 100 million doses are ready and in some places may already be in distribution. Imagine, if you will, what the count would be if the devil has held 10 of the 40-demon training sessions. The other nine would provide an additional 900 million doses, making a grand total of one billion. This would provide one dose for about one person in five in the whole of Earth or, given a week's supply for each addict, would supply 140 million addicts or about one-half the population of the United States."

"I'm sorry I asked."

"It is depressing," Deena said. "Anyway, let's talk about what I need you to do. First, a little background will help. There have been very few examples over the years of Customs violations by the devil. The last incident that I remember was when he tried to set up a communication link between Hell and his demons on Earth. This is strictly forbidden by Custom. The Custom was designed to prevent the devil from having direct control over his covert operations on Earth. She was furious and had the link removed and destroyed. As a penalty, She destroyed the next 6 ships full of tchadbe that left Hell. We thought he'd learned the lesson.

"What he's done now is even worse. He has violated the 10 demon rule. And maybe the communication rule, too, by setting up another link. Also, the use of REGEN might be considered a form of communication. So he's really done it this time. Unfortunately, it's also a time when he is as strong as he has ever been. So She is advising me to move slowly until we can get you back in to try to neutralize him. She still won't tell me what happened to you four on Hell. I did see the demons attack you when you landed yesterday, your first August 19.

"We're going to let Bennie's shipment go while we try to identify the other 9 centers that we feel sure are here. We know the identity of two more demons out of the 10, so there are seven to go. Those two are Grig, who is calling himself Manuel Gonzales and is in San Salvador, El Salvador. The other is Felc posing as Sidu Coulibaly in Bamako, Mali. I want one couple to go to Mali and the other to El Salvador tomorrow. Use extreme caution, because both of those countries are hotbeds right now.

"I know you have responsibilities, and we will try to help cover them for you. Of course we will get your documents ready and make all financial arrangements and reservations necessary, and will reimburse any unexpected expenses you incur. We had hoped to let you live in peace for a few days, but we need your help desperately. And immediately. As you now know, we angels can't get close enough without being detected. I can take you there by REGEN through Noah's Ark but you will have to be on real time while there."

Maggie said, "We have been talking about the children. If the devil is willing to violate some of the Customs, why not the one about children, too?"

"He won't. I am absolutely certain. She would use every resource She has in this universe if he bothered or hurt your children. He would be utterly destroyed and he knows it. In addition, he can't hurt them while I am here on Earth. So you can leave them with relatives or friends or, if you like, we'll take them to Noah's Ark."

"I guess I'll ask my Mom and Dad to come down and stay a few days," Jenny said.

"And I'll ask Mrs. Pearson, our housekeeper, to stay over. She's done it many times before."

"Good," Deena said. "Taking them to Noah's Ark would have its problems. I'll watch over them all."

twenty

Maggie and I drew Mali. Maggie had some French and Jenny some Spanish, so that decided it. We met at 7:00 on Thursday morning in the hot-tub room and went on to Noah's Ark. Mrs. Pearson had arrived, suitcase in hand, at 6:30. We told the kids we had a chance to visit Africa at a last minute bargain price and would be back in a few days. We never did explain to them why we kept them out of school. Maybe later. They didn't really seem to care much anyhow.

Right after we arrived at Noah's Ark, we left for our respective destinations. There was a five hour time advance in Mali, so we arrived about 1:00 in the afternoon. We materialized in an empty storage room at the Hotel Malien where a room had been reserved for us. We cracked the door, waited until the corridor was clear, and came out bags in hand. We circled around to the front and went to the front desk and checked in.

It was a large, old colonial hotel that was in surprisingly good repair. It had high ceilings with fans for cooling and it also had air conditioning that had been added at some point. There was a large gift shop with locally produced items including some beautiful hand-made silver jewelry and some amber as well.

I got a map of Bamako at the gift shop and we went upstairs to our room. We unpacked and went out on the balcony, which faced an unpaved side street. The heat was like a furnace; it sucked the air right out of you and it reminded me of the climate on Hell. A man leading two goats went slowly by with the goats pausing to drink from a mud puddle. It was still the rainy season, which lasted from June until early September. The other months were dry, so dry that it really didn't rain at all. By late May the place was completely parched. Only the hardiest vegetation survived.

"How do we locate Mr. Coulibaly? Did you look at the city map?"

"Not yet. I've got his address, though. He lives at 165 Rue du Jasmin. He's an African art dealer, you know, the wood carved masks and statues, tribal art mostly. Apparently he deals in the authentic stuff. I guess it's mostly reproductions these days."

"I want to buy a book on it. I've always liked it."

"There's a nice gift shop downstairs. They should have one. I'm off to get the rental car. Back in a few minutes."

"I'll go downstairs with you."

We got to the lobby and Maggie headed for the gift shop. I asked the man at the desk where the Voiture Rental office was located.

"It is not far from here. Did you have a car reserved?"

"Yes. A Peugeot."

"If you will give me your name, I'll have them bring it over."

"Sure. I'm Jack Warner, Room 204."

" I remember. You will need your passport and an international driver's license for the agent."

"No problem. How long will it take?"

"No more than half an hour."

"Would you call my room when it arrives?"

"Certainly, Monsieur Warner."

I thanked him and went to see how Maggie was making out. She was in the process of buying a book and was trying out her French on the young lady clerk. Purchase completed, Maggie was thirsty so we headed for the bar area. I signaled the desk man that I would be in the bar and he gave me a thumbs up.

We sat under a big fan on a verandah that had been glassed in to allow air conditioning. There was a view of the main street. The afternoon heat had slowed things down a little but there was still a steady flow of traffic, mainly mobylettes or what we would call motor bikes.

Maggie wanted a beer so I ordered two. The waiter spoke very little English but Maggie helped out. We were getting a beer brewed in a neighboring country, Burkina Faso, called Bravolta. I was a little apprehensive since most French beers are watery and either lack flavor or taste like flowers. Luckily, no Frenchman had a hand in the Bravolta. It was superb. Served in big one liter green bottles, ice cold, it was the best beer I have ever tasted. And I've sampled quite a few, let me tell you.

Just as we were finishing, the desk clerk stuck his head in and waved. I left some Malian francs and we went out to the lobby.

The rental agent was a big smiling man who spoke broken English with some Italian and French thrown in for good measure.

"Bonjour, Mr. Warner."

"Bonjour. Do you have the car?"

"Oui, yes. I got it out the door. I likea you pasaportes and driver licencia, s'il vous plait."

I gave him the two items, and he diligently copied off numbers from both and presented me with a form to sign. I did and he said, "It is the Peugeot green on the front of hotel."

I took the keys and thanked him by slipping him more than enough francs. He departed smiling and saying, "Merci, thank you, merci."

We went back up to the room and discussed our approach to Mr. Coulibaly. Maggie suggested we pose as tourists interested in buying African Art. We wouldn't be too knowledgeable, of course, and would have plenty of money. She would read her new book so we didn't appear to be totally out of it. If Coulibaly was as prominent as Deena said, we should cross paths fairly soon. It seemed like a good plan to me. I rested while Maggie scanned the book, then we changed clothes and headed out.

I stopped at the desk and asked about finding some art to buy. The desk clerk turned out to have 12 uncles and 23 cousins who were experts and had the real thing. I thanked him, told him we'd get back to him later and asked directions to the central market. We didn't need the car, as the market was just four blocks west of our hotel.

Bamako turned out to be a lively place. Although it was the capital of Mali, it was fairly small, with about 1.8 million people. The highest buildings were three stories and most buildings were stucco with whitewash or the natural desert tan. Green shutters were popular. The city smelled of raw sewage that flowed in the gutters. Off-putting to say the least, but we were surprised at how quickly we got acclimated to it. The people were dressed in brightly colored clothing and seemed happy as they went about their daily activities.

We had done some quick travel-brochure research back in the room, focusing on local customs, and found that shopping in Bamako, especially for food, is a daily routine and a valuable social outlet, too. Most Malians have no refrigeration, so perishables are bought only on an as-needed basis. Freshly baked baguettes are available each morning nearly everywhere, even arriving at your door on the back of bicycles in huge baskets. You could find most other food items in the small stores scattered around the city or at the central market. Pricing for most goods is not fixed but negotiated. It's fun but time-consuming.

We walked slowly but soon covered the four blocks. The central market is simply a huge city block devoted to a maze of small open-air shops or stalls. They are basically grouped, so that the clothing shops are clustered in one area, the food in another and so on. There are shops for nearly anything. And I do mean anything. We just wandered around for a while, taking in the unfamiliar but intriguing smells, sights and sounds that came at us from all sides. Maggie's appetite was off the rest of the trip after seeing the butcher shops where some kind of meat hung unrefrigerated, covered in flies. We saw stalls with bicycle parts, magic potions, and jewelry including antique ivory and amber and other beads.

Over on one side, we finally found a couple of stalls displaying woodcarvings on a colorful piece of cloth spread out on the ground. The sellers were all delighted to see us, greeting us like long-lost friends. It didn't take more than a few seconds for a couple of them to start the hard sell on what even to me was reproduction stuff.

Maggie asked for the real thing. The dealer looked pained but soon recovered and sent a man scurrying off to get more things. He came back with a statue and a mask.

"The statue is a Dogon male figure and the mask is Bambara," he said.

Since he was speaking French, Maggie responded. "They don't look well-used."

"They are very old. Look at the patina."

"How much?"

He gave us an outrageous price. We countered with about 10 percent and finally settled on about 25 percent. From his smile, I knew we had been taken but what the hell. It was Deena's money. Maggie then tried to get some names of dealers who had real art pieces. The third one he named was Coulibaly. He said that Coulibaly sat out every evening about six o'clock near the Hotel Du Segou, another major old hotel in the city and not far at all from ours. Maggie thanked him and we left with our 'treasures'.

We had another of those marvelous beers at a sidewalk cafe on the way back. When we got to our room, Maggie got into a chair and started to study the art book. I stretched out on the bed and mused on the approach we needed to use for Coulibaly. I was still a little uncomfortable about being direct with him. Maybe we should try to pick him up when he left home and follow him. Then I remembered the old FBI manual. It said, 'try not to tail someone in their own environment'. This was undoubtedly good advice, especially in a foreign country. Finally, six arrived. We dressed and left. The hotel was just two blocks east so we walked. I didn't want to show him our car anyway.

We had discovered that around every hotel, there was always a group of sellers of various items, most of them produced strictly for the tourist trade. . The Hotel Du Segou was no exception. We made the rounds politely until we saw a large man about 40 years old sitting off to the side of the hotel with art objects spread out on a sheepskin rug. This looked like our man.

"Mr. Coulibaly?"

"Oui. Ce moi."

"Do you speak English?"

"Yes, a little."

"A vendor in the central market recommended you to us. We are interested in starting a collection. We hope you can help us find some things."

"I have many pieces. What do you like?"

"We want to look at your best pieces."

"I have two very fine Bambara Chi Waras. They are very expensive, however." He gestured at two identical nice-looking carvings leaned up against the hotel wall.

Maggie said, "Excuse me, Mr. Coulibaly, but we're interested in genuine pieces and not the rare and incredibly expensive Chi Waras. We're new collectors, but we're not naive." He laughed and said, "Ah so. Perhaps these Chi Waras are not for you after all. You can't blame a man for trying, non?"

We both laughed and agreed it was worth a try. He got up and walked over to a well-used once-white Peugeot station wagon and pulled out a burlap bag full of what was no doubt the real thing. He pulled out a larger piece of material and began to spread the pieces out on that.

"This is all I have with me tonight, but I have more at home and at my warehouse in Mopti. Are you going north to Mopti to see the Dogon villages?"

"We probably will," I said. "It's supposed to be beautiful."

"Yes. I have been going there every weekend lately and if you are there Saturday and stay at the Motel du Mopti, as everyone does, I will find you."

"We may do that."

"See anything you like, Madame?"

"Yes, I like this mask very much. I believe it is Bobo, isn't it?"

This carving was an owl-faced mask with a large crest, painted in earth tones of reds and blues along with some white. It was faded and worn and had a beautiful patina. It was as vibrant and alive as the reproductions were dead. I began to see why people liked this art form.

"Good choice. An excellent piece. It is more precisely a Bobo Fing."

"I also like this pair but I'm not sure what they are."

"Another good choice. These are Dogon male and female fertility figures. Anything else?"

"I don't believe so. Jack? See anything you like?"

"I probably can't even afford your three! What's the damage, Mr. Coulibaly?"

He looked pained and said, "The pieces are very old, sir, but they are not damaged."

We had a good laugh when I explained the American idiom to him. He said that French was even worse. I agreed, but didn't tell him so.

We negotiated for a while and finally settled on about a third of what he asked originally. Deena still paid dearly for those three items. He brought up Mopti again and we agreed that we would probably be there Friday night and Saturday. He said he would see us Saturday. We walked back to our hotel for a marvelous dinner of couscous, fruit, and lamb. I hope it was lamb.

After dinner I bought a map of Mali and we went upstairs to figure out where in the hell Mopti was located. It turns out it is about 460 kilometers or 285 miles north of Bamako, right on the Niger River. I estimated it would take 7 hours to drive it. I called the desk and asked them if they could reserve a room at the Motel du Mopti for Friday and Saturday nights and they said they would try. Maggie and I tossed the trip around for a while. We both had a hunch that Mopti was the lab location. At 10:00 we called the kids. It was 5:00 at home and everything was fine. Deena had said she would come talk to us at 11:00 if the demon Coulibaly was out of range.

She arrived at 11:00, obviously somewhat depressed. No more demons had been located as yet. Hud and Jenny's demon was missing but they were still searching, and she was going to El Salvador to help them look as soon as she left us. We told her about our encounter and our tentative plans. She agreed that the lab, based on what she had been able to learn, was not in Bamako. Mopti seemed a logical choice to her since it was on the major north-south road in Mali.

The phone interrupted us and Maggie answered it. It was the desk confirming our reservation at Mopti. Deena said that she would come back at the same time again the following two nights if she could do so without detection, but she was concerned because Mopti was small and Coulibaly could detect her from about a mile away. I think that meant we would be on our own once we were out of the capital.

twenty-one

The trip to Mopti took nearly 10 hours instead of 7. We hadn't counted on the condition of what the Malians call roads. Months of unusually heavy rains had taken their toll on the cardboard-thin layers of blacktop. But it was an interesting drive, and we were able to see up close and personal what life was like on the leading edge of the Sahara Desert.

We pulled up to the motel about 6:00 and checked in. The rooms were a little seedy but they were the best Mopti had to offer. We went to the patio bar area and had a cold Bravolta. Deena didn't show at 11:00, so we had to assume Coulibaly was within a mile of us.

Next morning at breakfast, he appeared. "Good morning. I hope you both slept well."

"Very well, thank you," I said. "You're out early."

"I must go to Bandiagara, the main village in Dogon country, to meet a man who procures art for me. I thought perhaps you would like to go along. I can guarantee that you would have a really unique experience. We should be back in mid-afternoon and can go to my warehouse at that time."

"I'd love to see the village," Maggie said. "Thank you!"

"We accept. This will be a once-in-a-lifetime trip for us," I responded.

"Excellent. I'll meet you out front in 30 minutes. Please be sure to wear good– how do you say– mountain shoes."

"Hiking boots," I said. "We will. Glad you mentioned it."

The road to Bandiagara was not paved at all, and since it was the rainy season there were some dicey spots, but Coulibaly was not a virgin to these conditions. He and I sat in front. He leaned back, one hand on the wheel and the other arm sprawled over the well worn back of the seat, toying with shreds of the material that was beginning to disintegrate on the seats. As we drove, he began to talk about the Dogons, his English improving since he had apparently given this little talk many times before to other tourists.

"Centuries ago the Dogon came to this region" he said. "They settled on a broad plain below a rock escarpment that stretched for many miles. Wars with other peoples forced them back until they eventually resettled up on the escarpment itself. From that position, they could easily defend themselves. The problem was that the rocky soil was very unproductive. They proved equal to the task, however, adapted their agriculture to the adverse conditions, and actually prospered by local standards.

"Today, with the cessation of warfare between the tribes, they have successfully resettled on the plains. In fact, during the seven year drought of the late 60's and early 70's, they were the only tribe in West Africa to have already formulated a plan for a drought that severe. And they were the only people who did not accept relief food. Most remarkable people."

"Are these Dogon villages we're passing through now?" I inquired as we bumped our way past groups of small huts every few miles.

"They are. Some of the Dogon have stayed up on the escarpment. They grow onions to sell in Bamako and do quite well."

We flew along, figuratively and literally, and he continued to ramble on about the area, the baobob tree, the onion fields, irrigation, and a hundred other things. He was really quite knowledgeable and I had a momentary period of doubt about his demon status. But Deena said it was him, and she had proven to be correct every time before.

We finally rolled into Bandiagara about 11:30. He dropped us at a tiny restaurant in the village center and said he would pick us up at 1:00. We had some time before we needed to eat, so we walked to the edge of the escarpment and looked out over the plain. You could see for miles, and there were a lot of villages in plain sight. In fact, there was one about 1500 feet right below us, with a trail that looked relatively safe. But unfortunately we wouldn't have time to explore right now.

We went back to the restaurant and ate and then walked around the village until 1:00. Coulibaly picked us up and we started back to Mopti. He was less talkative going back but he did say that he had gotten some nice pieces and would show us at the warehouse. We arrived there at about 4:00.

We went into the warehouse and he turned on a light. From outside, the building seemed to be pretty good sized, but the inside was partitioned so that we couldn't really see the entire area. We knew we were in the front part, which probably made up less than a third of the entire structure. Coulibaly started talking, but I couldn't keep my mind on his art spiel because I caught a whiff of tchadbe cooking in the back. I was as excited and hyper as I had been on my first big drug bust with the Feds, and couldn't wait to make a move of some kind. We had identified the second lab!

Maggie took her sweet time picking out several pieces. She asked him to take them back to Bamako tomorrow while she thought about which ones we could afford. He agreed but said he was actually going back there later tonight. In the morning, we were to drive back to Bamako and were to meet him at the hotel at 6:00 tomorrow evening.

He dropped us back at our lodging and roared away. We showered and took a short nap. We had an early dinner at the hotel but it was pretty gruesome. I complained to the manager, but he seemed to have lost the power of speech. Still hungry, we bought some candy and gum and returned to our room about 8:00. It was Saturday so we called the kids early.

At 8:30 there was a knock on the door. A waiter was there with a tray and two glasses. He said, "Two cognacs, compliments of the manager. He's very sorry about your dinner."

"Thank him for us," I said and slipped him some francs. He thanked me and left. All of this was, of course, translated through Maggie. I'm a quick learner, but why bother for a few days when you have a talented wife.

I gave one to Maggie and said, "Might as well. It's hard to screw up cognac."

"It's really very nice of him."

We were just finishing the cognacs and had congratulated ourselves on finding the lab when the phone rang. It was Coulibaly.

There wasn't even a slight hint of salesmanship in his voice as he snapped, "Tell your angel that she isn't as smart as she thinks she is. The one you call Bennie found out from your housekeeper that you had gone to Mali and could only think of one reason why. He warned me this afternoon after you left the warehouse. I can't kill or even seriously injure you because of your angel, but I did arrange a little surprise for you. It will give me the 6 hours I need to shift operations. How did you like the cognac?"

I didn't say anything for a moment. I just looked at the two empty glasses. "What have you done, you bastard?"

"Now, now, now. Don't get nasty. I have arranged a night of bliss for you two. Each of you had one dose of tchadbe. And it should be taking effect right about now. Have a wonderful night."

I said, "You son of a bitch. I'll—." He had rung off.

"That damned Coulibaly is on to us. Bennie called him. He put a dose of tchadbe in each cognac. We've got to——Maggie! Maggie! Are you listening to me?"

The drug had already taken effect. Maggie was sitting in the chair with a far-off look in her eyes. She looked more relaxed than I had seen her in years. I wanted to tell her we had to do something, don't remember what it was of course, when I felt the tchadbe taking hold. I sat down on the edge of the bed and felt a sense of inner peace like none I had ever felt before. I was so relaxed, so peaceful, I could hardly lift my arms.

I looked over at Maggie and she stood up and took off her robe. She was nude; she started rubbing her body with her hands. I stood up and began to undress. My whole body tingled. I led her to the bed and, without haste, we began kissing. Then the kissing grew more intense and spread to all parts of our bodies. I was on fire and could tell Maggie was too. We flowed together and soon were spent.

I laid back against the headboard and wondered where this drug had been all my life. I said, "Whew."

"That's an understatement." Maggie began to rub me and kiss me and we were off again.

At 11:00 we were on the bed coupled together for the fourth time that night when Deena materialized. She said, "My goodness. You two must have lost track of the time."

Such was the power of the drug that I wasn't even embarrassed. I did manage to roll off of Maggie and sat up. Deena was nude of course and I remember wondering if angels did it.

"I'm sorry to spoil your fun but–what's the matter with you two?" She was referring to the fact that we had forgotten about her and had started kissing and fondling each other again. I guess she used some sort of mind control because I suddenly was clear headed again. So was Maggie. We were instantly embarrassed and pulled the sheet up.

"What happened, Jack?"

"We've been drugged by Coulibaly. He gave us tchadbe."

"My God. How did he find out?"

Between us we managed to give her the whole story. She thought a minute and said "I'll have to find him and take him to Her for banishment before he warns all the others. I'll also have to warn the Raines. But first, I'm sending you home. It's a little after 6:00 there and Mrs. Pearson and the kids went to dinner and the movies. Lock yourselves in the bedroom and leave a note saying you're home and very tired and you'll see them in the morning. I can't stop the drug except temporarily, so it will just have to run its course. Stand up and touch each other."

We did.

Deena said, "Have fun." And we were home.

I quickly wrote a note and put it on the refrigerator. We had no more than locked the bedroom door when the passion returned. We got into the hot-tub for a while and then progressed to the bed where we went on for most of the next four hours time after time. It must have been 2 am. when we finally fell into an exhausted sleep.

I awoke about 9:00 still feeling exhausted. Maggie was in the bathroom; I heard the john flush, and then she walked gingerly back into the room. "My God, I'm sore. I would never have believed it could be done that many times in a 6 hour period. The worst part of it is that I have a craving already to start all over again."

"Apparently it's pretty addictive, even after only one dose. Fortunately, there's none around."

"Jack, I think I'd take it if there were some.

"I know. Let's eat breakfast and see if the Raines are back"

I went out for the Sunday paper. It was raining so the paper wasn't bagged. At least Jeff Thompson was consistent. The headlines were about the increased use of meth in the Savannah area. They didn't know the half of it.

twenty-two

I was dozing in my recliner reading the paper when the doorbell rang. It was about 10:30 and I wondered who would be out in the rain making calls. I looked out and saw Jenny and Hud grinning at me from the front porch.

Hud was wearing a striped serape and a huge floppy sombrero. I opened the door and said, "Bienvenidos, Señor and Señora Raines," quickly exhausting my Spanish. "Come on in."

"How do you like my new look, Maggie?"

Maggie looked at Jenny and said, "He really got into the assignment, didn't he?"

"I swear, he's worse than a child. He's decided that he was a Latin land owner in an earlier life."

"No lie! I was! I'm going to confirm it when Deena has time to talk."

"When did y'all get in?" I asked.

"Last night about 8:30," said Jenny. "This is quite a story. Deena finally located Manuel yesterday and we were able to follow him to a small town about 40 miles east of San Salvador. He went to a building that looked like an old school. It was late in the afternoon, so we waited until dark to move in. About 6:30, a light came on behind a boarded up window, so we moved in for a look. There was a pretty wide crack between two of the boards so we had a front row seat.

151

"Manuel was there with two young couples. There were two beds and a nightstand, a camera, and two or three banks of lights. He gave each of the four young people a small pill to swallow and then everyone waited around for about 15 minutes. All of a sudden, the clothing started flying, and the couples began one of the most fantastic sexual performances I could even imagine. They didn't seem to tire at all. It appears that Manuel decided a little extra profit from porn movies was in order.

"We stayed for about an hour waiting for Manuel to leave. Before he did, though, Hud heard a noise off to our left, so we ducked down behind a nearby bush and waited. When a man passed by us, headed in the direction of the door, Hud took him from behind and knocked him out before he could alert Manuel. We took the machete he had in his belt and retreated to the car. We were relatively certain this was the lab since Manuel was there and he had certainly given those four young people tchadbe. So we headed for San Salvador.

"About five miles from town, we stopped for some cattle crossing the road and Deena suddenly materialized. She said we were in danger and should go home immediately. We told her the lab location and grabbed each other and REGEN sent us home. I forgot to mention that we had to wait for Don Diego here to retrieve his serape and sombrero from the car."

Hud just grinned and tipped his sombrero.

Jenny finished by saying that Deena was going to try to come by at noon today. If she couldn't make it, she'd try again at 6:00.

Hud said, "I still can't believe how the tchadbe affected those people. No wonder it's so addictive. I wonder what it's like?"

"Let me tell you our story," Maggie said. She went through the whole thing up to the cognac.

"Then," she continued, "Coulibaly called and said he knew who we were and had put tchadbe in the cognac."

"You're kidding," Jenny said. "My God, you didn't drink it, did you?"

"Every drop. Finished it just before he called."

"What was it like?"

Maggie paused again, looked at me, and said, "It was the most exquisite feeling I've ever experienced. It was incredibly intense but not frenzied." She leaned back and sighed and said, "I actually crave another pill. This could just be the most addictive drug ever discovered."

Jenny was on the edge of her chair. "This is incredible. How did Deena get you out?"

I said, "That's a little embarrassing. She appeared, right on schedule at 11:00, but we were, umm, kind of occupied."

They both had a good laugh.

We talked some more and a little before noon, I checked to see that the kids were in their rooms and came back downstairs. Minutes later Deena arrived. I know angels don't get tired, but she really looked exhausted. She sat down on the couch beside Maggie and said, "Are you and Jack OK?"

"We're OK, but not over it. I have to tell you I would probably do it again right now if I could."

"I know. Tchadbe's desirable effects overshadow its many deleterious outcomes. That's what makes it so addictive."

Maggie looked a little depressed. Deena continued.

"Let me bring you all up to date on where we stand. In Mali, after I sent Jack and Maggie home, I went straight to the lab. Coulibaly was, of course, gone or I wouldn't have come to your hotel. The four demons were the only ones there and I sent them to a holding facility on Noah's Ark. The bottles of tchadbe were gone. I tried but couldn't locate Coulibaly for quite awhile but then found him in Segou, about halfway to Bamako. I was several miles out when I detected him. I closed quickly so that by the time he detected me, I'd be right on top of him. I found him in a hotel room just jumping off the bed to meet my challenge. We struggled mind-to-mind for a few moments but there was really never any doubt. He gave up pretty quickly. He knew I would find him. That's why he didn't try harder to evade me.

"He also knew that he was strong enough to prevent me from forcing him to be truthful. I tried to find out where the bottles of tchadbe had been sent. I tried hard for the names of the seven others. But no way, Jose. By the way, I like your outfit, Hud. But to continue with my story, I sent Coulibaly to Noah's Ark for transfer to Her. She can compel even an elite demon to tell all.

"Now for Hud and Jenny. I went to El Salvador to warn you that Bennie had given Manuel your names and descriptions. That was the reason there was a man with a machete on patrol. After I sent you two home, I went back to the old school building. I went in quickly and Manuel surrendered without a whimper. The bottles of tchadbe, however, had already been shipped. Just like the ones from Mali. I sent Manuel to Her and the four demons to the holding area on Noah. I left the young couples there. They didn't even notice that anything had been happening.

"So, to summarize, we have banished two demons without learning anything of real substance. We have three shipments of bottled tchadbe hitting the market. And we don't know who the other demons are. The only thing we know for sure is that Bennie is the one who's been alerting them. One plus for us is that I believe Bennie still thinks he's in the clear." She sighed. "It looks like I'm not going to be a candidate for the Angel of the Year award once again."

I don't have a lot of experience in this area, but I know a discouraged angel when I see one. Maggie hugged her and told her it would all work out.

I said, "It may be time to pull Bennie in and send him to Her to get the other names and details."

"Exactly, Jack," Deena acknowledged. "That was my next step. The only problem is that Bennie has disappeared. I believe he is using the Tarcan REGEN to skip around the planet from place to place to cover up and move operations. Their REGEN, to give you some background, is primitive because it takes some time to calibrate for a jump, as much as several hours. We have ours down to seconds. Theirs also won't reach Hell directly, so they have to relay up to a ship, move the ship to the vicinity of Hell and relay down. We can go through the stations. I'm sure they would have pulled Coulibaly and Manuel out if they had a better REGEN.

"It is shielded because it's easy to do on Earth. But it's very difficult on Hell. We just recently developed a partial shield there ourselves. It has something to do with residual electromagnet particles in the air or soil or whatever. Heaven and the stations like Noah's Ark are closed to any REGEN other than ours.

"So we need a new strategy. Suggestions?"

I had an idea that I thought would have been considered already, but since I hadn't heard any mention of it, I said, "Why don't you trace the REGEN activity off the Tarcan ship? Or does the shield prevent that?"

"Jack, I don't know. I never thought of that. I'll check it now. Back in a few minutes." And she made her exit.

"You may have hit the jackpot with that idea," Hud said.

"They've probably tried it already, but I hope you're right."

We chatted for a while and eventually Deena popped back in.

"Well, Jack. I'll have to put you up for Angel of the Year! Apparently, these data are routinely collected, analyzed, distributed and filed away. I was inadvertently left off the distribution list. That's not surprising, though, since REGEN has only been used on Earth by the Tarcans for a few months. I really should have thought of this myself, but I didn't. My subordinates in Analysis should have gotten it to me, but they assumed I had it. Bureaucracy seems to be the same everywhere.

" I brought some of these results with me, and the Analysis section is working on others. What I have are movements in the last few days." She spread some numerical data out on the table. I'm not sure where she had been carrying them. "Now, we can see here that Bennie notified Coulibaly by phone at about noon, Clarksboro time, on Saturday and called Manuel a few minutes later. The REGEN records show a lift out of Clarksboro at 12:22 in the afternoon. Then they show an insertion at Winnemucca, Nevada about two hours later at 11:22 local time. That must be Bennie.

"This morning at 8:16 our time there was a lift out of Winnemucca. At 11:34 an insertion occurred at Perth, Scotland. That would be 4:34 in the afternoon in Scotland. Again, assume it is Bennie." She thought for a moment. "OK, kids, time to move out again.

We've got some new locations for you tourists."

twenty-three

Maggie and I drew Scotland. Our reasons and excuses to the kids were growing thin, so we decided to give them an edited version of what was happening. Without mentioning Heaven or Hell or angels or REGEN or anything else really happening, we told them that we were helping on a very important drug operation and would have to be gone again for a day or two. Mrs. Pearson agreed to come back. We left at 2:00 that same afternoon. That made it 7:00 in Scotland when we arrived.

Deena had us dropped in Balbeggie, a quaint little town about three miles from Perth. A rental Rover had been reserved for us and we were dropped in a little park a block away. It was cold and looked like rain, so we grabbed our windbreakers from the luggage and walked the block to the rental office. We picked up the Rover and headed south. Our destination was Perth.

The Tarcan REGEN records had actually showed the drop point to be about a mile north of Perth on a rural side road less than half a mile off to the east. It had all the ingredients so far for another farm location. Other than that information, we were on our own. It was Sunday, so most of Perth was closed. On the wall of a service station, I did manage to find a map that included Perth and Perth County. About seven miles north of Perth, there were two possibilities, one of them Flowers Road and the other, County Road 631. Neither branched out before a half mile so the lab should be on one of the two. By the time we checked into our hotel, it was nearly 9:00 and almost dark. The hotel was small and neat with large clean rooms. We dumped our bags and went right back to the car. We drove out to the two roads but didn't drive down either one. Both of them turned down from the side of a large hill where the main road was located. Even in the fading light, we could see down each for quite a distance and verified that they were indeed farm roads. We drove on another mile or so past the roads and stopped to talk.

"If we wait until morning," Maggie said, "Bennie might be in Hong Kong or somewhere else. But if we go down those roads tonight, we won't be able to see much. Plus, the people on those roads probably know who is in every car that passes. We'd draw a bunch of attention to ourselves."

"Right. But I could go in from the main road on foot. Half mile on each road is a piece of cake."

"The biggest problem with that would be the dogs. Each family probably has about 60 of them."

"OK, how about this? In the FBI, I found that people really want to spill their guts to strangers. Let's find a local or two who have lived here a good while and talk to them. Wasn't there a little store about a half mile back?"

We drove back to the little store and found the two owners getting ready to close for the day. An old lady was gathering up some fruit from a little table and putting it in a basket. A man about the same age was sweeping.

We went up to the little porch area, and the man, probably in his 70's, came over and said, "Come in, come in, we were just about to close, lad."

The lady was behind the counter, the basket of fruit nearby.

"What can we do for you," she asked pleasantly.

"My wife and I are looking for a small piece of acreage or a small farm we could live on in the summers. An acquaintance of ours heard that a place would be coming up for sale on either Flowers Road East or on East 631. He couldn't remember which. He did say the place was within a half mile of the highway. We just came from down there but it's dark and we can't see anything. We didn't want to drive down either road and alarm people living there. Do you think he might be right? If he is, we'll drive back out tomorrow morning."

They both thought a minute and the woman said, "Flowers Road is easy. There are three farms that own the right hand side and four on the left. The only one that sold was 10 years ago. On 631, I'm not sure. Most of that property is small farms and have lifelong owners, but one or two have sold. I don't know of any for sale now though."

"That little farm on the right about a half a kilometer down 631, you know, the one that belonged to widow McClain, may be for sale," the man said. "It's been tied up in court and the family finally leased it to a man from southern England about two months ago. I don't know what the damn fool wants it for. The neighbors say he spends all his time in the barn. It may be clear of the courts now. Might take a look at that one."

"Something funny about that man," chimed in the woman. "Mrs. Needham lives on the farm across the road and said that he never goes anywhere. Once he was out mending a fence and she walked over to talk to him but he was very curt. She said his accent wasn't Southern England, either."

"Anyway," the man said. "That's about the only place it could be. Land rarely sells around here."

We didn't want to overstay our welcome so we bought some candy and two magazines. I thanked them again and we left.

When we were back in the car I grinned at Maggie and said, "Bingo."

"You were right. Now what?"

"I don't know. What do you think?"

"We have to confirm. Isn't a night approach easier?

"Usually. Let's drive by again."

I cranked up the car and we drove to 631 and made a left turn. We drove at a normal pace and soon had covered a bit more than a half mile. It was right there where they had said it was. A small farmhouse sat about 100 feet off the road with a fair-sized barn in behind it. The driveway was circular with an offshoot around to the barn.

There was one light on in the house but I couldn't see anyone. It looked like there was a small woodlot behind the barn but I couldn't really tell in the dark.

As we passed our target, the road curved to the right and skirted some heavy woods, again on the right and bordering or actually on the McClain property. Although I shrank from the prospect, I knew I needed to work my way in to try to confirm. I drove on down the road, turned around and came back to the edge of the woods. I stopped before we could see the house and far enough back that the Rover couldn't be seen, either. I was dressed for the job, and had a pair of high-powered night glasses. Hopefully, I wouldn't need to approach too closely. I just needed to get the lay of the land.

"It's about 10:30. If I'm not back by 11:30, you'll know I'm in trouble. Go back to the hotel fast. If someone approaches the car, don't stay to chat, either. The hotel is out of Bennie's detection range if he's out here, so Deena will show up to meet us at midnight. You need to be there to meet her and tell her where I am. Just in case. Don't worry, because I plan to be back. Any questions?"

"No questions. Jack?"

"Umm."

"If there is any loose tchadbe lying around–."

I grinned and told her I'd look.

I struck off into the woods and began to angle to the right and slightly uphill. The single lighted window was soon visible through the trees. I used the glasses to look into the window but no one was in there as far as I could tell. I moved back a little further until I could see the barn and confirmed a woodlot behind it that joined the one I was in. I could see through cracks that there was a light on in the barn but there was no window open to see in. I continued my silent approach and finally reached the corner of the barn.

I was standing there getting ready to move along the back wall to a crack when a voice behind me said, "Evening, Jack. Out for a stroll I see."

My heart was in my throat. "Bennie?"

"Or Karg, if you prefer. You're pretty good, Jack. I've been on scan all evening and while I scanned you when you got about half

160

way into our little section of woods, I didn't actually hear you until you got right close here."

"You're not supposed to be able to scan me until I'm very close."

"A little advanced training from the devil," he chuckled. "Can we agree that I am the stronger of us and dispense with the unpleasantries?"

"You son of a bitch. You try to kill or maim me three times and set up that little scene with Jenny and you want me to be calm?"

"Now, Jack, those accidents were meant to scare you. I knew you were in Deena's 'wing of protection' and, as for the lovely Mrs. Raines, you've been wanting to fuck her for years. I just helped out."

He turned toward the side where the door was and said, "Come on in."

"Bullshit."

"You're being tiresome, Jack."

He grabbed me with his mind. I felt this searing pain in my head and found myself walking towards him. We went inside and found another man about 50-years-old dressed like an English landowner, tweeds and leather and all. He looked me over, turned to Bennie and said, "Do we kill him?"

"Can't. He's under an angel's wing. Did you hear from the Tarcans?"

"About 11:30 is their best estimate."

"Those bastards need to learn how to calibrate that machine. Every minute increases the possibility that the angel will show."

"How about it, Jack. When is she due?"

"I thought she'd be here now so that all I'd have to do is remove the bodies."

That earned me a backhand from Bennie's cohort; his ring cracked my upper lip . It began to bleed impressively. I got out my handkerchief and daubed at it.

The English-looking demon gestured to the back rooms and said, "What about those four?"

"Leave them. They don't know anything. Let the angel give them free transport back to Hell. Damn, it's 11:05."

He paced around a minute or two and asked, "Where's Maggie, Jack? And don't bullshit me."

I looked afraid and said, "No bullshit. I left her in Perth at the hotel."

"I doubt it very much, but I'll let it pass since she doesn't matter anyway."

I decided to use my training again, which requires a captive to try to talk to his captor in order to obtain as much information as possible. I said, "If ten teams of demons is all the devil can muster in his bid to raid Earth for labor, then I call it a joke."

He turned toward me and said without thinking, "You believe 10 teams is all we've got?" He laughed heartily and went on, "We have many more in training." Then he realized what he had said and hastened to add, "But we won't need them since the campaign is already succeeding way beyond our expectations. I understand you sampled our little pills with the lovely Maggie. How did you like them?"

"They work," I admitted.

"You bet they do."

He walked over to a briefcase and took out a large packet and stuck it in my jacket pocket and said, "Here's a supply of the new formula, on the house. It's perfectly stable and has a shelf life of years. Perhaps you can share it with Jenny Raines, OK?"

I didn't say anything. I knew I should throw them in his face but I wanted those pills. And I sure did want to share them with Mrs. Raines. A beeping sound disrupted my thoughts.

The English gent went over to it and said, "Five minutes, Karg."

"About time. It's already 11:30. Jack, I'm going to cuff you to this beam. Your angel will free you. I always liked you and Hud, Jack. I'm sorry it came to this, but I have a job to do, too. Close that Johnson property deal and you'll make a fortune. Now, I gave you 1000 pills in that packet. If you and Maggie and Hud and Jenny get together and use them once a month, you'll have a 20 year supply. Once a month won't harm your system but don't take them more often. Understand?"

He had been cuffing me as he talked.

"One last thing," he said. "Have Hud see that my daughter, or rather Bennie's daughter, goes to Bennie's sister."

"Karg, now!" screamed the other demon from across the room.

Bennie grabbed his briefcase, ran over to the spot, touched the English gent and they were gone.

Deena and Maggie arrived 30 minutes too late.

twenty-four

Deena uncuffed me with a glance. She turned to the door leading to the back section, threw it open and froze the four demons there. Then she quickly questioned them. They knew nothing useful so she dispatched them to Noah's Ark. Then she asked for my report.

I told her about my approach, my capture, and Bennie's newly-found ability to scan for mortals. "I think he's the only elite who can do this," I said.

"I suspect you're right, Jack. Nevertheless, it's one more thing to worry about. What else?"

"I badgered him about why the devil could only come up with 10 teams for the whole of Earth and he coughed up the fact that they have many more in training. He quickly realized what he had said and clammed up, but I suspect some of them are already here."

"We may be able to tell from the Tarcan analysis. I'm going to pick it up in a moment. Anything more?"

"Yes, he told me that they had whipped the stability problem with the tchadbe pills. Now they are good for years."

"You're just full of good news, aren't you Jack? By the way, the new name is 'Wham'."

Maggie said, "What did you say?"

"The Atlanta police department started calling the tchadbe pills Wham. I wonder if it's from that old definition of a quickie, 'Wham, bam, thank you ma'am'?

I looked at her and must have looked surprised when she flushed and said hastily, "Angels are human, too."

We all laughed and Maggie gave her a quick hug.

She sent me to the back to see if the small pick-up parked there would run. I checked and it did, so I came back and reported the only piece of good news I had given her so far.

"Good. It's 12:30. I want you two to take that truck back to town, park it somewhere near the hotel and abandon it. Be in your room at 3:00. I'll return then with the Tarcan REGEN analysis. I also have to meet Hud and Jenny in 30 minutes, so I'll see you later."

We got into the truck and headed to town. Once there, we left the truck on a side street with the keys in it and walked around to the hotel. There was no food service at that late hour, but the desk clerk kindly opened the gift shop and let us have some crackers and cheese and drinks. We took our pitiful supper upstairs. Since we had nearly two hours until Deena arrived again, we showered and got on the bed and made love. Then we talked awhile about situations into which we had gotten ourselves involved.

Soon it was nearly 3:00 and Maggie said, "I'm going to get up and put my robe on. I don't want Deena to think this is all we do."

Deena arrived right on time and produced a schedule of Tarcan lifts and drops with REGEN over the last two months. There was a summary of statistical projections of probable drops that helped establish where the labs might be. They were pretty sure, 99 % sure, of the original 10. Five were Clarksboro, Bamako, San Pedro, Perth, and Winnemucca, which Hud and Jenny had identified. The other five were Hiroshima, New Delhi, St. Petersburg (Russia, not Florida), Auckland, and Recife. There were maps of the latter five showing approximate drop points.

In addition, there were 10 other labs spread around the Earth. Based on the statistics, the confidence levels ranged from 74 to 89 percent that they were new labs that were already operational. It sure looked like Bennie had given me good information, and that the second class had graduated and was on the job. Deena also had summaries of the interviews She had done with Manuel and Coulibaly. As expected, they knew nothing about either the number or the locations of any of the other labs. They did have some limited knowledge of the distribution channels, however. Coulibaly said he made a delivery to an address in Abidjan, Ivory Coast, to a man named Pierre. Bennie had also told him that there were several channels available for back up, but he wasn't given them. Coulibaly himself had shipped 10,000 bottles last week.

Manuel's story was similar. He had an address in San Salvador with a contact named Elena, and had shipped 12,000 bottles last week. As far as we knew, Bennie, too, had gotten off about 10,000 bottles, for a total of 32,000.

"Jack," Deena asked. "Did you get any clue as to where Bennie and the other demon were going?"

"Not really. But I remember thinking about it at the time, and decided they were going to Hell. I don't remember what made me think that, though."

"I think you may be right. We have a record of their lift to the ship, but the ship hasn't left yet. We are still watching. If it does leave, it'll take about 8 hours to reach Hell and to drop them off, and another 8 hours to return. That's a long time to leave the network of labs unattended, even if the devil has managed to set up a communication link to Hell. I suspect that Bennie has left someone in charge. Probably Drok. He's right below Bennie in the hierarchy. The question is, where is he?"

We all mulled this over a bit. Finally Maggie said, "I did notice something odd. One of the 10 new labs is in Waycross, Georgia. That's only about two hours from Clarksboro. Why would they put one so close?"

"Good question," Deena said. "I don't know. The other 9 are not at all close to any of the originals. I'll ask Analysis when I'm back on Noah. So, where do we go from here?"

Hud said, "I vote we go after the remaining original five. The new labs shouldn't be quite ready to put out any product yet, so I don't think we need to worry about them right now."

"That's true. They were only established last week. And only a couple of those have had enough drops to get demons and raw tchadbe in. We shouldn't have to worry about them, in my opinion, for at least a few more weeks."

Maggie said, "I'd still like to add Waycross to the list. I've got a feeling there's more there than meets the eye."

"I respect hunches. Let's add it. But we'll put it last because I want to stop further shipments from leaving the fully ready labs, if possible. So, guys, let's split this list up between you two and Hud and Jenny. You all take Auckland and Recife and then, Waycross. I'll be back here at noon with the latest updates, especially on that ship.

"One more thing. If Bennie comes back down, we need to be ready for him. I'm going to put angels two miles from each approximate drop spot for those last three labs. That way, if Bennie comes down, they should know it. If they drop somewhere else we'll just have to check that later. Get some sleep and mess around until noon."

We slept until nearly nine, and were so hungry we rushed to dress and get to the dining room. A good full Scottish breakfast was just what we both needed. I leaned back and sighed and thought momentarily about another nap in that soft bed upstairs. But something else was on my mind.

"Maggie, I need to talk to you about something. Promise you'll be reasonable."

"Who is she, Jack?"

"No, not that. Listen, believe it or not, Bennie was actually kind of friendly, and just before he left, he gave me 1000 tchadbe pills."

"That's really funny, Jack. You don't need to tease me. I was serious when I told you to look around."

"I know that. I am serious."

I reached into my jacket pocket and pulled them out. Maggie didn't know whether to believe me or not but she reached over and touched the package.

"Bennie told me that these were the new formula and would be viable for years. He also said one per month. Absolutely no more."

"Oh God, you're not kidding. I think I can live with once a month, but I won't be happy about it. What else did he say?"

"Not too much of importance."

"I'm excited just thinking about it."

"Yeah, but the question is, what do we do with it? If we go by REGEN, will Deena detect it and take it?"

"If she does, I've worked my last job for her. We are supposed to be helping to eliminate tchadbe, though, aren't we? Or does She just want us to figure out how to control it?"

"Don't know. I thought of sending it FedEx, but then it might be searched at customs or one of the kids might open it if we're not home. I just don't know how to get it there."

"We just take it with us. Deena won't be any trouble. I'll handle her."

And she would. Decision made, we walked out and became tourists for a while, spending a bundle on some fine woolen items. By noon, we were back in our room ready to go. Deena was about five minutes late.

"Sorry about that. We've found the Winnemucca lab so I had to get those demons off to Noah's Ark. It just took a little longer than usual. And it's the same old story. This time, 11,000 bottles are already gone. I sent Hud and Jenny off to Hiroshima. I've also contacted the Analysis group on Noah, but they're as puzzled as we are about Waycross. The Tarcan ship has made the three drops we predicted, but Bennie didn't get off. Since the ship subsequently left for Hell, I'd guess that's where Bennie is headed. I wish I knew why." She paused and frowned. "I guess I'll send you all to Auckland first if you're ready.

"We are," Maggie said. "But I need to get to Noah's Ark to put our purchases in our locker if that's OK."

"No problem. Let's go."

We reached Noah without incident and were stuffing things into our lockers in the visitors' wing when Deena returned.

"There's been a temporary change in plan. Hud just called. There's been a fire in the lab and the place is burned to the ground. I suspect there are the remains of four demons in there and the local police can't be allowed to find them. I'm taking a couple of angels out and bringing Hud and Jenny here. I'll leave the angels to cope with the authorities."

A little over an hour later, Hud and Jenny arrived. Deena was in Analysis and told them to wait with us. We were still in the visitors' area when they came in.

After hugs and handshakes all around, Maggie asked, "Anybody know what time it is? Or for that matter what day it is?"

"I think it's about 9:00 Monday morning at home. I'm not positive, though," Hud offered.

Deena walked in and confirmed Hud's time estimate. She said, "I've just been watching the analysis. Chances for capturing an elite or learning anything useful at the other five original sites have now dropped to 50 to 1. So we'll ride with Maggie's hunch. I'm going to send you directly to Waycross even though it will be nearly 10:00 in the morning when you arrive. Check into the Holiday Inn on Route 1 South. I will drop you right behind the place in a little wooded area. You have adjoining rooms reserved and two rental vehicles waiting with the keys at the front desk. Any questions?"

"What are we looking for?" asked Jenny.

"I know you and Hud haven't been briefed, but I'll leave most of that to Maggie. I do want to set some rendezvous times. How about tonight, Monday, at 11:00 for openers? OK. Now, Jack found out that Bennie has learned to scan mortals at about 25 feet. If Maggie is right and Drok is here, you won't be able to get close to your target. You'll know how I feel but for me it's a mile and not 30 feet. Anyway, take your regular binoculars and the night vision ones and be careful. I've arranged for maps and other briefing materials at the Analysis section offices, so go pick them up before you leave. I'll be back to see you off at noon."

twenty-five

We were pretty used to the routine by this point. We slipped into the motel, checked in, bought more maps and picked up a couple of brochures so we would look like real tourists, and went to our rooms. This time Hud and Jenny accompanied us. We briefed them on what we knew. Or at least thought we knew.

Hud nodded and said, "I agree with Maggie. Something made them put this lab here even though it's close to Clarksboro. Maybe it was to keep the two top demons close enough so they could cover for each other."

"Maybe," I said. "Anyway, let's get some lunch and go look at the drop site."

I reviewed the directions from analysis again. The site was south of Waycross, on the same side of town as our motel. We'd have to go about 18 miles down Route 1 to Echols Road, which turned off to the East. We would go about three miles down Echols and, supposedly, the lab would be somewhere off to the left about three-quarters of a mile off the road. It was a relatively deserted area, which in this part of the world meant paper company land with pines and pines and pines. Peaceful. Good place to hide.

We ate lunch in the hotel coffee shop, then selected one of the two Ford Taurus cars waiting for us. Hud drove, so we quickly covered the 18 miles taking us to Echols Road.

Hud turned left at a little corner market and watched the odometer until it read 2.9 miles. The area we were in now didn't look promising, however. The left side of the road had been almost solid pines from the time we turned onto Echols. Then a narrow county road cut right into the pines on the left. The ruts were somewhat overgrown, so it obviously hadn't been used much. We all looked down it as we passed and we saw nothing but pines on both sides. We went on for another mile of solid pines on Echols Road, then turned around and retraced our path. We stopped again at the only hint of a road we had seen for miles, but decided that this could not be the place. We headed back to the motel. It was already 3:30.

"Did you bring your camouflage gear, Jack?" asked Hud.

"No. Think we need to go in on foot?

"Don't you agree?"

"I can't see any choice. We'd stand out like a beacon in a car, if whatever there is to see is back there on that little road."

"When are you going?" Jenny asked.

"Dusk might be a good time. What do you think, Jack?"

"We need to start out a little earlier than that. If we do find a building, we'll need enough natural light to see the layout."

"There's a little market at the Echols Road turnoff and a roadside market at a farm just back from there," Maggie offered. "Jenny and I could hit those for more information."

"Good idea," I said. "You'll have to drop us off near that dirt road and turn back anyway. You can also go on south on Route 1 to a little town called Race Pond and check around there. But you'll have to be careful. These folks will be suspicious of two outsiders."

Hud turned into the Holiday Inn and parked. "Sounds like a good plan, folks," he said. "Let's get ourselves ready." Maggie and Jenny went upstairs and he and I went off in search of an army surplus or sporting goods store for clothes for our mission.

When we got back to the motel, it was nearly 6:00, so we collected the ladies and went for a light meal at the coffee shop. After eating, Hud and I donned our new camouflage clothing and we left for the site about 7:45. We got to the drop-off spot about 8:10, just as it was beginning to get dark. Hud and I jumped out and faded into the woods. Maggie and Jenny roared off with a promise to return at 10:00.

Hud and I slipped into the woods about 100 yards and then cut left until we sighted the little road. We turned right, paralleled the road, and went at least a half mile before we saw anything but pine trees. The first indication that any human had ever been here was a cleared area on the other side of the road, with the remains of a building that had burned years ago, leaving a brick chimney standing all alone.

Hud said, "We'd better hurry. It's been so long since I've been hunting that I forgot how fast the night gets here."

We went a little further and came upon a house across the road. They had their inside lights on and we saw several kids running around. Not too likely a prospect. And quite a surprise this far back off the main road. I guess they like privacy.

We moved on a couple of hundred yards and saw more lights off to our right. We moved on a little further and saw a lane going back to the lights.

I said, "Do we cross the lane and circle around to the right or backtrack and circle left?"

"I think we should back off a little, move up parallel to the lane, and see what we have here."

"Sounds good. Wait! Listen! Do you hear a car coming down the road?"

Just then I saw the lights through the trees. The vehicle turned into the lane. We hit the deck just as an old pick-up truck flew down the lane past us.

"Let's go, Jack. Maybe we can get close enough to see who it is."

We moved quickly up toward the lights. We were very aware of Bennie's 30-foot detection range and had decided to use 50 feet to give us the advantage. As we got closer, it was obvious that what we had here was a typical South Georgia hunting lodge, a rustic but fairly good-sized log building. There was an outhouse in the back plus a two-vehicle shed, in this case holding a tractor and jeep. A storage shed was attached to this. I smelled something cooking but it wasn't tchadbe. It was some sort of a barbecued-meat smell.

The guy from the truck walked to the back of the house and yelled, "Jimmy! Ya back there?"

"Who th'hell do ya think's cookin' this stuff, your old lady?"

"No way. Smells too good. Her slop smells like horseshit. When're the others comin'?"

" 'Bout 9:00, I guess. How 'bout gittin' me some more charcoal outa the shed."

He wandered over to the shed and said, "Fuckin' shed's padlocked."

"Tha's right. I forgot. They got sumpin' stored in there. I put the charcoal over there behind the tractor."

"Got it. Damn, it's heavy."

Another car arrived and then another. It was nearly 9:00 by now. Hud whispered, "What do you think?"

"I think we'd better circle around and look on down the road. This doesn't look like our target."

" Let's move."

We made a wide circle and jogged another half mile. We came across one more building, an old barn, across the road, but it hadn't been used in years and was nearly collapsed.

We turned back and as we made our way around the hunting lodge, we could hear the party in full swing. They had started a fire in the side yard and Hud and I moved in for another look at the participants. There were about 15 men eating barbecue and drinking longneck beers. The fire illuminated the whole area, so we could see their faces. We got out our night glasses to look more closely. I didn't see anyone I knew until a figure moved up to stoke the fire. To my surprise it was our sheriff, Mike Andrews.

Hud said, "Jack, that's Mike. What the hell?"

"I knew he was a member of a hunt club down here somewhere. I guess this is it."

"That's bizarre, though."

"Let's go or we'll be walking back to town."

We jogged back to the highway and arrived at 10 on the dot, but the ladies weren't there yet.

Hud was uptight immediately. "Where the hell are they? I hope they didn't get into trouble."

"They'll be here in a minute."

We waited five minutes, then heard a siren in the direction of Route 1. Soon a car came along. It was them.

"We were about to get worried," said Hud. "What happened?"

Jenny said, "About two miles up the road toward Route 1 we saw a sheriff's car and a group of people in the middle of the road. So we slowed to a stop. A deputy walked up and said, 'Just be a minute ladies. Pick-up truck rolled with three men in it. Two are hurt and the ambulance is on its way. What are you two ladies doing out here in the middle of the night?' I asked him sweetly if it was against some law to be here at this time of night. I guess I pissed him off because he didn't answer and just motioned us around. We moved slowly past and could see that the three were drunk as coots. One was complaining that they were missing the barbecue."

Maggie added, "We probably shouldn't go back that way. Is there another choice?"

I looked at the map and said, "Yeah. We can continue on this road and it will intersect Route 12 in about five miles or so. Then we go left to, let's see, Hoboken and left again to Route 82, then right into Waycross. We'll have to hurry though, or we'll miss Deena."

Maggie was driving so we weren't in any danger of being late. We arrived at 10:52.

We had talked over our findings on the way back and reached no conclusions. Deena arrived right on schedule and sat down on one of the beds. She had nothing new except confirmation that the original five we passed up visiting had all been abandoned or burned. I got elected to report and it didn't take long. We had nothing either.

"What do you suggest?" Deena asked.

"I have one idea," said Maggie "You go out and do a two mile circle of the site and see if there's an elite present. I know you can't pinpoint but we can go back knowing one is there somewhere."

"Show me on your map. OK. Be right back."

We waited awhile and back she came.

"There are two. Jackpot, Maggie. Congratulations. The problem is that I still can't tell exactly where they are. What should we do?"

Hud answered. "We can go back in tonight and look some more or we can wait for morning and go in and cover a lot more ground quickly. Jack?"

"Before we decide that, I had another thought. Do you remember, at that lodge we heard them say that the storage shed was being used for some purpose that made it necessary to lock it and put the charcoal in the garage? Now, that's a fair-sized storage room. Bear with me a minute. I'll try to connect my thoughts for you when I get them sorted out myself. Hud, think back. Remember the dog incident in Cedar Creek? Bennie was there and undoubtedly caused it. But he wasn't at the streetlight incident. At least you didn't see him. Who was there?"

Hud looked puzzled but Jenny jumped up and said, "That son-of-a-bitch Mike Andrews was there. He was sitting there in his car writing something when we went back and told the kids we were going to your house. He was still sitting there when we came back out. Then he pulled out of your driveway just as we approached the streetlight."

"You're right," Hud added. "And I thought it was just a wild coincidence that he was there last night. He must be Drok."

"Deena, can you handle them both at once?" I asked.

"I don't know. Probably not. There's really no need to chance it anyway. He'll go back to Clarksboro tonight or first thing in the morning to go to work. We take out the lab after he's gone, and then go get him."

"Sounds good. What time?"

"Let's say 8:00 in the morning. I'm going to call an angel in to monitor at two miles out. She can't handle Drok but she really won't have to. She can tell me when Drok leaves and that will let us know it's safe to go in."

Jenny said, "So we get a night's sleep for a change?"

"Unless something changes. See you at 8:00."

twenty-six

It was 11:30. We opted for bed and went next door to our room. Maggie began to undress and said, "I checked the locker. Pills are there, ready and waiting."

"Good. Exactly where did you put them, by the way."

She turned on the shower and stepped in as she answered. "You remember that little beaded purse I bought in Perth? Pills are in that, and I put them on the bottom under the new wool gloves and scarf."

She was in the shower, so I didn't answer.

I undressed, moved close to the shower door, and said loudly, "Leave it on for me."

The shower door opened and she said, "Come on in. I'll wash your back."

I did and she finally got me turned around to wash my back. It was tight in there.

She scrubbed away and said, "I get really hot every time I think about those pills."

I reached back and put my hand on her and ran my fingers through the black curly hair. She reached around to grasp me. It was a snug fit in the little shower but we managed.

Later, we relaxed in bed watching Letterman. Maggie had been quiet since the shower.

"Jack, how do you really feel about Jenny?"

"I don't know. Why do you ask?"

"Jenny and I had a long talk this afternoon while you and Hud shopped for clothes. She told me that you two had sex the night Hud and I were captives."

I had started to sit up and explain but she continued.

"I told her that Hud and I did too, in the storage building where we were being held. I had planned to tell you, but the time never seemed right. We've been so busy and under so much stress lately. Anyway, we did it and we enjoyed it. At the time, I rationalized that it was a comfort thing brought on by our predicament. But it wasn't, Jack. I wanted to before we were captured. I like him. A lot."

"Maggie, I love you. I love you more than anything on this Earth. I have no intention of hurting you in any way. I don't ever want to leave you for Jenny or anyone else. I don't want you to leave me for Hud or anyone else. You are my first priority in life and I think it will always be that way. But, dammit Maggie, I can't explain it, but I have fallen in love with Jenny, too. I don't know how it happened. I didn't even know it could happen. I know that many husbands and wives have cheated on their spouses by engaging in a little casual sex. It happens and a short while later it's over and has very little to do with love. But I love her in the same way I love you. It's driving me crazy."

I felt relieved having said it. I looked at Maggie and there was enough light from the bathroom to show that she was crying. I pulled her close and held her.

"I'm sorry. I hurt you, Maggie."

"No, Jack. You didn't hurt me. I have just been so confused. I'm glad you told me. I guess I'm not as certain as you are and as Jenny seems to be, but I think I love Hud, too. But like you, I'm still very much in love with you. But when I'm around Hud and we're by ourselves, I kind of ache down deep and I want to please him and be with him. I also want to have sex with him. Is this love?"

"I don't know. I can't describe what I feel for Jenny any better than you just did, but I can feel it inside me and I think it's love. I think yours is, too. What about Hud?"

178

"Jenny says he's had strong feelings for me for several years. At first, she thought we were having an affair. She confronted Hud and he denied it but told her he would, given the chance. Yet he never suggested anything or gave me any indication about that."

"I guess that proves he still loves Jenny."

"She's satisfied that he does and swears she feels the same about him."

"This is a mess."

"It's all of that and then some. We've got a lot to sort out if we ever get home and have time to work on it. I'm so relieved since you gave me the reassurance that our marriage is still sound. I was afraid you might want out."

"I know. Me too."

"Jenny was going to talk to Hud tonight. Maybe tomorrow night we'll be home and can all get together and talk it out."

"Maybe," I said yawning. "Let's get some sleep."

She moved close to me and said, "I may sleep well tonight for the first time in a long while."

twenty-seven

Next morning, Tuesday, we knocked on the adjoining door at 7:30 and yelled that we were going to breakfast.

"Two minutes," Jenny yelled back.

True to her word, in two minutes they appeared at the door, ready to go. Jenny and Maggie went on ahead when I realized I had left my wallet. I opened the door and got it from my other pants. I went back out and Hud was waiting. We started down the corridor.

"I understand," Hud said chuckling, "that you've been enjoying my wife again."

"I've got to keep up with you and my wife."

"Yeah, there's that."

"An interesting problem. I can't wait to see how we resolve it."

"I'm going to relax and let them worry about what to do."

I laughed and said, "That'll be the day." We were both clearly relieved. No tension here.

We reached the door of the restaurant, joined Maggie and Jenny, and went in to eat. During the meal no mention was made of our ticklish situation. Instead we talked about the morning mission ahead of us. We got back to the rooms about 9:00. Deena arrived seconds later, ready to go.

"Let's proceed this way. We'll all go in one car to the two-mile point. I'll call in my angel and get her report. Then if Drok is gone, you four take the car in. I'll arrive when you do and we'll have them."

We went to the two-mile point and called the angel. She did not appear.

"I don't understand," Deena said. "She should respond. We're well within range. Drok and the other elite are gone. Let's go in for a look."

When we got there, she jumped out and whirled into the storage room. She froze the four demons working there with a glance.

"Who's in charge?"

"I am," said an elderly looking male.

"Quickly, where's my angel?"

"Dead. Out back."

Chills ran up and down my spine at the demon's words. We followed her out the back door and sure enough the angel lay huddled in a heap under a tree. Deena ran to her but it was too late. Deena was crying and so were Maggie and Jenny. I had seen a blanket inside so I went to get it. When I got back, Deena was examining the body. It was nude, of course. After a moment I heard her say, "That son of a bitch raped her first. He'll answer for that. I'm going to send her to Charity for rebirth. I won't need the blanket, Jack, but thanks."

She mumbled in the direction of the sky and the dead angel vanished. I never even knew her name.

I asked, "What happens to her, Deena?"

"She'll be reborn in a new body with her memory intact. That's why he raped her, so that she would have to live with a horrible memory or have part of her memory wiped and lose some good memories as well. I can't imagine how she got caught."

We went back inside and Deena asked the demon more questions.

"Who killed her?'

"Drok."

"How did he catch her?"

"He was taking a walk in the woods and detected her. He was the stronger."

"Who raped her?"

"Drok."

"Where did he go?"

"I don't know."

"Where's the other one?"

"I don't know."

"What's his name?"

"Her name is Elsha."

Questioning over, she sent them to Noah without another word.

She was quiet for a minute or two, then approached us. "She was too inexperienced for this job. It was fatal and it was my fault for not requesting a seasoned angel. I should have realized she would have trouble if he moved around to within a mile of her. Let's go straight to Noah and the Analysis section. I'll have someone get your luggage."

When we turned around, we were on Noah.

By this time, it was pretty obvious that we were losing both the battle and the war. Wham, Atlanta's name for the tchadbe, had caught on like wildfire nationwide. It was still available only in certain areas in limited quantities but it was in demand on every street corner. The press had a field day playing up the sex part and caused everyone to want some. That helped the devil's cause enormously.

The Tarcan ship was still not back from Hell, so finding Drok was our only hope. Bennie might not even come back but you could be sure at least 10 new labs would be staffed from the ship. Maybe more. It was imperative that Drok be captured soon. After visiting analysis, we went down to the little briefing room and began to formulate some plans.

Deena said, "Let's brainstorm. Where would Drok be most likely to go now that he knows we're hunting him?"

Hud said, "Probably to one of the second group of labs far from Clarksboro. We pretty much know where they all are now."

I said, "Maybe he went to a third wave site that's not yet operating. We don't have a clue about those yet."

Jenny had been fidgeting around and now said, "Why do we keep messing around with this problem? The solution is to send in several squads of angels to cover each site like a blanket until he's identified, then go in and pluck him out. I can't see that the four of us are much help except that we can approach blind and set him up for a surprise, but it seems to me that the need for surprise is long past. Let's grab the bastard and wring him out."

That's our Jenny. Her world is black or white. No halfway. You were either a son- of-a-bitch or you weren't. There were no half sons-of-bitches. It's part of what makes her a good battlefield leader. The downside is that it makes her an impatient planner.

Deena was shaking her head.

"As appealing as that sounds, Jenny, I can't do it. First, I don't have that many warrior angels. We have never needed more than the 10 the Customs allow on Earth. There are plenty of angels, Charity for example, who can't be used for what I do. We're stretched to the limit now. That's why I used Reesa, who was our 10th and weakest, in Waycross.

"Second, the Customs only allow us 10 angels at any one time on Earth. I know you're wondering why we should observe the Custom when the devil has broken it repeatedly. One reason is that She likes to keep Her word. The second reason is that if this dispute should get out of hand and require outside arbitration, the one who keeps the Customs probably would win. This is a minor consideration and will be ignored if She feels action of some sort is required even if against the Customs, but so far my instructions are to keep them intact."

"OK. Then what do we do?" Jenny asked.

"Maggie, what do you think?" Deena asked.

"I think if I were Drok, I'd reason that the last place anyone would look for me would be Bennie's old lab right there in Clarksboro."

We tossed that around a bit looking at the pros and cons.

Finally Deena said, "No one has a better idea. Let's play Maggie's hunch. It's 11:00 now in Clarksboro, so I will send you home and rejoin you at 2:00."

"I want to visit my locker to get some purchases," said Maggie.

"I know you do, dear. Hurry, and we'll wait for you."

Since it was Tuesday, the kids were in school. Jenny's Mom and Dad were out somewhere so Deena sent us to their house and we walked over to ours and rang the bell. Mrs. Pearson answered and was duly surprised. We asked her to stay until evening since we might have to leave again. She didn't ask any questions but clearly thought we were crazy. She may have been right.

Maggie had made it off Noah with the pills intact. I had a feeling Deena knew but had let it go. We had a safe built into the floor of our bedroom closet that would resist the most experienced and persistent of burglars even if they found it. I had learned about safes in the FBI, so all those years weren't a total loss. Anyway, we put the pills into the safe and I felt immensely better. We ate some lunch and I took a short nap. At 2:00 we were at Hud's when Deena arrived.

"I made a run past the chicken farm three miles out, and Drok is there right now. No sign of the female, though. Shall we go out and take him?"

We all piled into Hud's Explorer and headed for Highpoint Road and the farm.

About three miles out, Deena said, "I've got him in range, and he's still alone. Slow down, now. I want out at two miles in case he's improved his range. Now we don't know precisely where he is. He could be in the house or the lab or outside walking. You four go busting up to the front of the house in the Explorer so that he will detect you. That should bring him out for a laugh. I'll be on my way in at the same time and when he gets me at one mile, it'll be to late. Any questions? OK. Let's go."

She got out and removed her clothes. She said they hampered her movements. We took off and soon were at the lane. Hud poured it on and we went roaring into the yard. We all jumped out and started yelling. He came out onto the front porch.

"What do you fools think you're—Arghh."

Deena appeared and said, "Give it up, Drok. I'm the stronger."

"We'll see," he grunted as he began to concentrate. They were locked mind to mind, leaving us free, so we began to move in on him. He switched part of his effort to us and we were frozen in place. But distracting him and soaking up part of his power was working. Deena had him on his knees, panting heavily, sweat gleaming on his face.

I felt his power beginning to fade when a vehicle slammed to a stop. A young woman burst out of the car and leaped over the hood. She stopped and focused her attention on Deena. Deena staggered and fell to her knees. I felt the surge from Drok as he tightened on us again now that he had help. This had to be Elsha, the elite from Waycross. Somehow they had tricked us. Deena was clearly no match for both of them, and it was she who had sweat running down her face.

Deena had been forced to her hands and knees, head hanging down when I heard her yell, "Stop her, Maggie. Stop her."

"What can I do? I can't move?"

"Yes, you can. You must try. I can't hold on much longer." She rolled into a fetal position, her face contorted. Drok had gotten to his feet and regained enough mobility to walk off the porch and over toward Deena. He kicked her hard in the rib cage. He drew back and did it again. Deena moaned deeply and rolled over onto her stomach.

Then it happened. Maggie was on my left frozen to the spot. She started to move and Drok was so startled he missed his next kick. Maggie stared straight at him. He clutched his head in agony and fell to his knees. Elsha moved toward Maggie but Deena was immediately back in control.

"Hold him, Maggie," Deena yelled. She turned to us and said, "Kill her quickly."

Hud was closest. He broke her neck almost before I could react.

Deena said, "I've got him now, Maggie. Help her, Jack."

Maggie was swaying and about to fall when I got to her. I eased her to the ground to a sitting position. Her eyes rolled up and she was out. I eased her on down to the ground. Jenny, seeing Hud take Elsha, had gone for Mike, or Drok as we now knew him, who was on hands and knees head shaking back and forth.

Deena screamed, "We need him alive."

Jenny said, "You son of a bitch."

She ran up to his backside and gave him a hard kick in the balls. He screamed and rolled over onto his side. She hauled off and kicked him again before Hud and I grabbed her.

She struggled to get free, shouting, "I'll teach that son of a bitch to mess with us. Let me go, damn it!"

We finally got her calmed down. Maggie sat up and wondered what had happened.

I helped her up, gave her a squeeze, and said, "Everything is OK, thanks to you." I related the basics of the action that had just taken place, emphasizing her role.

"How did I do that?"

Deena walked over and said, "Just take it easy, dear. I'll tell you about it tonight. Let's clean up here first. I'm going to take Drok up to Noah now and have him sent to Her for questioning. I'll be back in about 10 minutes."

We were four shaken mortals. We didn't even talk during those 10 minutes except to ask if everyone was OK. By the time I had covered the demon Elsha with a tarp I found in the garage, Deena was back. "I'll take care of Elsha. You all go home. I'll meet you in the hot tub room at 11:00."

We got into the Explorer and left. The drive back was silent.

It was 5:00 on a hot Tuesday afternoon as we made our way home. Normal people were just ending their workday and starting home for the afternoon drink. I must be part normal, because I went in and had a massive afternoon drink. The kids were home and glad to see us, especially since we had brought presents for both of them. I spun them a tale about being in Waycross with the FBI and how we had gotten some of the bad guys but might have to leave again. Maggie took a nap. Mrs. Pearson left with the understanding that we might have to recall her after 11:00 if we had to leave again. We caught up on the mail and papers. Most of it was the usual junk, but there was a letter from Earl Ray Butts, the realtor, informing us that we could close on the Johnson property anytime before September 10. And then we thoroughly enjoyed the first quiet evening we had in a long time.

twenty-eight

Deena arrived at 11:00. She said the hot tub looked inviting, so we all peeled off, showered and got in. It was designed for four but held five OK. We never had briefings like that in the FBI or I might still be there .

"Let me bring you up to date. Drok is with Her and we'll have everything he knows by morning. The Tarcan ship is due back in the morning, we think. They probably know about Drok's capture by now, so Bennie should be aboard. The third wave of labs will already have been moved since we captured Drok. Analysis says it's 87 percent certain that they will adopt a continuous drop routine to hide the real locations of the third wave and the relocated first and second wave labs. So once again, despite our best efforts, we're still losing the war."

Jenny asked, "What happened to Elsha?"

"She is being repaired and will be banished forever, just like Manuel and Coulibaly."

"It seemed so final looking at her lying on the ground all huddled up."

"I know. You never get used to it. Now let me take you back a bit. Do you remember that when I first recruited you, I told you there were several reasons why I specifically wanted you four?"

We all nodded agreement.

"And I said I wouldn't give you the last one until later?"

Again all nodded.

"Well, this is the time. Maggie is primarily that reason, at least she was in the beginning."

Maggie gave a start and said, "What happened to me at the chicken farm? Is that it?"

"Yes, Maggie. Let me explain. Angels have many powers. I've never really enumerated them for you, but you've seen me in action and know a lot of them from just observing. Let me give you some particulars about them. First of all is mind control. This is a broad term, but it means that I can influence you to do something. For example, I can make Jack's head go under water like this." Under it went. I couldn't stop it. "Or I can freeze you on the spot. I can make you cry, laugh, be hungry, want sex, and so on.

"The second power is teleportation, for want of a better word. I can move myself up to 20 miles in a single controlled jump. That means that if I want to be at the chicken farm, I can go right now in one hop. It's not instantaneous, like REGEN is. In fact, teleportation is a little like flying but very fast. I will admit that it's so fast that you think I am disappearing, but that's not what's happening. For jumps longer than 20 miles, REGEN is faster if you are connected to it, but for closer locations, such as the chicken farm, I can be there in just a few seconds using this power.

"Our third power is sensory awareness. To a limited extent, I can 'read' minds. I can actually sense whether a person is good or evil. I can sense the presence of a weapon or a harmful substance. Like the demons, I have to be in close proximity of the person, not as close as the demons, but still limited to about 200 yards. I can tell whether you're sad or happy. General feelings. Not specific thoughts, however. I can sense the presence of an elite demon up to three miles, as you know, and a mortal at about 200 yards. If the mortal intends to do me harm, that extends to about 300 yards because a threat generates a strong emotion.

"One of the most important powers is that of time travel. It is also one of the hardest to develop. And very hard to explain. I don't have it perfected yet, despite decades of practice. I get murky glimpses of the future from time to time with no regularity as to when or where they occur. It is only minutes or hours at best and very vague. I am trying to refine it with practice, but I haven't had much success, so far. You already know, though, about travel to the past.

"Another power is form alteration. I can change my physical appearance to some extent. I can't turn myself into a grizzly bear or a Bengal tiger but I can alter into most human forms. For example, Mrs. Angelo. Or a demon. Like short range teleportation, this is not instantaneous either. The first time you adopt a new form, it takes several days of trial and error and extensive practice. But once you have it 'programmed', you can change to it almost instantaneously.

"The final major power is physical endurance. Physically, I am capable of no more than you all are in your enhanced state. But you will admit that you are able to perform tasks that you could only dream about before." We were, of course, and told her so.

"Now this is a fairly complete list. I've just hit the high points, but you get the general idea. You should have some questions or comments or observations, right?"

Maggie spoke up. "But I can't do any of those things."

"Yes, you can, dear. The first time I saw you was by accident on a street in downtown Clarksboro. You remember the day of the accident when the drunk lost control of his vehicle and crashed into the crowded sidewalk?"

"Yes. He just missed hitting me. Five people were killed."

"He didn't just miss you, Maggie. He hit you head on, or at least he would have, but you teleported about 20 feet to another part of the sidewalk. In all the confusion, nobody noticed or was willing to believe what they saw. I thought you were an angel and reached out to your mind, but all I found was a confused mortal. You blocked the experience out."

"I do vaguely remember."

"I followed you home and went to Noah to get our resident expert on psychic power, an angel named Bishop, who is able to read a person's strength and potential for using our powers. Not all angels have the powers available to them, you see, and they are latent in others. Bishop can tell you about that some day. I took him to your house and he 'read' you and said you were the strongest mortal he had ever seen. In fact, he said that if you were to work on developing these powers, you would be far ahead of our strongest angel. And that's me."

Maggie was shaking her head and said, "How can that be? Wouldn't I know it and have used it to my advantage?"

I said, "You know, Maggie, you have in a minor way, now that I think of it. You never argue with the kids. I can tell Laurie she's too young to date a senior and I catch hell for hours. You can step in and tell her you agree with me and after a few minutes she will suddenly agree with you. I have watched in amazement for years. You tell me the grass needs cutting, and I know it and have no intention of doing it when I find myself heading for the garage. Or we'll be watching a baseball game and you'll say that guy's going to strike out and he does. I never gave it much thought before now."

"Are you saying I've been manipulating my family?"

I said, "I think so, subconsciously. Don't worry. It's been for the best up to now."

Deena continued, "Anyway, today it came into the open. That has never happened to a mortal. It is suppressed subconsciously because it is strange and abnormal and not at all understood. Successful gamblers usually have it to some degree. And battlefield incidents abound. But you are special because you apparently have the ability to develop control over it.

"Jenny happened to come over to your house while Bishop was here, so he 'read' her too. Jenny, you have a strong latent ability that Bishop can develop easily. It's not as strong as Maggie's, but could prove to be near or above my level.

"I showed Bishop's report on Maggie to Ruth, and She was astounded. Maggie may have been the principal reason She decided to save the Earth. She was about to decide that the Earth version of humans had progressed about as far as they were going to anyway. But Maggie changed Her mind.

"We don't know what you are capable of doing. Up to now, I have been the model, and I seem to be at my peak because I haven't developed or changed much in many years. New angels are routinely screened. In fact, people trained by Bishop screen all new arrivals. It's been some time since we hit one as high as Jenny, and of course, never one like Maggie. So that's the story."

Everybody looked at Maggie.

She sat there for minute and said, "Quit staring at me. I'm still the same."

Then she splashed water on everybody and started a short water fight. We were all relieved, because this was the same old Maggie. Nevertheless, I knew that this was her way of breaking the tension that Deena had interjected into the affair. I still wondered what she was really going to be like now.

Jenny said, "How do I learn? How long does it take?"

"You will work directly with Bishop, and Maggie will, too, if she agrees. It will never be over until, like me, you stop progressing. But a week of training should awaken about 60 percent of your potential."

Maggie asked the question I was afraid to ask. "What about these two uglies. Does it work with beings who have heads of solid bone?"

Deena gave her a thumbs down and said, "Strictly excess baggage. Jack and Hud, you were just part of the price we had to pay to get Maggie and Jenny."

Hud and I splashed her at the same time. She laughed and said, "Actually it could be worse. When I decided to recruit you two girls, I had Bishop come and check you out. Both of you guys have some latent ability. In fact, you're above average but much below Jenny. What is present can, over time, be developed to the point that you could handle an average elite. Not Bennie or Drok, however."

Hud said, "Oh well, my life has been dominated by that woman anyway, so nothing will change."

Jenny laughed and said, "Yes, it will. I'm going to run your buns off waiting on me."

I said, "OK, folks. Let's get back to the real subject. Deena, I don't see any way of stopping those tchadbe pills from being made and distributed with the resources we have at hand. The answer is to stop the supply of tchadbe from Hell. We have to go back in, don't we?"

"And Maggie called you a bonehead! That's exactly right, Jack. Analysis did a projection that Balzerch could keep around 18 of the 30 labs in operation in spite of our best efforts, with 82 percent confidence. And he and his demons will send more tchadbe soon unless we can stop the source. I'm arguing that we keep up the resistance here with our angels and get you four back to Hell soon."

"Deena, even that won't stop it. If the supply from Hell begins to dry up, then they will bring in seed and grow the tchadbe here. The Sahelian Region of West Africa, parts of the Southwest U.S., parts of China and many other areas will, I'm sure, produce great tchadbe. Drugs that are in demand, and this one is going to be, are going to be produced and distributed by someone despite anything we can do. I recommend that you put your labs to work on developing a form of the tchadbe that will not hurt the immune system. Then we hope the various countries here on Earth recognize that and legalize it immediately. That will take the devil out of the market here. I'm not saying that we abort our attempt to neutralize his powers. He has violated Custom several times and must pay the price."

"The labs on Noah and in Heaven are actually working on that," Deena responded. "But it's probably going to take a long time. You're right about the devil. He has to, as you say, pay the price no matter what. Well, where do we stand? I guess that we should wait for Ruth's report on Drok. That should come by morning. Also, I'm bringing Drok back to Noah so that Maggie can get some real life practice. Elsha should be ready soon, too. I'll plan to bring that report here tomorrow, Wednesday, at 9:00 and we'll make our final plan. Remember, on Thursday, your two time lines merge and I will be one again. I don't want to finalize our plan until I know how you made out in Hell."

"Well, I could tell you and save some time, you know," Hud joked.

"Don't you dare," she said standing up in the hot tub.

The water streamed off of her magnificent body.

She got out, toweled off, and said, "Oh, I almost forgot. I need a couple of minutes alone with Maggie. Come into the bedroom with me, Maggie."

Maggie climbed out, grabbed a towel, and went into the bedroom. A few minutes later she was back. Deena had gone. Hud and Jenny dressed and went on home.

"What did Deena want?"

"To tell me she had detected the pills. She said she thought she'd better take them. I told her they were mine and they stayed. She said she knew I'd say that but she had to try."

"Why didn't she confiscate them on Noah?"

"I don't know. Anyway, she cautioned us not to use them more than once a month, and I promised that we wouldn't. Then she said something odd. She said, 'Being an angel keeps me so busy I have no time to do anything. I am so lonely. I am human, you know, and have all the human characteristics. I get hot and cold, laugh and cry, get tired, get depressed, and so on. Yet I live a monastic life because I never have any personal interactions with anyone except in the line of work. I told Ruth I needed some time off and She agreed. Every time I think of seeing you and Jack making love in the Mopti Motel, I get weak in the knees. I want to make love again. It's been so long.'"

I was flabbergasted. "You're kidding! Do you think she meant she wanted to make love with us?"

"I guess so. It wouldn't be fun alone."

"I'll be damned. An angel. What did you say?"

"I wasn't sure what to say or do. I dropped my towel, stepped over and hugged her hard, and then kissed her full on the mouth. She responded and then pulled back, blushed, and said, 'I must go. Thank you,' and she was gone."

"I wouldn't have had the nerve."

"Me neither, except there is something to this sensing stuff. I could tell it was the right thing to do. Besides, so what if she's an angel. She's not necessarily an angel from a Christian background where sex is suppressed and sinful unless performed by two people that God has joined together in marriage. A vision of an angel conjured up by a Christian would never think of doing anything as nasty as having sex. Real angels don't seem to be that way.

"Jack, do you remember Hud talking about the tribe his father was trying to convert in Kenya when Hud was a boy? They were gentle and kind people, simple farmers with an extended family structure with multiple spouses, but their sexual customs extended beyond that and allowed casual sex between anyone who gave consent. It didn't matter to their god whether they were single or married, hetero or homo, or relatives. Hud's missionary father was incensed and spent long hours berating these people for their 'sins'. He explained to Hud that sex, as they practiced it, condemned all of them to Hell.

"Remember that Hud said he spent long hours trying to figure out why our God would send one of these gentle people to Hell? They were kind to each other, helped anyone who needed help whether they were friend or stranger, and spent lots of time in worship of 'their god'. All in all, they lived good, clean lives except that they had the audacity to have consensual sex with each other."

"I remember. It sustains me when I have guilt about Jenny. Which reminds me. I'm not sure I like you being able to read my thoughts. You may become hard to live with using all these new powers."

"Maybe. But these powers do have their advantages. Like right now, you're thinking about ravishing my lovely body and wondering if I'm in an agreeable mood. I am. Let's go to bed."

twenty-nine

The next morning was a rainy, gusty, and unseasonably chilly one. The girls concocted some fortified hot chocolate, and by the time Deena arrived, we were cozily settled in our living room. Maggie handed her a mug, and she seemed surprised and quite pleased to be treated like one of us. She curled up in one of our big, over-stuffed easy chairs, and started with the report on Drok. He knew the locations of the labs in the first and second waves, but since Bennie was coming back, he had not revealed the location of the third wave. Bennie would not come back here, of course, and was to contact Drok when he selected his next location. He thought five total waves were planned. Also, there were plans to let mortals establish labs and get training to process on their own. The Tarcans would supply the tchadbe. The mortals would be told it came from Africa or Asia. There wasn't much more except for some details on how a lab functioned.

"Do we have the go ahead for a trip to Hell again?" Jenny asked.

"Yes, but not until you all have a week of training with Bishop. Ruth is afraid to send you back without some powers."

"Where do we train? On Noah?"

"Yes, and this time, I don't want to suspend time. We'll work around your kids' schedules so you'll be home when they are.

I know you'll miss work but I am authorized to tell you that you'll never have another monetary worry again."

I said, "Hud and I still want to buy that Johnson property. We'd like time to close it this week."

"You'll have the time and also the cash to pay for it."

"Deena, I wasn't asking for money."

"I know you weren't, dear, but I have my instructions. Ruth wants to make sure your lives are as free from mortal distractions as possible so that you can concentrate on the job at hand. We will undoubtedly confiscate untold millions in the drug war. So enjoy. You'll have all you need and more."

She got up and paced a minute as though she were trying to make a decision about something. Finally she said, "Let's work in pairs. The two men together and you two ladies. Ladies, mornings, 9 to 12 and guys, afternoons, 2 to 5. Ladies, evenings, 9 to 11. Guys, there's only a limited amount that Bishop can do for you in such a short time frame, so three hours a day is enough. You guys can work mornings and baby-sit evenings."

"When do we start?" asked Jenny.

"Right now. I want to take you all up to meet Bishop first. Then Hud and Jack can come back for their 2:00."

Bishop was a scrawny man I pegged to be about 55. I know he's actually hundreds of years old, but he looked young. He wore a goatee and had white thinning hair with a pink bald spot on top of his head. He walked a little bit hunched over as if he were in pain. Hud said later that he was out of balance because he was hung like a stallion. I hadn't looked.

He told us that the latent powers we possessed were latent only because we didn't know we possessed them. The more we accepted them, the easier it would be to learn to use them. He said that initially, concentration was the key. Later, we would use them automatically and only have to bear down under extreme circumstances such as an encounter with an elite. Having met Bishop and been briefed, Deena sent Hud and me home.

Maggie came back at noon all pumped up and ready for more. She could teleport herself about five feet and jumped all over the room. Hud and I went that afternoon but it was not at all encouraging. Neither of us gave a scintillating performance. But I did feel some sensations of awareness of others around me without opening my eyes. Hud felt nothing.

Hud came over with Jenny at nine. Her parents were still there and her father wears on Hud after about 15 minutes, so he came over to watch the Braves play. Maggie and Jenny got back a little after 11:00 and suggested a hot tub. We accepted.

They both had had another good experience. Jenny had broken through and her powers were coming on strong.

Everybody was leaned back relaxing when Maggie said, "What are we going to do about this love quadrangle we've gotten involved in?"

We all looked at each other but nobody said anything.

Maggie tried again. "It's got to be faced before we go to Hell again. So who wants to start?"

Jenny said, "I will. We've got very few secrets from each other anymore. And this is going to get worse because it looks like Maggie may actually be able to read minds soon and I'll be close to it. This is going to be an awesome responsibility. We'll be able to choose not to read each other, but that's difficult, too. But to answer Maggie, here's where we are. We're all sensible adults who, through a unique set of circumstances, happen to love each other. I don't see anything wrong with that except our society frowns upon four-person marriages, which I personally see as one of our better options. Ruth doesn't see it as a problem either, since it happens in other cultures all the time. A four-person marriage doesn't mean we automatically all have to have sex together although we undoubtedly will. Nor does it mean Jack and Hud have to sleep together. I'd be amazed if they did. Finally, it doesn't mean Maggie and I have to sleep together, but we probably will.

"Our other alternatives include continuing like we are now with an occasional romp with each other's spouse. This would be easier on the kids but not as satisfying, from my standpoint at least. Besides, thinking of the kids, an extended family structure does have advantages. If one man dies, for example, there's still a father figure.

Another alternative is for Hud and I to move to California or some-where. Out of sight, out of mind."

Maggie said, "My views exactly. At first, I was the least certain about whether or not there was genuine love involved here. But even though I can't read minds yet, I can sense that all of us are now of one mind. It's still hard to believe, but there it is. Jack? Hud? Say something, guys."

Hud said, "Jack and I haven't talked about this in the same depth some of us apparently have. Be that as it may, I would vote for mov-ing in together now, but the kid thing does worry me. We're already deceiving them about this Hell project. I guess we really had no choice about that one. But it has bothered me. If we choose to live together and try to slip around and meet after they go to bed, we're setting both families up for an inevitable disaster."

I said, "I don't think trying to fool them is an alternative. Kids are amazingly adaptive, and if we do decide to live together, I believe they could accept it given a little time. If we can't be up front about it, I'd opt for an occasional romp until the kids are gone."

"Even if we agree to be open with the kids, we'd be fools to be open with society," Jenny said. "Imagine the fuss this would create in rural Clarksboro, Georgia."

"I've been thinking about that," I said. "And I've got a proposi-tion for y'all to consider. You know, we're buying the Johnson prop-erty this week. The old house is in bad shape and Hud wants to tear it down due to the expense of restoration. Now, apparently, we have unlimited funds to play with. That house remodeled would be more than big enough for two families. We could even make it into two separate residences on the ground floor so the general public could see how on the up-and-up we were."

"I've been nagging Hud to move to the country anyway. I'd like to see the house. Sounds like a good solid prospect to me."

Maggie said quietly, "It's a lovely old house in a beautiful set-ting. The property wouldn't have to be developed now that we're rich, and we'd have the whole–what is it, Jack, 56 or 57 acres?–to ourselves. Let's go look tomorrow at 5:00."

Everybody agreed. Maggie changed the subject. "I can tell that everyone is wondering whether or not we should go ahead and jump in the hay right now. I'd be game, if that's what everyone wanted, but I said 'wondering' because there's still some hesitation in all three of you at the moment. I'm going to suggest we stick to an occasional romp until after we come back from Hell. Our lives are complicated enough without taking on a whole new set of emotions."

There was agreement to this, and, if my new sensory apparatus was working correctly, a general sense of relief. Everyone was very tired and we had to be rested for the trip to Hell. I decided, however, to try to take that 'occasional romp' with Jenny this week.

After they left, I said to Maggie, "In spite of last night, I don't know if I like the idea of you knowing exactly what I'm thinking all the time. Can you really do it?"

"Almost. It's still kind of murky except with Deena and she helps. Jack, I've got to tell you that she wants to be with us. In bed. I don't know what to do. She hasn't said it, but I can read it. I don't know if she's sending the message purposely, or if I'm just picking up her feelings. What should we do?"

"We really are having this conversation, aren't we?"

She just smiled, so I continued. "I don't know anything about angels. From what we concluded last night, the breaking of the sex taboos of Christianity is not a deterrent to going to Heaven. I don't know the rules about angels with mortals. She must know it's all right or else she's willing to take a chance."

"I guess I'll let it go for awhile and see what happens."

"I expect that's best. Are you tired?"

"Not tonight, Jack. I'm exhausted."

I hadn't even had a chance to ask. Damn.

thirty

The training went better on the next day, Thursday, the day we actually got back from Hell. That afternoon, joking with Deena, I asked if I could go and meet ourselves at the REGEN. She laughed and said I was already there and in the repair chamber down the hall. She said she was coming back with Maggie and Jenny at 11:00 tonight to brief us. She was now the combined Deena. I was one confused mortal, but decided not to strain my brain to try to figure out which me I was right now. Go with the flow, that would have to be my new motto.

Hud and I made a little progress in the area of mind control. We both could knock a magazine off a table and squeeze an orange, at least a little bit. Bishop said not to worry about teleporting and form changing because, for us, it would take many months of effort and probably would never amount to much anyhow. Thanks for the positive comments, Bishop. I was still able to receive murky images and sense emotions from the minds of others. Hud hadn't progressed at all in that area.

It was raining at 5:00, so we postponed our trip to the Johnson property until the next day, Friday. Hud had set the closing for 9:30 tomorrow, so we'd actually own the property before the girls had a chance to explore it in depth.

I spent the evening relaxing in front of the tube. Can't tell you what I watched, though. My mind was elsewhere. Maggie, Jenny and Deena arrived at 11:00. Hud had wandered over a little earlier. The kids were upstairs, so we met in the living room.

Deena said, "Well, we're all on the same timeline again. That will make things easier for me. I can report that my angels are holding their own in the war on Wham. They have identified and closed three third-wave labs and two others which were relocated from the second wave. But there still is an amazing amount of product flowing through the traditional drug channels. Jack, you were right. They caught two demons in the desert south of Yuma teaching some Mexicans how to grow tchadbe. So we know the seed is already on Earth. In the big scheme of things, Balzerch doesn't envision earth as a big market for his tchadbe, but rather as a source of unpaid labor, since many people who use the drug will end up in Hell. He knows we can hurt his ability to export tchadbe to Earth, but we'll have real trouble if it's grown here as well."

"It had to happen," I said. "I had hoped we could get to him before it did."

"I've asked Analysis to prepare maps and building layouts on the devil's complex and on the opposite shore, that location where the residents go for vacation. I still haven't decided exactly where to drop you. There is a plus to report, though. As of yesterday, we can fully shield the REGEN on Hell. That will help enormously.

"You need to look over the maps and other materials tomorrow, then give me suggestions. By the way, that young woman, Ella, is still in place. We are hoping the devil doesn't decide to blood test for mortals as part of his new security binge. If he does, she'll be spotted. As for right now, though, we're OK on this point."

"When will we get back together?" Jenny asked.

"Starting at 8:00 tomorrow morning, I'm taking a day off. I will turn you all and your children over to my second in command, Carmen. I'm having nothing to do with this mess for 24 hours. Got to get the head clear for what's ahead of us. I'll meet you again on Saturday. Any questions."

"How do we get to training tomorrow?" I asked. Amazing! I managed to slip a question in on her!

" Carmen will see that you get up by REGEN. See you Saturday then."

Deena vanished before I could get her again, and Hud and Jenny left as well, so Maggie and I went up to bed.

"She really does need a day to think," said Maggie. "She hasn't had a day off in years. She read my question about sex between angels and mortals, by the way."

"What did she say?"

"She said sex was certainly not prohibited in Heaven. Consent between all parties was the only rule. As far as she knows, there's no rule covering an angel having sex with a mortal. She said angels ate with mortals, fought with mortals, worked with mortals, and so on. She sees no problem with it and really seemed surprised that I even asked."

"Well, I'm a little uncomfortable with it, Maggie, but if she decides to take the plunge, I'm game. If Ruth gets mad, I'll just have to learn to cultivate tchadbe." She had taken off her clothes, and as she walked past the bed where I had stretched out, I gave her a little smack on the ass.

She jumped and said, "You're probably going there anyway. You're evil." By the end of the hour, I think I had changed her mind on that point.

Friday morning's closing on the Johnson property was uneventful. Deena had arranged for us to get money by winning big at a Las Vegas casino that was laundering drug money. Getting the cash this way meant we could pay taxes and be on the up-and-up. Of course, we couldn't get to Vegas to get it for a few weeks, so we took out a short term loan through the First Carter Bank.

Our afternoon training session was pretty unremarkable. Bishop didn't say anything to Hud and me, but his disappointment was pretty obvious. My mind was on other things, and I guess everybody else had the same problem. We didn't make it to the Johnson property on Friday either. Actually I should say the Warner-Raines property. We needed to re-name it to cover our plans.

That evening, I took the kids to their respective activities. Laurie had a party across town and was then coming home to spend the night with Melanie Foster next door. Mark went to the skating rink with the Raines' boys. Hud would bring them all back at 10:00. I got home about 7:30 and spent a very restless evening. A billion bits of information were maneuvering for position in my brain, putting me on mental overload and keeping me from focusing on even the most inane of the night's sit-coms.

Mark came in at 10:15. We made small talk and watched the hapless Braves for a while. They were losing to St. Louis 10-2 in the eighth. Mark quickly got bored and went to bed about 10:30. I fidgeted around for the next 30 minutes locking doors, checking doors, turning out lights, checking doors again, and finally gave it up and went upstairs. I was pacing around the bedroom when at exactly 11:00, Jenny and Maggie appeared. Maggie claimed fatigue so I said I would show Jenny out. She gave me a quick kiss at the door and asked when I wanted to have our 'occasional romp'. I said "very soon", and watched as she walked the two doors to her house and went in.

I went back upstairs. Maggie had just finished her shower and was climbing into bed. I peeled down and got in the shower myself.

The next day, Saturday, Deena came back with Jenny and Maggie after their morning training session.

I said, "How was your day off?"

"I honestly didn't know what to do with myself. I finally selected a high, uninhabited Rocky Mountain meadow with a rushing stream and went there by REGEN. I walked and walked and even swam in the stream. It was wonderful. I'll take you someday."

Jenny had called Hud and he walked in just then.

I asked, "When do we leave for Hell, Deena?"

"Seven o'clock Wednesday morning. We'll suspend time again for the sake of your children. We decided that it's best to drop you in the vicinity of the vacation area and let you make your way across the sea toward the peninsula, since it juts to within a mile of the island. Even though it will be guarded, they'll be no match for Maggie.

"The plan is the same. Try to get the drug to Ella and convince her it is a harmless practical joke or something equally innocent. Remember that you can safely go to her barracks because it's about

100 yards from the residence, and you don't have fatal intentions that can alert them to your presence. We've tested Maggie and Jenny using Drok to see if their powers change the distance required for mortal detection and it appears that they don't, so you should be OK. Drok's range was actually about 50 feet, a little more than Bennie's 30 feet.

"I'll see you from time to time over the next three days and we'll have our final briefing Tuesday night at 8:00 at the hot tub room. Any questions?"

"Same training schedule?" asked Maggie.

"Except no session Tuesday night."

There were no more questions so Deena left.

That afternoon at 5:00, we finally got to drive out to the old house. It was a beautiful afternoon, and although it was still hot, the humidity was down, making the air relatively breathable. The closer we got, the better I started feeling about the entire plan. There was just something special about the place. Happened to me every time I went there.

The house had been built about a quarter-mile from the highway in order to get a river view. The big pines and moss-draped live oaks around the house provided plenty of shade in the summer and lent it a real deep-South atmosphere. The structure itself had been beautifully landscaped at one time, and much of what had overgrown could be pruned and saved. The exterior of the mansion was brick, so the walls were still standing. There had once been a front porch and balcony, but Bennie had trashed both these during his little escapade. You could still make out the front door through all the rubble, so we headed in.

"Be careful. The floors and stairs are OK but there's a lot of rubble," I said.

We entered a large foyer with a huge flowing stairway directly in front. Above us was a 10-foot ceiling that came out about six feet to provide an entry to the balcony. It then opened up to the full two stories revealing a huge old chandelier hanging down in front of the stairwell, which, other than being covered with dust and cobwebs and a spider or two, seemed to be in amazingly good condition.

There was a hallway or walkway on each side of the stairs on both levels. On the second level, there were railings around the open part.

On the left-hand side, large double doors opened into the parlor, a large and airy room with a fireplace. There were three doors out of this room. The first led to a large front room lined with bookcases on one wall. This had apparently been a library or study. The second door led to a room adjoining the study which stretched clear to the back of the house. We figured that had been a game room or family room. And the third door led into a room behind the parlor that was long and somewhat narrow, which had apparently been a sewing room and an artist's studio for Mrs. Johnson. The right side of the house was laid out the same way except that the long narrow room had been divided into a kitchen and a pantry. The main room was a dining room and the two at the end of the house were just rooms. We couldn't tell what they were.

I said, "You can see how we could have two separate residences, each with a huge family room plus a kitchen and pantry, a dining room and a study-studio room. I believe each side has 2200 square feet downstairs and almost the same upstairs. The upper level has four really large rooms on each side but, of course, we can repartition up there to make what we want."

"It's beautiful," Jenny said. "You're right, Jack. This would stop any gossip. To the world, all we would be sharing is a common foyer. And all apartment buildings have those."

"My only objection all along was the expense," said Hud. "Now that that's out of the way, I'm all for it."

Maggie asked, "How soon can we start, Jack? I've got so many ideas, I think I need to get them down on paper quickly."

"I could actually get an architect from Savannah to do some plans right away if everybody's OK with that. I'll get Beeker and Morton. They specialize in restorations. They're very expensive, but I've seen their work."

"Sounds good," Hud said.

We walked around the grounds for a while and then had to go back home to let Maggie and Jenny get ready for their training.

All was quiet on Sunday. Maggie had a training encounter with the newly revived Elsha. When Maggie fried her, she fell to the floor and gave up. Apparently it was no contest at all. She was scheduled to try Drok tomorrow.

Monday morning I called Beeker and Morton. I asked for Bob Morton since I had met him at a party several years ago. He was about 38 and a widower. His wife died of breast cancer last year. I think they had two kids.

When he came on the line, I said, "Mr. Morton, this is Jack Warner. We met several years ago at a Christmas party at the McDougald's in Baxley. I'm a contractor now in Clarksboro."

"Yes. I remember you, Jack. What can I do for you?"

"Do you by chance know the Johnson house near Clarksboro?"

"Johnson house. Let me think. Is that the brick two-story on the river off Old River Road?"

"Exactly. You've been there?"

"Yes. Several years ago. It was on a tour of homes at Christmas time. Lovely home."

"My partner and I recently purchased the property and want to consider a total restoration project. It's been abandoned and has really suffered since you saw it."

"I'd be happy to work with you on it. What do you have in mind?"

"Well, I'd like for you to come over and meet me out there for a look-see. I can tell you what we want changed."

"I can do that. Will you be the contractor?"

"Just the general contractor. I'll use my crew for some rough-in work but I want to sub-contract the rest to specialists. You can help me out with some contacts there if you would."

"Be glad to. When would you like to meet?"

"Is tomorrow morning convenient?"

"Let's see. I don't have anything solid until lunch. What if we meet at 9:00?"

"Perfect."

"Do you know John Riley?"

"Only by reputation. I hear he's the best restoration carpenter on the East Coast."

"I'd like to try to bring him along, if you don't mind."

"Not at all. See you then."

I spent the rest of the morning at a house we were working on at Cedar Creek. All was going well. They didn't need my advice at all but it made me feel important checking on everything. When Maggie got back at noon, we had a light lunch and talked about the old house a little bit. Maggie said she and Jenny would meet this afternoon and sketch out what they wanted and Hud and I could review their ideas tonight.

I asked Hud to go with me the next morning to the house. When we got there a little before nine, Morton and Riley were already poking around, making notes. I parked the car in the shade and we walked over to meet them.

Introductions were made and we began talking about the house. "What we want to do is a complete exterior restoration, exactly as it was when it was built. Inside, there'll be some pretty significant changes."

We talked about the exterior a few minutes, then moved inside. We explained that we wanted two separate residences with a common foyer and stairway. We showed him our sketches. Upstairs included separate master bedrooms on each side of the stairs and two bedrooms in each end of the house with a third room between them. Hud and I would construct a common area between the two master suites after the fact and keep its existence to ourselves.

Norton and Riley made some really good suggestions and we split up, with Bob agreeing to have preliminary plans for the interior in a week to 10 days and with John planning to submit a bid on the exterior work in about the same time period. I think John wanted to design the landscaping, too, but we told him we weren't quite ready to focus on that yet but we'd let him know. Truth was, we had just forgotten about it. I guess maybe we had other things on our minds. Yeah.

Hud and I had our last session with Bishop that afternoon. He wanted to talk about Maggie. She had taken on Elsha and Drok at the same time that morning and brought them both to their hands and knees, shaking their heads in pain. Deena had never been able to do that. Between Jenny and Elsha, it had been close, but Jenny prevailed. She was no match for Drok yet, but was getting closer each session.

He looked at us and said, "Stay close to your ladies and you'll be all right." I picked up a touch of pity in his voice. Great for my confidence.

We were apparently a great disappointment, and probably embarrassment, to Bishop. We did become proficient enough to detect a demon at about 50 yards and could win a power struggle with an ordinary demon or two. But Bishop's audible sighs at the end of our sessions were clearly not meant to encourage us.

Deena arrived in the hot tub room at 8:00 for our final briefing. We were already soaking and invited her to join us. She showered and stepped in between Maggie and Jenny.

"I am really nervous about this one. I hope I haven't overlooked anything. I've tried to be thorough, but things have been changing so quickly. Let's review the mission as it stands right now.

"We'll drop you about ten miles out from the main vacation complex. The bush is higher than normal in this region, plus we have selected a little grove of trees near the main road. You won't have any trouble joining the other vacationers on their trek into the complex. Once inside, you'll need to approach the food machine first to get clearance. Then do the same at the main vacation center. This is where you claim your saved-up days and gambling winnings. You still won't be able to buy food or more vacation days with these winnings, but you can use them on special things like movies, circuses, real hotel rooms and, of course, more gambling.

"In spite of increased security and better communications, the whole system is still operating in very relaxed way. They quit blood testing for mortals and they've stopped quizzing new people at the food machines. Of course, they could start again at any time, so you'll still have to be careful.

"To get to the devil's residence area, you have to cross the little sea. If you go 20 miles north, you come to the peninsula. It's almost exactly a mile across the water. Maggie and Jenny can teleport it with ease. You guys will have to swim. There are guards, but Maggie and Jenny will take them out easily. Remember, though, that in order to keep from alerting anyone, you should use a forgetter order on the guards. Then ease on in about 20 miles to the barracks.

You'll fit in OK, but you won't be able to use this particular food machine. It's reserved for palace workers only. We've put enough super-concentrated food pellets in your water bags to last about three days, so you should be fine.

"The young woman, Ella, has been instructed to spend about five minutes every evening at 7:00 near the main barracks entrance. She will walk out of the entrance at 7:00, walk toward the water spigot, and fill her jug. Then she will slowly return. You've seen her picture. And she's a natural redhead, so that will be obvious at both ends.

"You must not make her suspicious about what you ask her to do, or he will catch her instantly. And if he catches her, he'd be after you in a heartbeat. You might start by asking her to report on her activities. That's innocuous enough.

"What else? Let's see. Oh, recall. You still have the two buttons behind each ear. The only problem is that they may not work all the time. The devil's REGEN system has been expanded and there are beams shooting all over the place now while they try to get it under better control. These beams sometimes interfere with our recall signals. We're not sure whether this is intentional or not. It's probably beam leakage from the shoddy equipment the devil buys from the Tarcans. I know that's bad news, but there are about 20 spots in the area where we will keep a continuous watch. You each have a list in your minds. I had Bishop place them there today. If you can't make your buttons work, try to get to one of these spots. As soon as we see you, we'll bring you up. The same interference affects our ability to track you like we did before, so getting messages to you will be more difficult, too. Aren't I full of good news?"

"You're a real joy," Jenny said. "Has the devil started cooking and eating mortals or perhaps staking them out on fire ant hills?"

"Not yet," Deena laughed. "But he still likes mortal women, so be very, very careful. Any questions?"

"Is Ruth still adamant about not violating the customs?" I asked. Chalk up another point for me. I'm getting quicker on the questions.

"So far. But this may change soon. Why?"

"I thought She might let you come down and join us. Between the three of you, you might slow the old boy down enough so that Hud and I could inject him."

"Jack, you don't know how much I would like to come. But two problems. First, with his power he would detect me from 2-3 miles out. And the other is that the power of all three of us together is not nearly enough to even slow him much. He is not a demon. He is something else entirely. Even Ruth would not try to handle him without back up. The only thing that deters him is that he knows She has that back up and, while costly, She'll use it, if necessary. Remember, he's not like Bennie. Demons can actually be friendly. The devil is, decidedly, not friendly."

"What's he most likely to do if we're caught?" Hud asked.

"That's not at all clear. He's totally unpredictable. It could range from keeping the women and sending the men to a tchadbe forced-work camp to execution or banishment. Just don't get caught, then you won't have to worry about it."

I don't know about my colleagues, but this briefing proved to be a real downer for me. It must have shown on all our faces for Deena reached out and put an arm around both Jenny and Maggie. We all sat there quietly for awhile and then Deena stood up and said, "I've got to go. I've got a lot to do tonight. See you here at 7:00."

After Hud and Jenny left, Maggie and I went and spent some time with the kids and then went to bed and made love. We both slept fitfully.

thirty-one

After a terrible night's sleep, we finally gave up and got up about five Wednesday morning. We were ready when Deena breezed in at seven and took us to Noah before we even had time for hellos. She had our water bottles ready and also had one bit of news. It seem that a strange ship had appeared in the skies of Hell last night. No one knew what it was or who it was since it didn't fit any of the known types on file. Analysis suspects it just may be from the devil's home system. But in this case, no news is not good news.

Deena said, "Be very careful and don't hesitate to recall. We'll follow you to the best of our ability and send messages whenever we can." She kissed each of us and we were completely on our own.

We found ourselves in a grove of trees as promised in a driving rain that wasn't. The rain, and the fact that it was early morning, made it very cold. We wasted no time in getting our bearings and headed out at a brisk pace, primarily to warm up. We soon intersected the road, and after checking in both directions, saw that there was no traffic as yet. We wanted to arrive with others but it was so cold we decided to run for a while longer. After three or four miles, the rain turned to a light sleet. Jenny called a halt.

"This is ridiculous," she panted. "We're all going to have hypothermia if we don't do something quickly."

Hud said, "Let's find a place to bed down and try to warm up."

His teeth were chattering so badly I could barely understand him. We went into the brush and found one of those giant fern clumps. We knew the routine, so it wasn't too long before we bedded down for a while. The sleet turned back to rain and soon the rain slacked off and it began to warm up. We got up and stretched and as we did, we heard one of the convoys passing in the distance.

Jenny said, "Looks like it's clearing. Let's move closer to the road."

We did, and soon a group of four men and five women went by, followed by a couple, and then by a group of five women and two men. All of them had leafy vegetation wrapped around them to keep warm. One man was saying, "I've been in Hell for over 400 years and this is the first time I ever saw sleet." A woman's voice said she hoped it would be the last.

After they passed, we looked down the road but couldn't see anyone else, so we joined this last procession. They obviously had come from a night in the bush because we knew there were no settlements for at least 100 miles where there was a food station for vacationers.

Soon the sun was out, weakly but still better than nothing, and we had a leisurely walk to the vacation barracks. We arrived at mid-afternoon.

After selecting cubicles and taking hot showers, we went to the food machine to establish credit. Maggie went first again. The machine droned, "How many vacation days will you spend here?"

"Twelve"

"Do you have 12 days built up?"

"Yes."

"Press your hand on the screen."

Maggie did.

"Credit given for 12 days' meals. Move on."

The rest of us went right through as well. So far so good.

We went to the recreation machine and claimed our credits there, again without a hitch. The machines have no memory because of the truth injection. When we were asked for our vacation days and gambling balances, it took our word for it, since we weren't supposed to be able to lie. It programmed the recreation facilities and gambling machines to give us access up to our credit limit. It's just like using a debit card, except instead of a card, this system uses hand prints and your total balance. The hand prints taken on the earlier trip were recorded at the settlements we visited then and not transferred anywhere else. I would like to think that they're bright enough to be working on a system with central records which would provide more information and more control over individuals like us, but for the moment, I was pretty well satisfied with their antiquated methods.

We found a sunny place with benches overlooking the sea and sat down. The sea was a beautiful shade of deep blue and actually made us feel as if we were on a vacation and not in Hell. There were some small boats in a lagoon off to our right and Maggie said they were paddle boats for vacationers to use. Everyone passing by seemed to be having a good time. Hope the same would be true for us in the next few days.

"Sure beats our reception on the other trip," said Hud.

"It will be nice to eat regularly on this side at least," added Maggie.

Jenny said, "Maggie, I can sense two elites off to our right in the direction of the Administration Building. Am I missing any?"

"There are three more on the fringe of my reception down near the warehouse area. About four miles away, I think. This inability to pinpoint a location is frustrating."

"If they have the new ability to sense us up to 30 feet, we'll have to be careful, especially in the food hall. We'll sit near the back door and if one comes toward us we'll just have to leave. Analysis says it's probable that only Bennie and Drok have this ability so far, but we've got to be cautious. If they've got it widespread, Ella's caught already."

"Speaking of Ella, does anyone have an idea of how to use her?" I asked.

"Well," Hud said, "I've always liked natural redheads—.

"You're incorrigible," Jenny said laughing. "I can't see any way except mind control and Deena said she thought that the devil would pick that up as potential harm."

Maggie said, "I think I may have a new piece of information for us. On the afternoon Jenny was frying Elsha in training, I was talking to Deena about the mission and found out that there are six other mortals serving in the palace. Deena said they had no direct contact with the devil, so she hadn't mentioned them before. She said Ella knew who they were, and would tell us if we needed them. The code word is the same as with Ella, the word 'victory'. The response is 'garden'. I asked her what the others did and she said that most of them are outside workers. One, however, whose name escapes me at the moment, works in the devil's kitchen. Deena said that one of Ella's duties was to take the devil a glass of chilled juice twice a day, about 10:00 in the morning and 3:00 in the afternoon. Where does she get fruit juice? In the kitchen from a kitchen worker. Who works in the kitchen? Julia. Just came to me. That's the name."

"So we spike the fruit juice?" I said. She nodded in the affirmative.

Jenny said, "Won't work. Ella will radiate the harm in the juice."

"Not if we get Julia to put it in there on the sly, without telling Ella."

Jenny answered again, "Then Julia will radiate the harm."

"Not if she thinks it's just a harmless prank. Plus remember that she has no direct contact with him."

"That's true," Jenny said. "But what can we tell her it is?

"We've done all the work so far. Let's let the guys figure that one out."

"Damn good idea, Maggie." Hud said. "Two separate actions which add up to harm, but if taken separately, radiate no warning to him. Glad I thought of it."

"I know how we can do it," I said. "These mortals like Ella and Julia have never seen or even heard of a mortal with powers like Maggie has. We'll just call Maggie a 'mortal angel'. Now. Let's see. How about this. The devil has a 'previously incurable illness', and Heaven has just invented a vaccine which is a sure cure. Ruth despises the devil and would ordinarily let him die, but She needs him for a few more years to, uh—help me out here, somebody."

"Because She is trying to stop the tchadbe trade and needs more time to investigate all the channels and worlds involved before shutting down the main supplier," Hud added.

"Perfect," I said. "We'll tell her that the devil wouldn't trust Ruth if She herself offered him this cure, and he wouldn't accept something he knew was from Her, either, so therefore She had to send us in secret to save him."

"May work, outlandish as it seems," Maggie said. "Deena told me the seven people who are here weren't picked for intelligence or creativity. In fact, they are all a little bit dippy. Remember that every high school class had someone who was just a step out of line with the rest of the world. Believe anything you tell them. She needed that type of personality to allow them to spy without alerting the devil."

"I can give you an example from high school," I said. "When I got my dog, Buster, I asked some friends to come over to see him. This one girl, Martha I think her name was, had exactly the characteristics Deena's looking for. Everyone was down on the floor playing with Buster. He was rolled over on his back, legs spread apart, displaying all his glory to the world. And Martha seriously asked if he was a boy or a girl. Broke up the whole crowd. She couldn't help it. She was just like that."

Jenny said, "I believe we're onto something, but please, let's go eat. It's after 6:00 and we missed lunch. I'm famished."

No elites showed up for dinner so we relaxed and packed it away. Afterward, we waddled back to the bench and sat some more, groaning and digesting and thinking. This was a really beautiful evening with a glorious double sunset. It didn't even matter that it was getting colder by the minute. Jenny finally said, "The smart thing to do is let only one of us, or at the most two, contact Ella and let her point out not just Julia but some others as well so we don't focus attention on Julia. Then we'll all meet with Julia and try the big con. Anybody got other ideas or comment?"

"Just that when we finally do get to Julia, Maggie needs to act God-like and throw in a miracle or two to convince her we mean only good for the devil," I said.

219

"Probably a good idea. Damn, it's gotten cold," Jenny said. "Let's head for the barracks. Or do we burn some vacation credits on a real hotel room?"

Hud said, "Love that idea, but it would probably just draw attention to us."

We went into the barracks and found our cubicles still empty. And cold.

It was just a little past 8:00 and none of us were really sleepy yet. Since this was a vacation barracks, it had the luxury of several lounges with TV monitors playing old movies from the Earth countries. We wandered into one of these and watched a Japanese film with giant lizards and explosions and scantily clad ladies. It wasn't too inspiring when unclad ladies already surrounded you 24 hours a day. I finally got bored and went to take another shower because I was cold. They had plenty of hot water and another luxury—cubicle heaters.

I went into the shower room nearest our cubicle. It was almost empty. There were two women just finishing up and a man shaving. I got into the shower and got all soaped up when pair of arms encircled me from behind. It was Jenny, of course.

"The three of us decided you might be lonely. We started to send Hud but then decided on me. Really, Jack! You have no control at all! You had better turn the shower to cold before we get into trouble here."

She laughed heartily and grabbed the object of all the attention, but I can't say that it helped me regain control. She said, "My goodness! You'd better hurry and soap my back and get me to a cubicle quickly. You're in danger of exploding."

I was embarrassed as usual. The two women went cruising by and giggled which didn't help. We finished showering quickly and went to Jenny's cubicle. She was right. I did explode.

"Jack," Jenny said a little later. "You know, of course, that Maggie and Hud are next door. We kinda waited all week for you to make a move since you're the shy one."

"I guess I am. But I'm satisfied with the outcome of this nefarious scheme. Do I spend the night or slink home to mama?"

"Just try to leave," she said grabbing me and sending me over the edge again.

I guess I was shy or something because I really had trouble making eye contact with Maggie the next morning.

She knew it and walked over, mussed my hair, and kissed me and said, "I hope you slept well, Jack."

I felt better immediately.

We went to breakfast early and were finished by 8:00. We debated the best time to hit the peninsula and finally decided on about 6:00 that afternoon, an hour prior to shift change. We could eat a good lunch and make 20 miles easily by 6:00. That left us with the morning to kill so we became tourists. They had a lot to offer by Hell standards. There were movies, skating rinks, amusement parks, a circus, fishing and boating, and the casinos.

We tried a casino named the Sandstorm. After two hours it was Hud, Jenny, and me with losses and Maggie several thousand ahead. We accused her of using her powers but she claimed not. She always wins, so I don't know for sure.

We had lunch at 11:00 when the food hall opened, and noon found us well on our way. There was a coastal road used primarily by fishermen, and that suited our purpose very well. When we finally sighted the peninsula, it was already late afternoon. We slowly made our way through the dense foliage to the point. We stayed under cover until it was time to go. The plan was for Maggie and Jenny to teleport directly into the midst of the area and freeze the guards. They would hold them while Hud and I swam over. Then Maggie would give the forgetter order and we would leave before their relief arrived at shift change.

As evening approached Jenny said, "It must be close to 6:00. I see no reason to wait any longer. Let's go Maggie. Guys, guard any loose appendages against hungry sharks."

They counted to three and were gone. Hud and I waited a minute and then ran to the shore and dove in. It was cold but we soon warmed up. We made good time and soon were climbing the sand beach to the guards' outpost. There were two of them, a male and a female. They had a communication device but apparently hadn't been using it when the girls froze them.

As soon as we arrived, Maggie unfroze them and said, "Are you the only two here?"

No answer.

"Come now. Do you need some persuasion?" She had obviously learned Deena's ball-squeezing technique.

"We are the only two," said the male.

"What time does your relief arrive?"

"Seven."

"You will both forget that we were here. Each of you must say so."

Both said they would.

"And you will not move for 10 minutes."

And that was the end of that.

We moved rapidly away from the site both to avoid running into the relief demons and also to stay warm. Whoever coined the phrase "hot as hell" didn't know about this part of Hell. After about an hour we found a clump of our favorite ferns and retired for the night.

thirty-two

The devil's castle sat up on a small hill facing south toward the sea and the vacation complex. It was huge, with spires, and I swear, a drawbridge and a moat. Off to the northwest, the direction we would come in from, about 100 yards away from the castle was the human complex. There was a complex for demons on the other side of the castle housing both elites and workers. Here they had their own food hall.

We had covered the 20 miles easily but had started late because of the cold, so it was already past noon. Maggie picked up the devil about five miles out and Jenny read him a short distance later. The were both repulsed by the evil they sensed. They also reported six elites in the area of the castle complex. We had an excellent vantage point to see the castle and surrounding structures from atop a fairly high hill to the northwest of the castle.

We debated about whether to go into the barracks or sleep outside one more night. We knew that Balzerch had about 600 domestics housed here, so we should be able to integrate fairly easily. Deena had also told us that there was a boat that arrived every other day from the vacation side with new workers coming in on it. It usually arrived after lunch. The next one was due tomorrow. The workers were cleared by an elite on the launch side, and simply moved in and reported to their section leader. For example, a new carpenter would report to the head of structural maintenance. If we waited, we could enter the human complex when they did. That seemed to be the safer alternative, so we elected to sleep out in the bush. Maggie and Jenny had been strangely and uncharacteristically quiet since before we had reached the palace and this helped convince me to vote to stay out. I asked Maggie what was wrong, but got no response at all. I knew she had heard me. I didn't ask again.

We watched the castle from our vantage point for the next three or four hours, and when it began to get cold, backtracked a couple of miles and found a good clump of the fern with a large and soft interior base. We covered up and were reasonably warm. Maggie was restless and then I heard her crying softly.

I pulled her closer and said, "What's the matter?"

"I wish I could turn this damned sensing apparatus off. I'm just overwhelmed with this gush of evil that has to be flowing from Balzerch, I'm sure. It's terribly depressing and unbelievably threatening. It's all I can do to keep from trying a recall."

She began to shake violently.

Jenny rolled over and put her arms around Maggie and said, "I can feel it too, though not that strong. Don't worry, Maggie, we're going to get that son-of-a-bitch. I've already had enough of him to last a lifetime and we just got here. We haven't even seen him yet. If I get close to him, we won't need the drug. I'm going to rip his balls off with my bare hands."

"Easy, dear," Hud cautioned. "You'll set his alarm off from way out here."

"I mean it, Hud," said Jenny who was crying openly now. "I hate him. Upsetting my Maggie."

They held each other close and cried for a while and then everybody quieted down. I finally dozed off and before I knew it, it was morning. We didn't have to hurry so we got out into the sun to warm up a little bit and ate some of Deena's food pellets. They weren't very filling but would have to do.

Then Maggie said, "REGEN coming," and sure enough, a message capsule appeared. She got it and thumbed it open.

She read it aloud. "Good job, so far. Strange ship comes from world on fringe of universe where no one ever goes because those who did never came back. World name on charts is Mystery. Still believe it's home world of devil. Scans show three beings on board. They have done nothing so far. Wham traffic still increasing. Still can't find Bennie. Hurry and get out of there. I love you all. Deena."

Hud and I got a little lift from the message, I think primarily because now we knew they had obviously been able to track us. Maggie and Jenny were so down even this didn't help much.

I said, "I'm sure Bishop or Deena told you this already, but I remember Deena saying once that she had learned how to turn the sensors off or at least down in terms of how distracting they were."

Maggie nodded and said, "You're right but I wasn't much good at it. Bishop said it would come in time. I just hadn't thought much about it since. He said it was simply a matter of concentration within oneself. I'm going off by myself a little bit where I can concentrate and try it again. I'll stay within sight of you, though."

Maggie moved up a slight incline that was relatively clear of bush and sat down. She put her head down on her knees. I asked Jenny about her own reception this morning, and she said she was OK. I think she used anger to block out the incoming evil. I heard her telling Hud again what she would do to 'that bastard' if she were God.

Maggie stayed motionless for a good 40 minutes, then got up and walked purposefully back. She said she was a lot better, gave me a hug and said, "Thanks, Jack."

Hud said, "If everyone's ready, we probably should start in. It's already mid-morning. We don't want to miss the arrival of that boat, and we need to determine the best approach to joining the new people as they arrive."

"Maggie, are you OK to move closer?" Jenny asked.

"Absolutely. I'm much better. I'll tell you what I'm doing as we walk along. It may help you, too."

"OK. Let's go."

We made an approach similar to the one we made yesterday and wound up on a small hilltop northwest of the castle. We could clearly see the human barracks and the dock jutting into the sea. The bush went up close to the pathway from the dock to the barracks and was high enough that we could approach and fall in behind the new arrivals. There wouldn't be very many people there to greet them nor would their supervisors be there since it was the middle of a workday. We would let them pass at a spot where the path took a left bend and once they were a little ahead, follow them in. Of course, the damn boat was late. We soon got bored, anxious and restless all at the same time. So we re-read Deena's message, ate some more food pellets for lunch, and finally felt a little better. Maybe even a bit more patient. The boat finally appeared about mid-afternoon.

As it began to approach the dock, we crouched down and moved slowly into position. I hoped no one high in the castle had seen us. Fortunately, the bush was thick enough that we could shield ourselves from the castle pretty well.

We finally heard activity at the boat dock, and pretty soon a group of people began moving up the path. One woman was saying how she was sure this job would beat growing tchadbe. Her companion agreed and added it would at least be cooler. Then they were past. We moved out, still shielded from the castle by the trees at that left turn, and tried to look like four stragglers from the group. We saw them ahead of us as we rounded the curve and kept pace with them the rest of the way. No one even looked back that I could see. We watched as they moved into the barracks, then sauntered over and filled our own water jugs, then found a bench.

Jenny said, "I think we're OK. We'll let them all mill around a while and then go in and claim cubicles. Let's try to act like we already have ours, by just walking along and moving directly to an open one without hesitating."

Maggie didn't say anything, and I noticed that she looked awful. "A nap is in order for you, young lady," I said.

She just nodded.

We quickly claimed two cubicles. I got Maggie showered and bedded down. Hud, Jenny, and I went on a purposeful exploration. This place was pretty much the same as those in the settlements except for hot water and heaters, a concession to the cold. We located a bench from which Hud would be able to see the redhead up close and another from which the rest of us could just observe. When she showed up, Hud would go with her to get her to point out Julia. The plan was for him to bring Julia out, and then for all of us to walk to the beach for a casual late-evening stroll.

It was hard watching everyone go to dinner. We popped some food pills and raved about how delicious they were. That only worked a little bit, though. Maggie showed up, said she felt better and was more cheerful. It was about dusk when Hud went out and claimed his bench. We walked over to the one we had picked. Luckily, it was empty too. We sat down to wait.

Jenny said, "With a little luck, we'll be done here tomorrow and can go home."

Maggie mumbled, "Don't bet on it."

"What do you mean?" I asked.

"Nothing definite. I just have a vague feeling that there are problems ahead. Probably just the devil's evil causing it."

"I hope you're wrong," Jenny said. "But we have to try. Hey! Look! Is that her?"

A long, tall, smashing redhead was walking slowly toward the water spigot. It was a little too far to tell if she was red on the lower end, too. She must have been because Hud got up and walked over toward her with his empty water jug. He spoke and she turned and spoke back. They chatted a minute or two like old friends, then sauntered slowly toward the barracks together.

We sat tight, and in about five minutes, Hud emerged with a smallish, dark–complexioned lady with short black hair. They turned toward the beach, so we got up and followed. About halfway down the path we came to a little sitting area with several benches. Hud and Julia sat down on one and we walked up to join them.

Hud said, "Julia, these are the others, Jenny, Jack, and the one I was telling you about, Maggie. This is Julia." He pronounced it 'hooleea' and said she was from Panama.

"Maggie, are you really an angel but still mortal?" Julia asked.

"Yes, dear. I guess I am unique although Miss Jenny is in training to become the second. This is so important that Ruth sent us both."

"Golly. This is exciting! Can you do unusual things?" Deena was right on in her selection of Julia as appropriately naïve. Since no one was in sight, Maggie bounced to the other side of the path and right back. Julia was wide-eyed. Maggie quickly grabbed her mind, stood her up and made her touch her toes.

Julia gasped and said, "That's wonderful. I wish I could do that."

"It's possible that you could be trained someday, Julia. Would you like that?"

"Do you really think I could learn? I mean really?"

"You would have to be tested, of course. If you do a good job on your assignment here, we'll put in a good word for you."

"Oh, thank you."

Maggie then turned on her strong mother-figure.

She said, "Come sit over here by me and I'll tell you about our mission and the critical role that Ruth has chosen for you to play."

Maggie launched into our tale. "Several months ago, in a routine scan of Balzerch, Ruth detected signs of a disease called Bladen's syndrome, named after the angel chemist who discovered it, Dr. Rudolph Bladen. It was only known to exist on four or five worlds at the time of his discovery. Basically, a person develops terrible and constant joint pain similar to the arthritis of Earth. However, Bladen's doesn't stop there. The disease actually destroys the joints, fusing them into a masses of solid bone-like tissue. It then spreads to the body's organs and destroys them one by one until you are gone. Until recently, there has been no cure, and the disease has begun to spread to many other worlds. This is the disease that Balzerch has. No question about it."

Maggie paused and Julia said, "Golly, that sounds terrible, even if it is the devil."

"That's true. However, you know God is no fan of the devil and would not really mind under usual circumstances if some dread disease took him out. But circumstances are not usual. As you may or may not know, Ruth is trying to determine whether or not there are more like him. So far She has been unsuccessful. There are so many systems, it may take years to find his. If the devil dies, and he certainly will in the next six months, then a lot of work may be wasted. The best chance of finding his home world is if he provides some hint of it's location when meeting with God, or if he's visited by members of his world. Neither works if he's dead. Can you see Her problem?"

"Oh, yes. What can we do if he's already dying, though?"

"That's where you come in, Julia. You can have a very important role in this situation. Through many years of effort, Ruth's scientists have finally developed a cure for Bladen's syndrome, and have tested it extensively. It works, but only if the individual gets the vaccine in the early stages. The problem is how to get it to Balzerch before it's too late. And it absolutely must be given before the victim is aware of the disease. This is the stage the devil is in now. Ruth's problem is how to deliver it to him. If She just tells him about his Bladen's, he'll think it's a trick and laugh it off. As you well know, he listens to no one. If She comes down and forces him to take it, he'll know She wants him alive and this will give him an added advantage in their ongoing battle.

"So She has decided to give him the vaccine without his knowledge. It's for his own good, so it will cause no harm. She has sent us to get you to help. Will you help us, Julia? You are really our only hope. And this is urgent."

She gulped and said, "Anything. Anything at all."

"Good. Now here's the plan. We have the vaccine with us. It can be taken mixed in food or drink. Every day at mid-morning and mid-afternoon, Ella comes to the kitchen for a glass of chilled juice for the devil. Are you familiar with this routine?"

"Yes, that's right, every day. One of us squeezes the fruit about an hour ahead of time, and then puts it in a glass and in the icebox to chill. That's where Ella picks it up."

"Good. Now, if I give you the vaccine, can you put it in the juice completely undetected? No one, absolutely no one, can see you do this."

"That's not a problem, even if I don't squeeze it myself. I'm in the icebox a hundred times a day for something or other."

"Excellent. Ruth was right when She told me you could be counted on, Julia. I know She'll be very pleased and grateful. Now, you must be sure not to mention this to anyone, especially Ella and the other mortals here. Not anyone. We don't want any slip-ups. Without that vaccine, Balzerch is a goner."

"I understand. Golly, this is real exciting!"

"Yes. Now, I need to know if you carry your water bag to work."

"Yes, I do. Out of habit, I guess, but I always have it nearby."

"Good. I want you to change water bags with Miss Jenny. Hers has a special pocket with the vaccine ampoule in it. All you need to do is drop that ampoule in the juice. It will dissolve instantly and be completely undetectable. Show her your bag, Miss Jenny."

Jenny showed her the ampoule and they traded bags. Jenny had anticipated a switch, and had put her food pellets and other supplies in our bags. Maggie reached over and hugged Julia and told her how grateful we were and how lucky we were to have her on our team. Julia said she would do it tomorrow morning. She said she got off at noon tomorrow, right after the lunch was prepared, and she would meet us at the water spigot at lunchtime. We agreed and sent her on her way. It was full dark now but a bright moon shone from above. Four shivering people walked by on their way back from the beach.

Hud said, "Maggie, anytime you want to take the bar, I'll be glad to sponsor you. That was masterful."

Jenny and I agreed.

Jenny said, "All we have to do is wait until noon tomorrow and get confirmation from Julia."

"Do we need to confirm with Ella that he actually drank the juice?" I asked.

"If she gets off when Julia does, we'll meet her, too, but that's a frill and I want to recall ASAP," Jenny said.

"Amen to that," Hud added.

With that, we moved back up to the barracks and went to bed. Everything was in place now.

thirty-three

Next morning, Saturday, I woke up early, so hungry, I could have eaten an old shoe. I had some food pellets, so I consumed them and I guess they helped. Maggie stirred, so we got up and went to the bathroom and then the showers. We walked down to the lounging area where we had agreed to meet Jenny and Hud and sat on a couch. Maggie was in a dark mood.

"You're a real joy to be around this morning. What's wrong?"

"Jack, we've done our job. Don't you think we should recall now?"

"It's always best to confirm just in case. Julia struck me as a little flaky, at best. What's wrong?"

"I can't put my finger on it. I just have a bad feeling about today."

"Let's talk to Jenny and Hud and see how they feel."

A few minutes later, they came sauntering up and we exchanged greetings.

I said, "Maggie is still getting a sense of trouble for today and wants to consider recall now."

Jenny said, "It's tempting. What do you see Maggie?"

"Just darkness in the future line. That's the problem. I can't see anything definite, but it radiates trouble. It's probably connected with the strength of the devil's thought radiation."

"Maybe. But maybe we really are headed into trouble. Let's take a walk in the bush and see if a REGEN message arrives."

We moved out toward our last campsite, walking slowly and chatting casually. We didn't want to hang around the barracks too long and draw attention to ourselves because we weren't working. We walked out several miles, then turned and started back. We had covered about a mile on the return trip when a REGEN message arrived. Maggie grabbed it and opened it.

She began to read, "The starship dispatched a shuttle craft toward Hell about 20 minutes ago. Should arrive soon. One being is aboard. Starship and Tarcan ship have rendezvoused. One Tarcan has beamed aboard the starship. We don't understand this development. Assume you have initiated action. Try to confirm quickly and get out. If possible, get the aviatrix. Deena."

"Damn," Jenny said. "New fun and games. I guess we have to confirm."

"Looks like it," I agreed.

Suddenly Maggie said, "Do you sense it Jenny?"

"Yes. What in the world is it?"

"It must be the starship shuttle passenger radiating. It's not evil like the devil. In fact, I can't tell what it is. It's neutral and well shielded. It's not nearly as strong as the devil."

"Let's move on toward the barracks. It's close to noon and time to meet Julia at the spigot," Hud said.

"She won't be there," Maggie mumbled under her breath.

I let it pass.

We arrived at the barracks and claimed a couple of benches. A half-hour later, lunch was in full swing and still no Julia.

A few minutes later a short man with a long sad face came over and said, "Victory."

Jenny said, "Garden. Who are you?"

"My name is Walter. I am a friend of Julia. Last night she told several of us including Ella the plan. Ella didn't like it much but she agreed to go along. Something went wrong. The demons came for Julia and took her away. Can you help?"

"What else do you know?" Hud asked.

"Just that several squads of demons are about to leave the residence for a search. I guess for you all."

"Just what we need," Jenny said. "Thanks for the warning, Walter. Now haul your ass out of here before you're seen with us."

Walter left quickly and none too soon, because seconds later a squad rounded the corner and headed for the barracks door. We were off to the side and they didn't look toward us or maybe ignored us, one of the two. Anyway, they went on into the barracks. We jumped up and melted a couple of hundred yards into the bush.

Jenny called a halt and said, "Anyone against a recall? Do we try to help Ella and Julia?"

"We can't get in to help them," Hud said. "We'd just be surrendering ourselves to the devil. I'm for recall. Maybe Deena has an idea about we can do."

"Wait," Maggie said. "The shuttle from the starship is lifting. There are two aboard. The second is Balzerch."

"Yes," Jenny confirmed. "I have it too."

"Let's wait a minute," I said. "If he's gone, we can go in."

"It's definite," Maggie said. "I lost him in the sky moving outward. And the evil flow is gone. There are several elites still in the castle area."

"The elites won't bother you, Maggie. Even I can stop an average one. Let's go get those ladies and the aviatrix and get our butts home."

thirty-four

We cut back through the barracks yard to get to the path to the castle and, of course, the demon team came out and made straight for us. They were a team of five.

The leader, a tall male with an unbelievable set of protruding teeth said, "Halt!"

Hud stepped up and said, "What's the problem here?"

"We are looking for four outsiders that fit your descriptions. You will come with us."

"What if we don't choose to come? Does it take five demons to subdue four mortals?" Hud was having fun baiting them but we were short of minutes.

"Two of us could take you——."

He stopped because Maggie or maybe Jenny had frozen them.

It turned out to be Jenny and she said, "The people you seek are somewhere on the beach. When I release you, you will proceed directly to the beach and search."

She released them.

The leader said, "Come. They're at the beach. We must go search there for them."

Hud said, "That beats hell out of fighting them. Good job, Jenny."

"Let's move," Jenny said, and move we did.

We went swarming up the inclined path, stopping once to dispatch another group to the beach. Maybe they could find and arrest the first group. The drawbridge was down and we ran across. An elite with a team was on guard duty. The elite saw us coming and went for his communicator, but before he could get it, Maggie chopped him down like a tree. He was writhing on the ground when Jenny froze the other two guards. We sent the two to the beach to join the party; and, taking no chances with the elite, I sent him, temporarily at least, to join his ancestors using a big wooden club I found leaning against the wall.

Maggie ran toward a hallway off to the right, the rest of us on her heels. After going about 30 feet, she turned down a set of stairs that went down to the lower level. Once down, she turned right and ran down a hallway of what seemed to be cells to a huge door on the right. Hud grabbed the door but it was locked. Maggie splintered the inside wooden lock bar and the door swung inward. "Careful," Maggie hissed. "There's an elite inside."

This was truly a scene out of Hell. Ella and Julia were each handcuffed to a high ring on the left-hand wall of what appeared to be a large torture room. They had whip marks and burns all over their bodies and both had blood on their inner thighs from their genital area. They both hung there limply, like they were unconscious. I hoped that they were. A large demon with a set of handcuff keys was approaching Ella as we came in. Maggie or Jenny or both froze him and the other four demons on the spot.

There was another person in the room, probably the elite, sitting back in the shadows on our left. Suddenly, Jenny and Maggie both staggered slightly and Hud and I went down. I had a searing pain in my head. Maggie recovered and literally jerked the person out of the chair and dragged him into view. It was Bennie.

As soon as Maggie had control, Hud and I were released and got up. Jenny took control of the other five demons and made them lie on the floor and told them their arms and legs did not work. Maggie had Bennie on his knees and was pouring it on.

I stopped her and said to Bennie, "This is what you have become? A torturer of young women?"

Maggie relaxed her hold enough to let him speak.

"I know it looks bad, Jack, but it was Balzerch. I just gave each of them a sedative injection and ordered Huop to unlock them."

Jenny said, "Where has Balzerch gone."

"All I know is up to a ship. He wouldn't tell me anything else."

"How long will he be gone?"

"He didn't exactly know, but not long."

"Not long at all," blasted a deep voice from behind us.

I whirled and saw the others do the same. There before us was a being I had no doubt was Balzerch.

He was big, about 6'6", and with huge, well-defined muscles. His skin had a reddish-pink tinge and he had absolutely no body hair, not even on his head. His hairless head was a little larger than good symmetry would have dictated if designed on a drawing board, but he didn't seem too concerned by it. His face was a mix of demon and oriental earth features, small slanted eyes, a large nose and slightly protruding teeth. He didn't have a tail but what hung in front gave a pretty good imitation of one. I felt sorry for the chosen women of Hell.

I felt Maggie drop Bennie and turn her power on the devil. He staggered back a step and then grinned and fried Maggie. She fell like she had been clubbed and made little whimpering sounds as she writhed on the floor.

Jenny screamed, "You miserable fucker. You son-of-a ——." And she was writhing on the floor beside Maggie. Hud and I were frozen and just observers.

The devil looked at Maggie and Jenny and said, "Commendable power for mortals. Karg, can't you be in charge for fifteen minutes without trouble?"

"Sorry, your highness," Bennie said.

"I presume that these are the ones we sought information on from the two foolish girls."

"It would appear so, your highness."

"Good. Since when do mortals have powers?"

"This is the first I knew about it, your highness. I am as surprised as you must be."

"Well, no matter. It will make our intimate encounters even more enjoyable since we can share minds as well as bodies."

"Yes, your highness."

"Listen, Karg, We've got a problem. This damned inspection team from my home planet is fast becoming a pain in the ass. I went up to convince them our operation was operating within the rules and thought they would leave. I even paid the Tarcan ship captain to testify on my behalf but the bastards refuse to believe him either. Now they insist on staying on the surface for at least a week to do visual inspections. They don't even suspect the extent to which my powers have grown. I could smash them like bugs, but that would just cause them to send another ship and it might be a battle-ready. So two of them will be coming down in about two hours. We need to be ready.

"What do you want me to do, your highness?"

"I've just summoned the other elites to come here and prepare the castle. For you, Karg, a very special job. I can't have any prisoners, especially mortals, when they get here. I want you to take these six and the flyer woman and REGEN to Zinco 12. Then take a cart to the supervised farm, Yehlo 11, and tell the commander to put them to work. The two with powers won't have any powers for at least a month. I fried them pretty thoroughly. These two don't seem to have any powers to speak of, but the commander should keep an eye on them just in case. None of them is to be harmed. I wish I could keep the two women with powers here, but I can't. At least not right now."

He walked over and probed around on Maggie's and Jenny's bodies with his toes and sighed and said, "Waiting does have its advantages, though."

"Yes, your highness."

"When you get them settled, come back here."

"Yes, your highness."

"He turned to Hud and asked, "What was in that ampoule that she put in my juice?"

"Rat poison," Hud answered.

He turned his power on Hud, and took him to his knees.

Then the devil quit, chuckled, and said, "No hurry. Tell you what. I'll let you watch me thorougly enjoy myself with your wife and you'll tell quick enough. No hurry."

Bennie sent one of the demons for the aviatrix and assigned a female demon to each of the ladies. Maggie and Jenny could walk with assistance but Bennie's sedatives had Ella and Julia unconscious and they had to be carried.

To Hud and me he said, "Come along quietly."

We were assembled in the REGEN room. Bennie got everybody touching, called for transfer, and just like that, we were on Zinco 12. The commander was waiting for us with a cart. We were loaded aboard, given a packet of bread, and then left.

The cart ride was a six hour ordeal. When we left, it was already past mid-afternoon, so we arrived at Yehlo 11 well after dark. Jenny and Maggie were conscious and aware of the situation but had no powers left. Julia and Ella were both still out when we got there. Bennie must have used a strong drug on them. The lady flyer told us her name was Eloise, and that she was OK. During the trip, I tried to make small talk with Bennie but he wasn't buying it. I was getting increasingly concerned that Deena and her crew had lost sight of us, and that we really were on our own. I thought talking to Bennie might help me relax a little, but since that didn't work, I just sat there and worried.

We were unloaded and taken to the barracks. There were large lights over the compound and I could see a huge chain link type fence made of some sort of plastic around the whole structure. There were a few residents milling about, but they had a strange aura about them. Two demons accompanied Bennie and our group. They carried Ella and Julia over and simply dumped them on the ground in front of the door.

Aside to me, Bennie quietly said, "Be careful in there. This is not a normal settlement. It's the one where the lobotomies are sent. Some of them aren't too stable. Don't hesitate to kill them if they attack you. Good luck. I'll try to keep track of you."

What in the world?

thirty-five

Hud and I left the five women outside and went in to check the place. It was a typical barracks design, and didn't appear to be crowded. We walked slowly through and were greeted with blank stares by most we passed. There was a small lounge area, sparsely furnished. We selected two adjoining four-person cubicles on the third level and put out the occupied signs.

As we moved back toward the front, two men suddenly charged us from a restroom doorway. We had superior strength, but they fought like madmen. I finally remembered that I had some mind power and clamped down on the one attacking me. I didn't quite freeze him but I reduced him to a snail-like pace.

I managed to gasp, "Hud. Use your power."

Hud was on the floor, his man biting him on the shoulder. He finally managed to turn on the power and stopped his attacker, flattening him in a flash. My man was sitting on the floor, and I kicked him hard on the side of his head and put him clear down.

"What the fuck is going on," said Hud breathing heavily.

"I'm damned if I know. They didn't have any reason to do that."

"Let's go get the others and get them in here safely."

We went back to the front door, told them what had happened, and cautioned them to be careful. We all decided to travel in pairs, at the least. The bigger the group the better until we could figure out what was going on in this weird place. Julia and Ella were finally up and able to walk but somewhat unsteadily.

I said, "Let's try a recall first."

We touched each other and hit the buttons. Nothing.

"Nice try anyway, Jack," Hud said.

We moved inside and I said, "Let's go directly to the showers and work on Julia and Ella. The devil made one mistake: he let us keep our water bags, so we have the salve."

As we neared the shower, I noticed that our two attackers had been dragged off to one side and were beginning to stir a little. We went on past and entered the shower. It was the cold-only variety. Hud said he would stand guard. Maggie and Jenny were nearly useless so I got them under two showers and told them to help each other. Then Eloise and I got Julia seated in front of a wash basin and took Ella into the shower. She was a mess. There were burns, especially on her breasts and genital area, whip welts that had bled, and genital damage due to the size of the demons. We washed her gently with soap and our hands, as there apparently wasn't a washcloth in all of Hell. We moved her under a dryer and then stretched her out on the floor. I applied a thin coat of salve to all of her wounds while Eloise started on Julia. Julia got the same treatment.

I grabbed a quick shower and relieved Hud so he could get one. Jenny and Maggie were finished but were just standing around vacantly. I hollered to Eloise to put some salve on Hud's shoulder. Finally we were all through and moved to our cubicles. We managed to get everyone up the ladders and into the cubicles. We put Eloise, Julia and Ella in one and we four took the other.

"Where are we?" Maggie asked.

"Yehlo 11," I said. "It's where they keep the lobotomies."

"Then I'm in the right place. I feel like my brains have been scrambled."

Hud said, "If we can believe Balzerch, your powers will return in a couple of weeks. They were damaged by his attack on you but apparently not permanently."

Jenny said, "Why are we here?"

I explained the devil's problems with his home world inspectors, and how he couldn't afford to have us seen by them. I also mentioned his plans for us after he got rid of them. I didn't go into a lot of detail. Not necessary right now. "We've got to get out of here before he sends Bennie to get us."

Hud said, "You aren't kidding. Let's try to figure a way while we're at work tomorrow."

We talked a little longer and then went to sleep.

Sometime later I heard a scream from next door. Kicking myself for not posting a guard, I rolled out of the bed and started that way. Hud was closer and already on the way. I made one more step when a hard blow smashed into my right shoulder. I heard a pop, no doubt the sound of my collarbone snapping. I turned and there was the same son-of-a-bitch who had attacked us earlier. I grabbed him with my mind and this time froze him solid. By that time, Jenny was up and saw that he was frozen. She bounced over and kicked him hard in the balls. That unfroze him for a moment. He staggered backwards toward the door so I stepped forward and kicked him out. It was a 14 foot fall. I was pretty sure this one wouldn't be back that night.

I raced next door and found Hud down with a nasty head wound. The other man had Eloise down on the floor and was on top of her thrusting as he tried to enter her. I froze him in mid-thrust and Eloise pushed him off. Jenny was down beside Hud. Maggie gave this crazy a terrific kick, and she and Eloise pushed him out. He hit the floor with a sickening thud and began to moan. Julia and Ella were sitting on the bed holding each other.

Maggie joined Jenny in checking Hud.

I learned over to investigate the damage and asked, "How bad is it?"

Maggie answered, "It's pretty bad, Jack. I think it's a fractured skull."

Jenny was holding his head in her lap and crying softly. Maggie saw me listing to starboard and said, "What is it, Jack?"

"Just the collarbone. I'm OK. Help Hud."

"There's not much I can do except put on some salve to heal the open wound."

She proceeded to do that and then checked me.

"Good call, Jack. It is your collarbone. Hold still."

She made a thorough examination of the area and then probed and pulled and pushed until I felt faint. Then she fashioned a sling using two water jugs and injected an ampoule onto the break. She made me sit on the bed and said not to move around.

She had all the others surround Hud and gently lift him onto a bed where the light was better. She examined him again, then she and Jenny decided that the salve was not going to be enough in this case. She was actually afraid that there might be bone splinters in the brain. And a hundred other combinations of complications. We needed a repair machine quickly.

I said, "Everyone touch Hud."

We tried recall but no go.

"Don't they have a repair station here?" Jenny asked.

"I don't know. But I'm going to find out."

I picked up the club that had been used on Hud and got the one in my cubicle as well.

I gave one to Maggie and one to Eloise and said, "Watch the ladders. If someone comes up, knock his fucking brains out. Make sure it's not me, though!"

Maggie started to protest that my arm needed quiet but I silenced her with a glance and went down the ladder. I made my way around our two assailants, one of whom was moaning softly. The other was in no condition to moan. He appeared to be dead. I hoped so.

I went outside and saw no guards, so I moved toward the commandant's quarters. There was a demon on guard at the gate and he came at me with a club. I froze him on the spot.

"What is your name?"

"Lork."

"Where is the commandant?"

"Inside reading."

"I must see him now"

"She must not be disturbed."

Did you catch that? She?

I left him frozen, borrowed his club, and banged on the fence and on a plastic bucket that was sitting there.

"Lork. What's wrong?" she said from the doorway.

"He's temporarily out of commission. I must talk with you. It's urgent."

"You dare to bother me?"

She was an elite and didn't hesitate to turn on the power. I fell to my knees clutching my head with my one good hand.

She eased a little and said, "Speak quickly."

"I came in on the special convoy this evening. My friend has a bad head injury inflicted by one of the residents. We fear for his life."

"So he dies. We will just repair him. Go away."

"Wait. He's still mortal. And I know Balzerch's orders were to prevent damaging us. Is Karg still here?"

"No. He left. But you do speak the truth. Those were my orders and he may want mortals to remain mortals. Bring him to the side door here."

"I will need something to carry him on. I am injured with a broken collarbone."

"Stupid mortals. Lork, help him. There is a stretcher right inside the door."

She turned and went inside."

I unfroze Lork, then he and I ran to the cubicles with the somewhat primitive stretcher. The two attackers were still there. Lork gave a hard kick in the ribs to the one moaning and then dragged him to one side. Then he moved the other one. He didn't waste a kick but muttered something about us causing him extra work. I went up the ladder and we managed to get Hud strapped to the stretcher. I had the ladies lower him and went on down to help Lork. Jenny and Maggie managed to get the contraption stabilized enough so that they had him hanging only six feet above Lork and me, so we lowered him on down with no real problem. Except, that is, for my searing pain. Jenny came down and took one end of the stretcher. I warned Maggie to stand guard and we left.

We entered by the side door and I saw the chamber on the right. The commandant was fiddling with some dials and grumbling that it had been a long time since she had repaired a mortal. She tilted the chamber until it was horizontal and we eased Hud in.

She looked at the wound and said, "Nasty. That'll take about 10 hours." She checked out my shoulder. "Report to me after breakfast in the morning."

"All of us?"

"Of course not. Only you. The healthy ones have to work."

"I'll be here."

Next morning was Sunday, and when we got up everyone was starved, which was a good sign. Julia and Ella had healed overnight and were feeling considerably better. Maggie and Jenny were also much improved but without powers of any kind. We went to find the food machine and Jenny volunteered to go first. Nothing happened when she signaled the machine.

She said, "I want to get food credit."

"You must see the commandant."

We were just turning away when a female elite breezed in and said, "You are the mortals. I will fix it. After you eat, report to me at Gate 2 for work assignments." She fiddled with the programming buttons briefly, gave the base a kick, then gave us a thumbs-up.

Jenny tried again.

"Food credit granted. Put your hand on the screen."

We all followed suit and then ate a huge breakfast.

Gate 2 was down past the commandant's lodging. Jenny wanted to stop to see if Hud was all right, but we advised her against it as he wasn't repaired yet. There was no need to stir up the commandant, who was undoubtedly having her breakfast.

But as we passed, the commandant herself stepped out the side door and said, "You mortals, over here."

We walked toward the side door and out walked Hud with a big grin on his face. Jenny, followed closely by Maggie ran to him and hugged him and kissed him. The commandant looked pleased and then made another exam of my shoulder.

"This is amazing," she said. "The rest of you wait here while I make a picture of his shoulder."

We went in. She took the picture and said, "How do you explain this? That bone is 90 percent healed!"

"I've always been a quick healer."

"I'm tempted to break your leg and watch it heal."

"Remember what the devil said about my health." And I grinned at her. Tried to lighten her up a little.

She grinned back, at least I think that's what it was. It's hard to tell with a demon.

She said, "I remember. Tell Esor, the elite you saw in the food hall, to give you light duty at work today."

"Thank you for helping, my friend."

"It was my duty."

I went out a little confused about demons. Several of the elites I was now acquainted with weren't bad types at all. We went on to Gate 2 and there was Esor, already waiting for us. She assigned us to a planting crew and we walked with the crazies to the field.

There's not much to tell. We were handed water-type bags full of seeds and were told to follow a hoeing crew making furrows and holes in between the low shrubs that lived here. They would shade the young tchadbe plants as they grew. We dropped the seeds eight inches apart, and another crew followed and covered them. When you ran out of seeds, you got another bag. The bathroom was anywhere the seeds had already been planted. We had our own water. Lunch was bread. And as a final note, it was hot. As evening approached, we quit for the day.

On the way back to the barracks, we managed to join hands to try a recall, but again, it wasn't to be. We got back, had showers, and went to dinner. After dinner, we walked around the compound looking for an easy way out. There didn't appear to be one. We posted a guard at bedtime.

The next day, Monday, was almost a repeat of Sunday. We planted seed. Hot. Fun.

On the lunch break, while Eloise, Ella, and Julia were on a bathroom break, Maggie said, "I really don't mind this job. Just knowing what those little seeds can be turned into keeps me going."

I said, "I see you're beginning to recover. Sex has reared its ugly head again."

"I can't wait until the month is up."

Jenny said, "I'm dying to try one."

Then it was back to work.

About mid-afternoon, I took a pee break and was in mid-stream when a bush behind me hissed "Jack".

"Don't react, just listen." It was Deena. "I'm going to freeze the two overseers. No one should notice for a minute or two, so when you get back, I'll freeze them and you get your group moving this way. I'll take you to the REGEN spot. We've got to hurry, Jack."

I walked back to where Hud, Jenny, and Maggie were and said, "Don't look now, but Deena is behind that bush where I peed. When the demons freeze, go to her quickly."

To our team's credit, nobody said a word or even looked up. We broke ranks and moved over toward the other three. One of the overseers moved to intercept me and when he got close, Deena froze them both. I moved quickly to the three and said follow me. Eloise was instantly ready but the other two, especially Julia, started to argue and ask me what I meant. Eloise grabbed Ella and took off after the others. I clipped Julia on the jaw, grabbed her up and really moved out. Hud ran back toward me and took her for a while. He managed to ask breathlessly what had happened to her.

"I knocked her out. She wanted to have a full briefing before she would go."

About then she came to. Hud put her between us and made her run with us holding her arms.

She struggled for a moment and Hud said, "You'd better run or I'm going to dump you and leave you for the devil."

She began to comprehend that this was a rescue and started running. We let her go and really poured it on. Deena was waiting for us on a little knoll. We rushed in and made skin contact, and just as we faded out, I saw the devil fading in nearby. We had barely made it. Noah's Ark never looked so good.

thirty-six

We were a sorry looking group. All of us were dirty from the tchadbe fields. Eloise, Ella and Julia were a mass of scars from old and new wounds, mostly old in the case of Eloise. Hud had a nasty scar on his scalp. Apparently the devil's machines didn't repair scars or else the commandant hadn't thought it necessary. I had a huge bruise on my right shoulder. And my collarbone area ached. I probably messed up Maggie's job of setting the bone when we moved Hud.

Deena sent us to Charity to schedule repairs. She checked and dismissed Eloise, Ella, and Julia and told them to report back tomorrow.

She took one look at Hud and said, "We can do better than that. Jump in."

Hud said, "I feel fine."

"I'm not worried about the scar, but I am relatively certain that some of the minute bone chips were missed by their crude machine. So in you go."

Turning to me, she said, "Jack, we'll give you and hour or so to strengthen that bone and remove that bruise. That will stop the aching. Let's see. One chamber is taken for the night. It's about 5:00, almost dinnertime, so go get something to eat. Be here at 7:00 and Hud should be done."

I hung around while she talked to Maggie and Jenny.

"Now, as for you two, I'm in unknown territory. These machines are designed for physical repair. They can take a damaged brain and put it back in original condition. We're even working on a machine that cures psychological ills, but so far with little success. We can make you forget an event that's causing you distress, but you forget everything for that time period. We know that you all can issue for-getter orders for short time periods but we don't know how you do it. And you can't seem to tell us.

"Now, here's the question. Is your temporary lack of powers due to brain damage or to abuse of the mind itself? We know when you are hit by a powerful mind thrust, it's similar to a hand gripping an orange to squeeze it. We think some brain damage results from the electrical charge that seems to be part of the attack. The brain damage has, in our studies, been minimal. But we have so few studies that we can't be sure at all what happens.

"What I want to do is try the machine. If there is physical damage, it will be repaired. If there is some other damage, it shouldn't be made any worse by being in the chamber."

"I'm game," Maggie said.

"Me too," chimed Jenny.

"Good. Maggie at 8:00 and Jenny at 10:00. Go get some showers and dinner and relax."

We met Deena on the way out. She graciously agreed to let us shower and said she would have dinner served in the briefing room. I found out that showers are more fun with two ladies than with one. I just barely managed to keep myself in check. The hot water was nice, too.

We got to the briefing room about 5:45. Deena was already there. She said dinner would arrive at 6:00. Then she brought us up to date on her end of the operation.

"We were tracking you pretty well until you hit the castle. From that point on, though, our REGEN wouldn't penetrate long enough to get a look. We also saw the space ship beam the devil back instead having him use the shuttle, so we assumed you had been caught. We saw the beam that took you to Zinco 12 but couldn't pinpoint it well enough then to know for sure that you were on it. The devil keeps his captives for fun and games, usually.

"We continued to focus on the castle and saw the starship shuttle land with two beings aboard . Why they use a shuttle when they have REGEN is beyond me. A little later, the castle cleared and we realized you all weren't there. We watched their REGEN and about 4:00 this morning, we got an incoming from a settlement which we couldn't trace and then a few minutes later, one to the Tarcan ship. The ship left immediately for earth. They arrived at 11:00 this morning and started making drops.

"Now comes the strange part. I got this message here."

She handed over a message sheet. It said, "Try Yehlo 11. Be quick."

"Bennie," I said.

The others nodded.

I continued, "Bennie was the one who took us to Yehlo 11. He went back to Zinco 12, beamed to the castle and up to the Tarcan ship to come to Earth. Then he sent you this warning."

Deena said, "We didn't even know he was off Earth. Anyway, we didn't have any luck picking up Yehlo 11 for quite a while. So we took the latest photos, which are taken every 15 minutes, located your work group, and I went down on the nearest approach we could manage. You participated in the rest. The devil detected our REGEN poking around Yehlo 11. We thought we had him shielded out but apparently not completely or all the time. By the time I beamed down, he must have had his coordinates pretty well set, because as you may recall, he was arriving just as we left. Did you see him?"

"I did," I said.

Jenny and Maggie hadn't.

"Well, that's about it from this end. What happened to you all?"

Jenny looked at Maggie and me and we told her to tell it. She described our scheme for Ella and Julia in detail up to the point of execution and then paused.

Deena said, "It's absolutely inspired. What in the world went wrong?"

"It was that dumbass, Julia. She left us and went straight to Ella and several others and was so excited and impressed that she told them about the whole plan. Of course, Ella was suspicious, so this radiated to the devil. He pulled them both in. You saw the resulting scars. We don't know if anyone else was compromised or not, but it seems likely. You may wish to recall them. I recommend you give that harebrained Julia an early retirement."

Jenny went on to explain why we were sent to Yehlo 11 instead of playing with the devil. Deena was extremely interested in the inspection team and, as soon as Jenny finished, she excused herself to go communicate this to Analysis and to Ruth.

It was pushing 7:00, so I went on down to Charity's for repair. Hud was just finishing and I told him where to find Maggie and Jenny. I jumped in and by 7:45 was done. The ache was gone. I waited until Maggie came in and kissed her luck, then went back to the briefing room. Deena had just returned.

"Well, the 'you know what' just hit the fan. I neglected to tell Ruth that I was going to Hell. The devil filed a protest about Custom violation with Her about an hour ago. She is mad mostly because I didn't tell Her ahead of time. She told the devil when he got his demons off earth, She would worry about the angels.

"I pleaded lack of time to notify Her and then reported what you said about the aliens. That saved my butt, because She has been very curious about who they were and what they were doing. She is also curious about Bennie. She said to get him. That will be the first assignment when you all catch up to tomorrow morning."

"Is the original 'you' going to work our tails off as usual?" Jenny wanted to know.

Deena smiled and said, "You know I can't tell you. You'll have to be surprised. Remember if you do see my earlier self, don't mention this trip to Hell."

She paused and thought a minute. "Jenny is not going to be done until nearly midnight. Why don't you all stay in the dorm tonight and I'll take you home in the morning to Wednesday, September 3 at 7:05 AM, five minutes after you left to come here. That way you'll be rested to begin your day. If I take you now, I would still have to drop you a little after 7:00 on the same morning and you'd start the day with no sleep."

It made sense to me and Hud and Jenny agreed. I tried to remember what I needed to do on that Wednesday we were going back to rejoin. It was a little blurry. We had an hour to kill until Jenny had to go, so we went to the recreation lounge. Eloise, Julia, and Ella were there.

When we walked in, Julia came cruising over gushing all over the place. "I just want to thank you all so much for getting me out of there. I apologize for telling the secret, but they were my friends and I didn't think it would hurt, Miss Jenny."

While she was babbling on, I eased over and sat down by Eloise. Hud followed my lead and sort of migrated toward Ella. That left Jenny with the loony. She was talking, and so was Jenny but we weren't close enough to make out most of what they were saying. I did clearly hear Jenny say "Cut the crap". Wonder what that was about?

I asked Eloise, "What do you think you'll do?"

"I don't know, Jack. My timeline on Earth is 50 or so years ago but I can't imagine rejoining it. The devil used his rebirth machine to hold my age at about 35. He didn't know if it would work on a mortal or not but it did. I guess I'm still mortal. The damned machine may have killed me during rebirth for all I know. Anyway, I do have the younger body as an asset to go along with all those years of experience."

I have neglected to describe Eloise for you. She is tall, about 5'8", and weighs about 135. Those pounds were very well distributed by the designer. She is beautifully proportioned with breasts above average size. She is a brunette and has a smattering of freckles on her face and upper chest. She has what the guys in high school used to call a "classy chassis".

"Your body's most definitely an asset, Eloise. We've been so busy I hardly had time to notice, but I can assure you that it's absolutely perfection."

"Well, thank you, Jack"

"Back to your problem. What does Deena think?"

"We've barely had 15 minutes together, but she said I had several choices. One is to go to Earth and rejoin my family in current time and explain as best I can what happened. Bad choice. My former husband will be in his 70's and remarried if he's still living, and I had no kids or close relatives anyway. I doubt he'd be glad to see me.

"The second option is to remain here and work for someone like Charity as an assistant, but that sounds dull.

"The one with the most appeal is to go back to earth, assume a new identity, and begin to build a new life. Deena said money would never again be a problem and I might be able to grab an off-earth assignment from time to time. It sounds good but 50 years is a long gap to bridge."

"Quite a dilemma. But I understand why you favor the third. Let me talk to Maggie, but maybe you could come down with us for a week and we could start to reintroduce you to old mother Earth."

"That would be fabulous, Jack. But it would be a terrible imposition on you and Maggie."

"Let me ask her and we'll see. I'll speak to Deena, too."

We chatted a little more. I managed to catch Jenny's eye and gave her a big grin and a wink. Have you heard the expression 'If looks could kill'? I don't think I need to explain more. Julia was still pattering on about something and Jenny was clearly bored to death. I saw her look at her watch. I glanced at mine and saw it was almost 10:00. She got up, pried Hud loose from the redhead, and made ready to leave. I think he really did have a thing about redheads. I told Eloise to wait there till I got back.

I joined Jenny and Hud on the trek to Charity's.

Jenny said, "I won't forget what you two clowns did to me in there. You'll pay for sticking me with that dingbat. And to make matters worse, imagine the two of you behaving like schoolboys around the new girls in town. Shame on you both. I'm going to tell Maggie."

Bishop and Deena were there for the unveiling. Bishop gave Jenny a buss on the cheek and inquired about how she was and so on. Then, without much enthusiasm, he shook hands with Hud and me. I think he figured he'd be stuck training us again.

Charity helped Maggie out of the chamber and asked, "How do you feel, dear?"

"OK. Let me test for a minute."

Maggie concentrated and said, "You don't have to tell me, Jenny. It's written all over their faces even if I couldn't sense it. Guilt. And lots of it."

Jenny laughed and Deena said, "What in the world?"

Jenny said, "Watch yourself, Deena. No female under the age of 75 is safe around these two."

When things calmed a little, Bishop asked, "Am I to assume that you two have your powers again?"

"*I* do. At least for the most part, and they're growing stronger all the time. It would appear that there was considerable physical damage involved, so healing in the chamber did the trick."

"That's wonderful, Maggie," Deena said. "Let's try Jenny and see if it's the same."

Charity put Jenny in the chamber and started the cycle. She said to come back about midnight.

Bishop left and the four of us strolled down the hall. I had barely started to bring up the Eloise thing when Maggie said, "It's fine with me, Jack. She can use our help. But it's really up to Deena, you know."

Deena had apparently been preoccupied for she said, "What is? Oh, I see. That's a good idea, Jack. I'm glad that she doesn't want to go into the past. I could send her back, but she was famous and is now a different person than before. Her reappearance now could significantly change the timeline. That's why Ruth is so careful."

"Eloise is a realist, Deena. She can take it. And she could be trusted not to reveal what happened on Hell in the last week."

"I'll talk to her. I want to help her in any way we can. She's been through so much that I can't believe she's not a basket case."

We went back to the lounge and Deena asked Eloise to join her in her office. Julia was gone but Ella was still there. Hud said he was going to run over to Analysis and check on something and would be back before midnight. We talked to Ella awhile and realized that she was pleasant and much more aware than Julia. She wouldn't have blown that assignment. She got sleepy pretty soon, and headed for the dorm, leaving Maggie and I alone. There was a vending machine of sorts in the lounge. I managed to figure it out and got a sandwich and a beer for each of us. I wanted some ice cream but couldn't make that happen.

"Are your powers still strengthening or can you tell?"

"It's strange. I feel that I'm going to be stronger than ever. You didn't say anything, Jack, but did you notice that I actually read your thoughts about the Eloise thing? And Deena read yours and mine, but I think it was through me. I couldn't do that before. I could only make an educated guess based on the type and strength of the emotions involved."

"How about the others?"

"I can't tell yet. They're still sort of numb."

"Can you really tell exactly what I'm thinking right now?"

"It's jumbled, but yes, I think I can. You're wondering what you can do to the stupid machine to make it give ice cream. You're wondering what Deena and Eloise are talking about. And you're wondering what life is going to be like with a freak for a wife."

"Now just a minute. That's a little strong. I don't think of you as a freak, but you'll have to admit you're going to be different. It will impact on our relationship."

"I know, Jack. But Bishop says he thinks I'll be able to turn it off whenever and with whomever I choose. It will be like any other sense. If I don't want to see, I close my eyes. I plan to tune you out unless we agree on a specific time or action where we both want to use it. For example, Bishop says your ability will soon strengthen to the point that you will be able to read emotions and to actually bond with someone with strength like Jenny, Deena, or me. Bond, in the sense that we would share the emotions of a common experience and actually intensify that experience. Sex is one example. Or grief. Or happiness."

"It's going to be different. I hope you're right about the difference being positive. I didn't know Bishop thought I could do anything right."

"Actually, he has high hopes for you and Hud. He just doesn't express himself well. He's also very excited about me because of my potential."

"Whatever you say. I'm glad to hear it, though. In any event, let's take this a day at a time. I still love you, even though you are weird."

"I'll show you who's weird."

She leaned over and gave me a long hard kiss and I was just beginning to register a reaction when Deena and Eloise came in. We sat up quickly, I with my hands in my lap.

Deena grinned and said, "Don't mind us, folks. Go on with what you were doing. We'll just sit here and watch."

"Perverts," Maggie said.

Everybody laughed and Deena said, "It's all set for Eloise to go with you. That is, if she still feels safe around you two. I even cleared it with Ruth. I'm going to be real careful around Her for a while or you'll be working with Carmen."

"It's not that bad, is it?" Maggie asked.

"Not really. But She's definitely not happy and hasn't let any opportunity pass to let me know. Anyway, I have explained to Eloise the problem of inserting her into the 1950's and she understands and agrees. She also knows that Ruth has made a short term exception on the part of you four, and she realizes that she can't talk about the trip to Hell with anyone except you four until all of you catch up.

"I'm giving Eloise several thousand in good confiscated drug money. Come to think of it, I'll give you four a few thousand each, too. Eloise, you can be thinking about your new identity this week, and when you decide, we'll create a past and present for you in terms of papers, property, family, and so on. It won't be a problem for us."

"We're very pleased and we'll try not to corrupt her too much." Maggie said. "Can she go with us in the morning?"

"I don't see why not. When Jenny is through, Eloise, we'll pop you in the machine for repair. It may take most of the night, but you will come out of it rested. Also a blood scan was automatically performed when you arrived, and you are definitely still mortal. The devil's machine did a good job, but without the boosters you will begin to age again, and will die like other Earth mortals."

Hud came wandering back about then, and we went down to pick up Jenny. She wasn't quite through and so we made small talk with

Bishop and Charity. Deena cleared with Charity the overnight use of the chamber for Eloise. We agreed that everyone would meet at REGEN at 7:00 in the morning for departure.

Jenny came out feeling fine and about the same as Maggie, in terms of her powers. Eloise was popped in and we went to the dorm to sleep.

thirty-seven

When we arrived in the hot tub room, it was a mere five minutes after we had left for Hell. We decided we would introduce Eloise as an old college friend of Maggie's from Missouri who was thinking about relocating to the Savannah area. She would be recently divorced, without children, and would be using her maiden name, Ernhart. She had her own money from running a successful mail order business in Missouri where she and her husband had lived, selling household furnishings. Fifty some years is too long a gap for her to claim she was a pilot, so she would have to start over on licenses and so on to get some of that part of her former life back.

We left her in our hot tub until we got the kids off to school, figuring she could arrive during the day. Maggie told the kids an old friend would be coming in today and would be spending a few days with us. Laurie could have cared less and started to complain that a weeknight curfew was unfair because 'everyone else' could stay out until midnight. She was going to a party tonight and wanted to be free to tell everyone she could stay out if she wanted to. Maggie said no. Laurie said "OK".

We went back upstairs with a breakfast tray for Eloise. While she was eating, we talked about getting some new clothing for her. Well, I really just listened. She was just a little taller and fuller than

Maggie so Maggie searched her closet and found a couple of outfits that were too large for her. Eloise fit into a summer dress and a pair of well-worn, but well stretched flat shoes. They decided to go shopping that same morning.

We spent the next hour touring the house and explaining what things were to Eloise. She knew about TV but had never seen one in color. Microwave ovens were magic, and actually pretty hard to explain. The Lincoln and Maggie's Windstar were luxurious, but the CD player and the GPS were too much for her to fathom. Satellite TV, cell phones, ATMs, ipods and x-boxes were so far beyond where she was that we didn't even attempt to explain these either for the present. And so on.

I finally decided to go to work. The girls went to Savannah for some serious shopping, an area of expertise for Maggie. The house in Cedar Creek was coming along nicely. Tom Raith, my construction foreman, was exceptional and I could trust him to get things done. He was there, sitting in his truck talking on his cell. He finished and got out.

"How's it going, Tom?

"Good, Jack. How 'bout you?"

"Can't complain. When'll you finish dryin' her in?"

"If it doesn't rain again this afternoon, we'll have the roof trusses up and the sheeting down. It'll go pretty fast after that. Prob'ly early next week. Why? You got somethin' else?"

"Yeah. I want to show you the Johnson house. Can you break away for an hour or so?"

"No problem. Billy! C'mere a minute."

A tall skinny guy of about 25 came ambling over.

"Howz it goin', Mr. Warner?"

"Just fine, Billy. Looks like y'all 'bout got it under roof."

"If it don' rain, we'll have 'er today."

Tom said, "Billy, I got to be gone for an hour or so. Keep the guys busy puttin' up them trusses."

Billy ambled off to get back to work and Tom got in his truck and followed me to the Johnson place. He had never seen it and I wanted to show him how to start.

"Damn, Jack. Don't you want a demolition crew?"

"You're almost right. But we can bring her back."

We wandered around and through the old house and I showed Tom the basic plan for the interior.

After we went back outside, I said, "So what I want you to do is get started by cleaning up the debris from the balcony and the porch. Save any wood molding and structural beams that are not severely damaged. Save the heart pine, too. You can put them in the old garage, but we'll have to do something about the leaks in the roof in there first."

"I'll go down to Lowes and get a big tarp. What about the rest of the exterior?"

"What do you think?"

"We'll go over it carefully and remove any damaged molding. We'll also need to check where the roof has leaked to see if there is damage to the structural support system. And the foundation and floor support will need checking. I can already see there's a bad spot on the far left hand corner. The floor is buckled there. How about the rest of the inside?"

"We'll have to wait for the architect's new plans to be sure, but there's some obvious water damage that will have to be cleared out and some windows need work. Most of the finish work will be done by a restoration crew out of Savannah."

He grinned and said, "After we do the dirty work, they get the easy job.

"Yeah, and they charge more, too. Actually, I hope they will work with you and maybe Billy so y'all can learn how it's done. I'd like to get into restoration work. I'd like to have you on my team, too."

"Sounds good to me. I'd better get back. I'll pull Billy and one other off and put them over here. That Benson boy has been aggravatin' me to put him on. If it's OK with you, I'll give him a try and that will make three here. I think he'll work out."

"Billy'll keep him busy. Go ahead."

He left and after wandering around a little, I left too. I met Hud for lunch at Burton's and we sat with Earl Ray. He said he was going to give Bennie one more week to work out his problems and then he'd have to hire someone else. He had planned to retire and sell the business to Bennie. We told him we hoped it would all work out and, on impulse, I told him if he decided to sell, to give me first chance. He looked surprised but said he would if Bennie didn't come through.

I spent the afternoon catching up on bills, running errands for the business, and looking at a problem one of our home buyers was having with a water leak around the chimney. I called Tom and told him to get the roofer over to fix it. At about 4:30, I went home. I showered and put on some shorts and was reading the paper when Maggie and Eloise arrived. I was sent to the van to get a load and take it upstairs to the spare bedroom. When I got there and walked in, there was Eloise in the buff getting out packages of new panties and bras. Such was my ingrained habit of being shocked at nudity that I found myself blushing and turning my head aside. It was ridiculous but there it was.

Maggie was opening packages and said, "Sit down and relax, Jack. Eloise has some serious modeling for us. Wait till you see her new outfits."

Eloise was pulling on a pair of racy, high cut panties and then selected a lacy bra of the same color, a midnight blue.

She said, "It feels so strange to have clothes on again. I'm not sure I like it but the shopping sure is fun."

Eloise tried on nine or ten new outfits and looked smashing in every one.

Later, we introduced her to the kids and there was an instant rapport evident between them. Eloise was careful about asking questions that would label her a time traveler. That night we ordered pizza, watched some TV and just had an old-fashioned family night.

It turned out to be a quiet four days. Deena came by and told us that we would be left alone for a few days. She didn't know how many because this was the earlier Deena. She did tell us there was little we could do at present to help the war on Wham, which we were still losing. She couldn't find Bennie, so that became her focus for the next several days.

We spent a lot of time with Eloise trying to adjust her to 2015. She did well. Maggie's powers returned to full speed and even seemed to be accelerating. We needed to see Bishop soon.

On Monday, September 8, one day before we rejoined ourselves in the present, three significant events occurred. First, Bob Morton called. He wanted to bring the plans and meet at the old house at 3:00. I agreed and called Jenny to tell her and get her to call Hud. Second, Maggie talked to Deena who called from Africa saying she was taking another vacation day today and wanted to spend the night with us. Maggie had talked about it with Jenny and Hud and they were OK with it. So Maggie told her to come to the hot tub room at 9:00. Finally, while fixing lunch Maggie dropped the coffeepot. Before it hit the floor, something grabbed it and placed it back on the counter.

There was a pretty long, silent pause. Maggie finally said, "Jack, come help me in the garage for a minute."

I agreed and we went out.

"Jack, did you stop that coffeepot from falling?"

"I wish. You know I can't do that."

"Listen, Jack. I didn't either."

"What do you mean? You think I did?"

"No, I think Eloise did."

I staggered and grabbed my head and said, "Oh, no. Three wacky females with the power to control me and read my thoughts is enough. I just can't stand another one. I'm not so young anymore. All this stress is taking its toll. I found six more gray hairs this morning."

Maggie laughed and said, "Quit whining. All you've thought about for the last 3 days is how and when you could get her into the sack."

"That's not true. Besides you promised not to read my thoughts unless I agreed."

"I've kept my promise. That observation comes from years of reading you without reading your thoughts. Request permission to read your thoughts."

"Permission denied," I said grinning.

"I knew it. Go ahead. She is a lovely person."

"If I do ever decide to try, you'll be the first to know."

"Thanks, Jack. Now what do we do about the coffeepot incident? I don't think she even knew she did it."

"Let's take her to Bishop tomorrow if we go up to Noah. Or if not, Deena can take her."

We went back and had lunch. Nothing more was said about the incident. I hoped nothing like that would happen around the children until we had time to explain more to them.

At three that afternoon, we met Bob Morton at our old house. There were five of us because we took Eloise along. We introduced her to Bob as a divorcee from Missouri just as we had planned. Bob had outdone himself, and we were really impressed, especially with the master bedrooms. Since they took about one half of the floor space on each side of the upstairs, they were huge, about 1100 square feet each including bath. In addition, we had a room about 25' by 25' feet partitioned off at the head of the stairs to the back of the house.

Bob was explaining, "Now, the master bedroom is at the front and accesses the balcony. You can access the room by coming up the staircase and using the door off the walkway beside the stairs or go straight into the master bath by using the private elevator in the kitchen. The master baths have huge Jacuzzi tubs, double showers, two lavatories and a make-up table, toilets and bidets, skylights, and so on."

It would take two trips to Vegas for money. Oh well, I liked Vegas.

"I didn't recall you having any instructions about this space between the two master suites at the back. It could be partitioned into two storage spaces, or two sitting areas, or one large common sitting area, or something else."

I said, "We were actually thinking of an exercise or recreation common room but really haven't decided."

"That's fine. Let me know if you want us to finish it up for you. Now the other two bedrooms each have a small bath and a common set of stairs set between the study-studio room and the dining room. These bedrooms can also be accessed from the master bedroom by a door that opens onto the stairwell.

"If you all approve, I'll get an estimate from John Riley and two other firms that do good work. I've got John's bid on the exterior, and it can be adjusted to fit the amount of work you want your crew to do."

"Good. Let me keep a set of plans and I'll call you tomorrow. I'll also call John and discuss the details of who does what and then get him started."

After he left, we stayed around a while discussing the plans. Some minor changes were suggested and adopted.

Then Hud said, "Let's grab a plane to Vegas tomorrow morning for the money. We shouldn't commit to this unless we can show that we can afford it."

"Sounds good to me, but don't we need to go to Noah in the morning for more briefings?" Maggie asked.

"I forgot about that. I'll make some plane reservations for after lunch, and if we can't do it, then we'll cancel."

That decided, we went home.

The evening went by slowly. Hud called and said he had the plane tickets for Vegas and reservations at the Mirage for two nights. He and Jenny would come over at 7:00 tomorrow morning to go to Noah.

About 8:45, Maggie came down the stairs from checking the kids. She yawned and said, "I think I'll go to bed and read a while. I'm tired tonight."

"Good idea," I said. "Think I'll do the same if Eloise will excuse us."

Eloise said, "No problem. I'm tired, too."

"Don't forget we are going to Noah at 7:00 tomorrow morning," Maggie reminded her.

"I'll be ready."

Maggie and I went on back to the master bedroom. We showered and were sitting in the hot tub when Deena arrived, right on schedule. She showered and joined us.

"I'm nervous as a school girl," Deena said after we had soaked for a while. "It's been so long since I met anyone I really wanted to be with, I don't know how to act."

Maggie said, "Let's dry off and get on the bed."

I highly recommend sex with two ladies.

thirty-eight

At 7:00 the next morning, Tuesday, we went to Noah. Deena had left at 5:00 to prepare for our briefing, so Carmen took us up. We met Deena in the briefing room.

"The time lag is over," Deena said. "You've had a good rest and now our job is to find Bennie. He's the key. We think he may be in California, but can't be sure. One of my angels detected two elites in a lab in San Diego. This is the lab that we know is being set up to process the Mexican tchadbe when it matures. Usually two elites means that either Bennie or Drok is present. We know it's not Drok but of course he could have been replaced by a third one. So all we can do is try. I'm going in today and I want you four to be available to help with the interrogation if it turns out to be Bennie. I have a feeling he'll talk to us this time."

Hud said, "Can we go to Vegas and be available from there? We need to pick up the jackpot and get the taxes paid so we can use it on our new home."

"I don't see why not. I'll send you out there after lunch if you can make arrangements for the children."

We told her we had already done that. Hud quizzed her about using the plane to leave a paper trail of our trip.

"Why waste the time? I'll arrange for it to show that you came in on the 9:15 morning flight. And I'll drop you right at the Hertz lot. I can keep track of your location, so just enjoy until I have Bennie. I may have him before you leave, but if I don't get him by midnight tonight, I'll come to one of your rooms to report. Any questions?"

Maggie asked, "What about Eloise?"

"Let's go see."

We wandered down to Bishop's office and went in. He and Eloise were talking over coffee.

Bishop said, "Here's another one. Her potential is about the same as Jenny's. It's incredible that she spent all those years in detention and didn't realize that she had powers."

"What do you propose we do?" Deena asked.

"I'd like to keep her around for two or three days and work with her. How about it, Eloise?"

"I can stay until Friday. Friday night I have a date in Clarksboro."

All eyes turned on Eloise, and Maggie said, "Good for you. Who's the lucky man?"

"Bob Morton. He called me after we met at the old house."

"That's wonderful," Deena said. "If I'm not here, I'll have Carmen take you down Friday morning."

Deena took us back home to pack.

We talked about Eloise for a bit, all of us amazed that her "re-entry" was already so successful that she had a real date. Pretty soon, though, Hud and Jenny left for their house. Deena stayed on for a minute and said, "I had a wonderful time last night."

Maggie said, "We did too, Deena. I'd like to do it again sometime."

"Well, I've got to leave. I'll be back about 12:30, hopefully with good news about Bennie."

We busied around until Jenny and Hud came back for lunch. At 12:30, Deena arrived and said the elite at San Diego wasn't Bennie after all. Just a ruse. A few minutes later, we left for Vegas. Deena dropped us behind a little warehouse building on the Hertz lot and we moved cautiously around to the front. A shuttle pulled up and disgorged about 10 passengers. We eased in behind them and went on in. After a short wait in line, we secured the keys to our Lincoln and left.

The Mirage is on the Strip and really not that far from the airport. Hud had reserved adjoining doubles for us, reasoning that we wouldn't have rented the huge suite Jenny wanted on our current incomes. She accused him of being a stodgy old lawyer. We dropped the car with the valet, got our bags, checked in and went to our rooms. It was 10:30 Tuesday morning, local time.

We went for an early morning swim in the pool and had a late lunch. Then we went and played the slots for a couple of hours. Jenny, Hud and I lost about $200 each and Maggie was up nearly $700, as usual. It boggles the mind. Not exactly complaining, mind you. After dinner, we caught a cab to our target, the Golden Swan casino. They specialized in the old coin machines, which pleased me since I've always liked the sound of coins falling into the tray. Something comforting about that. We arrived about 8:30.

The casino was fairly well-packed for a weeknight, so we moved into the dollar slot area and managed to find seats close to each other. Tonight there was a progresso worth about 3.4 million lump sum. This was unusual because most jackpots of that size were on a 20 year payout schedule. Deena had arranged for one of the angels, a man named Terrence, to meet us there. He was able to manipulate a slot machine to achieve a jackpot through mind control, much like Eloise lifting the coffee pot except much more refined. He was standing at a bar near the dollar slot area. We signaled him and he nodded OK. We got some dollars and sat down at four of the Blazing Sevens machines.

It was exciting not knowing which one of us was going to win or when. We had played about half an hour and I had just borrowed some of Maggie's winnings for the third time when the sirens went off and I had the jackpot. It was me! I was as stunned as I would have been had it been real. People began to crowd around and the machine was shrieking out music and kicking out dollars. What a great sound! Eventually the machine ran out of coins just as a smooth, smiling casino representative oiled over with several young pretties in tow.

He congratulated me and asked me to wait while they got a photographer there.

After a series of stupid posed pictures and endless questions, we were taken to a casino office. There they weren't so friendly. I got the impression that they were sure that the jackpot wasn't supposed to hit until some date in the far distant future. They were suspicious but had nothing to go on. I told them that we wanted to split the jackpot between Hud and me based on an agreement we had made earlier. We agreed to meet the following morning at 10:00 to receive our checks and pay our taxes to an IRS representative. We would each net a little more than a million dollars.

So away we went with an elaborate but legal I.O.U. Hud made sure of that. Final line was, though, that we had no choice but to trust the casino. Oh, and I did have about $350 in actual coins that the machine had managed to spit out.

We finally ditched the last reporters and hucksters and got back to the Mirage. Hud had called and asked them to move us to their best suite. We got there about 11:45 and quickly settled in to wait for Deena, who was due at midnight.

She came on time and was all smiles. She said, "Is this the suite of the millionaire Warners and Raines?"

"If we live through the night," I said. "They weren't amused."

"I should think not. They had the thing fixed so it wouldn't hit until next year sometime. They'll have a long night rounding up the money, but they'll find it. They won't dare do more than have you all investigated but of course they won't find a thing."

"Any luck finding Bennie?" asked Maggie.

"No, but I'm trying a new approach. I let the two elites in San Diego go free and told them to tell Bennie we were in Las Vegas at the Mirage and wanted to talk to him. He knows I'll get him if he stays on Earth, so maybe he'll respond."

"Hold on a minute," Maggie said, "I've just picked up three elites entering the city. Wait. Yes. One of them's Bennie. No question."

"You're getting stronger and stronger, Maggie. I don't even have them yet."

"Me neither," said Jenny.

It took Bennie about 30 minutes to make his way up to our suite. He knocked. Hud opened the door, saw that he was alone and ushered him in. He waved Bennie to a vacant chair and asked him what he wanted to drink. He fixed two gin and tonics, gave one to Bennie and then sat down himself with the other one.

Deena said, "You showed good sense coming in like this. Why did you decide to do it?"

"I got tired of running from you and wanted to work out a deal."

"What sort of deal?"

"Let me give you some background first and then we'll see."

"Go ahead, Bennie. We're listening."

thirty-nine

"I am Karg, fourth in line for the leadership of my home world of Horvak. Horvak is out on the fringe of the universe, not too far from the devil's home world of Kosark, the system your charts call Mystery. His name is Balzerch. He comes from a gentle race of people who have a strong desire for isolation and privacy. My own race is somewhat the same.

"Balzerch is a deviant. Some time ago, he decided to leave his world, which astonished his leaders since that had never happened before. Of course, people left occasionally if they had business in our sector of the universe, but they always returned as quickly as they could. In any event, Balzerch finally got permission to emigrate, but was told not to do anything that would discredit his people. He floated around the universe for many years searching for the right deal until he met the Tarcans.

"It was these Tarcans who told him about Earth and the evolving human species that your God, Ruth, would be judging soon. She had created a Heaven on a planet near the Earth but had not decided what to do with those who didn't qualify. Balzerch, with the Tarcans' help, negotiated and purchased the next planet toward the sun from heaven. It was hotter and dryer but well suited to what he had in mind.

"You need to know that not only is Balzerch a deviant, he apparently is a mutant as well. He had tremendous latent mind powers, which he worked hard to develop. Maggie and Jenny have already felt that power. Ruth respects that even though She could, given enough effort and help, defeat him. You already know about how he established Hell and the tchadbe trade using free labor from Earth.

"Now, a brief sketch of your God. Ruth is one of a select few who control the many galaxies and solar systems in this universe. She happens to be one of the most powerful, with several hundred systems under Her rule. She has angels from each system working for Her, since it would be an impossibility to handle everything Herself. Deena is the leader of the Earth angels.

"Ruth reports to Her superior, who controls our universe. I don't know much about what happens at that level of activity. All I know is that our God reports to Xerma, the same second-tier God as does Ruth."

Bennie took a pull on his drink, thought for a moment, then continued.

"Now, Balzerch has become the major producer of tchadbe in the universe. He is not really condemned for this since tchadbe is legal in most places. His current difficulties stem from his introduction of tchadbe to the people of earth against their will. Nor has he lived up to his agreement with my home world with respect to his treatment of my people. These two complaints against him reached his home world at about the same time.

"At this point, Ruth didn't know his home world, so She put out an alert to the other Gods in this universe to try to find out what Balzerch was doing. Word of this inquiry eventually reached the authorities on his home world of Kosark. They were appalled and immediately opened an investigation.

"Secondly, my people had begun to investigate the Tarcans and Balzerch with respect to their treatment of the demons leased to them. My home world has a chronic labor surplus, especially since the long life procedures have proven to be effective. They adopted a contract procedure where a demon, either elite or worker, can be leased for long term employment on other worlds. The Tarcans were selected to negotiate the terms of each agreement within a given set of conditions, and to transport the demons to the employing world. It worked very well up to a point.

"Balzerch, in his greed, has violated the agreement repeatedly by working the demons more days per year and more hours per day than called for. He has also used physical abuse on some and forced sex on some of our female members. I was placed into the labor stream flowing to Hell as a special agent for my government to investigate the situation. I have been here many years and have managed to rise to the top of the demon hierarchy on Hell, so I have been able to observe the situation first hand. Many of your years ago, I generated a report confirming these abuses, and when my people read that report, they notified the government of Tarcan to get the situation corrected. As you know, bureaucracy always moves at a snail's pace so, of course, nothing has happened as yet. I was asked for an updated report recently, and I sent word to them that instead of improving, the situation was worsening. This prompted my government to not only make further protest to the Tarcans but to notify the government of Kosark as well.

"This brings us to the present. Because the Kosarkians are strong advocates of human rights, they were upset by the tchadbe trade and incensed by the labor abuses. They commissioned an investigative team to come to Hell to see firsthand what was happening with their errant citizen. That team, as you may know, is in the skies of Hell as we speak.

"The Kosarkians, despite all their good intentions, are somewhat naive. They believe they can simply show up and force Balzerch to mend his ways or force him to come home for punishment. They don't have a clue as to the extent to which his powers have grown. He is trying to appease them and get rid of them before they try anything that will force him to reveal his strength because he does not want an open confrontation with his homeworld. They do have a strong military and are not without allies. They have our God as well who has strong powers but, I must admit, is not up to the power of Balzerch. Still his preference is to pull the wool over their eyes and send them home with the promise that he will correct any minor abuses that they may uncover. He knows it will take years to send another team due to the slow workings of the bureaucracy, and by then he will have accomplished his objectives.

"This tchadbe thing on Earth was inspired on his part. And it's going to work beyond his wildest expectations. Ask Jack and Maggie about the power of the experience. It sickens me to have been a part of it, but I was given a role to play and had to perform whatever actions Balzerch dictated. Whenever I could do so without risking my mission, I have tried to soften the impact. I put Drok where I knew you could get him because he was a brilliant tactician and was making the plan work all too well for Balzerch.

"I personally burned seven of the labs with the tchadbe still in them. And I alerted you all to the seriousness of the problem by arranging the accidents so that they drew attention to me. Most of my people are decent, hard working people. They do, however, have to follow the orders of the one who has them under lease. If told to attack you, they will do it, as you already know.

" There's not much more to tell. I'm finally finished with my spy role on Hell. I can't return because he now suspects me and will kill me if I go back. I have gotten by all these years because I didn't have any intention of harming him. But now that I have met with you, he would sense my betrayal immediately. I have been instructed by my superior on Horvath to join forces with you to stop Balzerch. The demons on Earth have been placed under my control, but I can't change things too drastically without alerting him and causing him to take some action we might all regret. But somehow, we must act quickly to stop him. Then and only then will we be able to work on the tchadbe problem here on Earth."

Bennie leaned back, reached over and picked up his drink. It was empty so Hud and I got up and fixed another round for everyone including Deena who ordered a scotch on the rocks, first drink I ever saw her take. She took a healthy slug and launched into a coughing fit. She was embarrassed and everybody laughed at her. She was game, though, and took a tiny sip with much better results. If she stayed around us much longer she would wind up totally corrupted.

Deena said, "A remarkable story. I have a couple of questions. What are the chances of meeting with Balzerch's countrymen on the spaceship?"

"I don't know much about them, but I think they'd be interested."

"Also, how would you recommend we go about stopping him? You know him better than we do."

"I guess I do, but no one really truly knows him. What was in that injection you tried to give him?"

"A substance that creates permanent sexual impotence and a basic indifference to life in general." Deena then proceeded to explain the aborted plan to Bennie.

"That still seems like a good approach to me," replied Bennie. "Killing him would be next to impossible without the direct intervention of Ruth and Her support from other worlds. It would be very costly to Her."

Maggie said, "How do we get to him especially now that he is wary?"

Bennie thought a moment before replying. "I don't know. None of us can take it by ourselves. He could read any of us easily, and would know we had bad intentions toward him. I believe it may require an innocent like your Ella. Or it will require enough of our concentrated powers to hold him long enough to do the job. He could easily defeat you and I and Deena combined, so we need to have at least four, probably more, with strong powers."

"Don't be too sure," Deena said. "Maggie is much stronger than I am, and her power is growing every day. Jenny is approaching my level and Eloise, the aviatrix, is on a par with Jenny and me. The five of us might be able to hold him long enough for Hud and Jack to inject him."

"Maybe," Bennie said. "How long does it take for the injection to take effect?"

"About an hour. But we're not quite sure about reaction time in his race."

"We'll never hold him for an hour. He'll kill us all before it takes hold."

"I'll ask the lab if a powerful sedative can be included in the ampoule, one that could knock him out for an hour or two. That would solve that problem."

"All right. What should we do now?" Jenny asked.

"Let's see. Tomorrow is—no, today is Wednesday since it's already 2:00 in the morning. I want you four to stay here a couple more days to give them time to investigate you thoroughly, and then, when they find nothing, they'll chalk it up to machine malfunction and write it off. What do you want to do, Bennie?"

"This is going to sound silly, but I would like to go back to Clarksboro to my home and arrange to buy the realty agency from Earl Ray if he hasn't sold it yet. I'm going to ask Ruth for permission to stay on Earth and finish raising my–Bennie's–daughter. I may even marry Marie if she can handle the truth about me. I have kept in touch with her and my daughter and told them I would explain when I got back."

I said, "I told Earl Ray not to sell until he gave me a shot at the business, so I know it's still waiting. I thought there was a chance you might want it, and he was getting nervous about you being gone."

"Thanks, Jack."

Deena said, "You probably shouldn't use the Tarcan REGEN again. They might pull you up to the ship and deliver you to Balzerch. I'll take you home on my way to Noah. I'll report to Ruth. I'm sure She will want to talk to you, Bennie. I'll try to set it up for Thursday, OK?"

"Sounds good to me. This will be a tremendous burden off my mind."

Deena said to us, "Don't mess around with those casino types. If they send someone to bother you, fry them. Let's meet at Jack's house at noon on Friday. Eloise will be down and I'll send Carmen out here for you all about 8:45 local time. Bennie should be in Clarksboro, too. Any questions? Ready, Bennie?"

We all knew better than to ask a question when she was in a hurry. But no matter. We were getting used to it.

After Deena and Bennie left we talked a few minutes about the casino's potential reaction. We all had harm protector powers which functioned, so we really weren't too worried. We just didn't want to call any more attention to ourselves than we had to. We were all tired so we called it a night and went to bed.

The next morning was really a comedy routine. We had breakfast at the Mirage and took a cab to the Golden Swan casino, arriving about 9:30. With some time to kill, we got some dollars and began to feed the slots. Within five minutes, Maggie hit a four thousand dollar jackpot. An attendant came over and congratulated her and started making arrangements to pay her off. About then, Mr. Doman, the head manager from yesterday showed up with another attendant. He was steamed. He ordered us to follow him to his office for payment.

I said, "You seem upset. I think we'll just take our payment here. Isn't that the normal practice?"

He moved over close to me and said in a low voice, "You're asking for big trouble you son-of-a-bitch. I don't know what you all are up to, but we're going to find out. Count on it."

"You shouldn't get excited like this. It's been known to cause strokes. Or worse," Maggie warned.

He swung around to her and said, "You stay out——."

He grabbed his head and staggered backward, falling to the floor. He rolled around moaning and holding his head. Jenny knelt down beside him, looked up at the attendant and said, "Get a doctor quickly or call 911!"

"What a shame," said Hud. "And I was just beginning to warm up to him."

A small crowd was gathering by then, and a security team moved in to disburse it. A small man of about 50 moved in and said he was a doctor. He bent over the victim and about then, Maggie relaxed control. The manager's pain began to let up immediately. He struggled into a sitting position and asked the doctor, "What happened?"

The doctor shrugged his shoulders and said, "I don't know, but we'll have to run tests. Probably a small cerebral hemorrhage from the sound of your symptoms."

Maggie said, "He seems to be under a lot of stress. Probably needs a good vacation."

Doman gave her a look designed to kill. But the ambulance attendants arrived to save the day, buckled him up and carted him off.

By then it was after 10:00, so we told the attendant we would be in the main office waiting for our payoff there. A smiling receptionist greeted us, said we were expected, and ushered us right in. We were led into a small but very plush conference room done partially in red velvet. There were three people present. A tall man in a gray suit and red tie stood up and said, "Please be seated. I am Mark Strickland, Assistant Manager of the Golden Swan. Mr. Doman has become ill and can't be here."

Maggie said, "Yes, we were there when it happened. He seemed so stressed right before the attack. I hope he's OK."

"Yes, to be sure. Now, let me introduce Mr. Roberto Gonzales of our parent company and Mr. Holcomb of the IRS." Holcomb produced his IRS credentials, which Hud perused.

We all nodded to each other in greeting.

Mr. Strickland continued, "Let's dispense with the payoff so we can get Mr. Holcomb on his way. Here's a breakdown of the various payments. It's split evenly between the Warners and Raines as requested. The IRS amounts have already been taken out. Are there any questions? No? Then here are the checks. Two are for the IRS, one is for the Warners and one for the Raines. You need to leave, I believe, Mr. Holcomb?"

Mr. Holcomb put the checks in his brief case and left without having said one word.

After he left, Mr. Gonzales said, "Let's cut the crap, Mark. I don't know how you four did this, but we'll find out. And when we do, I can assure you that we'll take care of you."

Hud said, "That sounds like a threat. All we did was win a jackpot. I thought that's how it worked in Vegas. You all act like spoiled children."

Mr. Gonzales turned red and hissed, "Shut the fuck up. I'll do the talking. Now, like I said, we will——what the hell do you think you're doing?"

His question was addressed to Hud, who had taken a small recorder out of his pocket and was checking to be sure that it was running.

Hud said, "Just making sure I'm getting all this down."

Mr. Gonzales lunged across the table at Hud shouting, "Give me that, you hijo de puta!"

Hud pulled back. Mr. Gonzales missed his mark and sort of flopped on the table. Mark helped him get back in his chair.

After things calmed a little, Maggie said, "You need to be very careful, Mr. Gonzales. This stress you exhibit is very similar to that of that poor unfortunate Mr. Doman."

"Bullshit."

Hud said, "I'm an attorney, and if you persist in bothering us, I can assure you that we will sue. We came to your casino and won a jackpot. You all seem to be implying that the jackpot was fixed so that it couldn't be won and that we did something to change that. We didn't. But I'll bet the Nevada State Gaming Commission will be interested in my tapes from yesterday and today. How's that for bullshit?"

Mark took a more sedate tone. "Now, now. Let's all remain calm."

"Shut up, Mark," Mr. Gonzales ordered. "All right. We over-reacted. Three point four million is a lot of money. Of course the machine was honest. It's just that the odds were that it wouldn't hit until next year. We got upset when it hit so early. Take your winnings and enjoy them." He stood up and said, "I'd like to have those tapes if you don't mind. I'd like to review them."

Jenny walked around the table, motioned for Hud to turn the recorder off, and approached Gonzales. He turned to face her and she continued. "Now listen closely you mangy little fucker. I'm sick of you and your casino. We keep the tapes and if you bother us, this is just the beginning."

And she stepped back and kicked him right in the balls. He grabbed his crotch and slumped into a chair, moaning. Mark was undecided about whether to rub Mr.Gonzales' balls, attack Jenny, or stand and wring his hands. The latter won.

Mr.Gonzales, purple faced and gasping for air, managed to say, "Mark. Get them the fuck out of here."

Mark turned to us and said, "I think you should leave now."

And we did. In the outer office, the attendant had the four thou-sand dollar check ready for Maggie. Apparently Mark had not been informed about the jackpot from today, and as we left, was quizzing the attendant. We had a group of reporters waiting outside the office and so we stopped and held up the checks for pictures. Hud told them that there had been some confusion due to the attack suffered by the casino manager but that the assistant, Mr. Strickland, along with a representative of the parent company, a Mr. Gonzales, had carried on admirably. This would always be our favorite casino. About then, Mr. Gonzales appeared at the door to the office looking somewhat colorless.

Maggie said, "There's that nice Mr. Gonzales now. I'll bet he has a statement for you."

A big blonde female reporter shouted, "Let's get a group shot."

They put Maggie and Jenny on either side of Mr. Gonzales with Hud and I next to them. Maggie and Jenny had one arm around Mr.Gonzales and their checks held out in the other.

Jenny said in a low voice, "Isn't this cozy, Mr. G.? Smile."

He wasn't amused and mumbled that same word he used in the office, the one that sounded like 'poota'. I'll have to brush up on my Spanish.

After the pictures, we begged off and left.

The rest of the week was uneventful. We heard no more from the casino. According to the papers, Doman had a miraculous recovery. Maggie hit a $2000 jackpot at the MGM. We caught an excellent show at the Mirage. And finally, it was 8:45 Friday morning. We checked out on screen and Carmen came and took us home.

forty

It was nearly noon when we got there. Eloise and Bennie were sitting in the living room chatting as we arrived. A few minutes later, Deena arrived, looking radiant as usual.

"I see everyone is here so let me bring you up to date. First, Eloise had a great set of sessions with Bishop. And her powers are about at Jenny's level, as we expected. Next, Bennie had a debriefing session with Ruth, and She gave him permission to live on Earth as long as he desires, just so that he lives in such a way that he causes no harm to an Earth human. He will, of course, have our protection. Congratulations, Bennie."

Bennie was clearly pleased.

"Finally, the casino crowd. How did you make out with them?"

Hud said, "Jenny had to reason with one of them and another had what the doctor called a possible cerebral hemorrhage. Other than that, all went well. We didn't exactly part friends, but there shouldn't be any follow-up."

"Good. Now, on to the main problem. We have made contact with the Kosarkian ship and arranged a meeting with the lady who has remained on board. Since she is alone, we'll have to go to her ship. We can shield the REGEN from Balzerch and we warned her not to communicate any of this to the surface. That meeting is at 8:00

tonight and I'm going to take Jack, Hud, and Bennie. I'll get you all in the hot tub room at 7:00, OK?"

We all nodded agreement.

"The other two Kosarkians are on the surface and due up tomorrow for a rest and a report to the home planet. We don't have anyone in place who can give us a report on Balzerch. We tried to get a report from some of the elites through Bennie, but they have already been warned not to talk to him. I'm going to try to catch an elite today who has just come up from Hell and interrogate him or her.

"I met at length with Ruth, and She wants to wrap this up as soon as possible because the Wham situation on Earth is rapidly getting out of control. It has been about a month since Wham hit the streets, and there is already a significant increase in child neglect cases. In addition, hospitals are reporting immune system breakdowns and genital damage cases at record levels.

"We discussed our possible approach to Balzerch and have just about decided on a direct one. It seems unlikely, with the people we have left in place, that a scheme like the Ella-Julia one is possible. Ruth believes that the six of us—Carmen has agreed to come on board—the six of us with strong powers can hold him long enough to administer an injection, providing that we take him by surprise. For that we need the Kosarkians help. We want them to bring him up with their REGEN to their ship and keep him occupied for about two hours. We eight will go to Hell and sedate all of the elites, and then set up to take him the instant he reappears. We hold him while Jack and Hud inject him. We have been able to include a sedative that acts instantaneously and lasts four hours. That should cover all the contingencies. Any comments?"

Bennie said, "I'll go, but I still believe he's too strong for even six of us. You don't know him like I do. Especially when he's angry."

"You may be right," Deena admitted. "Analysis put the odds at 5-1 against us. But Ruth knows that. Here's the situation from Her standpoint. She knows that She will lose a lot of Her influence if She has to call in angels from other worlds to help stop just one being. You know that no one will believe his strength. But that would encourage 'devils' on some of Her other worlds to rebel, and many more lives would be lost. So She's really asking us to take the risk to preserve Her power. In other words, She needs to act as if She considers Balzerch just a minor annoyance, easily eliminated without Her intervention. It's not pretty, but there it is. If we fail, She will then be forced to handle him directly, so if we can stay alive for a few hours, we'll be rescued."

Eloise spoke for the first time. "I can assure you that if we fail, it won't be a fun few hours before we're rescued. But I want to try."

Bennie said, "One point. Balzerch has a system he uses when he goes away by REGEN. Prior to his return, an elite on this end receives a query from the devil to determine if everything is in order. The elite must send him a confirmation code. I just happen to know this code. I doubt that he's thought about changing it."

"We'll have to chance it. We probably won't have time to interrogate an elite to find out," Deena said. "I wonder what else we don't know that is critical."

No one said anything for a few minutes as we mulled over the fact that without that seemingly small bit of info from Bennie, we would have failed before we even started.

Finally, Jenny said, "How strong are Carmen's powers?"

I haven't told you much about Carmen. She was a native of Monterey, Mexico and died in a train wreck in 1910. In a relatively short time, she rose to the position of an Assistant Head Angel. Physically, she was short, about 5'3", and a trim 105 pounds. She had short black hair, dark eyes and unusually small breasts. She was outgoing and had a very pleasant personality. She was a little like Jenny, quick to anger and an advocate of direct action. Deena said, "She is below you and Eloise, but still respectable."

"What about Bishop?" I asked.

"He can read power levels in others and teach others, but his actual powers are similar to those of Jack and Hud," Deena said. "It pretty much comes down to the six of us."

"How close can Jack and I get to him as he materializes?" Hud asked.

"About 10 feet. And you must wait until the beam turns off or you will be injured. I'll watch that beam and scream 'go' when

I'm sure it is safe. We six can start our mind control a second or two before the beam quits. Any other questions? If not, we'll meet tonight here at midnight to set the time to go to Hell. It will depend on the Kosarkians. I'll pick you guys up at 7:00."

The rest of the day went by quickly. I checked in with Tom. They were making good progress at the old house. They had temporarily finished at Cedar Creek and had the whole crew moved over to our house site. I asked Tom about the structural damage and, other than that one corner, there was nothing else major either in the floor or roof systems. Tom said the beams were mostly heart pine and would be there forever. No need for replacement there. He had also seen John Riley and they had talked about how they could work together. He said Riley would have an estimate on the interior in a day or two.

I left there and just drove around a while. I was feeling uneasy since our briefing with Deena, but couldn't put my finger on just why. It was like we were missing something very important. Then I had it. When we had broken up our noon session, I moved over to say a word or two to Carmen. None of us had ever really talked to her. She was standing beside the TV looking at some books on a shelf.

"Do you like to read?" I said.

She turned and smiled. "Yes, I read a lot. I've about exhausted our library on Noah."

"You're welcome to borrow some of ours anytime."

"Thanks, Jack. I'll take—damn!" She exclaimed and slapped the back of her neck.

"What is it?"

"A bug or something landed in my hair. Take a look, would you please?"

Whatever it was had disappeared, but I dutifully examined the back of her head parting the hair in several spots to look carefully. All I saw was an old scar completely hidden from view by her thick dark hair.

"Don't see anything. Must have taken off."

She brushed the back of her head with her hand and said, "Thanks for checking, anyway."

About then Deena called her and they left. From that point on I had been uneasy. Now I knew why. Charity's machines didn't leave scars, but the devil's machines did. What did it mean? Maybe she had been on an earlier version of the machine here that didn't erase scars? Or maybe something else. I made a mental note to ask Deena at seven. I got home about five to find Maggie in the kitchen cooking.

"I'll have something ready about six so you can eat before you have to go."

"Good. Listen. I've been thinking about Carmen."

"Are you never satisfied? I saw you over there groping her after the meeting."

"I wasn't groping her. I was looking for a bug she said flew into her hair. Besides, since you like to sleep with angels, I figured we'd have her in bed soon."

"Not that slut. You can if you want to, but not me. She's strange."

"You may be right. She may be even stranger than you suspect. When I was looking through her hair I found an old scar on her scalp."

"So what? Lots of people have—Oh, yeah, I see what you mean. Charity would never have left that. That's very interesting. What should we do?"

"I'm going to tell Deena tonight and let her deal with it. It could be perfectly innocent, but maybe not, too."

About 6:30, Bob Morton came for Eloise. He looked natty in a dark blue blazer with a pair of tan pants and an open-necked blue and white seersucker shirt. I let him in and sat him on the couch. I felt like giving him the standard fatherly talk about how to treat the daughter, but decided against it.

"How 'bout a drink, Bob?"

"No thanks. Nice house you have here."

"We've enjoyed it, but we're sure looking forward to country living."

"How's the renovation going? I haven't talked to John Riley for a while."

"We're well under way with the rough stuff. The structural parts are basically sound so we're cleaning up the porch and balcony mess, removing all that damaged exterior molding, and taking out some interior petitions so we can rough-in the new ones. John will have his estimate on the interior soon."

"Sounds good. I want to see it before you move in."

"Sure. Let me know when you want to ride out there."

Eloise appeared at the head of the stairs and undulated down. She really looked smashing in a deep red dress with white lace peeping out of the top of the low-cut neckline. Maggie had sent her to the hairdresser. He had pulled her hair into a bun at the back, which looked great on her. After they left, Hud and Bennie arrived and we went to the hot tub room to meet Deena. Maggie came along. Deena arrived about when we got there.

She asked, "Everyone ready?"

"Can we talk for a few minutes and still be on time?"

"Of course, Jack. We have plenty of time. What is it?"

I proceeded to reveal what I had seen on Carmen's scalp and why I was suspicious.

"Oh, shit! So she's the leak. And I never suspected. Damn!"

Bennie said, "She's probably a demon. It's always been rumored that Balzerch had a spy placed at a high level in Heaven."

"It must be her," Deena said. "Now that I think about it a little, it all seems to fit. Fortunately, we've been together all afternoon and I just left her to get a briefing from Analysis. She's had no chance yet to send our plan to Balzerch. We must go immediately and take her before she leaves Analysis. Quickly now. Maggie. Come with us. Time won't pass for you."

An instant later we were on Noah We made a beeline for Analysis. Carmen had just walked out of the Analysis office door when we spotted her. Deena called her name and asked her to wait for us.

"Don't you all have to go to the Kosarkian ship?"

"Carmen, turn around. I want to look at your scalp."

"Look at my scalp? What is this?"

"I want to see if you have a scar on it."

"Of course I have a scar. I had a scalp wound in the train wreck. That's what killed me."

"Our machines have always repaired all scars. Who are you?"

In an instant, Carmen had turned the power on Deena, who staggered and almost fell. Maggie looked toward Carmen and fried her, putting her on the deck moaning and shaking.

Deena had recovered and was once again in charge. She had really been caught off guard.

"She's obviously not going to talk to us, so I'm going to send her directly to Ruth. We should have a report before our midnight meeting. I suggest we go ahead and meet with the Kosarkians under the assumption that Carmen didn't have an opportunity to make contact with Balzerch. If that proves false, we will have to regroup. I'll run into Analysis and check on her activities after I left her."

She was gone for several minutes and then reappeared.

"They said that she hadn't done anything that could have involved sending a message to Hell, so maybe we're all right."

"We'd better go," I said.

"Maggie," Deena said. "Take Carmen to Bishop. Fill him in on what has happened, and tell him to send her directly to God and get me a report by midnight Then Bishop can take you home or you can wait until the rest of us get back."

"Consider it done."

Maggie got Carmen up and led her on down to Bishop's offices. We made our way to the REGEN room. It was just about 8:00 when we beamed to the Kosarkian ship. We arrived in a large, pleasantly lit room with several pieces of furniture in it. Seated in a large chair was the Kosarkian lady, Mesarch.

"Welcome to my ship. Please be seated."

We moved to seat ourselves and the lights went up a little. Mesarch stood and asked if we wanted refreshments. We settled on coffee. As she poured, I couldn't help staring at her. She was big, probably 6'2" and about 180 pounds. Like Balzerch, her body was reddish and completely hairless. She had large breasts and her waist was narrow in proportion to her overall size. Her facial features were more refined than his were and the teeth barely protruded at all. She was nude, of course, and because she was hairless her gender was not in doubt. In human terms, I would put her age at about 40, but that could be way off. She finished serving the coffee and sat again.

"I understand you wish to confer about Balzerch."

Deena said, "Let me tell you what has been going on for the last several months."

And Deena proceeded to relate a very concise but complete summary of what had taken place. Mesarch said nothing as she listened, but I could tell from her change of posture that this was very distressing to her. At the end, she gave a little sigh and said, "He's certainly been a busy little fellow. We had no idea."

"I'm sorry."

"No, we want the truth. You must be mistaken about his powers, however. We all have some powers. Most of us are about the level of an elite demon. How could he be so strong?"

"There's no mistake," Bennie said. "One on one, he could defeat Ruth, although it would take considerable effort. He was hoping to send you back to your home planet without revealing his strength to you."

Mesarch stood and paced a moment and said, "There's no question. He must be stopped and returned to Kosark for trial. But if what you say about his strength and his powers is true, we can hardly be expected to stop him. What do you propose?"

"You are the leader, are you not?"

"Yes, I lead."

"Good. We have a plan in mind."

"What do you propose?"

Deena proceeded to outline our plan. She wrapped up by saying, "Now let's discuss the details."

"Let me interrupt for a moment," Mesarch said. "Is there no antidote for the substance you plan to give him? As you probably know, we Kosarkians are reluctant to alter any being permanently regardless of the crime until they have been tried. Then we may take any action up to and including the death penalty."

"We have an antidote", said Deena, "but we are the only ones who have it. Since we developed the drug, it is extremely unlikely that anyone else will discover it. We would, however, make it available to you before his trial or whenever you wanted it."

"Good. Proceed with the specifics."

"We need your help on the setup. We must get him out of Hell for a couple of hours. We know that your team is due up tomorrow for a rest and for some time to digest what they have seen. On Sunday, we would like for you all to call him to the ship using your REGEN and stall him for two hours. Then send him back. We will be waiting and hopefully will have enough power among ourselves to hold and inject him. We lost one of our members tonight, so it will be close.

"To make it work, you will have to do some play-acting, Mesarch, and be absent while he is here. If you're here, he will sense from you the upcoming harm and will take some sort of counteraction. So we will take you to Noah's Ark for a short visit. You will also have to be very routine in instructing your team. You can read and discuss their report with them on Saturday and come up with several things that need clarification and suggest they call Balzerch to the ship on a courtesy visit while you are gone. Or some other plan might occur to you. In any event, your team must not suspect foul play or Balzerch will sense it immediately. What do you think?"

"There is no problem on this end," said Mesarch. "My team will do exactly what I tell them to do. I can tell them without arousing their suspicions. I just want to make one small change."

"Of course. What is it?"

"Instead of going to Noah's Ark to wait, I will accompany you to Hell and be that missing team member. I am as strong as your demon, Bennie."

Bennie gave a start and said, "How do you know I'm a demon."

"I've worked with demons for many years. You project an aura which differs slightly from these humans."

Deena said, "Ma'am, we really don't expect you to expose yourself to danger for us. This mission has only a one-in-five chance of success. If we fail, he will exact a high price from us, if you know what I mean."

"I can imagine. But child, don't worry about me. What you don't know is that we on this ship are a military team and I have seen many things in my years of service. I was instructed that we should pose as a diplomatic mission but to take action if I found the rumors about Balzerch to be true. Helping you is my definition of taking action."

"In that case, we would be honored to have you on our team."

We stayed for another hour talking and feeling each other out. Her race was remarkably like us in many ways and strikingly different in others. She showed us some short videos of Kosark and talked about their culture. Their race was several thousand years older than ours and had developed into a mature society where crime was practically non-existent.

They had adopted the long-life drugs and suffered the usual period of too rapid a growth in population that most systems experienced. They had solved this with a strict transformation of another planet in their solar system. Their original planet was earth-like and about the same size. It was the original Kosark. Kosark II was the transformed planet. It was the size of our Jupiter with a Mars-like climate. They had plenty of room to expand when Kosark II was finished.

They had gone through a phase of violence and war in their developmental stages. The settlement of Kosark II must have been much like the development of our West minus the Indians. They had outgrown the violence and had evolved into a gentle race where there was little crime of any kind. They also adopted an isolationist policy, which explains why so little was known about them.

The videos showed a way of life somewhat similar to ours. There were farms and cities. They used a vehicle that could be loosely called an auto although it also resembled an army tank. They had developed REGEN to the point that most inhabitants with sufficient income in the cities had given up cars and used the public REGENways. In rural areas it was still too expensive for the average person. Their homes were single family dwellings but their architecture was wildly different from ours. Straight lines seemed to be avoided at all costs. Symmetry wasn't popular, either.

Mesarch seemed to be typical although she was somewhat smaller than the average Kosarkian female. The men averaged about seven feet tall and weighed about 350 pounds.

Almost all work was done from the home using computers. So was most shopping. The only real reason to leave home was to recreate. We spent the next hour learning more about the people and their customs. About 10:00, Deena called a halt and we said our good-byes and left for Noah.

Deena took us down to our house, including Maggie, who had waited behind on Noah to help Bishop with Carmen. Deena promised to be back by midnight with the report. Since it was still only 7:00 at home, we had five hours to kill. Bennie asked Hud to go to his house and look at the papers on the buyout of Earl Ray's agency. I sat down to pay some bills.

forty-one

About 11:30, Eloise and Bob returned. I offered him a drink but he said he'd have to take a rain check and left.

"How did it go?"

"Very well. He's a marvelous man. I like him."

Maggie walked in from the kitchen doorway where she had been standing and said facetiously, "Did he ask you to marry him?"

Eloise blushed and said, "Not yet, but soon."

I asked, "Where did you eat dinner?"

"A little place called Heather's on 57th Street. It was really good."

"Among the top five in Savannah. We've been there several times."

"Well, girls, it's pushing midnight," I said. "Time for our visitors."

The doorbell rang and Hud and Jenny were there. A few minutes later, Deena arrived.

"I have the preliminary report on Carmen. She is a demon and her real name is Hilb. Hilb was at the train wreck as a bystander and when she went in to help, she saw Carmen. Carmen was the daughter of the vice-president of Mexico and Hilb knew that. Carmen was still alive when Hilb got to her, so her original thought was to take her place as the Mexican's daughter.

295

"She took Carmen away from the scene and headed directly to the hospital. But Carmen died along the way so Hilb disposed of her body. Then it occurred to her that she might be able to penetrate Heaven. Of course, Carmen's soul went to processing for a new body and a trip to heaven. Hilb had detected that Carmen had latent powers prior to her death and assumed she would immediately be selected for angel training. Hilb took her place during a routine training exercise on Earth. Interestingly enough, the scar that had exposed her at the cocktail was a scar on her own head which somehow had gotten transferred to her Carmen replica. She should have been detected much earlier, but she wasn't. We've got some angels with some explaining to do.

"Anyway, Carmen was interrogated by Her and we seem to be OK in terms of our plans. She hasn't reported to Balzerch for two days. To do that, she has to use a Noah link to Hell, and getting undisturbed access is difficult at best. She doesn't get many opportunities. So we're covered there. But she's of no help on Balzerch's plans or actions because she rarely receives a message from him. Her reports have been valuable to him though. One of her reports to him explains why there were demons waiting the first time you landed in Hell. She sent them the plans for shielding a REGEN. And she made contact with the Tarcans to warn him when you entered his palace. They reached him at the Kosarkian ship and he immediately went down by REGEN. Who knows what else."

Maggie asked, "What happened to the angel, the real Carmen?"

"Balzerch arranged for the Tarcans to take her to their homeworld and imprison her. She's probably still there but we'll get her soon. The Tarcan's world is about halfway between here and Kosark. They act as agents in nearly any transaction you can visualize and between any number of parties. They are a really curious race. They have no real powers, far fewer even than Jack and Hud. They tend to be fairly honest, but will bend a rule or law for a quick profit. We think Balzerch must have something on them that would explain their willingness to help him in things like kidnapping Carmen, because they normally wouldn't do that type of thing."

Jenny asked, "What do they look like, just in case we run into them?"

"They are much like you all except considerably smaller. A four-foot Tarcan would be a large person. They are personable and always willing to help, for a fee of course. Because of their size, they make very desirable space travelers since they eat less, take less oxygen and so on. Nearly all their travel and freight transfers go by space-ship as REGEN is just too expensive for most trade goods, so Tarcan ships are much in demand.

"That fills you in on some details, but we need to get back to our immediate plans. I've conferred with Ruth and we're in agreement on the procedures for the trip to Hell. We'll leave here as soon as we see that Balzerch has been sent up to the ship. Mesarch will already be there waiting for us on Noah. We expect all this to happen about 2:00 in the afternoon on Sunday. Tomorrow. We'll have approximately two hours to immobilize the nine or ten elites who will be at or near the palace. We need to get the two on communications and REGEN first. Maggie and I will take those. The rest of you will take them as you encounter them. You will give them an injection which will sedate them for about eight hours."

Hud and I were to stay out of the way except for helping with the ordinary demons. We would have to use the power of suggestion on the humans and worker demons to send them to the beach or someplace else out of the way. Bennie said he understood the operating procedures to receive a REGEN and knew the code, so that would be his job.

Finishing up, Deena said, "I will pick you at 12 noon, Sunday. Any suggestions? Any questions?"

"Time will not pass for us, as usual, right?" asked Hud.

"Right. For all of you."

She left with a promise to update us if anything else new came up before noon Sunday.

Everybody left to get some sleep.

Early the same morning, Bob Morton called and said he had just spoken to John Riley. Apparently, there was some confusion about the drawings they had done. He wanted me to meet him at the old house to straighten out the problem. We agreed on 1:30.

Maggie overheard, and proposed we have a picnic out there. About then, Jenny called and Maggie got her on board. Eloise, learning that Bob would be around, signed on. Bennie stopped by with his daughter, and Maggie asked them to join us and told him to invite Marie. For some reason, I was elected to take a picnic list and go to the Piggly Wiggly. That set me back $185. For a picnic! I don't know why I worry about it now that we are financially secure, but actually spending money still causes me pangs of economic distress. Maggie had also said everyone was bringing something, so we would have enough for lunch for about a week. Overkill as usual. I called Bob Morton back and told him to arrive at 1:00 if he wanted to eat with us. He did.

At 12:30, we loaded up kids, dogs, food, tables, chairs, and so on and headed out. When we arrived, we drove around to the garage and set up in the back yard under a massive live oak tree where we had found a couple of round stone tables. The others soon arrived, and by the time we laid out all the food they had brought, we really had a feast. I ate way too much and would probably suffer half the afternoon. The kids went off to the river and the others wanted to tour the house. I met with Bob for a few minutes and all he wanted to do was change the stairwells up to the two bedrooms on the ends. That didn't prove to be a problem so we joined the tour. It was a fun afternoon, and about 4:00, we had a snack and some more dessert, then everyone loaded up and went home. No word from Deena. No news is good news, they say.

Sunday morning was rainy and a little chilly for mid-September. The newspaper was in a shrub beside the door, unbagged as usual in the rain. It was really wet and I considered calling the office to complain, but instead, I laid it out to dry. We had brunch about 10:00. I ate a good bit because I didn't want to eat again before we went into action. I admit to being a little more worried about this trip than the others seemed to be, I suppose because we were going to tackle Balzerch directly. And we really didn't know whether or not we could win. How would the kids feel if Maggie and I came back and had aged 20 years as captives of Balzerch?

Just before noon, we visited the kids' rooms and told them we were going to nap a while. Laurie kind of smiled and said for us to "sleep well." Sometimes I think that child has an overactive imagination.

The others arrived quietly and soon we were in the hot tub room, all peeled down and ready to go. Deena arrived and took us to Noah. She sent us to the briefing room and asked us to wait. A few minutes later, she and Mesarch arrived. Deena went over the plans again and asked Mesarch if all was in order.

"All went according to our plan. Better, in fact. One of my team actually suggested late yesterday that we bring Balzerch up to the ship to explain several points we had discussed, and to show him videos relating to the facts. I agreed and suggested 2:00 this afternoon. I told them I was coming here at noon and expected to be back but to just carry on if I was late. I said keep him until 4:00 and then if I'm not back, tell him I will come down tomorrow to finalize any details. The 2:00 beam-up has been confirmed by Balzerch."

"Excellent. Here are the packs with your ampoules for the elites and for Balzerch. Just so there's no confusion, the red ones are for Balzerch. The stick-on packs work well and absolutely won't come off until swabbed with a fluid at the lab. I always put mine on the outside of my right thigh. It really doesn't protrude much and is designed not to catch on things. Any questions?"

We were loose for a while, so we just wandered around trying to keep the tension down. Finally, it was time and we all gathered in the REGEN room. There was a scan waiting for Balzerch to REGEN up to the ship. Right at 2:00, the attendant said that a REGEN had just gone to the Kosarkian ship. A scan of the ship showed three life forms of the same type. He was there.

We all touched Deena and were in the palace on Hell.

forty-two

We landed in a central courtyard just inside the main entrance. Deena and Maggie went off to communications and REGEN to secure them. Everyone else disbursed. Hud and I scouted around and found a group of humans in a dining room, mostly kitchen help and servers. They were agitated and seemed frightened by all the activity going on around them. We "suggested" them to the beach and moved into the kitchen where we found two demons. After a short struggle, we sent them to the beach to join the others. The palace was a bee-hive of activity but after an hour we had emptied it and the demon and human barracks as well. Maggie and Deena jumped to the vacation side and took out the four elites over there. They disabled the boat and left the rest alone. If anybody wanted to swim the 20 miles in the next hour, let them come.

By 3:10, we were all in the main REGEN area, a converted recreation room as big as a gym. The staging area was in the far right hand corner. It was a huge platform with large double doors to the outside to handle freight or whatever. There was a circle with a diameter of about 15 feet in the center where the people-traffic arrived and departed. On the back wall, to the left of the staging area, was a raised platform with a huge chair on it, apparently used by Balzerch to receive dignitaries. We discussed tactics for a while and positions were established. Generally, the ones with powers were spread around the staging area on the two open sides. Bennie was along the right hand wall at the controls. Hud and I were to be on adjacent walls about five feet from the corner. The theory was that Balzerch would be so busy he might overlook Hud and me. At 3:45, we declared ourselves ready.

I was already tense and of course he was late. By 4:15, the tension in the room was palpable. I saw Mesarch begin to do toe touching exercises and some of the others were walking in little circles shaking their hands and twisting their heads to relieve the neck and shoulder muscles. I gave Hud a grin and he said, "I'd rather be in Vegas."

"Not me. I love this sort of work."

Just then Bennie got the signal and I saw him send back the code. It worked. Bennie gave two thumbs up. There was a metallic whine, and then we saw Balzerch begin to emerge. This was the real deal.

A heartbeat later Deena screamed, "Go!"

I went. Two steps later I was frozen. I was standing where I could see everything and I first saw Hud frozen just like I was. Then, I saw Balzerch go to his knees, his face contorted with effort. Looking past him, I could see that Jenny and Mesarch were down and out. Bennie and Eloise were on the floor but their heads were still up. Maggie and Deena were on knees and were struggling. Time passed as if it had been reduced to slow motion. Eloise went out next followed by Bennie. Deena went down, followed by Maggie. Just like that we were out of guns.

Balzerch rose slowly shaking his head from side to side.

He looked at Hud standing off to his left and walked over and said, "Well, now. It's the wise ass who tried to give me 'rat poison'." He gave Hud a vicious kick in the balls and Hud dropped like he had been felled by an ax.

He turned and gave me a smile and said, "I'll save yours for later."

He turned again and walked over to Bennie and said, "My favorite little traitor."

He then kicked him several times and left him wriggling and groaning on the floor. By then, all of the others except Maggie were conscious again but frozen in place. Most of their powers were fried, eliminating them temporarily from any action. He looked at the line-up of ladies like a football player looks at an all-you-can-eat buffet.

"What have we here?" he asked himself. "A lovely array if I have ever seen one."

He moved past Bennie, gave him another kick, and turned off the REGEN. Then he moved out to the staging area again and came upon Mesarch first.

He bent over her and said, "Well, well. Even my own have turned on me. I can take it, though." He put his big hand on her crotch and started squeezing and stroking her. She tried without luck to move enough to free herself and gave a voiceless scream. "We'll have such fun together over the years ahead. It will be nice to have one of my own."

Next in line was Eloise. Apparently he had had enough of her because he passed on to Deena. He bent down and did the same to her as he had to Mesarch and with about the same reaction from Deena.

He was saying, "I haven't had an angel since that Carmen we sent off some years ago."

He moved on to Jenny. "I missed you on your previous trip by just an instant. I'm glad you came back. I like my women small and lively."

He put his hand on her as well and relaxed his control a little bit so she could speak.

Predictably, Jenny screamed, "You miserable bastard! You get your fucking hands off of me!"

He gave her a couple more strokes and squeezes and said, "That's the way. Struggling increases the pleasure."

He stood up and was obviously aroused. To say he was hung like a horse was an understatement. He bent back down and grabbed Jenny's arms and dragged her up on the staging area toward me. He stopped and stood for a moment looking at her and listening to her calling him vile names and telling him how she was going to rip his balls off. Then he kneeled down, relaxed control a little bit so Jenny could resist, and moved to enter her. I saw Hud make a determined

303

effort to move and I did the same. No go. Balzerch pushed and Jenny let out a loud agonized scream.

Then I saw Maggie rise to her knees. Her face was a mask of rage.

She said loudly and clearly, "Get off of her you son-of-a-bitch!"

He lunged back and focused on her. Maggie's strength must have increased enormously for she had him temporarily stopped. Then he refocused and began to relentlessly regain control. About then, near the chair on the raised platform off to my right, a bright light appeared and Ruth emerged. She joined Maggie and soon Balzerch went down, releasing us from his control. I had him injected in an instant. Hud was up and, seeing that I had made the injection, limped over to Jenny. She was crying. He took her in his arms. I made a beeline for Maggie and saw that she was dazed, but all right. Deena got up and staggered over to Bennie, who proved to be OK except for possible cracked ribs and a pair of very bruised balls. All this in the space of just a few seconds.

After her initial moves, Ruth just stood there through all the action and watched. I saw that She was as old as Mrs. Angelo. Her hair was white and She had wrinkles on wrinkles. I reminded myself of how Mrs. Angelo turned into Deena, but somehow this was God.

I looked over and saw Mesarch and Eloise getting up. Deena shifted to them and made sure they were OK. The best thing I saw was the devil sleeping peacefully on the staging pad. I was walking over toward him when I felt a whoosh of air go past me. It was Jenny. She bent over and grabbed his balls and said, "I told you, you son-of-a-bitch," and she began to tug.

Hud limped up and we moved over and each grabbed an arm. We managed to break her loose before she actually pulled them off but he was going to hang much lower in the future. As we dragged her away, she was yelling, "I told that bastard!" She managed to give him one solid kick as we pulled her away. A good hangover would be a pleasure compared to what he was going to wake up with.

We sat Jenny down. I looked over toward Ruth and saw that She was getting ready to speak. We hushed Jenny and turned to listen.

"I am pleased with the heroic and selfless effort made by all of you. Let's try to sort this out. Mesarch. Do your people want him?"

"Yes, your highness."

"Please call me Ruth. I'm not royalty. Do you want to take the antidote with you or have me send it only if you need it?"

"I'd like to wait."

"Fine. Call your ship and arrange to be picked up. Please tell Balzerch there's nothing for him here, and if he ever comes back, I'll kill him and destroy his soul. He has untold amounts of money stashed on Tarcan. He can and must retire."

"Yes, yo—-Ruth."

She called her ship on the REGEN communicator and said, "Pick up two."

A voice came back and said, "Right. Five minutes. Mark on the 10 count. Nine, Eight."

She went over and touched Balzerch and the count went on, "Two, One, Mark. Good. Pick up in five minutes."

She walked over and hugged each of us. She whispered something to Jenny that brought a smile to Jenny's face. Then it was time. Mesarch and Balzerch faded out.

Ruth had seated Herself in the big chair and now began to speak again.

"I want all of you to go to Noah for repairs and a little rest. Then, Bennie, you come back to Hell as temporary administrator for one month. Remember, that was part of our deal."

"I remember."

"Good. I will hold time for you, Marie, and your daughter. But I want you to live the month on Earth while catching up in time in Hawaii or somewhere. I don't want you around the Warners and Raines for that month. It's too easy to let something that is going to happen slip out and foul everything up."

"We need a vacation, but I'm broke."

"Deena's not. You can have all you need for the rest of your life. Just ask."

"Sounds good to me. Thanks."

"You're welcome, Bennie. I want Jack and Maggie and Hud and Jenny to meet with me in Heaven on Friday, the 19th at noon. Deena will get you all to Noah and bring you to Heaven. Thank you again."

She stood and faded away in bright light.

Nobody said anything for several minutes and then Deena said, "Let's go up and see Charity."

It was 6:15, exactly two hours since Balzerch had arrived.

forty-three

Charity wanted to treat everyone but me. She took Bennie and Jenny first for two hours. Bennie's ribs were only cracked but he was in obvious pain. Jenny was only slightly damaged physically but was still without her powers. The rest of us went to dinner while they were in the chambers.

We used the food machine in the recreation room.

While we were eating, Maggie said to Hud, "Don't worry. Jenny is going to be fine. She's a tough bird."

"I know. It's a shame any of you ever have to go through ordeals like that."

I asked, "Does it strike anyone else as strange that Ruth didn't arrive until She did? Why didn't She come when Balzerch did?"

"That's a damned good question, Jack," Hud said. "I believe I'll put that one to Deena."

We chatted and drank coffee until it was about 8:30, when Bennie showed up. He said Jenny needed to stay in the chamber for 15 minutes more. Eloise and Maggie were to go at 8:45, then Hud was due at 9:45.

Deena breezed in and said, "It will still be noon Sunday when you get home. Do you want to go after Hud is through or sleep here and go early tomorrow?"

We tossed it around and opted to go tonight. After all, we had told the kids we were going to take a nap.

We invited Eloise to come back with us to our guest room while she decided whether or not to settle in Clarksboro. She accepted.

At 10:15 we went home and sent Hud and Jenny on their way. Bennie had elected to go on to Hell and get started on his month. He would still get home at noon today after his month. Eloise headed to the guest room for some sleep and Maggie and I went to bed. About 3:00, I woke up and heard Maggie in the shower. After a while, she came out toweling herself.

"Oh, you're awake. Good. I've been thinking. Ruth's arrival time was actually for my benefit."

"I know."

"What do you mean you know?"

"I just know. It was timed so that you would be forced to expand your powers by the crisis with Jenny or whomever Balzerch happened to select for the honor of his company. She knew you all couldn't defeat him without Her. Tough on Jenny. Looks like God doesn't subscribe to the 'don't harm others' rules She requires of us."

"You're pretty smart for a husband. That's what I was thinking, too."

"She pulled the same trick at the chicken farm with Elspeth and Drok. To save the situation, you were forced to use powers you didn't know you had. Or maybe it wasn't set up and just happened that way. But Ruth knew that sooner or later a situation would arise which would trigger your powers. I'm sure She thought it would happen on the first trip to Hell, but in spite of everything, we managed to get by OK without powers."

"I think it almost did work when Hud and I were captured. I remember thinking I would not allow them to rape me or abuse Hud. I didn't know how, but I knew I could do it. But as it turned out, they treated us pretty well."

"Have all of your powers increased?"

"Jack, you just wouldn't believe it. It's actually scary. After Charity's chamber fixed the physical damage, they have been increasing more rapidly than I can keep up with. It's only three. Let's run out to the house and I'll show you."

We told the kids that we would be out of the house a couple of hours and would bring home Chinese for dinner. We also told them that Eloise was sleeping in the guest room if they needed anything. We got into the Lincoln and cruised out to the house. We got out and walked around a minute and then Maggie said, "Didn't I hear you say that big tree over there had to come out?"

She was referring to a large old live oak tree that was nearly dead. We planned for the pool area to be over there. The trunk diameter at the base was about 4 feet.

"Yeah, it sure does and it's going to be tricky. It leans right toward the house and will land on it if they don't fell it properly."

"Which way do you want it to fall?"

"That way," I said, indicating the path toward the river.

I turned back, heard a grinding, crunching sound, and saw the big tree fall right in the river path. I was speechless.

Maggie grinned and said, "How's that? Told you I was stronger!"

"What else can you do?"

"I really don't know. I have no real feel for the future except the murky stuff I always get. I feel certain I can teleport more than the standard 20 or so miles. I can take a mind apart and read present and past thoughts. I tried it on one of the Analysis technicians while Hud was in the chamber. I can also control my on-off switch much better. Yours, too. And yours is still set to 'off ' until we mutually agree to change it."

I sighed deeply and said, "What does all this mean?"

"I don't know, but I expect we will find out on Friday."

"I hope we like what we learn. I had another thought. What if all humans had latent powers they were unaware of? Like Hud and me, for example. Is it just a coincidence that you and Jenny happened to marry two guys with latent powers? All we have is Bishop and Deena's word for it. Wasn't it odd that Eloise just happened to have latent powers too?"

"You have a knack for complicating things. I don't know, but I would like to ask those same questions. I'd also like to know how

Bishop is able to read powers. That's a sub-power, apparently, and I'd like to have it, too. I do remember that Bishop told me once that it was easy. Instead of trying to read a person's thoughts, you focus on the physical structure. There is an area of the brain that he looks at to get potential. It's partially the size of the area and partially the density."

"Why can't you do it?" I asked.

"I may be able to. Permission to examine your brain."

"What the hell. Go ahead." We sat down on a nearby bench and she told me to relax. For several minutes she didn't move or hardly even breathe.

Then she mumbled, "There you are. On the right side, down there. Good. Good. OK."

She raised her head and said, "It's there all right. The problem is, I don't have a benchmark like Bishop does. He has literally looked at millions of brains."

"Let's go home and you can look at the kids and Eloise. I'll call Hud and Jenny to come over as well and bring their kids too. We'll have some supper and you can show off your newest talent. But do you think those folks may not want their minds read?"

"I didn't have to read your mind to find it, so no problem there. Remember, I'm looking for powers. I don't plan to read the kids' thoughts and none of our other friends either. But normal curiosity sure makes it hard to resist trying! I'd be satisfied now with just the ability to find powers."

We got in the Lincoln and started home. I called Hud on the cell. He said Jenny had already cooked but they would come over about 8:00. Their kids had other plans, though. Then I called the Chinese place to order our supper and headed in that direction.

When we got home, Eloise was up and around so we all ate Chinese. At 8:00 sharp, Hud and Jenny arrived. We sat in the living room and I explained to them the things Maggie and I discussed. Everybody agreed to let Maggie have a look.

During the next few minutes, Maggie looked at all three, leaned back in her chair and said, "I may not know what I am doing, but here it is. Based on size and density, Jack and Hud are about identical to Jenny and Eloise."

Jenny asked, "What does that mean?"

I said, "It may mean that Hud and I were held back from fully developing our powers without our knowledge. Why, I can't imagine."

"It may also mean that Jenny and Eloise are near the norm for humans and only Maggie is the exception," added Hud. "But why not tell us?"

"We'll find out on Friday," Maggie said. "Jenny, Eloise, have either of you experienced an increase in powers since the chamber last night?"

Neither had.

I said, "Maggie has. Hud, you know the big oak tree at the old house? The one that has to come down?"

"The one where the pool is going?"

"That's right. Take Eloise and Jenny out in the morning and see the results of 'Maggie's Tree Service'."

We chatted a little longer, then they left and Maggie and I went to bed. Eloise said she would turn out the lights.

A little later, we were stretched out in bed and I was nearly asleep when Maggie said, "I've been doing some calculating. On Tuesday, the 16th, it will be thirty days since we had the pills in Mopti on August 23. Remember that we had those double days because of our trip to Hell."

"Time does pass quickly," I said sleepily.

"Not quickly enough. I can hardly wait. Should we invite Hud and Jenny to join us here or do you want to get a plush suite in Savannah or Jacksonville."

"It's kind of awkward with Eloise here. Maybe a shopping trip to Jacksonville is in order. After all, we're millionaires now."

"I agree. Maybe Eloise will agree to watch the kids. How about calling and reserving a suite for tomorrow?"

"I'll tell them to expect us about three in the afternoon."

"I'll call Jenny now and make sure they can go."

They could.

I got up early the next morning and called the hotel in Jacksonville. They had a huge two-bedroom suite available for tomorrow night so

I reserved it. I ate a bowl of cereal and had some orange juice and headed out for the old house. On the way, I called John Riley's cell number and got him on the first ring. I needed to find out about his estimate.

"Got it ready, Jack. I was going to call you later. When can we meet?"

"How about this morning? Is that possible?"

"Let me check in with my crew and get them started, then I'll run on over. Say about 9:30?"

"Great. I'm on my way there now. See you then."

When I arrived, Tom and crew were on the job. He walked over and said, "I see you got that old tree to fall in the right direction."

"I got a guy from Hinesville who really knew what he was doing. He put a cable up in it and pulled it over with his backhoe. He had to leave though, so I need you to get Edgar or somebody to cut and split it. Let's stack it in that lean-to on the back of the garage. How's the house coming?"

"We knocked off at noon on Saturday. Haven't done too much since you were here Friday. I need to talk to Riley soon, though. We're about ready to rough in the new walls."

"How would 9:30 suit you?"

He grinned and said, "I guess I can wait another half an hour."

"They're supposed to dig the footing for the Reynold's house in Cedar Creek today. We should have the slab down by next Tuesday or Wednesday and then you'll have to pull off here and frame that one."

"Yeah, I talked to Jesse, the slab man, about it already this morning. He said the plumber's been holdin' him up, but it looked like he'd about caught up. We'll be there when he finishes."

We walked over to the house and Tom pointed out a couple of new but relatively minor problems. We had them solved pretty quickly. We were just finishing our tour when I saw John's truck coming down the lane. I moved out on the driveway where I could meet him. We went over his estimate and reached an agreement. I called Tom over and told him what part his crew would do and what Riley's responsibilities were. I also told him that I wanted him and

Billy to work with them whenever they could so they could start learning restoration techniques. After that, John left, promising to start on the exterior trim work about Friday.

Tom and I were going over the rough framing of the new balcony and porch again when Hud, Jenny, and Eloise drove up. I went over to meet them and we walked around the house to where the big tree was down.

"I don't really believe it myself, but Maggie did that standing right here where we are now."

"I'll be damned," Hud exclaimed. "How can she do something like this?"

"I don't know. She made it look easy."

We took a quick look around, then they had to leave. I checked in one last time with Tom and then I left, too. I went by the men's store for some new shirts and slacks and wound up at Burton's for lunch with Hud. Earl Ray joined us and said he and Bennie had struck a deal that pleased him because he had always liked Bennie. After lunch, I went to the bank to see about paying off the Johnson property loan. It was a busy day.

That night Maggie had a roast for dinner and we talked about school with the kids. Laurie was in the running for junior high class president. Mark won a science award for his turtle exhibit. And so on. We went to bed about 10:00 and Maggie was unusually quiet.

Finally, I said, "What's the matter?"

"Nothing."

That means ask again.

"I know something is wrong so why not tell me now?"

"It's really nothing."

That means one more time.

"Well, when the kids got home from school, I took a reading of their latent powers. Mark's are about like yours but Laurie's far exceed yours. I can't read myself—I mean I never tried to read myself. I can only go on what others tell me. But I can read her. She is strong, so strong it's scary."

"Why don't you try to read yourself?"

"OK."

She concentrated for a while. "I can't be positive but her powers seem to be close to my own. God, Jack. What the hell is going on?"

"I don't know, but I'm going to find out when we next see Deena on Friday. Two super powers in the house at the same time? Give me a break!"

"Laurie doesn't know about this yet, but I'll bet she's using them to a limited extent to get what she wants."

"I don't want to talk about it. It's too depressing. On top of everything else, now I have my daughter reading my mind!"

"She doesn't know she has the powers yet, so relax for now."

"When I see Bishop, I'm going to punch him out for starting all this."

"That's fine dear. Now go to sleep."

I did but I wish I hadn't. I dreamed that Bishop was giving everyone I knew super powers but me. And I lost the ones I had. He was laughing hysterically when I woke up sweating. I didn't sleep too well after that.

forty-four

The next morning we packed a bag and got ready to go to Jacksonville. Eloise was staying with our kids, so we were all set. We picked up Hud and Jenny about 11:00 and left. We arrived at the hotel about 2:30 and were shown up to our suite. Jenny and Maggie wasted no time at all, and immediately left to go shopping. Hud wanted to go to a museum, if you can believe that, but I opted for a nap. I slept for about an hour without Bishop's interruptions of last night, and woke up feeling pretty good. I went out for a river walk and killed another hour and a half and then went back to the suite. I guess I dozed off again, because when I heard the door open, a re-run of Mr. Rogers was on TV and I rarely watch Mr. Rogers on purpose. It was Hud.

"Getting a little education there, Jack?"

"Funny. Must have dozed off again. Any sign of the ladies?"

"We'll have to go see Mr. Gonzales again before they're through!"

And just then, in they came with armloads of packages. They were followed by one of the bellmen pushing a luggage cart with more boxes and several large dress bags. The girls were in high spirits, and this must have spilled over onto the tip because the guy literally danced out of the room, almost singing his thanks.

"We never had so much fun," Maggie said. "I like being a millionaire. I really like it."

"We figured that much," I said. "Hud was just saying how we would have to see that nice Mr. Gonzales again."

"That little asshole," Jenny said. "I should have kicked him twice."

"Anyway," Maggie said, "this time we were spending Deena's money, remember?"

"What's the dinner plan?" Hud asked.

"Let's just skip it," Jenny said.

"Patience, patience," I said. "I figured since we're wealthy now, we needed to have a club affiliation, so I had Bob Morton arrange for us to have dinner at the Ocean Club tonight as potential new members. Top floor. I've been there so I know you'll enjoy it. The view of the whole city and the ocean from up there is worth the trip. We're due there at 8:00 which should put us back here at 10:00. Plenty of time."

We got ready and went to the club in a limo. It was a clear night and we had a window table. It was beautiful and the food and drinks were superb. We finished about 9:30 returned to the hotel.

Once in the suite, Maggie went to her make-up case and got the four pills. She gave us each one and we retired to our respective bedrooms. We each took a pill and then quickly showered. Sure enough the feeling of calm and well-being soon took over. Then the gradual increase in desire began to build up. My skin tingled and I began to breathe heavily. Maggie was already on the bed and she said, "Come here, Jack."

I did. And did. And did.

It was every bit as fantastic as the first time. We stayed active for the entire six hours. I woke up at about 10:00 and saw that Maggie was still asleep so I quietly went into the bathroom for a shower. Then I went to the living area and ordered a huge brunch for four. I was nearly starved.

Soon Maggie came staggering out and said, "Just as fantastic as I remembered. I hope they find a safer version you can take more often. Luckily the four of us are able to monitor our use of it. But I can see that the average person would not have the mental strength to resist it."

Next came Jenny.

She was walking gingerly and said to Maggie, "You said it made you sore. You weren't kidding."

"I took the liberty of ordering brunch for us. Should arrive soon, if you ladies want to shower first."

They both did and about the time they finished, room service arrived. I had the servers set it up on the balcony and summoned the troops. Jenny dragged Hud out of bed and we settled in for another feast.

Buttering a muffin, Jenny said, "I can understand the problem of drugs and addiction better now. It's a good thing I don't have access to those pills because I'm not sure I could always wait a month. How in the world do people take them day after day and not have burnout and excess wear and tear on the equipment?"

"Beats me," I answered. "But there are cases where people have taken them daily for several weeks in a row until their immune systems burned out and they were too sick to go any longer. It's a powerful drug."

"It's just beginning to cause the effects everyone feared would occur on Earth," Hud said. "I read a report the other day which said that immune system breakdowns were up almost 80 percent over the same period last year in the cities where Wham was first introduced. Same sort of numbers with other problems. If I remember correctly, child neglect cases were up about 70 percent, VD about 40 percent, genital damage over 200 percent, and rapes up around 15 percent."

"It's not going to go away," Jenny said. "I know that now. But apparently it isn't harmful used once a month like Bennie and Deena said. Instead of prosecution, maybe we need education. But of course people have been saying that for years about all the drugs. Alcohol and tobacco, too."

Buttering a last piece of toast, I said, "What's really needed is a one hour version of the drug that doesn't affect the immune system. There's no way to keep this drug completely off the streets."

"I'm afraid you're right, Jack," Hud said. "Look at us. Prominent members of the community of Clarksville, defenders of the law, sitting here discussing an illegal drug problem and what should be done, just hours after taking the same drug illegally. It's kind of interesting, isn't it? I'm going to work harder for the drug users I defend."

"You mean it would be OK if our kids had access to it?" Jenny asked.

Nobody wanted to comment on that, so there was a period of silence and then I said, "Speaking of Clarksboro, we better hit the trail."

About 30 minutes later, we were on the road home.

forty-five

Thursday was quiet, and we spent Friday morning leisurely getting ready to go to Heaven. The best part was that we didn't have to decide what to wear. Deena sent word that she would pick us up at 10:00 so that she would have time to brief us before we went to Heaven. We were all ready when she arrived.

Once on Noah we went straight to the briefing room. We passed Bennie in the hall on the way and Hud asked him how things were going on Hell. Bennie said it was a 'helluva mess' and got a laugh. He had come up to confer with Analysis on some problem he was having with the food shipping schedule. We went into the room and a minute later Deena breezed in with an update.

"I just want to tell you what's been happening since Sunday. The Tarcan ship captain had been called before Ruth and She really laid him out on the carpet. No more tchadbe shipments to Earth. No more demons imported. No more use of REGEN without permission. And they have to stay in orbit around Heaven until an ambassador from Tarcan arrives next week.

"When the Tarcan captain heard that Balzerch was gone, he secured a huge quantity of seed from the demons on Hell and sold it for an enormous profit to the growers on Earth. We managed to get some of it, but the bulk went underground quickly. The upshot is that we have stopped the supply, but only temporarily and only after a huge quantity got away from us. We just can't stop the flow of Wham for very long. It's so frustrating. If it isn't one thing, it's another.

"Bennie reports chaos on Hell, but he has the demons back on the job and everyone is working. The other Tarcan ships are arriving with enough food supplies most of the time and taking away the tchadbe, so the economy will survive until we can institute reforms. We want to give all the demons a chance to leave if they so choose. Apparently, some were not asked if they wanted to work on Hell.

"And finally, I don't know exactly what Ruth is going to talk about this morning so we'll just have to wait. Any questions?"

"Yes," Maggie said quickly, almost before Deena got her question out. "Will we be able to ask Her questions?"

"I really don't know, but my guess is that it will be OK."

I asked if I had time to talk to Bishop for a few minutes before we left.

"Sure. We won't leave before 11:45 so we have half an hour. Let's meet at the REGEN machine at 11:40."

We moved out to the hallway and Maggie said, "What are you up to?"

"I'm going to ask that bastard why he held back my training on purpose. Do you want to come along?"

"I guess I'd better so I can keep you out of trouble."

Bishop was pleased to see Maggie and tolerant enough of me to shake my hand.

"What can I do for you two today?"

I said, "Why did you tell Hud and me that our latent powers were way below Jenny's and Eloise's when, in fact, they are nearly equal for all four of us?"

"What makes you think that?"

"Maggie took a reading and compared."

"Maybe she's mistaken."

"I may be," Maggie said. "But I want the truth, Bishop, and I don't want to have to read your thoughts to get it."

"All right, all right. Those were my instructions. But I can't tell you why because I wasn't told."

"Have you read my daughter's powers?"

"Yes."

"Well?"

"You already know."

"I'm not real sure of myself yet. Why don't you tell me?"

"Except for you, Maggie, she's the highest ever recorded. Ever. And her powers will expand during the next seven or eight years. She will probably be a notch above you. Incredible as it may seem, at the present time she doesn't have a clue."

"What the hell's going on, Bishop?" I demanded. "I'm tired of the bullshit."

"Calm down, Jack. I'm just a pawn. I'm not told much. Maybe you'll learn more this noon from Ruth."

"I hope so."

We went to the REGEN room, and when Deena arrived, we all left for heaven. The REGEN room on Heaven looked just like the one on Noah. We entered a corridor, turned right, and after a longish walk, entered a big room. In one end was a raised platform with a large chair on it, obviously not designed for any of us. Scattered around facing it were an assortment of chairs, sofas, and some other things I couldn't put a name to, obviously intended for other races. It was an elegant room, done in shades of gold with some purple and green splashed around. Reminded me of Mardi Gras in New Orleans, but more regal.

As we stood around talking, a bright light appeared on the stage, so bright you couldn't see the chair. When the light dimmed, God was there. She told us to sit down and then She just sat quietly and looked at us for a few moments. I finally realized She was reading us openly to speed things up. Then She began to speak.

"I have much to tell you and it will take a while. Some of it you have already guessed or detected on your own, I see. Deena knows part of it, but I think she will be surprised at much I have to say. Let me give you some background first.

"As you know, I am Ruth, God to several hundred solar systems in this galaxy. I have been functioning in this role for more years

321

than I care to relate. I have the ability to split myself into many parts for purposes of judging the dead on their fate. I am, in fact, in many places as we speak right now. Fortunately, most of my worlds have been civilized for thousands of years, so they require little intervention on my part. Even the judging is relatively easy because most are good people. Of course, having fantastic Head Angels like Deena also makes my job easier."

At this She paused and looked at Deena, who blushed all over. Then She continued.

"So, all in all, my job is demanding but workable. Now, there are a number of Gods in various galaxies of this Universe, each of us with many solar systems. We all report to Xerma, the Supreme Being for this segment of the universe. She in turn reports to someone in charge of our entire universe, but I really don't have much knowledge of what happens at that third level. I do know that our representative is a man named D'Lorn. I also know that the decision to replace one of us or whether or not to let us resign is made solely by Xerma. Now to the situation we have here.

"Several thousand years ago, I was going through a down cycle. I was having trouble on several worlds and for some reason, just didn't want to face the problems. Because of this indecision over the problems, I thought that the best choice was for me to resign. Well, you don't just resign from God duty, so I was given the chore of finding my successor. As the years went by, no one really suitable emerged. And of course the problems continued, too.

"It would take hours to tell you what we look for and I won't even attempt a full explanation except to say the person chosen must have exceptional mental powers. This is rarer than you might think. Nearly everyone on all my worlds has powers at a level below Bennie's. The few that exceed that level are frequently unstable or otherwise unsuitable. The stable ones like Deena and Bennie and Eloise gravitate into jobs like head angel or fourth in line for the Ruler of the demons, or chief spy in Hell. Maggie and Jenny, with powers beyond normal levels, will be offered more work in the future. In any event, I was having trouble finding anyone to replace me.

"About that time, I checked on the evolution of life on the Earth, which was one of my worlds. Many, many thousands of years ago when the human form began to evolve, a team sent by Xerma's predecessor visited the Earth. They artificially inseminated several thousand young women in these primitive tribes using sperm from several worlds with advanced human cultures. It was an experiment designed to observe evolution in a primitive world. We have had, over time, some interesting mutations that have proven to be extremely useful from the primitives. For example, tchadbe, for better or worse, came from a primitive. So did many of the life extension drugs.

"Earth had evolved to the point that intelligent life was emerging when Balzerch showed up. We took a routine reading of his powers and zoom—they were off the scale. I was not his God, but since he appeared in my universe, I got permission from his God to pursue him. He was looking for a project site and the Tarcans had just shown him the next planet in from here. He knew about tchadbe, which was just beginning to be introduced in our universe, and the planet he was considering was ideal for growing it, given a labor force. He approached me about setting up Hell for the Earthlings and using them to grow the tchadbe.

"I needed a Hell for the Earth and this actually seemed to fit my needs. But I was so fascinated by his emerging powers that I got careless. He demanded many things and I gave in on some which I shouldn't have. For example, I agreed to not send angels to Hell. I think you are all familiar with the Customs. My original plan, if you can believe this, was to mold Balzerch into a pattern that might ultimately result in him succeeding me. Then I had problems on several worlds at once, problems which dragged on for years. In the process, my dissatisfaction and boredom went away, and I withdrew my request for resignation. I paid little attention to Earth and Hell during this period. Both seemed to be evolving nicely and we had begun processing souls, so all was well.

"But Balzerch had a deviant streak that I didn't detect. Even in those early days he could mask his true self. One day, upon the advice of my head Angel at that time, I had a report on Balzerch's operations prepared from all the data which were collected routinely from Earth and Hell and got a real surprise. Balzerch was violating our Customs at will. He was importing demons and turning them into virtual slaves; he was cutting corners on amenities, even food quality; and was using the female demons and the Earth female residents of Hell as his own personal harem. Sex was being forced, and my rules say it must be consensual.

"On Earth, he was supposedly limited by Custom as to what he could do to tempt Earthlings to violate my rules and wind up in Hell. But he repeatedly exceeded his quota of demons on the Earth. He introduced the poppy to Earth, and he was responsible for much of the new weaponry and other life-taking technology that emerged over time. I was staggered and called him in to account for his actions.

"His powers had by now matured. Their rate of increase had slowed to a trickle, but by then it was too late. His powers exceeded mine. Bishop managed to get a reading on him the day Balzerch came up. I wasn't too worried because I have access to many people with powers to help if needed. But calling in help causes a loss of confidence on the part of one's followers, so I let him off with a stern warning that if he didn't stop violating the customs, I would end his existence.

"He realized that I truly was capable of this, and agreed to return and abide by the Customs. For a while he did, but he just had this compulsion to expand and increase his profits, so gradually he began to cheat again. I notified Horvak, Bennie's home world, about Balzerch's treatment of the demons and Bennie was sent to investigate. He filed several reports. Balzerch's home planet, Kosark, was also notified many years ago, but they move extremely slowly. It took all this time for them to finally get a team sent here. Before they arrived, however, he had the tchadbe scheme well under way on earth. I enlisted the help of you four and Eloise and used you shamelessly to try to stop this debacle. I have been almost maddened by my inaction, but there are other priorities that caused me to avoid bringing in outside powers.

"He, of course, knew of my position in the other worlds. What he didn't know was whether or not I would act, and this was a deterrent at least for a while. But he got bolder and bolder. Finally, Deena conceived of a plan to send a team of specially selected and trained mortals to Hell. I had been observing one potential candidate for some time and I wanted to see how far her powers could be developed once she became aware that she had them. This mortal was Maggie.

"Even though the team was built around Maggie, you three were included with good reason. Jack had FBI training in drug enforcement, Hud had Special Forces training in the military, and Jenny, you were read to be a natural born catalyst. You make things happen, provoke emotions, and are a leader. All in all, you give us a good mix, especially when you consider that Maggie is also a trauma center nurse. Even so, we didn't really give the first mission much chance. It was unfortunate that Carmen blew the whistle on your team, but fortunate that everyone survived and made it home."

She paused and asked if anyone needed refreshments. Before anyone could answer–no surprise there– She rang a bell and several servers appeared. They were all female and had the usual equipment, but had a lot of coarse-looking body hair. They also had six fingers on each hand. And I don't know what else. I always hate to stare. Well, almost always. With drinks served and trays of hors d'oeuvres on the tables, Ruth continued.

"Then came the confrontation with Drok and Elsha. In spite of all the trauma on Hell, Maggie had failed to awaken up to that point. But the sight of Drok and Elsha frying Deena did the trick. It wasn't a set-up as you suspected, Maggie. Deena might have had a permanent injury if you hadn't intervened. And we thought Elsha was gone.

"Once you realized you had powers, we could move ahead on that front, developing your powers to their full potential so that you could help bring down Balzerch. Your work with Bishop progressed well but you weren't making the quantum jumps we had hoped for.

"The second mission to Hell was also real. Part of the purpose was to have you face a situation where you would be stimulated to use your full powers, but that situation actually proved to be too stimulating. Of course, I'm referring to the direct encounter with Balzerch. He defeated you easily, but he would probably have defeated me, too, so that's not a criticism. He froze your powers, and until Charity's chamber, you were out of action. Still, you did gain some strength from the encounter with him.

"The last trip to Hell was real, too, but we neglected to tell you everything. I plead guilty to that one. We knew that the Kosarkians were livid over what Balzerch had done, especially his treatment of the demons, and so we enlisted their help. You all met with Mesarch and set up the diversion timing and everyone knew their job. The thing I didn't tell you was that you didn't have a chance. I hoped Maggie would make the next jump under the stress but she didn't. She was able to protect herself from burnout and to hide that fact from Balzerch. Our plan was that if she did not immediately make the jump, I would come in and all of us together would have taken him. That would have occurred almost immediately after he arrived and before he injured or fried anyone. Sorry, Maggie. This did not go exactly as we planned.

"You see, I was poised in the REGEN circle on a shielded ship in orbit when I suddenly blacked out. Now I know that Gods are not supposed to black out nor are angels or residents of Heaven because we have conquered physical illness and are well on our way with mental illness. But I started having these episodes about 50 years ago and have one about twice a year. The machine can't cure it. My physicians can't even diagnose it. They say it must be mental. It does not occur at any particular time of day, with any food type, or in any given situation like when exercising or under stress or whatever. It usually lasts just a few seconds and I go right back to normal with no after effects.

"But when the crucial time came for me to join you, I was laid out on the REGEN circle instead of showing up to help you. Of course, you all know better than I do what happened then. When I regained consciousness, our monitor showed him dragging Jenny up on the platform and spreading her legs. I screamed 'Go', just as Maggie began to speak, and arrived in time to help her put him down. I apologize to each of you who suffered an injury as a result of my inadequate performance, especially Jenny."

She stopped and looked at Jenny.

Jenny said, "That's all right, Ruth. I'm just glad you got there when you did."

Jenny seemed to be pretty comfortable calling God by her name. I hadn't totally reached that point yet.

"Thank you, Jenny. In retrospect, I made another mistake. I instructed Deena to tell Bishop to limit the powers developed by Hud and Jack. I felt that Maggie and Jenny would evolve more quickly if they knew the safety of the group depended on them. It did work that way up to the final encounter. If Jack and Hud had both been up to power, the extra delay in Balzerch's victory would have enabled me to get there before anyone got hurt. I guess the old saying, 'live and learn' still applies. Anyway, that's the story." She leaned back in her chair and sighed deeply.

Nobody said anything. She just sat there as if She were asleep. Finally, Maggie stood up and said, "Ruth, I need to ask a question."

"Go ahead, Maggie."

"Why are you so concerned with the development of my powers? I'll be glad, of course, to help more in this tchadbe mess. We all will. But am I missing something?"

"I thought you knew. I've decided to resign again and I'm considering recommending you for my job. You would be the new God."

forty-six

The room was unnaturally quiet for a few moments. Maggie looked at me and I saw a tear running down her cheek. I reached out for her and her eyes rolled up and she fainted. I eased her gently down onto the sofa. I got her legs elevated and Jenny ran up with a cold napkin she had stuffed in her ice water. She put it on Maggie's head and looked up at me, tears welling up in her eyes. I had been fighting it, but now I stood up, looked around and saw it was nearly unanimous. Deena and Hud were standing there either crying or trying not to.

After a moment or two, Maggie rejoined us. She sat up slowly and Jenny gave her some water. Suddenly she remembered where she was and who she was with and she stood up and said, "I'm sorry, Ruth. This is a complete and utter shock."

"Are you OK?"

"Yes, I think so."

"Please sit back down. I must finish my story quickly."

Everyone moved to their seats and got settled again.

"Maggie, dear. Don't be alarmed. It may never happen and if it does, it will be many years. Besides, you absolutely have to want to do this before the final selection is made. All I wanted to do was to let you know you are near the top of the candidate pool. So is your daughter Laurie, although she won't be officially notified for several more years.

"First, I want you to do something important for me. I have the authority to delegate duties for any of the systems under my control to mortals who qualify. I do this fairly regularly on most of my calmer worlds. But I want to give you the Earth, which is decidedly not calm. This means that you will assume all of my duties with respect to Earth, including the administration of Heaven and Hell and decisions about who goes where. The angels will be under your control and so will the administrator of Hell.

"Earth is so out of control that I came close to eliminating it all together. Several times. Deena and others convinced me to try again. I just don't understand Earthlings. You are not typical primitives because you are evolving so rapidly. Other worlds have spent a thousand years doing what you have done in the last hundred. But the negatives have begun to overshadow these positive advances.

"In the past 40 years on Earth, there have been significant increases in violent behavior including murders, rapes, child and spouse abuse, and wars. People cheat and lie routinely about nearly every facet of their lives. Drugs and the associated criminal behaviors are out of control. Family structure in many societies is breaking down. In short, it's a mess. I take part of the responsibility because of my negligence. Balzerch gets a major chunk of the blame, too. But the people themselves have been greatly at fault. They have proven to be weak and susceptible to any evil put in front of them. They have all but abandoned their religions in most developed countries. As I said, it is really a mess.

"We Gods prefer not to intervene directly into the daily lives of our subjects. We would rather save judgment for death. And that's basically what I tried here, but it failed. Maggie, if you accept this position, you will have to intervene and have a pre-death judgment process to clean up the world. How you carry it out will be up to you, but I'll be interested in your plan. I did it once years ago and that was the origin of the Noah story. But it's a much bigger and more complicated job today. You're up to it, however, or I wouldn't be making this offer. And you have a solid support system here already in place—Jack, Hud, and Jenny.

"You will have to confer with me on any major decision, especially the use of the past to alter the present or future. But otherwise, you'll be on your own after a short training period.

"What I want you to do is begin your training for the job with absolutely no firm commitment required on your part for several of your months. I will start you off with Bishop, and have you working with him to fully develop your powers. Bishop thinks this will take an hour a day for about three months.

"At the same time, a second hour a day can be spent with Deena studying the history of my worlds and their peoples, with an intensive look at Earth. Much of that, of course, can be implanted, and Deena can be there to answer your questions. Finally, you would have to spend two days a month with me, observing and asking questions. We can do all of this in suspended time so that you don't lose real time on Earth. But you would have to adjust to a 26-hour day. I don't think that will be a problem. You've already experienced that before. Are you willing to try?"

"Ruth, this is so much to absorb. I'll need time to think it over. It's not every day that I face a decision like this."

"That's sensible, Maggie. Take all the time you need. I can see you any Friday at noon if you tell Deena a week in advance. In the meantime, please send questions to me through Deena and I will send you an answer.

"Now, let's continue. Maggie is the chosen one, as you now understand, but you other three will all have to be on board. You are essential to the plan. For that reason, I want you to continue to work with Bishop, especially Jack and Hud. I'm sorry I held you back as long as I did. By the way, call it coincidence or whatever, you four and Eloise are all above the average Earth inhabitant in terms of powers. Possibly the presence of the potential to develop powers had something to do with your attraction to each other. We really don't know. But I understand that you have, in effect, all four married each other. Is that right?"

I said, "Yes, Ruth. We can't do it formally in our society but that is virtually what we have done."

"I don't think that presents any unusual difficulties. There are just three spouses instead of one. I have two myself. Anyway, here's some more background.

"First, God is a mortal. Always. That is a rule. That surprises you, doesn't it? It was set up that way for a good reason many thousands of years ago. The belief was that a mortal would have more insight into why mortals do what they do with their lives. An immortal would be out of touch with mortal feelings and could make poor decisions as a result. Of course, this was what was happening before the life-extension drugs were developed, when medicine was still relatively primitive. A God who took care and used all techniques available might have lived up to 200 of your years in those times. That rule is outdated because I myself am about 8000 years old, and it's getting harder to argue that there is much difference between an immortal and me. Nevertheless, an assistant like you and the new God will be mortal.

"Yes, I am about 8000 of your years old. I have been God for nearly 4500 of your years. As I said, with the conquering of physical disease and the long life drugs, mortals can almost become immortal. We age about one of your years for every 100 years that pass. That makes me physically about 80 years old. I can alter my form at will, of course, but what you see right now is the real me. No drugs or machines can stop the inevitable end result of mortality, which is death. And I will die within the next 2000 years. Before that day, though, I want some time off and that is why I will resign. I want to be a tourist on worlds I haven't seen, meet people who don't know I am a God, maybe live for a while on a primitive world where people have fun, like gamble on Earth at Las Vegas. I need a vacation.

"Back to you all. For mortals who work under me, the rule has always been that spouses get the long life drugs and have access to the repair chambers. They also have full privileges in all heavens and worlds under God. If there is a split-up, they are given the choice I gave Eloise: work on a station like Noah or remain in current time on their world or some other world. They lose the long life privileges unless their home world or adopted world has developed their own.

"Kids aren't a problem for you all, because they will be grown before Maggie would take over. The best plan anyway is to live on your home world and use REGEN to move around. Most days, I work about 12 hours and sleep four, leaving the other eight for personal things and my family. In a pinch, you can hold time for a couple of hours a day and still get eight off, but it's tiring. Earth will soon have long-life drugs so you won't stand out as being different because you're not aging.

"There is only one rule handed down that you must follow: 'Reward those who live in such a way as to cause no serious harm to another, punish those who do not'. Beyond that, you are accountable for your actions, but are rarely questioned about anything. If you are unsure of a specific action, you can ask for advice. The two days you spend with me each month will help define the word 'serious' in the rule. If you perform unsatisfactorily, you will be asked to resign. This has happened only on rare occasions, and usually occurs only if you develop a mental problem that we are still unable to cure.

"There is so much more, but I suspect you've had enough for now. Deena will help you all she can and try to answer your questions. Let me know when you decide."

She sat back in the chair, the lights came up, and She was gone. We just sat there not really knowing what to say.

Finally, I looked at Maggie and said, "Well, you said you wanted some answers."

"I did, didn't I. I kind of wish I hadn't come. I don't know anything about being an assistant to God. The whole thing is so preposterous. It's so ludicrous. It really can't be happening."

"It'll take some getting used to, I suspect," Deena said. "But you can do it, boss."

"Boss, my ass. I might just want to go home," Maggie said.

We went back to Noah and then home. Deena said she would be in touch and left. Maggie said she was tired and needed a nap but wanted to talk to all of us after supper. Hud and Jenny agreed to come back at 8:00. We all sensed the new authority in Maggie's voice. Subtle but distinctly different.

I ate lunch and made some phone calls on my way to the old house to check on things. I mainly wanted to see if John Riley's crew had started. I got there about 1:30 and saw that John's truck was there. I parked and walked over to the house. Tom and John were standing near the new porch talking.

"That's what I like to see. Progress," I said.

John said, "It's slow but we're workin' on it."

I looked around and saw both crews working, mine on finishing up the new porch and balcony and on the inside partitions and John's on the exterior trim. The roofer had been there and said he would start his crew on Monday.

"We need a place to work on those interior doors and windows," John said. "Can we use the old barn?"

I haven't talked at all about the barn. It was a replica of a Pennsylvania Dutch bank barn but only about half the size. This one was a faithful reproduction right down to the beams, each one hand-hewn heart pine. Must have cost a small fortune.

In case you're not familiar with them, a bank barn is actually built on a slope, or a bank, with the main floor entrance at the top of the bank. Under this main level is another level that has been cut right into the bank. This was usually the stable area since it was relatively climate controlled. A second floor above the main level was for hay storage. The main floor was for equipment storage or whatever.

"Y'all can use the main floor, but put plywood over it where you work to protect those planks from damage."

"No problem. We can use the plywood later on for the garage roof."

I told them I planned to come out again Monday and headed for home. Maggie was fixing dinner. I walked by her and gave her a goose. She jumped and threw a potato peeling at me. I ducked neatly. Good training, excellent reflexes, and lots of practice, you know. Then I went upstairs and took a quick shower and changed clothes. I was in a pretty relaxed mood for a change.

Eloise left to go to dinner with Bob, and the kids went to the movies. Maggie and I ate dinner alone and at 8:00 Hud and Jenny arrived. We got settled in the living room and Maggie began to talk.

"I want to hash over the whole situation. You know that I'm totally blown away by this thing and don't even know how to evaluate it. My first reaction is to tell Her to shove it. Why do I need that kind of grief? I'm already a millionaire and have a new extended family. About all I have to gain is a long life, but who wants to live 8000 years?

"But on the other hand, how can I let this opportunity escape? Just think about who will have to answer to me. The big drug dealers who buy their way out of convictions. The serial killer suspect who goes on killing because no one is sure if he did it or not. I will know, really know, and can really act on my knowledge. The seven year old girl being raped and beaten by her father won't have to suffer anymore. He will be gone. This may make it worth the effort.

"But the real question I want us to discuss is what kind of a God would allow a place under Her rule to become as fucked up as the Earth is now? I mean look at the human misery around the world. If you had the power to change this, and Ruth does, why let it go on? Oh, I know what She said about Her noninterference policy, but that should have been abandoned before the middle of the century, 70 or 80 years ago. When a Hitler emerges, someone needs to act, if that someone is really in tune with what is happening.

"She purports to worry about these things and has responded to the new challenge presented by Wham on a limited basis, but why didn't She root out the bastards responsible for illegal drugs, for example, and eliminate them? How can I work under someone like that?"

Hud tackled that one. "I think there are two reasons for the problems on Earth. One is the fact that Earth was progressing rapidly but along satisfactory lines when She began to focus on the other worlds' problems. Remember that She admits negligence here. Then, secondly, when She saw how bad things had become and saw what Balzerch had done, She decided on termination. If you're going to terminate anyway, why waste any effort on straightening up the mess? So She left Earth alone until She could resolve the Balzerch problem. That has been going on for some years now. Those two reasons add up to one fucked up Earth."

"I think Hud is probably right," I added. "It doesn't excuse Her, but it does help clarify the situation."

"I think it was precisely for Maggie," Hud said. "She now has a reason to be optimistic and wants Maggie to succeed Her. It all fits."

"Maybe. But I am still blown away by the idea."

"It doesn't make Her look any better for Her negligence, but it does explain what happened," Jenny said. "Many religions on Earth predict that God will send someone to judge their members someday. It looks like that day has arrived and you are that someone, Maggie."

"It has to be a big mistake," Maggie said quietly. "How could it be me?"

Hud said, "It had to be someone."

Everyone was quiet for several minutes, each thinking about the implications of what Maggie had to do.

Finally, Hud said, "It seems a shame to have to suspend citizens' rights to fair trials and so on just when we got it working pretty well."

"That's just the point, Hud," Maggie answered. "That's you the lawyer talking. But it's not really working. If you're a rich celebrity and you kill someone, you can buy your way out. If you're a criminal like a drug dealer, you can probably bribe someone in law enforcement establishment and escape arrest. But the real point is that if I'm sitting in judgment and they come before me, I would know the truth instantly. God judges the person after they die, after they have created considerable human misery. Why not judge them all the time? Those who don't measure up, lop off their heads. Well, maybe that's a little bit extreme, but you get the point. We're not going to be replacing the judicial system. We're just going to reduce their caseload. And it will frequently come before the fact and not after. Fewer victims, you know."

"I suppose you're right about stopping those we know are guilty, but you're wrong about the current system. It's not designed to get the guilty, it's designed to protect the innocent. And we do a good job of that. Some guilty do slip away in the process."

"With me judging, the innocent will be fully protected and the guilty had better beware. This has gone on long enough."

"What about religions?" Jenny asked. "The Christian religion allows a person to screw up time after time. Then when they're 85 and about to die, they can suddenly realize the error of their ways and repent. After they have screwed up the lives of countless others, of course."

"Fortunately, I don't think Ruth buys into this when She judges," I said. "She judges the person on the degree of harm but doesn't allow unlimited repentance, as I understood Deena to explain it."

Maggie frowned and said, "It all sounds so simple. All I would have to do is apply the rule and worry only about those who cause harm to others. But how much harm? What type of harm?" She sighed. "I'm really unsure about taking this job."

Hud said, "It's not so bad, Maggie. Just a matter of degree. We do it all the time in the judicial system. The 'punishment fits the crime' philosophy."

"I know that, Hud, but what punishment would I have access to? It's kind of on or off. Either I let the offender live or take them out. Here's an example. Suppose we have three sex offenders. Offender A raped and beat a woman until she was nearly dead. She lost an eye and was scarred all over. It was his third offense. Offender B broke into a home and raped the woman inside. He was careful not to hurt her otherwise and it was his first offense. Offender C caught a woman in the alley and gave her a quick feel and let her go. Which ones get eliminated? Obviously A does. What about B and C?"

Hud hesitated a moment or two and said, "Put that way, that is to die or not to die, I don't know. In our system, A would get life. B would get 10 years and serve maybe two. And C would get probation. I don't know how it would work with us judging."

Jenny said, "I would eliminate A, really eliminate him, and let the other two sit and watch me for a few days while I dished out other punishments. Then re-check their minds to see if they have remorse and are serious about reforming. If not, as you say, lop off their heads."

"I tend to agree with Jenny," I said. "But why couldn't you set up an adult halfway world like Ruth has for kids under 18 who don't qualify for Heaven. This world would be for mortals like B and C who aren't quite ready to be sent to Hell. You could staff it with immortals from Heaven, including a large group of psychologists and psychiatrists to assist the ones who are mentally ill. Those who reform come back to Earth. Those who don't are terminated and go to Hell."

"Not a bad idea, Jack. I'll run it past Her when we talk. But what about A. What if he is just mentally ill and curable?"

"I don't know about that one," I answered. "I guess if he were really cured I could live with him, but it would have to be a real cure, not an 'Earth cure' like we have today. Can you tell if a person is cured or not, Maggie?"

"I think I can, but I'll definitely need some practice. I thought I had cured you of lusting after other women, but the last time you let me read you, you weren't."

"Who's Jack lusting after now," Jenny wanted to know.

"Most anything in skirts!"

"I would have thought that three women on a fairly regular basis would be enough," Jenny said, laughing.

"You would think so, but I warned Eloise to bolt her door at night!"

"Y'all are a real riot," I said. "If I pass through your judgment line, my life would be read as being so dull, I'd probably get sent to Hell just to give me some excitement."

"Jack, That's brilliant. You have just named the court I'll hold: the Judgment Line," Maggie said. "It's perfect."

Hud got up and stretched and yawned and said, "Tomorrow's Saturday, but I have to get some work done if I'm going to continue to practice law. So 'nite, folks, it's my bedtime."

As they were leaving, Maggie said, "Thanks for listening. I'd like to continue to chew it over with all of you until I can make up my mind."

She already had. She just didn't know it yet.

forty-seven

The next week passed quickly enough. I spent most of it at the old house and at Cedar Creek catching up with the contractor business. I made a couple of trips to Savannah and Hud and I had a couple of encouraging sessions with Bishop. I could feel my powers beginning to emerge. Maggie was quiet all week, still trying to come to grips with the carrot that was dangling in front of her. We talked several times but it really was a difficult problem for her, to really want to do something but at the same time to be afraid to do it. I really think it was that she was afraid she couldn't do it. Fear of failure has lots of times held her back.

Deena visited on Thursday night. The four of us were at Hud and Jenny's relaxing after Jenny had served an excellent meat loaf. Yes, I said an excellent meat loaf. We briefed Deena on the ideas we had been throwing around, especially on God's apparent negligence. Deena commented that she herself had been worried about Her for the last 60 years or so. She had been afraid to bring it up except when it came to fighting for Earth's survival.

"I have you set up to see Her tomorrow at noon," she told Maggie. "That hasn't changed. What has changed is Her insistence that you other three come along. I just can't understand that, because usually She tries to keep meeting participants to a minimum. I don't know

339

what to do because She is certain to pick up from one or more of you those negligence ideas we just discussed. You three can't block your thought processes yet, and that worries me."

Maggie said, "Why don't we just tell Her they're busy?"

"You can tell Her. Not me. No one is too busy to meet with God."

Maggie sighed and said, "I suppose not. Well, we'll just have to play it as it falls."

Hud asked, "What's new with the Wham campaign?"

"Not much. We've cleaned out the last of the demons, we think. The supply of Wham has dipped and the price is sky-high, so now we've got a rash of petty thefts. It will get worse until the local plants mature. The lab still hasn't come up with a safe version but they're hopeful."

I said, "I wonder what would be considered a 'safe' version. Even if the immune system problem is solved, the other effects, like child neglect, go on."

Deena nodded in agreement. "That's the education problem. Maybe Maggie's upcoming Judgment Line will create some incentive for people to be responsible. By the way, I like that Judgment Line idea."

"You've been reading us again," Jenny said.

"Not really. Not me. Bishop got it from Hud or Jack. Anyway, I like it."

Maggie said, "Well, let's not worry about tomorrow right now. If She's unhappy with us, Bennie can always use good farmers."

Deena said she would collect us at 11:00 tomorrow. Maggie and I went on home.

We got to Noah the next morning at 11:00 and immediately went to see Bishop to ask for any hints on how to more effectively block our thoughts. He wasn't too helpful, explaining that, in addition to having enough power, it simply takes time to learn. We had about an hour's practice. Not nearly enough. Just a teaser.

At noon we went to Heaven. We were in the same room as before and the servants brought lunch as soon as we arrived. We had just begun to eat when Ruth arrived in the usual blaze of light.

"Go on with your meals and I'll talk for a few minutes. Being God, as I told you, has its rewards and also its disappointments. It is lonely since you really don't have a chance to make friends or to be able to share your problems with someone else.

"I have been uncomfortable enough with my negligence concerning the Earth, and then last night, my chief angel carried some bad thoughts about me."

Deena turned red all over and sputtered, "How did you—How could you——?"

"I never told you I couldn't read you. You just assumed it, because I didn't comment on things you thought I should have. We Gods need a few secrets, too, you know! The only ones I have never been able to read were Balzerch and the demon, Bennie. In Bennie's case, he had the normal powers for an elite demon except for the incredible ability to almost completely block his thoughts. Bennie tells me he thinks some other elite demons and a few select earthlings are close to developing this power."

She turned to Maggie, looked at her intently for a few moments, and added, "And now Maggie. My goodness, dear. How much have your powers increased this week?"

"I don't know, Ruth. I just know that every day they are stronger."

"Well, it's remarkable. Anyway, Deena's conversation with you all was open for me to see and I looked. It made me think about the last 70 years, and I see that all of you are smarter than I am. And I am slipping even more. No doubt about it. I had Analysis run a complete check on my decisions over the past 500 years. They found that I was consistent until about 80 years ago. Since then, I have been erratic and indecisive. I never realized it and, of course, no one had the courage to tell me."

She sighed deeply and just sat there.

Maggie said, "It seems to me that the fact that you realize there is a problem and have faced it means you aren't really in bad shape."

"I hope you're right. In any event, I have already notified Xerma of the situation and She is arranging advanced testing on my blackout episodes. She feels that there may be a connection of some type. Maybe it can be fixed. It does make your training more imperative than we thought, Maggie. Deena tells me that you are ready to start but not ready to commit. Is that right?"

"Yes, Ma'am. I need more time for a commitment. How long will your medical tests take?"

"I'll be gone about one of your weeks if all goes well."

"I think I want to wait and see what the outcome is before I make my final decision."

"I would, too. Deena will watch over things here while I am gone. Any questions?"

Maggie asked, "Do you feel like talking about the assistant job a few minutes?"

"Of course."

"Well, I'm having trouble with the interpretation of the Rule. What constitutes enough 'harm to another' to justify elimination and a trip to Hell? How do we define "another"? Are we only considering harm to humans? Harm turns out to be a very slippery concept."

"Welcome to the club, Maggie. I can't give you a precise definition or draw a magical line between harm and no harm, or humans versus other living beings. But you will learn with time and experience working with me. But even after many years of making judgments, someone you would send to Heaven, I might send to Hell. Gods are not perfect or above making mistakes. One important factor is to determine the intent of the accused. Did they cause the harm to someone without premeditation? Or was it planned? Did it do a temporary harm or were the scars permanent?"

"A couple more questions. What about mental illness? Many of the so-called harms are committed by people who have been harmed themselves, and, as a result, have no self-control. A good example would be the child abuser who abuses because they themselves were abused. Also, does it make a difference whether or not one is judged while still alive versus after death? It seems to me that if someone is still alive, they could possibly repent if left alone long enough. Or not."

"Again, there is no clear cut answer to any of those points, Maggie. I will tell you that repentance is overplayed in the judgment process. Most repentance isn't real when you look deep down into the person. But some is. For example, a person who killed the enemy during a war may actually repent. Each case is different.

"Mental illness? What is that? Is it a person who deviates from the norm and can't help it? If your uncle suddenly announces that he is a rutabaga, but is otherwise harmless, is he mentally ill? Or is it a person who uses it as an excuse to deviate from the norm? We have found that curing mental illness, when it really is mental illness, to be difficult, even at this level. All too often on Earth, a person who kills a child, for example, is pronounced 'cured' and released only to kill again. It is hard to deal with and extremely complicated. If this all sounds like we work on a case-by-case basis, you'd be correct.

"But I have adopted a procedure that seems to work. If the person involved is really mentally ill and a candidate for Terminus, I may let our psychiatrists try a cure. If they succeed, instead of destroying their soul, I will try Hell. In Hell, if they kill it really doesn't hurt anything and I can always remove them. The hard part is sending a mentally ill person to Hell when they might have been a candidate for Heaven. This is why we have to take them one at a time and look at the whole picture. It all takes time, Maggie, but that's really all we can do."

"I think I understand," Maggie said. "I'm actually mulling over an idea to create some sort of halfway world between Heaven and Hell for the living who must be removed but may be mentally ill."

"I have considered that too, and it could have merit. I have a lot of unemployed psychiatrists and psychologists in Heaven who could help. When you decide to accept the job, we'll consider it in detail. I hate to stop here, but I must go. I'll be back in a week or so to talk to you again. I appreciate Hud, Jenny, and Jack coming with you, and will continue to include you since Maggie's decision affects you as well."

We stood up and She left.

After a moment, Deena said, "I might have known She knew what I was thinking all along. That's kind of embarrassing."

"Don't worry about it," Maggie said. "She's used to reading negatives about Herself."

"I suppose so, but I still feel bad. Let's go back to Noah and make some plans."

During the next week, Bob and Eloise got engaged. No real surprise there. Eloise was trying to decide how to tell Bob about her past and planned to discuss it with Deena soon. The house was progressing nicely. Ruth had come back from medical testing and related that the prognosis was not good. Deena said that She had a gene defect affecting an obscure area of Her brain, and that it was not correctable at present. The black-outs would get worse and the mental processes would be affected even more. Ruth's doctors told Her that She should resign in the next 50 years, so Maggie had a little time before having to decide on the God position.

On Friday, Maggie went up alone to meet with Ruth and agreed to start off with the assistant job. She also agreed to train four hours a day instead of two and to meet with Her four days a month.

On Saturday evening Deena came down to our house to meet with us and with Bob and Eloise. Deena came early to brief us on some procedures and protocol. She was dressed in a sharp-looking coral matching skirt and sweater.

Deena said, "There really has never been a case exactly like this, like Bob and Eloise, because Ruth wouldn't OK it in the past. Mortals have always worked for us but were usually on their own when reinserted into their time. But She feels a special obligation to Eloise and agreed to bring Bob into the circle. She had a long talk with Eloise last week and they are in agreement. Bob will have to get the whole story. She wants you all to be present to help him believe me when I relate the story."

The doorbell rang and I went and let Bob and Eloise in. I took their coats, Hud served mulled wine to everyone, and soon we were all seated. There was an early October chill, so I had laid out a small fire in the family room fireplace. Felt pretty good.

I started by saying, "Bob, we invited you here tonight because we want to tell you a story that will be hard for you to believe. I can assure you, though, that it is 100% true. This is Deena. She is an— Well, I'll let her tell you."

Deena began, "Bob, I am an angel."

Talk about getting right to the heart of the matter!

I could see Bob reacting about like we did when Mrs. Angelo arrived. He glanced around to see if anyone was laughing. No one

344

was. He looked trapped, like he were in a group of demented persons. He asked Hud for a stronger drink.

"No one ever believes me at first." She stood up and became Mrs. Angelo and said, "This is how I first appeared to the Warners and Raines."

Bob almost fell out of his chair. "I don't know about the angel part but that is pretty damned unusual. I don't know about this."

Deena switched back and sat down again. She gave him the standard spiel about Heaven and Hell, how they started and so on. She then gave him a concise recounting of how Hud and Jenny and Maggie and I became involved up to our trip to Hell when Eloise was rescued.

"Bob, by now you have begun to realize that you jumped into the middle of a unique situation," Deena said. "Before I tell you more, I must ask you to affirm a vow of secrecy and your commitment to Eloise."

"Well, 'unique situation' is an understatement! I am either dreaming or have finally lost it." He paused. His second drink was already gone. He began to speak again, slowly and deliberately. "Assuming this is real, my commitment to Eloise has not changed even though I suspect I'm going to hear things about her which you think will bother me. As to secrecy, no problem. But what if I decide to just get up now and walk away?"

"Maggie or I would wipe all of this and Eloise from your mind and send you home."

"Yes, I thought that might be the case." A longer pause. "Well, I reckon I'm in it for the whole ride. I love Eloise. I doubt anything could change that."

"Good. Hold on."

He took one of Eloise's hands in his, took a deep breath, and looked directly at Deena. He had a 'hit me with your best shot' on his face. Deena did.

"Eloise was born in 1937, married in 1956, and disappeared in a plane crash in 1958. She had become a famous aviatrix, and that crash was a worldwide event. But in reality, I simulated that crash because I had enlisted her to work with the Angels Corps. After training,

I sent her to Hell to try to take out the devil. I didn't know it at the time, but she never had a chance. She was captured and imprisoned and abused until last month when these four got her out. God elected not to send her back to her actual home time for fear of altering the future. Also, after more than fifty years, even if we adjusted her age to 21 again and reinserted her, she would be a different person. She agrees and now will stay here in this time and place."

Bob was visibly shaken and turned toward Eloise, who had begun to sniffle. He took her in his arms and held her tight. He asked if there was a place where they could be alone. I took them into the den and closed the door.

When I got back Maggie was saying, "That was pretty rough but I think he'll be all right. He's a good man."

After about 10 minutes the den door opened and they came back in. Both had red eyes.

Bob said, "Everything's fine. We have a lot to talk about, but this wedding is definitely on."

"Wonderful. Let me wrap up then," said Deena, and she brought Bob up to date including Maggie's acceptance of the assistant's job to Ruth. It was a lot for one sitting but Bob took it pretty well.

Finally, Deena said, "I want to take you to Noah so that Charity can run you through the repair chamber and give you any injections you might need. I'm sure She will OK the long life drugs if you two agree to be agents for Heaven in the future, but She hasn't confirmed that yet. Also, I want you both to work with Bishop on your powers. Bob's powers according to Maggie will be similar to Jack's and Hud's. Any questions?"

Bob said, "How do I explain my absences to my colleagues and family?"

"I forgot to tell you about time. Look at your watch."

"Why, it's stopped exactly where it was when we arrived!"

"We can take you away for weeks at time and return you to the same instant you left. We don't like to do it for extended periods of time due to the chance that the future could be altered. Eloise can explain all that to you. Anything else?"

Maggie asked, "Will they be assigned to the Judgment Line?"

"That's my current plan, boss, but you have to approve it."

Maggie playfully threw a cushion at Deena, but it stopped in mid-air and floated to the floor. Deena said she'd love to have an all-out pillow fight, but right now, they had to go.

I said, "One more thing. Bob and Eloise, the four of us have talked and would like to make you an offer that you can think about. We have a lot of room at our new house site and would like for you two to consider building there if you want to. Just let us know."

Bob said, "It's a lovely spot and we appreciate the offer. I think we'll probably take you up on it."

"Whenever you're ready."

Then Deena gathered up Bob and Eloise and they left for Noah. I felt empathy with Bob. I knew what feelings he was having, at least to some extent. Difference was that I had weeks to digest it all, and he had mere hours.

Maggie asked Jenny and Hud to stay a while so she could bounce ideas off of them. Hud and I fixed drinks and I got some corn chips and pretzels. I put one more log on the fire, and then we all sat down. Very comforting to be home.

Maggie said, "The more I consider the problem of judgment, the more confused I get. The news stories just this week alone are enough to make you sick. One was 'Mother tortures and kills 2 year old daughter'. That person, by any definition, must be removed from society. But is she mentally ill? Is 'mentally ill' so broad that every deviant is included? I have been practicing by walking through the mall and reading people. I have discovered that I can detect in a person whether or not they have harmed another one, even to what extent. I can also see if they have repented or not. In other words, I can tell 'good from evil'. But are they 'evil' because they are mentally ill? I'm not sure about that."

Jenny said, "Can you tell if a person who has committed some kind of harmful act did so intentionally, or accidentally due to circumstances that might be beyond their control?"

"Yes, I think so. For example, at the mall the other day I read a guy who was planning to kill three people he didn't even know for pay. A true hit man. So I called the police, told them he looked suspicious, described him in detail, and believe it or not, they got him. Luckily for the intended victims, he turned out to be wanted for another murder. Now that was obviously going to be intentional. Mentally ill? I doubt it but it depends on the definition. Can this person be cured? I talked to the top psychiatrists in Heaven and they say probably not short of a lobotomy. Here's another story. Several years ago a woman who had been confined to her house and beaten by her husband every day for six years had managed to get hold of a kitchen knife and killed him. She was remorseful but I don't think repentant. She doesn't appear to be a threat to anyone else. Mentally ill? Not really. Send her to Hell? I couldn't. But she did harm another. How do I judge her fairly?

"One more. A man about 40 walked by radiating depression. About six months ago he had left a party drunk, drove off, hit another car and killed the driver. He tested just a little below the legal limit. He got off with 2 year's probation and a suspended license. But he's so consumed by guilt, it's ruining his life. Obviously repentant and no threat to society. But he did harm another. Mentally ill? Not until it happened. Send him to Hell? That's what is driving me crazy."

"What if he had been dead drunk and was still repentant?" asked Hud.

"That's what I mean. How can I say for sure? I guess it boils down to a judgment call. Like Ruth said, case-by-case decisions, with some of them really difficult to judge.

Hud said, "That's what it almost always is in the various judicial systems around the world, Maggie. We let judges and juries make the call. They make mistakes. So will you. But you have two advantages. One, you know for certain whether or not a person is guilty or innocent. And secondly, you will have your halfway house to use as a buffer between Hell and a further stint on Earth. In the first case, you really have only to decide the degree of guilt or harm a person has caused and whether or not they have repented. If in doubt, you use the halfway world."

"I think Hud's right," I said. "Our current system sometimes lets innocents get punished and lets the guilty go free. At least, you won't be making those mistakes. The halfway world should catch most of the mistakes you might have made. By the way, how about calling the halfway world Reprieve?"

Hud offered the name Last Chance. And Jenny's, the unanimous winner after much discussion, was Uncertainty. We broke up for the night at that point and agreed to go to the Mall with Maggie tomorrow to see for ourselves.

forty-eight

Bob and Eloise were married on a beautiful Saturday afternoon in early November in the gardens back of the old house. Although the house itself wasn't due to be completed until mid-December, the outside was looking good and we had a functional bathroom for guests to use. I had the grounds cleaned up, pruned the shrubbery myself, had some flowers set around, and hired a caterer to do the rest. Then we hoped for a pretty day. It couldn't have worked out better. It was sunny and about 75 degrees. Eloise was stunning in her white gown and Bob looked nervous. Typical stuff. In my opinion, a good time was had by all.

By mid-November, the Judgment Line was coming along nicely. Bennie had agreed to a second month on Hell, and Maggie had worked out a deal with him to use the northern polar region of Hell as a temporary halfway world. She named it Uncertainty, which really pleased Jenny. About half of the workers on Hell had been pulled off tchadbe production and were building a fence around Hell at a 200 mile limit from the North Pole. The fence could be made of metal since Balzerch's ban had been lifted. Construction of barracks and food halls was also underway. The plan was to use the residents of Uncertainty to work on food production not only to feed themselves but also to supplement Hell and save money there. A piece of

Uncertainty was being sectioned off and reserved for those children under 18 who were to be removed from society. Enough construction would be completed by January the first to allow our operations to begin.

Setting up a Judgment Line is an enormous undertaking as we all found out during the last month. I turned the construction business over to Tom, and Hud acquired a junior partner, a young lawyer named Melissa Turner from Tennessee. He was turning the practice over to her. We just had to free ourselves to work on this new project. Luckily we weren't on our own. Ruth, Deena, Bishop, and many others were right there in the middle of the planning.

There were a million expected and unexpected problems for us to address. The first was the element of time. For example, how do you evaluate nearly six billion people in a short period of time? If Maggie saw one per minute and worked 12 hours a day with no vacation it would take 22,831 years to judge them all. Even if Maggie learned how to split herself into several parts as Ruth did, assuming 10 simultaneous lines, it would take more than 2000 years. And this assumes no population growth and no long-life drugs. So we obviously had to come up with something else on this front.

Our solution was, of course, to set up judgment lines in each country–as many as needed to do the job in a few years. It would be easy to staff these with angels, because there were more than enough with adequate mental powers to determine guilt or innocence and intent. And we would provide specific guidelines for them to follow. They could leave a person on Earth or send them to Uncertainty but could not terminate them and could not send them to Hell or Terminus. That was left to Maggie and her designates, all of who would be mortals. In other words, only the incorrigible would be passed on to the final Judgment Line. This figured to be a small and manageable percentage of the population.

The current judicial systems would be left in place since they would have to function during and after the purge, but the judges themselves would be among the first to face the Judgment Lines in each country, along with current prisoners. Next would be the police forces around the world, in order to eliminate those who are corrupt.

The remaining police would then be required to submit a list of suspects for all 'serious harm' crimes such as murder, rape, and child or spousal abuse, and these persons would be brought in and judged, with the innocent going free and the rest sent on to Uncertainty or to Maggie. These procedures should flush out most of the problems, especially if the police consulted battered spouse, foster parent, and other similar social agencies in making their lists.

Last but not least of the groups to be singled out early would be the politicians and the military brass. After that, the rest of the population would be slowly processed and Maggie's job would be simplified since many of the candidates for Hell and Terminus would already be gone, processed in one of the more preliminary judgment lines. And before anyone would get to Maggie, one of the three of us, Jenny, Hud or myself, would have another go at any people who, for one reason or another, just couldn't be judged adequately by the lower courts.

The logistics of making all this happen were a nightmare. First was the problem of announcing that a universal judgment process was about to begin, and explaining that absolutely no one would be excluded or could avoid the process. Using the various media for the announcements, especially TV, would reach most of the people but we felt that they wouldn't take it seriously. Nor could we put 'miracles' on video since people would believe that they were faked or caused by some new technology.

We finally decided to pre-announce a 'miracle' and then perform it on a worldwide scale for everyone to observe. To carry this out, Ruth arranged to have several asteroids moved into a position to partially block the sun for five straight days for 2 hours per day in order to avoid major disruption of crops and temperature levels. It would be announced and performed on a precise schedule in all countries of the world. And this announcement would be disseminated through the media two weeks in advance. This would give scientists ample time to study the skies and discuss the impossibility of such an event occurring.

After the five days, Hud, Jenny, and I—the advance people— would go to each Head of State to arrange for Maggie to be received

353

by each of them and to appear on video. Maggie would then arrive in each country, meet with the Head dignitary, and formally announce the Judgment Line process. The angels would move in and immediately begin the judgments. The five-day event was set to begin on December 27, 2015 . Judgment would begin with the New Year.

Deena was in charge of recruiting angels to staff Uncertainty and to act as judges, and on November 17, she told us she wanted to meet at our house that evening. She arrived at 8:00, just as Hud and Jenny arrived. Deena began by saying she wanted to review exactly where we were in the process.

"The angels will be able to provide up to 43,000 candidates with sufficient mental powers to judge. This will make the judgment line a three or four year process assuming that they all work 300 days per year and see about 120 people per 10-hour day. Angels can work long hours and not tire easily, so it could be done even more quickly if you want."

Maggie said, "I don't see any reason to hurry. If it takes four or five years to do it right I wouldn't be upset. I think the four of us can handle that, assuming we only have to see a minute percentage of the population. It's hard to tell what our actual load will turn out to be."

"What's this 'four of us' stuff?" asked Jenny. "I thought you were the final judge."

"I have decided to share the wealth, if you all agree. Hud and Jack, Bishop tells me, have progressed to the point where they can read thoughts and intent quite well."

Jenny said, "I don't recall you telling me that, Hud."

"I have been practicing on you for weeks," Hud responded with a big grin on his face. "You are a most interesting subject."

"I'll get you for that," Jenny responded. "What do you have in mind, Maggie?"

"At my last session with Ruth, She said I could use other mortals as judges for anything except a trip to Terminus. She suggested you three since you have the powers now as well as an understanding of the process. It has to be mortals, because angels can't send a mortal to Hell. It makes sense to me, because it will cut my load way down. I'll get the ones who are the worst cases. You can sit through the first several cases with me and we all will vote for a while to try to get some consistency. It should work."

Hud said, "I'm game. It should be a fascinating experience. I suspect, though, that it'll also be depressing as, well, as hell."

"Seems worth a try," I said. "I have been worried about your load, Maggie."

"Yes, I've been doing some figuring myself. I think we'll need to establish 43 district courts. We haven't discussed that before."

"Oh, my," Deena said sighing. "I smell more work."

"Just a little. Let's do some projecting. I don't know how many people destined for Hell or Terminus will flow to me, but I believe it's going to be more than we had assumed. It might take the four of us many years to see them all.

"Let's assume that just one-tenth of one percent of adults get sent forward. That's probably high, but assume it. If the population is six billion and 38 percent are below 18 years old, that would be 3.72 billion adults. One-tenth of one percent would be 3.72 million. If we each saw one every ten minutes for an eight or nine hour day, that would be about 50 each or 200 per day. Working 300 days a year would cover about 60,000. Now 3.72 million divided by 60,000 gives an estimate of 62 years. So even though one tenth of one percent is probably high, we're in way over our heads. I need more mortals with powers, but there don't seem to be any. So I have come up with a new plan.

"We'll set up a district court for every 1000 lower courts. This would be 43 district courts. Then we'll send all 3.72 million through this level. At 40 per judge per day for 300 days a year it would take 2.4 years to do them all. This would give us some cushion to absorb normal population growth."

"Won't help," Deena said. "They can't send them to Hell."

"I know. But a few will be kicked back to Uncertainty. Let's say ten percent. That will leave roughly 3.35 million. Of those, probably a high percentage will be targeted for Hell, say 90 percent or roughly three million. Jenny, Hud, and Jack can group scan them and spot any unusual cases which should be looked at further. Evil, or the complete absence of it, really stands out, even in a group. So I am confident, they can each handle 100 every ten minutes or together about 15,000 per day. At 300 days per year, they could do them all in less than a year. Of course they'll be spread over three or four years.

"That leaves me with the other ten percent recommended for Terminus. I'll give them an initial light group read 100 at a time and kick out any that should go to Hell or the psychiatrists and send the rest to you three for a deeper read. I'll need more angel help to have the groups ready when we are.

"I've got a good supply of those," Deena said.

"That's good. I've decided we'll only work eight hour days even if it takes an extra year or so. We still have kids to raise.

"That makes sense to me," Jenny added.

Deena broke in. "Let me tell you now my thoughts on procedure. First, the problems of getting people to court. In the beginning, when we target specific groups, I can provide almost unlimited angels to act in a policing role to bring in the desired individuals. As people see the Judgment Line progressing, those with nothing to fear will accept the inevitable and report in on their own.

"The major problem is how we can identify those who haven't been judged without creating a mountain of paperwork for our staff. Remember, in many countries, births aren't even registered. I asked Analysis for a solution, and they recommended a small injection at the time of judgment that will cause the person to appear red in a wide-beam scan. We can easily set up a series of scanners that will blanket the world. All we would have to do is have an angel team on the ground ready to move across a designated sealed-off area. Everyone in the sector not judged would show up as green and could be corralled. Those bound over to Maggie will be injected to show up as blue in case one escapes. It should work since I have all those angels to help."

"Sounds simple, and it should work," Maggie agreed. "But we would have to institute border control between areas that have been searched and those that haven't. We'll have to keep the areas small and not round up too many at one time or we'll have the problem of housing and feeding them while they wait their turn. The general populace should prove to be helpful, since everyone not yet judged will look green to them, too. I guess we can use angels for border patrol, don't you think?"

"Shoulder to shoulder, if necessary," Deena said. "Now, your location should not matter. We are in the process of building Noah II which will have several REGEN machines as well as additional processing space for those headed to Hell. The REGENS can be used to bring the incorrigible to wherever you set up."

"In that case, I want to be near here," Maggie said. "With the REGEN we won't need much holding space and with a few angel guards, we should be OK. Anyone know of a suitable location?"

"I can think of two right now," I said. "One is that old rural school building on Jenkins Road. It could be ready in 5 or 6 weeks for our purposes. The other is Bennie and Drok's chicken farm. The one building is already partially ready and the other two could be ready soon. These two sites assume you want it to be a low-key process using primarily video."

"Suppose I want high visibility?"

"Then I think you would want to move to Savannah to better service those personally wanting to observe."

Hud said, "There really won't be much to observe. The whole process will be done by reading the accused. They'll have little to say. The few reporters who want to come could be accommodated in Clarksboro. I'd like the locals to get the business."

Maggie agreed. "There are definite advantages to starting out low key. We'll make it hard to visit and let most rely on some video by the others. Old school or chicken farm?"

"I vote for the old school," I said. "More room for parking and considerably larger. Plus there's something, um, gross about setting up a court in a chicken house. The school would make it seem more official to the public, don't you think?"

Hud and Jenny agreed.

Maggie said, "Jack, can you take charge of construction and put a rush on it?"

"No problem. My crew is not doing much now that can't be postponed. But we'll have to run out tomorrow and look at it and also get Earl Ray to lease or buy it from the county."

Maggie looked at Deena and said, "Does that mean another trip to Vegas?"

Deena laughed. "No such luck, Maggie. We have scads of confiscated drug money right now. I'll have a batch sent down and Hud can set up some phony firm bank accounts to feed it through. Hud, use a forgetter order on the bank employees when you open that account and tell them not to report that the deposit was in cash. Their books will still balance and no one will be the wiser."

"Can do," Hud said.

"What else?" Maggie asked.

"Those destined for Hell can be REGENed up to Noah II for processing and those for Terminus go to Heaven through Noah II," Deena said. "How will you organize who's in charge of what, Maggie?"

"You're in charge of everything except the judgment process itself. I want to be directly over the angel judges with one person under me in charge. Bishop recommends an angel named Chastity. I met her the other day. I liked her but wanted your opinion first."

"She's a good choice. I'm considering her to replace Carmen. She has excellent powers. Almost up to mine. I'll send her down to meet with you."

Maggie agreed and said, "I also want the top psychiatrists from Heaven to be at the old school to evaluate any Terminus bound cases before sending them forward. If they are truly mentally ill and believed to be curable, then I want to know it. It's a little cumbersome, but will help avoid mistakes. As to the others, you need to pick those who work under you. I would think you'll need a person in charge of the specific group roundups, another in charge of the general populace roundup, one for security, and one for REGEN. I would like to meet these four, or however many you decide you need, before we start."

"Where will we physically locate the lower courts?" Jenny asked.

"Most countries are going to need several locations," Deena said.

"I'll ask each head of state for a list of locations from which the lower court judges can choose. We'll spread the courts out proportionately to cover each country," Maggie decided. "Speaking of Heads of State, I plan to judge them while I am making the announcement in their country. I'll take them out immediately if absolutely necessary right then and there. I'll only do it, though, if I think it's imperative to save lives. If I take out too many in a short period of time, it may disrupt the world economy more than necessary."

"What about Heads of State who refuse to help us with the process?" Hud asked.

"We simply use mind control and threats to compel them to comply," Maggie said matter of factly, right to the point.

"Nothing like a little pressure on the balls to bring them around," agreed Jenny.

"On that note, I think I'll leave," Deena said. "You've given me about two years work to cram into a little more than a month! See you all later." And she breezed out.

After she left we tossed around several more ideas and potential problems. The most urgent and serious was what to tell our children. Up to now they had no idea of what was really happening.

"I think we're going to have to tell them. And soon," I said.

"I agree," said Jenny. "They've got to know before Judgment is announced. We also need to tell them about our move to the old house and our new relationships. I've given this a lot of attention in the last few months. And I've come to the conclusion that while it's going to be a whole lot for them to digest at one time, there's no real way to sequence this except to tell them the whole story in one package. Lay it out as clearly and succinctly as we can for them, and answer questions as they come up."

"One question I can think of right off the bat is that they will want to know about their own power levels and, in Laurie's case, that could prove to be a problem," Hud said. "That really may be too much for her to absorb right now."

"I agree, Hud," Maggie said. "And I have been worried about it for some time. The other three kids read to be as high or higher than you guys in terms of power potential, so they're also likely candidates for problems."

"Nevertheless, we need to tell them right away," I insisted. "Maybe a trip to Noah would help explain things to them. Let's think about it and decide tomorrow."

Everyone agreed, and on that positive note, Hud and Jenny left. Maggie headed for bed and I called Earl Ray about the old school. He said no problem with the county. He promised that by noon he would have it tied up for five years, with guaranteed renewal rights for three more five-year periods. I also told him to buy it if he could. He said he would try, but that might take a full board meeting. I told him time was important, but money was no object. He said he understood and rang off.

Then I called Tom and asked him to meet me at the old school at 8:00 in the morning. No problem. Then I went to bed myself. Details were falling into place pretty neatly right now.

forty-nine

Next morning was rainy and cold, with an ugly leaden sky and about 36 miserable degrees. We get snow once every couple of years and all the weather people had said it could happen today. The kids were up early hoping for a day off but so far it was still too warm to freeze the roads. I got to the old school at about 8:00 and found Tom waiting in his truck. .

"Nice day for ducks," Tom said.

"Don't forget the penguins," I agreed.

"Right about that. What's up?" Tom wanted to know.

"I've got a burning desire to attend a rural school again so I decided to use this one," I joked.

"Maybe I'll go with you. Never learned much the first time 'round."

I laughed and said, "Seriously, I've got a client who's hot to use this as office space and needs it in a real hurry, like yesterday. We need to look it over, decide what can be done, and how much time it will take. Once again, money is no object."

"OK. I'm ready. Let's do it."

I threw a rain poncho over my head and we walked over to the schoolhouse. It was 4-side brick construction with a two-story main building containing 16 good-sized classrooms and a set of offices

361

on the first floor and 18 classrooms on the second. There was also a second building that had been the gymnasium and the lunchroom. The roofs were still intact and there were no major leaks, but they needed some attention. As near as we could tell, both buildings were structurally sound. Most of the windows had been knocked out by vandals but would be OK to use with new glass. A good cleaning and a new paint job would do wonders for the main building. The gym needed a new floor because the old one had buckled badly near the center and on one side, as a result, probably, of rain and moisture coming in through those broken windows. The old foldaway bleachers were gone, as was the scoreboard. It was just a huge empty room. I could see that this would easily serve as the main detention or holding hall. The locker rooms and showers were repairable, mostly cosmetic stuff, and the cafeteria kitchen could be restored as well, if we decided we needed them.

Tom and I began a list of immediate actions needed as soon as Earl Ray was able to move on the acquisition. Tom didn't ask what this client's business was, or even question why lockers and restrooms would be needed. Guess that by now he was used to my odd requests.

"Tom, I'll go to Savannah this afternoon and talk to roofers, heat and air firms, and some electrical and plumbing contractors. They'll have to start right away so I'll have to promise big bonuses to get them. What about the rest?"

"I can arrange for new glass, cleanup and paint, any carpentry using our crew, and concrete work, and everything else. But a new floor for the gym worries me some. What do you have in mind? What do you plan to use it for?"

"Let's tear it out, repair any damage, and put in a rugged commercial carpet. I'll see someone in Savannah about that, too." I ignored his second question.

"What about the well? Should I get Farnam to come out?"

"Yeah. He probably drilled the original one, anyway. What else?"

"Carpet in the main building, too?"

"Yeah, but maybe not all commercial. I'll give that some thought and add that to my Savannah list. And by tomorrow, I'll be able to give you any plans for changes in walls and so on. Then you can order any new doors we'll need."

"OK. What about the spec house in Cedar Creek?"

"Where do you stand on it?"

"We're under roof but still lack doors, windows, plumbing, electric, and of course, the shingles."

"Bring in the subs for plumbing and electric and get a sub for shingles. Leave Billy and one man to do the doors and windows and bring everybody else over here tomorrow. When we finish here, we'll have made so much money that we might not need to finish the spec house."

"Must be some rich client."

"You'd never believe it if I could tell you."

After Tom left, I decided I had so much to do in Savannah that I would go directly. I called Maggie to report in.

"It's in pretty good shape, Maggie, good bones and all, but it'll take all the time we have left to renovate it. Can you round up Hud and Jenny and go out and decide on interior partitions?"

"Sure. I can do that. Jenny has an appointment to take Wayne to that specialist for tests at 1:00. He's been feeling worse the last few days. Probably late this afternoon will work. That OK?"

"Good. I'm on my way to Savannah now, but I should be home by dinner. Talk to you later."

I had unusually good luck with the various firms in Savannah that day. Most of the ones I talked to had enough time to do the job before Christmas and welcomed the extra money. I'd already spoiled them, apparently. I did have to promise some particularly lavish bonuses to the plumbing and electrical contractors. All of them agreed to meet me at the old school the next day, Wednesday. I had called Earl Ray after lunch and he had worked out a five-year lease to start with. He said that actually buying it would require board action. He told me to sign the lease so work could begin, and when the board met, they would consider the purchase request, almost certainly favorably. You see, the board loves money just a bit more than the average person does. I promised to stop by to sign between 5:00 and 6:00 that evening. I got there about 5:30 and he was ready.

"I got the five-year lease with a three-time 5-year renewal option. So you're protected for 20 years in case the board doesn't sell. What in hell are y'all going to do with that old school house?" Earl Ray wanted to know.

"It's a secret, Earl Ray, but you'll be among the first to know.."

He sighed deeply and said, "That damn Bennie talked me into covering for him for two months instead of one. Thank God, he's due back this week. I've been more tired this fall than I can ever remember. It'll be good to retire!"

"You can fish every day then."

"You got that right. That's exactly what I'm going to do."

"Thanks for putting the rush on this one, Earl Ray. Good job as usual. And good luck on your retirement. Someday I may actually have time to go fishing with you."

"Let's plan to do that," he said as I went out the door.

I turned the Lincoln toward home and thought about Bennie. God had made him take a two-month vacation in Hawaii with Marie and the real Bennie's daughter. He planned to reveal everything to Marie and it must have gone well, because we received a notice of their marriage on October 26. I had forgotten when they were due back, but looked forward to seeing them again. I pulled into the driveway and started to get out when Laurie ran out and said I was to go directly to the Raines. Since it was still raining, I stayed with the Lincoln and drove over.

Maggie met me at the door, visibly upset.

"What's the matter? What happened?" I asked anxiously.

"The specialist told Jenny that he's 99 percent certain that Wayne has leukemia. She just got home after a full afternoon of testing, sitting and waiting. Hud is in Brunswick and not answering his cell phone yet. Jenny is devastated."

"Why?"

"Why? What a stupid question. What do you mean why?"

"I repeat, why? All we have to do is take him to Charity and the repair machine. We're planning a trip to Noah anyway and I planned to run all the kids through the machine anyhow. Mark's asthma will be history, too."

"I thought of that, of course, but Jenny and I recall that Ruth said only spouses get those privileges. Don't you remember? She more or less dismissed the addition of children."

"She'll take our kids or She'll be hunting for four new suckers to play assistant. Anyway, She was assuming the kids would be grown before you took over."

"I don't know, Jack. But I agree with you. And that's a good arguing point. She'll have to come through on the kids or I'm out. Even if it means becoming a farmer in Hell for blackmailing God." I could see some of the tension melt.

"Agreed. Now let's tell Jenny and try to calm her down."

After we explained our position to her, she did relax a little. I was mixing some drinks when Hud came in and caught hell for not having his cell phone turned on. He was shocked and then said the same thing we all had about going up to Charity.

"We'll just put him through the repair machine on Noah," Hud said.

"That's what I thought," I said. "But Maggie and Jenny are worried that those privileges are reserved for spouses only. We've all just agreed that kids count or we're out of the game completely."

"Exactly," Hud said. "But I think kids were included anyway."

"I'm not sure," Maggie said. "What if it were my father or my cousin? Would they be eligible?"

Hud said, "I guess She has to draw the line somewhere. But not with our kids."

Everyone agreed, so Maggie put out a call for Deena to come as quickly as possible. Then she and Jenny started fixing dinner while we waited to hear from Deena.

Our kids came over for dinner and afterward walked back home to do homework. Or whatever it is that kids do in the evening. Wayne seemed OK, but I don't think the true gravity of his condition had set in yet. Deena answered and said she would come at 9:00. She arrived right on schedule.

"What's up? You sounded pretty worried, Maggie."

Jenny said, "It looks like Wayne has leukemia. We had the tests run today."

Deena walked over to the sofa and sat down by Jenny and hugged her and said, "Don't worry. Charity will take care of it."

Maggie said, "We weren't sure children were included in the offer."

Deena frowned and said, "She really didn't say so, did She? But I'm sure that they must be. Ruth worries about kids more than anyone else."

"Well, they better be," Hud said.

"I'll go now and try to see Her," Deena said. "But I think it will be tomorrow afternoon before I get a chance. I'll call when I know something. In the meantime, try not to worry. I'm really optimistic, so you can be, too."

After she left there was really little more to say. We talked about the old school but so far, only Maggie had gotten out to see it. She showed us a sketch of what she thought would work, and we spent a few minutes discussing and revising it. Hud said he would try to stop out first thing in the morning. Jenny was too distracted. Understandable. We didn't press her. After that, we went home.

The next morning, Wednesday, it was 34 and still raining. What miserable weather! By the time I ate breakfast, it had dropped to 31 and was spitting snow. I hollered at the kids and they came racing down, turned on the radio and heard their fate with respect to school that day. At 7:00, the announcer gave them their wish: no school.

I had my first appointment at the old school at 8:00 to get an estimate from a heat and air company. I had seven others lined up for various times throughout the day. I left home at 7:45, so the roads were still too warm for ice to form, and I had no trouble at all getting there. Tom and crew were there setting up a portable heater in one of the school rooms where the men could take thaw-out breaks. I decided right then that it would be a good place for our headquarters. I immediately called the power company and arranged to get the electric turned on the next morning so that we could set up more heaters. Warm workers would be better workers.

The heat and air man was Bunny Hopkins, the same guy I happened to be using on our old house. I had just finished showing Tom the sketches and revisions we had made for changes when I heard Bunny arrive.

"Yo! Where ya'll?

"In here," I shouted sticking my head out the classroom door.

He came stomping into the room cursing the weather and blowing on his hands. He made a beeline for the heater and stood there a minute warming his hands. "This is the sunny South? Bullshit! It's colder 'an a frog's ass sitting on the North Pole. And snowin' on top of that!"

"Good to see you out and around and in a good mood, Bunny. You'll survive it."

"I dunno. I'm not so young anymore. Take last night. I was positively drowsy after my sixth beer. Usually I c'n drink ten before that happens." He laughed and his mood clearly lightened.

Bunny was about 6'5" and weighed in the neighborhood of 290 pounds. He had played football with the nearby Georgia Southern University Eagles when they won the Division 1-AA National Championship in 1985 and 1986. He was from Alabama but had loved Savannah so much that he opened his business there in 1986 and was doing really well. Quality work, for sure. Kept his beer cold for after work.

He grinned and continued, "Well, Jack. Let's look'er over. I got to be back in Savannah about 10:00 and this damned weather is supposed to get worse."

We made the tour and decided on what we needed. Unfortunately, the big unit required for the gym had to be ordered and shipped. The process had never taken less than about two months in the past.

"No quicker way?" I asked Bunny.

"Well, yeah, we could ask them to air freight it, but that would cost you your left one. Take about two weeks that way, I think."

"Don't worry about the freight cost. Bring it in by air. I told you this is a rush job and we're willing to make some extra expenditures to insure it's done on time."

"Must be some kind'a rich client. What in the hell they gonna do with it?"

"Can't tell you now. It's a surprise. You be careful on the road," I said as he ducked low to get into his van. We shook hands on the deal and I promised him the nice completion bonus. We agreed to attend to details when the weather was a little more friendly.

He said, "I'll get a crew out tomorrow to start to take out the old systems. We'll somehow make it before Christmas."

He roared off, fishtailing a little on the now-slippery roads. They'd soon be really bad. Roads down here are constructed for hot and dry not cold and wet. I moved back to the heater. A few minutes later, Hud came in and I got him to the heater. I made a mental note to bring in some chairs.

"Any word from Deena?" I asked.

"Not yet. But she said it'd probably be this afternoon."

"Right. Well, what do you think of our new offices?"

"I hope they'll be warmer than they are now. Let's look around."

I grabbed the sketches and we walked through the main building first. Maggie wanted the front office complex to be staffed with angels to fend off the media types who insisted on being here in person. Behind the office would be space to be used by the psychiatrists from Heaven. This would take a total of three classrooms of the seven on the office side of the hall. The fourth classroom would be a conference-break room and the last three would be reserved for Maggie's large courtroom. On the other side of the hall we planned on a waiting room for media and a public restroom taking up the first two rooms. The third would be split into a small bunk room and storage for us, and the last six would be turned into three courtrooms for Hud, Jenny, and me. Each of the four courtrooms would have a private bathroom. Since this was a slab floor we were lucky that they had run plumbing to nearly all of the rooms.

The second floor would be repartitioned into eight large rooms holding 100 people each to use when we did group reads. This would take 16 of the existing rooms. The other two would hold a REGEN which could move about 100 people at once as quickly as you could get them assembled.

Hud agreed that it was workable. We went to the gym and I showed him the floor and told him that I thought carpet was the answer. He agreed.

"We've got a huge budget, so why not?" Hud said. "And since we do have plenty of money, I think I'll institute a search for some antique benches for us to use. What do you think?"

"Good idea. Get a real impressive ornate one for Maggie."

"Agreed. What kind of furnishings do we need in here? This is a really big space to fill."

"I thought we'd create a detention area partitioned off in one corner with a set of bunks for those accused who are held over for some reason. That should take about one-fifth of the floor space. We could put a dorm-living area with some small private rooms on the opposite end that would be for the angel guards, the office angels, the psychiatrists, and visiting angels. They won't be allowed to leave the premises but will REGEN up every week or two for a break. Now, this would take about one-half of the floor space leaving the rest for two REGEN machines." Hud asked about a power source for the REGEN machines but I had to admit I didn't have a clue about that. We'd need to deal with it asap before all the crews started their work.

"Do you want me to handle getting the furnishings for this room and the offices and courtrooms?" Hud asked.

"That would take a lot of the load off of me. Do you have time?"

"I think so. Melissa is finally beginning to take hold and we're pretty light right now anyway."

"It's all yours except for the kitchen equipment. I want to promise that to the plumbers to give them a little more profit incentive."

"Good. I'll get on my part right away."

We headed back to the heater. When we glanced out, we could see that the snow was coming down even heavier, those big, fat, fluffy flakes that were only pretty until they hit the ground. Hud decided he'd better go before it was too late. I was tempted but the plumber, Jake Gilmer was due about now and I really had to be here. I told Tom and crew to leave if they wanted. Only one of the guys left, though. His wife was due in a few days so he was understandably worried.

About 10 minutes later, Jake came wandering in. We toured the place and he took a lot of notes. He agreed to give me an estimate soon. I told him to deep-six the estimate and take it on cost plus, because I wanted him to do the job. I also promised a really nice bonus if he made the Christmas deadline. He was the only acceptable firm to even agree to come out and bid. There are lots of plumbers but only a few good ones, so I wasn't too worried about choosing him right up front.

We made the deal, and after he left, I started calling the others who were due to come. Only one, Rod Smith, the electrical contractor was on his way. I told the others to wait until next morning. Rod arrived and said it was really getting bad. He was going to go to his grandparents' house here in Clarksboro as soon as we finished, so we made short work of it. I offered him the same deal as Jake. He was reluctant because of the time factor and all the other work he had committed to do, but the bonus won him over, as I knew it would. He laughed and said he guessed he would give up sleeping for that kind of money.

After he left, I told Tom and crew to go home before they had to spend the night. We all left at the same time. I was really pleased at how well the day had gone.

I grew up driving in the ice and snow up north, and there are just three basic rules: anticipate, anticipate and anticipate. Every upcoming move. Here in south Georgia, snow happens once every four years or so, and it's usually a very small bit that lasts just a very short time. But people simply don't have a clue about how to drive in it. They roar up to stop signs and bash on the brakes just like any normal day. I wasn't having any trouble with the road but was held up several times by a rash of fender benders. One accident was pretty serious and I wound up helping get the injured out of the cars. I finally made it home about 1:00 after leaving the school at about 11:00. It was usually an easy 20 minute drive.

Maggie and the kids were home but still no word from Deena. I ate some cold leftover roast for lunch and was contemplating a nap when Deena announced her arrival. The kids were upstairs so she came on in.

She sat down on the sofa and said, "I talked to Ruth a little while ago. It's a tossup. She said She hadn't really anticipated such a thing, so it's always been spouses and no one else. Of course, She did admit that She had used very few people with kids over time so kids had never come up in this way before. She has turned down brothers and sisters, parents and so on, but never kids. She has decided to mull it over until tomorrow."

"She'd better 'mull' Her way to the right choice or She'll be hunting a new assistant," Maggie said.

"I told Her you would be more than unhappy, but by that time, She was too preoccupied to respond. I gently kept after Her, and She finally said to bring you up at 9:00 tomorrow morning. I think She wants you to state your case in person."

"That suits me just fine. I have a few things to tell Her which may serve to influence Her decision."

"Who's going to tell Jenny and Hud?" I asked.

"I really need to leave. I'd appreciate it if you could talk to them."

"Chicken," Maggie said. "Go on. I'll do it. Do you want me to meet you on Noah a few minutes before 9:00 tomorrow morning? Since I learned how to use the REGEN, I haven't really had a chance to do it unsupervised."

"That'd be great. How's the old school going to work out, Jack?"

"I think we can make it in time. I do have a question. What kind of power do I need for the REGEN machines?"

"We use atomic power packs which last about six months. They can be REGENed down as needed. Anything else?"

"That's just the answer I needed, Deena."

"I'll see you in the morning," Maggie said and Deena left.

Maggie called and briefed Jenny on Ruth's decision to wait and said that she was going to go see Her in the morning. She told Jenny not to worry.

fifty

The next day, the snow was just a memory, and the sun was shining. The kids were bitterly disappointed, of course, but I myself was due at the school again at 8:00 and didn't want to slide all the way, so I was glad the roads were completely clear. It had warmed up during the night, clear up to 42 degrees, so most of the snow was gone. Just a few pitiful little bent over snowmen and a couple of small snow piles under the biggest trees. I told Maggie to have fun with Ruth and left, humming and in a really good mood.

When I got there, Tom and crew were on the job. I saw Jeff Holt's truck. Jeff owned our local demolition firm. They were already working on taking out the old gym floor. There was another truck there and it turned out to be Edward Jarvon, one of the two roofing firms I asked over. I didn't know him well but heard they did good work. I explained the time crunch again, and told him to figure on a new roof for both buildings and he went out to get some measurements.

"How'd you get Jeff so quick?" I asked Tom, who had strolled in to see me.

"He had a house to take down but the weather's made it too sloppy to work in the yard area so he agreed to come and knock this out. He'll take out the old gym floor and clean out those old kitchen fixtures. They should finish tomorrow. Where do you stand?"

"Heat and air goes to Bunny. Plumbing to Jake and electric to Rod. The roof will go to Edward or Al's Roofing, whoever can do it the quickest. I've got two carpet guys coming today."

"Sounds good. I talked to Farnam's son and they're going to check the well and put in a new pump, if the well's OK. If not, they'll drill a new one. Ground's not frozen, so it won't be a problem for them. Jason's Glass is set do the windows. I told him to measure and get the order in pronto. Let's see. What else? Oh, yeah. I talked to Emmanuel Tarver. about the painting and he thinks he'll have time. I told him to start on the exterior trim anytime. He may be out today for a look."

"Good work, Tom. You've covered just about everything. That leaves the parking lot and driveway. I'll call Harley Danson and get him to give us a quote. Anything else?"

"How high did you want us to set the interior walls in the gym?"

"I think about 12 feet should be enough, don't you?"

"Yeah, some sound will filter over but it shouldn't be too bad. We can put in some drop ceilings pretty easily if it turns out to be a problem."

About then, Edward wandered back in and said he would have me an estimate by noon. I told him the estimate of when he could start and finish was as important as the price and that I would have both bonuses and penalties in the contract. He said he understood and left. I spent the rest of the morning with the other roofer and the two carpet people.

I met Hud for lunch at Burton's at 12:30 and Bennie was there. He looked tanned and fit.

"All done with the job?" I asked Bennie.

"All done and glad of it! I'll tell you, that was an ordeal. Back to the real world, though. I met with Earl Ray this morning and took over the business. He seemed a little older and wearier than normal."

The waitress came over and took our orders and when she left, Hud said, "I was telling Bennie about the old school project when you came in. How's it going?"

"Very well. Great, in fact. I think I've got commitments on everything except the roof and I should have that early this afternoon. Oh, and I need to check on the paving."

"Harley's the man for that," Bennie said.

"Yeah, I agree, I'm going to call him after lunch."

Our food arrived about then so our table was pretty quiet for a bit. The owner, Bill Adams, came over and asked our opinion about going strictly non-smoking. We all said he should, but he quickly said he wasn't sure, since some of his best customers were diehard smokers. He thanked us for our opinions anyway. Wonder why he even bothered us? He had his mind already made up, and didn't really want to hear what we had to say.

When we finished and were ready to leave, Bennie said Marie wanted to have us all over for dinner Saturday night. We said we'd check with the girls and let him know. Hud was on his way to Savannah to check on furnishings for the old school. As I made my way back, I decided that we needed to come up with a better name for that school. My entry was Reckoning. No more time for musing, though. Back to work. I called Harley on the cell phone. We agreed to meet at 1:30.

When I got back, Tom was with the painter, Emmanuel. I walked over and talked to them for a few minutes.

"How's business?" I asked.

"Been a little slow, a little slow, you know. Spring's the killer time for us. Even so, I'm not sure I can promise a job this big in the time frame you want."

"Promise your men a Christmas bonus and take it out of the bonus I'll give you personally to finish before Christmas."

I mentioned a figure and he whistled and said, "Yeah, well, OK then. We'll start today. My crew may have to work weekends and nights, but we'll get 'er done in time."

"Good. One thing, no bonus if you don't get done. Agreed?"

"Agreed. We'll start pressure washing and scraping this afternoon. See you later." He almost ran to his truck.

I turned to Tom and said, "I love having an unlimited budget. By the way, you can tell our crew that if they work hard it will be a green Christmas for them, too. We'll undoubtedly have to work some weekends and nights."

"How green?"

I told him and he said, "That's green enough. We'll be available."

Harley came by about 10 minutes later and we made a deal for the paving. He really wasn't that busy, so he would earn his bonus easily. I left to run some errands in town and stopped by the house to see if Maggie was back. She wasn't, but she REGENed in while I was in the bathroom.

"Took you long enough. What happened?"

"I stayed to interview Chastity and some psychiatrists for the old school."

"Reckoning."

"What did you say?"

"Reckoning. That's the name I'm proposing for the old school. I meant what happened with Ruth?"

"I recorded it. Do you want to listen?"

"You bet. Where is it?"

She got the recorder off the dresser and tossed it to me. I turned it on and heard Ruth's voice.

"I'm glad you and Deena could come, Maggie. Please sit down and I'll ring for coffee. Or would you rather have tea?"

"I'd prefer tea, if you don't mind. Thanks."

Ruth continued, "The hardest part about my job is making decisions about mortals even though I am mortal. The rules that I operate under allow me to make such decisions, but I am supposed to use restraint. If a mortal does a job for me, I can reward him or her in many ways. Some of these include the repair machine, the injections against all disease, the long life drugs, and so on. My policy has always been to extend these privileges to the spouses of these people and it has worked well. I have had requests to include parents, siblings, aunts, uncles, neighbors and, you name it, but I have routinely refused. You can see that it could easily get out of hand. I do admit that in all these years, I have never been asked to make a decision about children. There have been a few children of course, but none ever had an illness that local medical technology couldn't solve. So there it is."

"Does that mean you have decided against allowing the children to see Charity?"

"Deena tells me that you'll be mad and probably resign."

Maggie broke paused the recording here and said, "I was so mad at this point that I couldn't even speak for a moment. I actually contemplated trying to fry Her. Then I regained control and– well, listen."

"You can bet I'm mad, but I'm not going to resign. Instead I want to talk about my job description. Check me if I'm wrong, but my title is assistant to God. I have been given the Earth to administer as I see fit and consult with you only if I had a problem I couldn't resolve. The one thing you said I couldn't do is alter the past to change the present or the future. You said if I didn't perform satisfactorily, I would be relieved. I was to have all the resources of Heaven at my disposal. Is all of this true?"

"Yes, dear. That's the essence of it. What are you trying to say?"

"Just this. Have I been relieved?

"No, dear, of course not."

"Then why are you making my decisions for me? If I decide to bring a mortal to the repair chamber, that's my business. And Charity is, you remember, at my disposal. Are you prohibited from letting our children visit Charity? No. That just happens to be your own personal rule. But that is not one of the things I was forbidden to do. The only condition was about altering the past and this doesn't. I'm going to bring them to Charity and if you see fit to relieve me for that, so be it. I'm not sure I want this job as you describe it anyway."

"Well, well, Deena. Looks like she has some Godlike qualities after all."

Deena and Ruth glanced at each other and laughed.

"What is the matter with you two?" Maggie demanded.

"I'm sorry, dear," said Ruth. "I know you'll be miffed but I've just been testing you. I can't read you anymore and don't even know if I could defeat you if necessary. But I do know that in all the hours we've been together you have not questioned me or challenged me on one thing. You have been much too reverent. When Deena told me about little Wayne, I decided to test you to see how far this reverence extended. I found your boiling point. But I had to know. I may have caused Hud and Jenny a small hurt, and I'm sorry about that, but I think they'll forgive me when I explain it to them. The bottom line is that you must be able to make decisions on your own, and now I know you can and you will. Forgive me this little transgression."

"You never intended to refuse Wayne and the other kids?"

"Heavens, no. Children are as important, if not more important, than spouses to those who work for me."

Maggie said, "Deena, did you know about this?"

"I'm afraid so. And I told Jenny and Hud yesterday that all was well, but also told them that they couldn't tell you or Jack."

"I'll get you for this, Deena," Maggie said chuckling. "I owe you one."

Deena laughed and said, "Don't blame me."

"All right. You two are one up on me. In the future, though, I'd appreciate some transparency. Now, what else do we need to discuss?"

Deena said, "The only problem is money. I can feed some through the banking system and not be detected but it's going to be harder with the tremendous amounts we're going to need."

"Hit a couple more of those drug-involved casinos," said Ruth. "They're each good for several million."

"Good idea. I'll set it up," Deena said.

The rest of the tape was apparently all small talk so I shut it off.

I said, "She may be slipping but She's got a few good curveballs left."

"I still don't know whether to be relieved or mad, but at least it's over. I'll admit that I do feel better having confronted Her."

"Are you going to play this for Jenny and Hud?"

"I think so, don't you?"

"Yeah, I do."

"I'll call Jenny and see if she and Hud want to bring their kids over for pizza. And afterward maybe we can tell them the whole story. Tomorrow's actually Friday, so they could miss school. We could all go and see Charity."

"Sounds good. Have any ideas about how to approach it?"

"I don't know, Jack. I just want to be honest and answer all their questions."

"I guess you're right. They already know we're moving to the country and probably have guessed the rest."

"I'm sure Laurie has. Oh, well. Let me call Jenny."

fifty-one

We all sat around enjoying pizza and some funny stories from the kids. Afterwards, we sent the children upstairs to mess around while we prepared ourselves for the unveiling. We tossed it around a while, and Hud finally said, "Let's get it over with. I think just start out with something, anything, and play it by ear."

"I agree," Maggie said and she got up, went to the stairs and called the kids.

They all four came down and Maggie got them seated.

We all looked at Maggie and she shrugged and said, "I guess it's up to me."

She looked at the kids for a moment and began.

"We have some very important things we want to tell you. One of them you already know. We've shown you the big country house we're remodeling, but we haven't told you that it's designed for two families. Two apartments. We are all going to be moving there in just a few weeks.

"The reason is more complex. Our religion and our society impose certain standards on us. Some are strictly based on custom, such as going to church on Sunday or eating our food with silverware or celebrating Thanksgiving. Others are based on law. You are punished if you drink and drive or if you neglect a child. Part of both

379

our customs and our law is that you may marry but it must be to only one person. Custom frowns on multiple-spouse marriages and it is basically illegal in most the U.S. This is not necessarily true in other cultures and with other countries' legal requirements. But it is here.

"Now, peoples' lives and emotions don't always conform to the customs and the law. They discover that they are different. What I am trying to get to is this. The four of us have discovered that we love each other, and if it were legal, we would all four get married together. Again, this is not as unusual as you may think. As I said, there are many types of marriages around the world which involve more than two people. But it isn't legal in the U. S., so we are doing it without the formalities of a wedding.

"To keep up appearances in Clarksboro, we will continue to live separately in two apartments in the big house. This will have very little effect on your lives as long as you don't tell anybody about it. It does create more security for you since you will each have two mothers and two fathers. In practice, however, you will still answer to your own father and mother on a day-to-day basis."

She stopped and waited a few moments. Jimmy turned to Laurie and said, "You were right. They've been sleeping together." Laurie turned red and Mark and Wayne shifted uncomfortably.

Maggie said, "We knew Laurie suspected something was up and I guess you were right, honey. Now I'm telling you that we love each other, and sleeping together is one way of expressing that love."

Laurie said, "It's all right with us, but don't you think you should have talked to us before the decision to combine families was made?"

"No, Laurie," Maggie said gently. "It was our business and our decision. As I said, it will impact little on your lives unless you spread it all over town. Then people will take notice and it will impact us all. Does that make sense?"

The kids all nodded, but I could see that they were going to have to talk it over among themselves before they really could decide where they stood on the situation.

Hud, ever the lawyer, jumped in. "What Maggie is saying from a legal standpoint is that while it is not illegal for four people to decide to live together, it is still frowned on by society, particularly a rural society like Clarksboro. Only if we took formal wedding vows would we be illegal under the bigamy laws. But Maggie is right. You must keep this to yourselves."

"We will," Jimmy said. "You don't have to worry about that. I'm not even sure anybody would believe me." Everyone else chimed in their agreement.

Maggie began again.

"We'll talk about this all you want in the next few days. But now get comfortable and be prepared, because we have something else extremely serious and important to tell you. As you all know, we've been away a lot recently. We haven't been quite open and honest with you, I'm afraid. I think you all had suspicions here, too, but we have been reluctant to drag you into it. Now we must. Where do you think we've been going? What do you think we've been doing?"

"We don't know, but we noticed some strange things going on," Laurie said. "Aunt Eloise talks like a woman from one of our history tapes from the 1950's, and she's never heard words like rap or BFF or dope or droid. We wondered what planet she must be from."

Jimmy added, "And we can tell that all of you are in better shape than you've been for years. We saw Dad lift the old wood stove in our garage and move it all by himself. I remember when he and Mr. Warner together nearly died moving it. Yeah, that's more than a little strange."

Mark said, "You're different, too, Mom. I mean, you still like us but you're different."

Wayne agreed that his Mama had changed, too.

Maggie took the conversation back.

"I guess we weren't as clever as we thought. Brace yourselves. This is going to take a while, and it will be quite a ride."

Maggie started in July with Mrs. Angelo and went right up to the present. Precise and concise. Just the facts. I had trouble believing it myself. And the kids were clearly overwhelmed.

When she finished Maggie said, "I know this is a lot to absorb. I'm sorry, but you had to know, and you had to know now. You must not talk to your friends about this in any way before New Year's Day. Not a word. We weren't going to tell you until then but

Wayne's illness forced our hand. We are taking you all up to Noah tomorrow morning to visit Charity and to use the repair machine. You will also get several injections against further diseases."

"We don't have to go to school tomorrow?" Mark asked excitedly.

Maggie laughed. "No, but I do have one piece of bad news for you. No one on Noah or in Heaven or Hell wears clothes."

Laurie gasped and said, "You mean we have to go——?"

Maggie laughed and said, "That's it exactly. We all peel down before we go."

Jenny said, "It's actually quite comfortable when you get used to it."

"I know you have a million questions but I'd like for you to hold most of them until tomorrow. Anyone have one that can't wait?" Maggie asked.

"What if you wear clothes anyway?" Jimmy asked.

"You would stand out like a sore thumb," Jenny said. "When did you get so shy? Weren't you the one who told me about skinny dipping at the beach last month?"

"That was just a bunch of guys. This is different," he said stealing a glance in Laurie's direction.

"You'll live through it and learn to like it, so don't worry," Hud said.

"Let's meet here at 9:00 in the morning and I'll take us up," Maggie said.

With that, the Raines went home.

The kids were really wound up and wanted to discuss the whole thing in detail but Maggie stalled them off on most points. Laurie did ask about her own powers and Maggie simply told her that they would develop in time. We finally chased them off to bed. Only to have Laurie return about 15 minutes later.

"Mom. What day did you first find out you were a candidate for God?"

I almost jumped out of my skin. That was a piece of information Maggie had chosen to withhold. I feared the worst.

"What makes you think I am?" Maggie asked her.

"You said so."

"No, I purposely did not say so."

"It was October 17, wasn't it?"

"If that was a Friday, that was probably right. How do you know?"

"I just knew it that day and wrote it in my diary. I was going to ask you about it, but it seemed so ridiculous. Until tonight."

"Laurie, it seems that your powers are beginning to emerge. I had hoped you would not awaken for several more years because they are an awesome responsibility. Just relax and let me know if anything unusual happens to you. OK?"

"OK."

Maggie got up and hugged her and told her goodnight again and she left.

"So it begins," I said shaking my head sadly. "Pretty soon she'll know my every thought."

"Maybe. But she has always been a responsible girl. I'll work with her as much as necessary to teach her the ethical use of her powers."

I got up and stretched and said, "I'm tired and really strung out. I think I'll go on to bed and try to rest. How about you?"

"Me too. It's going to be a long morning. But I'm really excited about it. I think we've turned the page to another chapter."

Despite exhaustion, I slept fitfully that night and finally got up about 5:30 and worked a while on the books. I called Tom about 6:45 and told him I wouldn't be out until late afternoon and to keep things moving. We had breakfast about eight. Just as we finished, the Raines arrived and it was time to go. Everyone was dressed and only Maggie was missing. She breezed in wearing a robe and said, "Everyone ready? Good. Then off with the clothing."

And just like that, she was nude. The rest of us started undressing and soon we were all naked and embarrassed. Maggie gathered us all together, we all touched, and we were on Noah.

"Neat," Mark said.

"This way," Maggie said. She turned and walked toward Charity's lab.

When we got into the lab, Deena and Charity were over by the repair machines chatting. Jimmy looked at Deena and said 'Wow', which earned him a dirty look from Jenny. Maggie introduced the kids to Deena and Charity.

Charity said, "Let's begin with Wayne and Mark."

She put them into the Chambers and started their cycles.

"Wayne's leukemia is confirmed and will be eliminated. It will take about three hours. Mark has asthma and a heart murmur. An hour and a half should do it for him."

Maggie said, "We'll come back about 11. Let's go on a little tour."

We spent the next hour and a half meandering around Noah. Deena promised some live footage of Heaven and Hell as soon as everyone was out of the Chambers. We stopped by to visit Bishop, who was his usual self. He seemed very glad to see Laurie. He told Maggie privately that Laurie was even higher than at his last reading. We got back to Charity's about 11 and Jimmy took Mark's place.

After two minutes Charity said, "He's healthy as a horse. The only thing to treat is athletes foot and some jock itch. He'll be out in 15 minutes."

Laurie took Jimmy's place and Charity began the cycle.

"She's got a bad knee from an injury in the past and we'll correct that. Otherwise nothing. We'll need about an hour for her."

We left again and escorted Mark around a little bit. At 12:30 both Wayne and Laurie were done so we went to join Deena for lunch in the briefing room. Deena had the long-range cameras from Hell on screen and you could see the work being done on Uncertainty. The buildings were well underway and the fence was essentially complete. She also showed some video of Heaven including a short clip of Ruth talking to Maggie. The kids were much impressed. Deena answered questions until about 2:00. She told the kids again how important it was to keep all this secret, and said she was very impressed with their sense of responsibility. Then we left for home.

The next three weeks were incredibly busy. By Friday, December 12, we were about ready to tear out our hair. First was the old house project. We were due to move in this weekend but it still wasn't ready. It was the painters and the carpet and tile people holding things up. There was one decent tile man for a hundred miles in any direction and he was always overwhelmed with work. Fortunately, I had set a December 18 deadline and had a really stiff penalty clause. It looked like he would make it. The carpet we wanted was back ordered but the guy hadn't bothered to tell me. He said it would be shipped Monday. Not acceptable, I told him, so I sent one of our crew with a truck to Rome, Georgia, yesterday to pick it up. He was due back this morning. I fired the painter. How can you be so sorry you don't want to earn money? I found another who was on the job this morning. He said he could pull in his whole crew and could finish by Tuesday. So maybe we could move in by the 18th and be settled for Christmas.

The second problem was Reckoning. It was not a problem of being behind schedule, because things were pretty much on course. It was just a case of "if it could go wrong, it did". The plumber found a leak under the slab in the office area and we had to tear up a section and repair it. The roofer found some structural damage under the shingles of the old gym. We got that repaired. A delivery truck backed into a brick wall on the main building and we had to hunt up a bricklayer to repair it. Nothing really huge, but so on and so on. Still, it looked like we would make the Christmas deadline in spite of everything.

The third problem area was the Judgment Line process itself. There were endless things to do and we all worked like demons, pardon the pun. Deena got the lion's share and had everything on course. Jenny, Hud and I divided the world into three parts and scheduled our Heads-of-State visits. On paper, that is. We decided the best physical plan was to arrive unannounced and use mind control to force our way in. We were going to visit 10 to12 per day each, so it would take us about a week.

During that week, a message announcing the Judgment Line process would be broadcast several times daily on TV and radio and published in all the print media. Judgment would actually begin in each country immediately after Maggie herself had a chance to visit each of the specific Heads of State and had broadcast final local messages. All of these messages were partially canned ahead of time in the local languages. Maggie had spent long hours reading them onto tape. Following the announcements, Deena would move in with her angel judges and set up the courts needed.

We scheduled Maggie's visits to occur every 30 minutes, so it should take about two weeks. By then, Deena should have the courts operating in the first countries that Maggie had visited. And Chastity was down for a visit during that week. Maggie had liked her and gave her the assistant's job. She would help the judges get started after Deena had the courts set up. So we really were making progress.

Finally, the kids nearly drove us crazy with questions. It wasn't their fault. Their lives had been turned upside down and they were excited, confused and worried all at the same time. Mark asked me if he would go to hell for fighting with Johnny Eason. Laurie wanted to know how Maggie could be God when she was guilty of adultery here on earth. They both wanted to use powers to do school work or, more correctly, to avoid schoolwork. Mark desperately wanted to spill all the secrets to his buddies. And so on.

I came home one afternoon and Maggie was crying. Apparently, Laurie had come home and announced that she was going to have sex with her current flame, Robert. She said if her mother could do it, so could she. Maggie, of course, got mad and they had a big fight. I went upstairs and knocked on her door.

"What?"

"It's me. Can I come in?"

She opened the door and I saw she was crying too. I hugged her and we sat down on the bed.

"What's the problem, Pumpkin?" I asked.

"I'm so ashamed of Mama for sleeping with Mr. Raines." More sobs.

"How about me? I slept with Mrs. Raines."

"Men do those things. Mothers don't."

"Men need women to do those things."

"Not my mother, they don't." Dramatic heaving, sobbing sighs.

"Laurie, I'm not going to try to tell you that you shouldn't be upset. That's normal when something happens which is outside your experience and your training. But let me try to explain. Your mother and I met many years ago and fell in love. We decided that we would marry and spend our lives together. We had you and Mark as a result of that love and now we share that love with you two. Understand that so far?"

"That's how it's supposed to work. That's what I'm told, anyhow. How would I know?" There was more than a touch of sarcasm in her voice.

"Good. Now try to picture this. I meet another woman and after spending some time around each other, we discover we are in love. It has nothing to do with my love for your mother. It's just a new relationship that happened."

"How can you love two people at once?" Sobbing begins again, but I notice it's more controlled now.

"Do you love me?"

"Yes."

"Do you love your mother?"

"Yes."

"How can you love both of us?"

"That's different. I don't love you in the sex way."

"That's true. And it is possible to love someone without having sex, right?"

"Well, yes."

"Laurie, I loved Miss Jenny for a long time before we had sex together. I wanted to be around her, to talk to her, to touch her, to share her life. Our first sexual encounter was not planned or even sought by either of us. We were thrown together by the demon, Karg, against our will, as were your mother and Mr. Raines. But it is a normal desire to have sex with someone you love and inevitably, we did. All I can tell you is I love your mother more than ever and I also love Miss Jenny. Now, the problem is that our society and religion dictate that I must choose between them. Either I stay with your mother and forget Miss Jenny or I divorce your mother and marry Miss Jenny. Either way it's a mess for everyone, including kids. Maybe especially for kids. But in our situation, it's fortunate that Mr. Raines and your mother feel the same way about each other, so we can come to terms with what could be a problem without disrupting lives. If they hadn't, I would have been forced to choose. I would have chosen your mother and Jenny would have chosen Hud but we would both have been very sad.

"You are upset because we aren't conforming to the way we were taught by society and by the Christian religion. You may have to make similar choices yourself someday. In fact, what you announced you were going to do with Robert is against society and the Christian teachings, isn't it?"

She was crying again, but she nodded her head in the affirmative.

"Then you already have had to face the kind of pressure we felt before we made our decision. Bear in mind that our society and religion are not shared by most of the world's people. In some other societies and religions, multiple spouse marriages are not only common but expected and even necessary. Premarital sex is condoned and sometimes encouraged. Laurie, Ruth told us She has two spouses. She didn't say what sex they were. So you won't go to Hell for having sex with Robert and we won't go to Hell for wanting to marry our neighbors. So relax."

"You mean you think it's OK if I have sex with Robert?"

"Do you love him?"

"No, I don't think so." A pretty quick answer to that one, thank heaven.

"There's nothing wrong with recreational sex. Of course, I'd prefer that you wait until you have some more experience in predicting what might happen. But I can't and won't try to stop you. You're old enough to make your own decision. Talk to your Mama. She's pretty wise for a sinful old woman. I'll send her up."

I got up and she jumped up and hugged me and said, "I do love you, Daddy, and I love Mama, too. Thank you."

I went downstairs and Maggie said, "How is she?"

"Fine. She needs her Mom now. Do you want to go up?"

"Yes."

Maggie spent about an hour up in Laurie's room and when she came back she said, "You missed your calling. You should have been a shrink. You must have said all the right things."

"I was just honest with her."

"I know. She'll be all right. No question about it."

fifty-two

"We interrupt this program to bring you urgent and important information," an authoritative voice on the TV announced. It was Simon, the angel whom Deena had chosen to take over all TV and radio stations for the announcement. Maggie and I were sitting in our living room with Hud and Jenny and all the kids watching that night of December 13. The screen faded and an image of Maggie seated in a throne-like chair came up. The lights were set so that it was hard to really focus on her face. She was dressed all in white, and looked very Godlike. She began to speak.

"My name is Maggie and I am a representative of God. She has asked me to initiate the judgment process for all the peoples of the Earth." She paused here for effect, and did the same throughout the broadcast. Very effective. She continued. "Most of your religions have predicted that someday God or Her representative would come to Earth and that at that time, everyone, without exception, would stand in judgment. That time has now come. Judgment will begin with the New Year. You will each be judged individually. No one will be missed or excused. You will be judged on the basis of whether or not you have harmed others and to what degree.

"This judgment process will take 3 to 4 years to complete. Most of you will pass through unaffected. It will be nothing more than a minor time inconvenience. Those of you who have caused serious premeditated harm to others will be removed from the Earth community immediately. Courts for this judgment will be set up in all countries. Details will be forthcoming.

"In order for you to comprehend that I am serious and not promoting a new movie or some fanatic with enough money to buy TV space, God has arranged for a 'miracle'. Beginning December 27, for five days in each country, there will be a total eclipse of the sun for two hours. Details will be published in newspapers and magazines. During the first two weeks of January, I will appear on TV and radio in each country announcing the location of the courts and the procedures you will need to follow for the Judgment Line."

The voice on the TV said, "We now return control of your TV to your normal programming. It will resume exactly where it left off."

"Bravo," Hud said "It sent chills down my spine and I knew what was coming."

"Listen," Jenny said. "The network has broken in on the programming now."

We were watching CBS and now the friendly face of their news anchor, Jim Marshall, came on. He was in a slightly rumpled shirt and his tie was loose. He had delivered the news about an hour earlier and thought he was done for the day.

"Good evening again, ladies and gentlemen," he said with a smile. "We don't know anything about the message you have just seen. We were not consulted. Somehow, it was substituted for our regular programming without our knowledge or permission."

Someone off camera handed him a note, which he looked over quickly. He continued, "According to our news team, this message preempted programming on all TV channels and radio stations, including the satellite feeds."

Another note.

"And it happened in every country of the world in their local language as nearly as we can tell. I can't imagine what group has the technical expertise to do such a thing."

Jim paused, listening to someone in his ear.

"I'm being told that we will rerun the message while our analysts try to make some sense out of this."

Maggie came on and delivered the message again. Back to the network.

"This is really extraordinary. Let's bring in CBS analyst, Diane DePlene. What do you make of all this, Diane?"

"Well, Jim, I believe it's the work of a religious sect with unprecedented access to communication technology. Several prominent sect leaders have been predicting that God would appear soon and now one of them has made it happen."

Jim reads something passed to him from off-camera.

"Diane, I've just been handed a note stating that Professor Hamrich of the University's physics department has said that the technology to perform such a feat does not exist at the present time. He says it can't be done."

"Well, Jim, he's obviously wrong since it has been done."

"Let's assume he's right for the moment, Diane. What other explanation is there?"

"I refuse to attribute this to some God. Maybe it's an alien encounter. I just don't know."

Another note.

"Thank you, Diane. I've just been informed that Professor Hamrich will join us in about 10 minutes. Perhaps he can shed some more light on this mystery for us. In the meantime, let's take a break for messages from our sponsors while we try to get a handle on this situation for you." First commercial: three huge pro football players drank some Crystal beer in some bar and became so desirable that six gorgeous ladies couldn't stay away from them. This was followed by an ad for an automobile that is so impressive that just buying one causes beautiful women to throw themselves at you. Then came toilet tissue soft as a gentle breeze, dog treats that were homemade in some grandma's farm kitchen, and a new miracle drug to treat arthritis. Then we were back to Jim.

"Welcome back to a CBS special report. We are going to run this announcement one more time for those who may have missed it before."

Again, we watched Maggie do her thing. The kids were alternatively entertained, impressed, and sobered by the whole thing. We once again reminded them of the importance of complete secrecy. This time, I believe it sank in with all of them.

"Well, this is still a mystery. No one seems to be claiming responsibility for this extraordinary event. Wait. Here's another note. Ah. I've just been informed that a group of right wing religious fanatics called the Doom Predictors has claimed responsibility for this message. This is the group that predicted the world would end last year. I guess they're still around. Diane, what do you make of this?"

"Well, Jim, it's a possibility, but I don't recall them having the resources to pull off something like this. Reverend Cayle, their leader, has been predicting a judgment day for several years, however. So maybe they've found a way to recruit some scientific talent."

"Yes, well, thank you, Diane. I see Professor Hamrich has arrived. Welcome, Professor. I understand you to say that the preemption of all satellite channels and local TV and radio stations is not currently possible. Why is this?"

"Well, Jim, such a feat would require that one simultaneously override literally thousands of satellite feeds and local TV and radio signals. And I believe that text messages were also sent to every cell phone. But this literally can't be done."

"Yet it apparently was, Professor. Who did this?"

"Maybe she was just who she said she was, a representative of God. Maybe she is a member of an advanced civilization and chooses to appear as a God to us primitives. Who knows? I really don't have an answer for you right now. I don't even have a plausible guess."

"What about this eclipse claim? Is it possible for anyone on Earth to create such an event? I assume it's not a natural phenomenon."

" No, it's definitely not natural. Eclipses, of course, do occur, but not on the same day in every country and not five days in a row. If this event occurs, I'll be willing to admit to a God or some other superior being causing it."

"Professor, I thought most men of science didn't believe in God."

"After learning that our galaxy has several billion stars with planets, and that there are billions of galaxies in our universe, many of them just discovered using the Hubble telescope, it would take a fool to believe we are the only intelligence around. Call them gods or whatever, something is certainly out there. There may be many other universes for all we know. It looks like we are finally going to encounter some of them. Exciting times ahead, Jim, really exciting."

"Yes, well thank you, Professor. This just in. President Tilson has issued a statement asking citizens to be patient while, and I quote, "this hoax is being investigated. We expect to expose the perpetrators within the next few hours". So there you have it. We'll keep you informed throughout the evening of any developments in this story. Jim Marshall, CBS news."

"See what's on CNN," I said.

Maggie switched over, but it was more of the same. Their expert analyst thought that the Soviets had changed their stripes again and had devised this method of creating chaos in the U.S. Of course, he neglected to explain why they ran it in their own country alarming all of their citizens. Amazing the lack of depth in some of the media. Anything for the ratings.

Hud and family left soon thereafter. We continued watching for another hour or so and then went to bed. We did set the tv to record all night, just in case these "perpetrators" were located.

The next week passed quickly with everyone still working day and night. The house was ready on Friday, at least ready enough to move in. We had finally named it Arrowhead after Arrowhead Creek, which ran through the property. Indians had lived there at one time and we frequently find arrowheads in the creek area.

Reckoning was going to be done on time thanks to some subs working 18 hour days. They were well compensated, but it was hard duty. Of course time passed pretty quickly with all of them bandering about their own ideas concerning the Judgment.

We hired a transfer company out of Savannah to move us and they spent all day Thursday packing. They loaded Thursday night and moved us in on Friday. They were done by 3:00 that afternoon.

The house was purely magnificent. We had spared no expense and it really showed. Except for the antiques both families had collected, we had purchased all new furniture, and that was nice, too. The kids had huge rooms with private baths and they were pretty well pleased. Our common room, the parents' private room that is, was a result of a lot of effort on all of our parts. Entry was from either master bathroom. No kids allowed. They never even knew it was there. The roof in that room was about 80 percent skylights, and allowed us to get sun during the day and watch the stars at night.

That room was furnished with sofas and lounging chairs, two large beds, several exercise machines, a large four-person hot tub, and a bar-kitchen area. It was a huge room with no partitions except silk curtains in various places.

At midnight that Friday night we finally got our chores done, got the kids in bed, and were in the new room soaking in the hot tub. The sky was clear and the stars were bright. We had not used our Wham pills this month yet so that we could save them for tonight. Our month was actually up last Tuesday the 16th.

Maggie said, "That was really a good idea to wait on the pills. This place is hard to believe. It's so perfect."

"Where are they, Maggie," Jenny asked. "I can't wait any longer."

Maggie reached over to a low table and got one for each of us. Within ten minutes, I was ready. I never in my life felt anything that good. Maggie and I dried and took one of the beds. Hud and Jenny took the other. It was a long and extremely satisfying night. The effects wore off about 6:30, so we got up and fixed some breakfast. I was ravenous as usual after such a session. After eating, we slept a couple of hours and then Hud and I left for Reckoning. The antique courtroom furniture was due in today, and I sure didn't want to miss that.

When we got there and I saw Hud get out of the car, I had to laugh. He looked and walked like an 80-year-old man.

"What the hell are you laughing at?" he said with a grimace. "You really ought to see yourself."

"I know. I hurt all over and I'm sore in a spot I never knew could get sore."

"I feel the same way. And I needed more sleep."

As we walked toward the front door, we saw the trucks bearing goodies turn into the driveway. Hud was excited. He had actually found several antique judges' benches and had bought the best four. He hadn't actually seen them in the flesh since they came from New York, but he had seen videos of all of them. Once I caught a glimpse of them, I knew why he was excited. They were going to be stunning.

One was a real prize, and was reserved for Maggie. It was a Supreme Court bench from one of the former British colonies in Africa. It was very ornate black-red mahogany, with a lot of hand carved relief work and beautiful patina. He hadn't told Maggie. He wanted to get it installed and then surprise her. They barely got the truck doors open before Hud was inside. I let him have some fun alone.

After a minute, he stuck his head out and said, "I can't believe this. They're even better than I thought."

I jumped up on the first one for a better look. It was obvious that they were beautiful pieces although you couldn't see all the detail yet. We got out of the way and let the workers get started. While they were unloading, Liz Adams, the dealer who located them for Hud, arrived to supervise the installation. All four sets included witness boxes and jury areas, neither of which we needed, but Hud wanted to install them anyway. I think there may actually be a designer lurking in there along with the usual lawyer crap. There were even matching benches for an audience and tables for the lawyers. The furnishings for the main office, the second floor rooms, the reporters' lounge, our bunk room, and the psychiatrists' offices had arrived yesterday. So now the main building was essentially complete. The old gym area still needed carpet, and some other minor chores remained, but it would be completely ready by Tuesday.

That afternoon Hud's new Ford Explorer arrived and I took him over to pick it up. Mine was due, too, but hadn't come in yet. When we got home, Hud rounded up Jenny and I got Maggie and we took a ride in it. I wasn't surprised when we pulled up at Reckoning.

"Some furniture came in today and I want to see how they placed it," Hud explained, telling a little white lawyer lie.

We walked up to the front and went in. The offices were arranged and looked great. So did the lounge. We walked on down to the door to Maggie's courtroom and stopped.

Hud said, "Your courtroom, Madame," and ushered Maggie into the room.

She drew in her breath. "Oh, Hud! I'm speechless! Where in the world did you find this? It's magnificent!"

"It came from Africa to New York. I bought it there."

She gave Hud a hug and said, "Thank you for this. I'm really touched."

She walked over and climbed the steps to the high seat and sat down.

"Let me turn on the lights and we can get the full effect," I said. "There. That's just right."

Maggie was bathed in light and her face was there but hard to make out from the area in front of the bench. In a white robe, if she wore one, she would appear quite holy. She made Jenny sit up there so she could see the lighting and said it was just right.

We looked at the benches Hud got for the rest of us and they were nice, too. They were smaller and less ornate, but each had been used for many years and had its own individual character. We were all pleased.

That night we went to Bennie and Marie's for dinner. She served a spectacular curry. And as usual, I ate myself sick. The two of them seemed to be very happy. Bennie said that despite the sorry state of the economy, he had actually been very busy with the real estate business even though this is usually a slow time of year. I didn't mention to him the fact that four of the seven other real estate businesses in town had closed up shop. He also told us Earl Ray had lung cancer, but that they weren't hopeful about his recovery. He was in Augusta at the University hospital. We hashed over some more news and gossip, then left for home, our new home, about 10:30. I wanted to watch the late news.

The media had been having a field day since Maggie's announcement on the 13th. Every expert on God and religion, the occult, communication technology and planetary movements had been ferreted out and interviewed multiple times. The consensus was that one of 13 religious groups had somehow pulled it off and that the eclipse thing was going to be a hoax. There was universal agreement that the eclipse as announced by Maggie was not possible as a natural event. No less than 30 'Maggies' had been identified as the 'one' and had given interviews. They hadn't even come close to us although one of the subs, Rod Smith the electrician, had told me that it looked like Maggie. I laughed it off and said "I wish". No more was said.

Somehow, in all the confusion we managed to put together a Christmas for the kids. Bob and Eloise came for dinner and it was a quiet and pleasant day.

fifty-three

On December 27, it was clear and cold in Clarksboro. The eclipse began precisely at noon as predicted and lasted two hours. The same thing had already happened or was soon to happen in all countries where the weather was clear enough to observe it. By evening the news media was in utter chaos.

We watched old Jim again on CBS at 6:30. He was overwhelmed. His first analyst was Diane and she concluded that she had nothing to conclude. She talked for two minutes and said nothing. And admitted it. The professor was there again and said it was the work of an advanced civilization of beings we never met before. President Tilson told us not to worry because our armed forces would be able to handle any threat to world security whether it came from aliens or not. Jim asked him if he thought it was God and he said if it didn't originate on Earth, then he hoped it was God, but he seriously doubted it.

We had decided to begin Monday the 29th making appointments with the Heads of State. I was taking the Americas, Hud had Europe and Africa, and Jenny was covering Asia and Oceania. We weren't really making appointments. We were simply informing them of when Maggie would be there. No discussion.

Deena had arranged for angel interpreters for every language we would encounter and they would accompany us on each visit where help was required. They wouldn't really be needed at court since one's goodness or badness was universal and would be detectable regardless of the language. Nevertheless, it was our intention to have one available in case the defendant wanted to speak. This was done mainly to mollify Hud, ever a stickler for legal details.

We would be moved by the REGEN machines on Noah II that were finally complete. To move about by REGEN with no receiver or transmitter on the other end is more difficult since it must have the precise coordinates. We won't have that problem at Reckoning since we will have two REGEN stations there. But for these state visits, we would be picked up in the common room at Arrowhead and beamed through Noah II to a predetermined spot in the office of the Head of State. Noah II personnel had the ability to monitor to make sure he or she was there, which would certainly be helpful. And last, any resistance could be instantly detected and dealt with quickly by freezing them in place.

My first visit was to President Tilson, as Maggie wanted to start at home. I was up and ready by 8:00 the next morning and REGENed up to Noah II and down into a cabinet meeting at the White House. I arrived at one end of the room and was an instant hit. The president yelled for guards. Secret Service types came through the two doors. I froze them and told them they couldn't move. The cabinet members were just realizing something was happening when I froze them. I told them they couldn't move but could listen and remember what happened. Wow! This power would have been great in the FBI. I liked it immediately.

The president pushed a button for more guards and some Marines rushed up. I let them join the Secret Service. The president finally realized something unusual was taking place. He had urinated in his pants and was shaking all over.

"Please sit back down, Mr. President."

"Who the fuck are you?" he asked in a shaky voice.

"I am Jack, husband of Maggie. You know from TV that she is assistant to God and also your Judge."

"Bullshit. There is no God."

"She'll be interested to learn that She doesn't exist. But you're wrong. I have had the honor of meeting Her and assisting Her in forming the Judgment Line process."

"Bullshit."

"How do you think I'm able to stop all your guards and freeze your cabinet?" I spoke now directly to the cabinet members. "Gentlemen and Ladies, you can move your heads. How many now believe in God– shake your heads yes or no."

Only two nodded no. Both were men.

"Only three nonbelievers in the whole room. To you three, please tell me how am I able to squeeze your balls like this?"

Three contorted faces and one agonized scream. That was President Tilson since the other two couldn't talk.

"Stop. Stop. What do you want?"

"Maggie will be in your oval office on January 2 at 7:00 in the morning. You and she will make a joint TV and radio broadcast to the nation at 7:05 announcing details of the upcoming Judgment Line procedures for the U.S. All networks and stations must carry this program. All you have to do is agree with anything she says. And you will arrange for the media coverage, of course. Go with Maggie to the press room at 7:03 for the 7:05 airtime. Begin announcing this event on December 31.

"Now listen carefully. Fuckups will not be tolerated. If Maggie arrives to a roomful of Marines, you're going to be held personally and solely responsible. Maggie has a stronger grip than I do and much less patience."

I gave him another little squeeze. He groaned and slumped a little more.

"We know where you are at all times. We hope you cooperate. Any questions?"

"Do I announce that both of us will be at the press conference?"

"It isn't really a conference, it's a decree. Yes, announce both Maggie and yourself."

I walked to where I had appeared and pressed the button on the little communicator I carried and said, "Watch how I leave and remember what I said. No screwups."

And I was on Noah II. And Maggie was there waiting on me.

"What happened?" Maggie asked anxiously. "Did you have any trouble?"

"No problem. The president's going to cooperate. I wouldn't call him a believer yet, but he'll come around."

"Let's wait for Jenny and Hud."

As she spoke Hud came through from England.

"Whew." he said. "The prime minister was not pleased. She needed some extra convincing I'm afraid. She'll be ready, though.

"What happened?" Maggie asked.

"Well, I figured if squeezing men's balls worked, something was needed for women so I pulled hard on her pubic hair and it got the desired effect."

Maggie and I both laughed. Then Jenny appeared. She had been to Japan.

"What is so funny?" Jenny asked.

Maggie told her and she had a good laugh, too.

"How did it go with the prime minister?" I asked.

"Very well. The interpreter makes it take more time but it worked out OK. He was a little reluctant at first but became very reverent before I left. His balls may hurt a smidge for a day or two."

Maggie said, "Glad no one had any trouble. Remember we are mortal and can be killed if we drop our guard. Deena isn't watching now that we have our own powers."

"I'm not likely to forget," Hud said.

Canada was next for me but our scan showed that the Prime Minister was still in bed sick so I took Mexico first. The president was up very early for a meeting with the military brass and I came in while they were having breakfast. This time when they screamed for guards nothing happened since I had frozen them the instant I landed. The Generals reached for weapons and I froze them as well. President Garcia was made of sterner stuff than President Tilson. He went for a hidden gun and I had to tell him that his arms and legs didn't work in order to quiet him.

I then gave him the basic message and told him to be ready on January 2 at 7:30. He said something starting with 'chin–' which my angel interpreter said, meant 'fuck you'. I put some strong, steady pressure on his balls and he began to see it my way.

"Don't even think about trying to avoid this meeting with Maggie. If you foul it up, well, let's just say that Maggie is less patient than I am." I used that line before and it worked, so why not make it part of my little arsenal.

And I gave him another little squeeze for good luck.

"We know where you are at all times. Just do what I told you and all will be well. Comprende?"

He said he did and we left.

Canada was next, and the prime minister was up and dressing. I appeared in his bedroom. He yelled for guards but again I was ahead of him. His wife ran in from the bathroom, buck-naked. I froze her and a valet and a breakfast server who also ran in. I told the p.m. to sit and gave him the message. I let his wife and the other two listen. He didn't even argue. He said he had been expecting someone like me and was going to cooperate. I thanked him and left.

That first day we worked 12 hours and averaged visiting 20 countries or 60 in all. We thought we could probably finish on the 31st if we went hard tomorrow.

On the 30th, we did 70 more and on the 31st we finished about 6:00 that evening.

Maggie had invited Bennie and Marie and Bob and Eloise for New Years Eve, and they arrived for dinner about 7:30. Ordinarily we would have had 10 or 11 couples, but we discovered that it was uncomfortable being with people who were not on the inside. Among ourselves we could feel free to discuss our respective activities. That was kind of sad since I always have enjoyed a good social party with lots of friends and conversation. Deena was also invited but there was some bash in Heaven she wanted to attend. I was so tired I barely made midnight before going to bed.

We mostly loafed and watched football New Year's Day. Maggie finished her speech and would start with the U.S. at 7:00 tomorrow morning. President Tilson had made the announcement yesterday as instructed. She was nervous and jumpy all day. Finally, I told her I thought I would go with her to this first one. She said fine and actually seemed relieved to have some emotional support.

Next morning, we dressed and went to Noah II about 6:45. Maggie was wearing a pure white long dress and really looked stunning. Deena was there and said everything was just about ready. The courts would begin operation next week on a limited basis and build up to full speed as Maggie finished these visits. Then it was 6:58. Time to go.

We arrived in the oval office and President Tilson was there, looking well-groomed, pale, and very nervous. There were plenty of secret service around but they were not interfering with us. I froze them anyway along with anyone else not in the press room. Maggie scanned the press room and froze one reporter who she said had evil thoughts. At 7:05 we went in.

You could have heard a pin drop when Maggie approached the podium. There were reporters from all the media, as usual. They had been told that there were to be no questions today. Maggie began.

"Citizens of the United States of America. Greetings. I am Maggie Warner, Assistant to God in charge of the planet Earth. God is unhappy with the Earth and has decided to take immediate action. Judgment is upon you and will begin late next week. To accomplish this, there will be about 45,000 courts spread around the world. More than 2000 of those will be here in the U.S. Specific announcements about when and where you will be judged will be made regularly by your news media. We will begin the Judgment Line with all judges at the federal, state, and local levels. This will be done simultaneously with all current prisoners.

"Unless you have harmed another person in a serious and premeditated way, you have little to fear from this process. This is not, however, a trial by jury procedure. Your mind will be open to your judges, and you will not be able to hide anything. Absolutely no one will escape judgment. In your first appearance, the judge will make one of two possible decisions. First, the judge may decide you have not caused enough harm to be punished. In this case, it is over for you this time around, and you go back home and resume your life as before. The other possibility comes about if the judge decides that you have caused serious harm to another. If the decision is that you are mentally ill but curable, or if you are a borderline case, you will probably be sent to Uncertainty, an institution on another planet for treatment and observation.

"If the judge decides you are guilty but neither mentally ill nor treatable, you are sent to a district court of which there will be 43 worldwide. Here the finding of the lower court that you deserve Hell or worse is either confirmed or overridden. If confirmed, the district court will recommend either Hell or Terminus to the highest court. This court, called Reckoning, is my personal court, and represents the very final point in the Judgment Line. If I decide you are guilty, I will order your life terminated and send you to Hell. In extreme cases, I may order you to Terminus for termination and soul destruction. Be assured that when I am finished, Earth will be a safer and more pleasant place to be.

"There is no escape or appeal. Judgment is going to happen in all countries of the world to every individual. Those who have completed the process will be given a harmless injection that causes them to show up on our scanners as red in color. Those without the injection will show as green. We will scan every inch of this Earth before we are finished, so running will not save you. Wealth will not save you. All will be judged equally.

"Children will also be judged. If it is determined that they must be removed from society, they will be sent to a special section of Uncertainty where they will remain until cured, if mentally ill, or until they turn 18 and can be judged as an adult.

"Any resistance to this process will be dealt with severely. Please cooperate and come when you are called. You may not like it, but I'll see some of you very soon. That completes my statements today."

The reporters all started talking at once but Maggie took us out fast. Back on Noah II, Deena was waiting.

"Good show," she said.

"I was so nervous," Maggie said. "Jack had to hold me up."

"It actually went very well," I said.

"Well, I'm due in Mexico," Maggie said. "El presidente awaits. Where is my interpreter?"

"Here I am, Senora. My name is Lourdes."

"Good. See you tonight, Jack." And they were gone.

fifty-four

I REGENed down to Arrowhead and turned on CNN. Maggie had been a big hit. The commentator was asking a senator from the Midwest what Congress thought of the Judgment Line.

"Senator, most of those who we interviewed believe that this is a mass deception and that President Tilson has, to put it kindly, 'lost it'. What do you and your colleagues think?"

"Well, Jeannie, I am a God-fearing member of the Baptist church and have always believed in the predictions in the Bible of a judgment day. But this is not at all like I pictured it. I don't know this young woman but I wouldn't be surprised if she were a hoax."

"Perpetrated by whom? Who could cause the eclipses to occur?"

"Well, Jeannie, that I don't know, but science doesn't always have all the answers. Maybe it did occur naturally. Who is the young woman? Maggie, isn't it?"

"She has just been identified, Senator. She is a housewife from a small town in Southeastern Georgia. Let's see. Ah, here it is. Clarksboro, Georgia. We have a news team on its way there now."

We had prepared for this predictable invasion by fencing in the whole front of the property and installing electronic surveillance devices around the rest. An angel security team was on duty and a guardhouse was in place at the front entrance. Hud had activated and tested everything this morning. No one was coming in here unannounced.

Hud walked into the room and said, "Fascinating, isn't it?"

"It's all of that. One of the qualities of a Senator is the ability to ignore evidence that goes against your own beliefs and biases. That one is a master of the technique."

"Yeah. They had the Director of the FBI on earlier and he is going to 'locate that young woman and bring her to justice'. What does it take to make them believe?"

"Believe what?" Jenny said as she breezed into the room.

"The Judgment Line," Hud said.

"They'll believe soon enough," Jenny said. "I've got the kids settled. They watched the whole thing on TV. And believe me, they understand very well the importance of silence right now. Fortunately, school doesn't start back until Monday."

"I still wonder about Maggie's decision to go public," I said. "But she's probably right. Sooner of later, someone would have found out. We've got good security and an angel net thrown over the area, including the town itself, to protect against bombs, missiles and the like. The kids get an angel's wing of protection, as do all of our close relatives. We'll make out."

"Speaking of invasions," Jenny said, "Mark Hansen from the Clarksboro Herald and Millie Grimes. from WCLK local TV are at the front gate. When do we want to see them?"

"I'm inclined to let them in now," Hud said. "We are going to change this town and the lives of its citizens for good and we all agreed that they deserve first crack at the truth. Maggie said to use our own judgment, that nothing happening on Earth was secret."

"I agree," I said. "But we'd better wait until we can get Bud Ellis from the weekly newspaper and someone from WADR radio and give Hud's document to all four at once."

"Sounds good," Jenny said. "I'll tell the guard to admit those four at 11:00."

I would have preferred to hold the briefing outside but it was too cold and damp so we held it in the foyer. Hud and I already had some chairs in place and at 11:00 we were ready.

They arrived and introductions were made all around. Kay Winder represented WADR.

Hud leaned back and said, "Before you start, I want to discuss some legal issues with you." He opened a file and took out some notes. Looked more official that way. "The actual interview process will be delayed until Monday for all media personnel including you four. This will give you a definite edge on the competition and will also create unbelievable profit opportunities. We don't expect your firms to profit unreasonably from this, so we are going to impose some simple rules." Hud scanned the papers from the folder. "You can keep five percent of anything you can get from the networks, newspapers, and so on. The rest must be donated to the city and county governments for use by the whole community. There's going to be increased need for police and fire protection, plus more infrastructure, so this should pretty easily defray that cost and leave some additional funding for special projects. I have prepared a legal document outlining this procedure which must be signed before we begin. Also, you must pass any deal you are going to make with outside sources through a lawyer selected from this list before you sign. It's all laid out here in detail, and I want you to read it thoroughly before you sign."

Hud had included only those lawyers that Maggie had read as being honest. It was a fairly short list.

Hud continued, "That doesn't mean you can't let your own attorney look at this document if you like. But you must get approval from one on our list prior to signing any other agreements related to this entire situation. Does everyone understand?"

Mark Hansen said, "I don't think I can sign that. It'll have to be Mr. Harrel."

"I know," Hud said. "We'll meet again at 3:00, right here."

By 3:00, there was a gathering crowd of media outside the front gate. We admitted only the four mentioned earlier plus a camerawoman named Alison Sloan. They each had a signed document for Hud.

Hud leaned back and said, "OK. Fire away."

Millie had been elected to start with the TV coverage. She introduced each of us and explained Maggie's absence. Then she began, "How did you all become involved in this judgment process?"

Hud was prepared to take this one, "We four were selected by God's head angel to do a job for God." They all glanced at each other. "I know it sounds ridiculous, but there it is. Simple and straightforward. We agreed and completed that job successfully several months ago. Now, the four of us had been selected specifically because it was discovered that we, especially Maggie, had latent powers not common among others on Earth. One of these powers is the ability to read thoughts and emotions. After that first assignment, God called Maggie to Heaven and asked her to set up and administer a judgment process for the Earth. God, whose name is Ruth by the way, has become displeased with the performance of the people of Earth."

"Why is that?"

"Look at your headlines and lead news stories. Rapes, murders, abuse, drugs, gangs, corruption, and so on. Not a very pretty picture. Normally Ruth prefers to delay judgment until death, but She eventually decided that Earth wasn't progressing very well under that formula. So we got elected to do a Noah."

"A Noah?"

"I'm making reference to the Biblical story of Noah's Ark, when God was so displeased that She wiped out everything except those on the Ark. In the present campaign, She is only wiping out those who have caused serious harm to others."

"Mr. Warner, we know that you've been renovating the old rural schoolhouse. Is there a connection?"

"Yes, there is. This is the location of Maggie's court, the final court. We call it Reckoning. And it is ready for us to start the process."

And so on for about two hours. They all left delighted with their scoop. We were going to catch hell from the national media because they normally won't pay for news, but we had saved the citizens of Clarksboro from the significant financial burden which was inevitable to handle the influx of visitors. Our four locals banded together and, so help me, auctioned off the video rights. CNN made the high bid and had been given a two hour lead before it was released to the others. USA Today bought the newspaper rights for Saturday, necessitating a special edition. All the others could use it Sunday. Time magazine went for magazine rights and planned a special edition for release Monday. There were also foreign rights sold. All in all, they raised many millions of dollars.

Maggie got home about 8:00 that night and we had a big meal ready and waiting.

"Well, how did it go?" Hud asked.

"Very well. I managed to visit all the ones we had scheduled and only ran a little bit late. I'll tell you, I had a spot of difficulty in one of the Eastern European countries and unfortunately, President Tomorova had a sudden heart attack and died. Strangely enough, the head of the military expired at about the same time. I pretty quickly found out that those two were hatching a plan similar to that of Hitler and had already imprisoned and tortured dozens of the opposition. They carried out a lot of the torture personally, and I just saw no reason for it to continue."

"I got some of that when I set up that appointment," Hud said. "Remember, I told you to give Tomorova a deep read?"

"I remembered, and you were right. I told the next in line, who I read to be a decent person, that we would be closely monitoring them. Otherwise, it was fairly routine. I'm not sure that all of the Heads of State I visited will make it through judgment. They're not a pretty bunch."

"What about President Tilson?" I asked. "I didn't sense any real evil."

"A politician through and through. In his mind, he has never harmed anyone. He really believes that all of his actions have been in the interest of the people. He is, in reality, a lightweight, totally manipulated by 'advisers'. If he survives, I suspect he's going to have some new 'advisers' soon."

"Based on today, do you think you can stay on schedule and finish on the 15th?" asked Jenny.

"I don't see why not."

"Then we probably should open Reckoning on the 16th even though it's a Friday. If the lower courts open on the 8th as we planned, there'll already be a week's backlog by the time we start."

"I know," said Maggie. "And I think that backlog will be larger than we thought. I've just about decided to open on a limited basis until the 15th. I asked Chastity to come down with Deena tonight and discuss procedures for that week."

You haven't really met Chastity yet. I don't want anyone to get the idea that all of Heaven's female agents are knockouts in the physical beauty department, but Chastity was another stunner. She had chosen to hold her age at about 40 and she was the best-looking 40 I had seen in a long time. She had long auburn hair and greenish eyes. She had a beautiful body, and when she arrived with Deena that night, she positively glowed in the subdued lighting of our common room. I was glad Maggie still maintained that she wasn't reading my thoughts.

"Good evening," Deena said. "We're running a little late. Sorry about that. Our new boss has given us too much work!" She grinned at Maggie.

"Angels aren't supposed to get tired," Maggie said laughing.

"Don't you believe it," Chastity said. "Deena has worked me half to death and I'm already dead!"

"If you think I'm bad, wait until Maggie gets through with you. I haven't had a minute's peace since she started this job," Deena said. "I'm thinking of petitioning for transfer to Hell and the life of a tchadbe farmer. I believe it'd be easier."

Maggie grinned and said. "I'll go with you. Seriously, I do want to talk about the period from January the 8th to the 16th. We have about decided that the backlog facing us on the 16th may be too large."

"We talked about that, too," Chastity said. "Many of the ones that you all will see will be in these first waves."

"Right. How many immediate subordinates do you have now, Chastity?" Maggie asked.

"I have 43 or about one for every thousand courts. These are the ones that you will meet with tomorrow night for training. I call them the B level."

"Have they appointed a layer of subordinates yet?"

"Yes. Each one has about 25 or roughly one for every 40 courts. These are the C level."

"Let's see. Forty-three times 25 is 1075 at the C level. How many can you seat at one spot on Noah II?"

"Roughly 500 in the auditorium/training room," said Deena.

"Good. Chastity, let's get you to set up training sessions for two groups of 500-plus C levels. That should be the judges under about half of your B level subordinates for one session and about the same for another. I want to test them on consistency. Set one up for Sunday night and one for Monday night. Then they will have another session on Tuesday and Wednesday nights. On Thursday, the 8th, all the remaining judges, about 40-some thousand of them, call them D level, will be on Earth and will meet with their C level superior, one of the 1075 that we have trained.

"The trained C level judges can give them some intensive training in how to make decisions consistent with my wishes. The best way, I've decided, is for each of the 1075 C levels to open one court in their assigned territory, that's 1075 courts worldwide. Each of the C's let all of their assigned forty D level judges observe an actual court session. The D's then vote to see how they compare. That will take about 4 intense days. That done, we'll plan to open the rest of the courts on Tuesday the 13th. That will improve our process by building in some consistency, and will halt the potential backlog. What do you think? Any questions?"

"Will you address the two groups of C level judges?" asked Chastity.

"I will in the first sessions. You can handle the second which will be practice based on the first."

"What time?"

"Seven o'clock those two nights. I'll hold time and be back home at 7:00. There's a PTO meeting and open-house at Mark's school on Monday." Maggie insisted on staying grounded in reality for her family's sake.

In addition to working with Bishop, Hud, Jenny and I spent a lot of time at the mall just sitting and reading people. It was amazingly easy to do once you had enough practice. We kept notes on what the disposition of selected targets would be and compared after we had done a certain number. For example, on Monday we read 20 people. On comparison, Hud had 18 free and clear, one for Uncertainty and one for Hell. My numbers were 17, 2, and 1 respectively. Jenny was

15, 3, and 2. Hud and I had disagreed on a man who had raped a 29-year-old woman seventeen years ago when he was 19. He had not been caught. We both agreed on Uncertainty for a woman who had abused children while baby-sitting. We both thought she was curable a deserved a try at treatment. We also agreed that a man who had paid to have his wife tortured and killed deserved Hell. Jenny was a little harsher than we were. She also would have sent the child abuser to Hell.

We talked each case through and after those four days, rarely differed. By Thursday, Maggie was tired of her visits but still had a week to go. Courts opened in those countries which had received a visit from Maggie, with each C level judge instructing their 40 or so D levels. Sounds complicated but it actually worked very well, and put everybody on the same page at the same time. Consistency was crucial.

Hud and I acted as troubleshooters in these court openings and traveled some. I had to go to Bolivia, for example, to straighten out a family dispute that left us without a courtroom. The President's brother had been told to provide one of his office complexes and he refused at the last minute. I'm not as nice as the angel judge. I went in and reasoned with the brother and he saw it my way pretty quickly, so I didn't have to spend too much time there.

Somehow Maggie managed to finish on the 15th and that night we all took a spin out to Reckoning to see if all was ready. When we arrived about 8:30, all the lights were blazing. Deena was there making last minute changes and adjustments. There were about 100 reporters camped out waiting for us, but we had a secure private entrance through the breezeway connecting the two buildings. Maggie was introduced to the office staff first, headed by an angel named Gilbert. He had a staff of ten already on board. Three of the psychiatrists were also there: James, a middle-aged angel from England; Ping, a 50ish lady angel from China; and Rosario, a 30-year-old Venezuelan.

We went on back to the old gym and met Francine, head of the security force, and George, in charge of the kitchen and the domestic staff. All were angels. Twelve prisoners, three women and nine men, were already in the detention wing. Each had a bunk, and was secured to the bunk by a handcuff. They didn't look pleased. Most of the staff were done for the day and were just loafing around. Maggie pronounced Reckoning to be ready. We left for home.

fifty-five

Next morning, January 16, the four of us assembled in Maggie's courtroom. The plan was to see the first 12 together to see if a consensus could be reached. Hud and Jenny and I sat in the old jury box and gave Maggie a thumbs up sign when we had made a decision on each case. Then we got together and discussed our positions.

The first case was a male about 35 years old named Donald G. from Taos, New Mexico. He was serving a 20-year term in the New Mexico prison system and had been convicted of raping and brutalizing at least three women. He was led in by a security team and told to stand in front of Maggie. Like all who were to appear here, he had been stripped of his clothing and jewelry and his head was shaven.

Maggie said, "You are here to be judged."

"I want my lawyer. I know my rights. I'm up for parole in another year."

Maggie just ignored him and we all took our read. I was appalled. I had seen some evil at our sojourns to the mall, but this man radiated evil. I could see that he had over the years raped and abused many more than the three for whom he had been convicted and had also killed a 16 year old girl in Arizona. Remorse? Repentance? He was looking at Jenny and thinking exactly what he would do to her given a chance. Fortunately, that chance would never come.

"Take him out. We'll call for him later," Maggie said.

"What about my rights? What about my lawyer?" The defendant screamed as he wrestled with the security team.

Maggie partially froze him and said, "Remove him."

Then she turned to us and said, "Isn't this going to be fun? I can't imagine what I'd be doing if I weren't here. Oh, well. Time to vote."

We each wrote our choice on a slip of paper and handed them to Maggie who had done the same.

Maggie looked up and said, "Three to one for Terminus. Let's discuss it."

Hud said, "I voted for Hell. I think it was because this was our very first case, and I'm still uncomfortable with the lack of a defense."

I said, "I don't have any doubts about his guilt. He spent his life harming others and doesn't seem to care. He doesn't appear to be mentally ill in the curable sense. Even Hell can do without him."

Jenny said, "I have to agree with Jack pending the psychiatrists' opinion."

Maggie said, "Hud, is he guilty or not?"

"Guilty. No question about it."

"What could he use as a defense except insanity?"

"Nothing."

"Well, he gets that chance with the psychiatric team. I'm also going to ask him back to defend himself."

She mounted the bench and pressed the button for her bailiff, Hilda.

Hilda appeared and Maggie said, "Bring the defendant back, please."

The security team brought Donald back and stood him in front of the bench.

"Now is your opportunity to defend yourself. I find you to be guilty of at least 32 rape-torture incidents one of which resulted in the death of a 16 year old girl. Is there anything you wish to say in your defense?"

"You bet there is. This is a fucking joke! No lawyer! No jury! No clothes! I should be turned loose for violation of my rights!"

"Did you do what I accused you of or not?"

He grinned and said, "I could show you a good time if we got together later. I could make you cry for more. You're a good looking bitch."

Maggie looked at us and said, "Any questions?"

Hud said, "Do you feel any remorse for what you have done?"

"Why should I? They all wanted it and I gave it to them."

Hud persisted, "What about the girl who died?"

"Fuck you. Fuck you all. How about my rights?"

Maggie said, "Hilda, take him to the psychiatrists."

After they left Maggie looked at us and said, "Any vote changes?"

Hud said, "Yeah. One here."

The second case was a 28 year old woman named Wanda H. from Alliance, Ohio who had been convicted of killing two husbands at the same time. Apparently, she had married both, one in 2007 and the other in 2008. She was living in two different apartments when the husbands each found out about the other. She invited them to dinner to hash out the situation. She poisoned the wine and got both at the same time. I did get a feeling of some remorse and no feeling that she was a real threat to do it again, so I voted for Hell. Maybe her ex's were there and they could have a reunion. The others voted for Hell too. Maggie had her called back and said, "You were found guilty by the people of the State of Ohio. I also find you guilty. I order your life terminated and send you to Hell. Hilda, send her to Noah II for processing."

Hilda brought in a white envelope and handed it to Maggie. It was the report from the psychiatrists on Donald.

Maggie glanced at it and said, "All three agree that he is a deviant but not mentally ill. Hilda, bring him."

The security team dragged him back in and stood him before the bench.

Maggie said, "Do you have anything to say before Judgment?"

He just glared at her and started mumbling curses under his breath.

Maggie said, "Donald. Hell is too risky for one of your kind. You might in the future manage to escape and I won't chance it. You are sentenced to Terminus, which will end your existence forever. Send him to Noah II and then transfer to Heaven for execution of sentence."

As they dragged him out he was shouting, "No! No! I'm up for parole next year! You bitch! You whore!"

After he was gone, Maggie said, "This is pretty intense, guys."

Jenny said quietly, "It is traumatic to say the least. But one thing's for sure. He'll never, never, never rape or kill someone else's wife or daughter. That alone is enough to keep me going. Just imagine. That son of a bitch might have been paroled! He could've come to live right here in Clarksboro."

"Thanks, Jenny. That helps put it in perspective, doesn't it?."

The third was a Judge from Louisiana named Richard J. He had a thing against prostitutes, and had been involved in framing and imprisoning more than fifty over the years. A few of them weren't even prostitutes. He was in cahoots with a police captain and his underlings to manufacture evidence against the prostitutes, and had even framed three for murder, managing to get one executed. Several others had committed suicide. He was also a frequent visitor at Madame Jasmine's, a house with a questionable business reputation, which seemed to me somewhat of a paradox. I decided he was mentally ill, but I have little faith in cures for those of his type so I voted for Hell. Surprisingly, the others did also. Maggie sent him off.

The next several were clear cut cases of premeditated murder and were dispensed with quickly. Case number eight is worth mentioning, however.

It involved a young woman of 19, Becky Anna S., who was in prison in Tennessee for her part in an armed robbery that resulted in the death of the store owner. She was from Nashville, and along with her boyfriend had robbed a jewelry store in Memphis last March. What hadn't been exposed before was that last year she had given birth to a little girl in February, one month before the robbery. She had let her boyfriend dump the newborn baby in a dumpster where it was found dead the next day. Had she been remorseful, she would have been sent to Uncertainty by the angel judge but she apparently wasn't. I read her IQ to be about 80 and she showed signs of mental illness. I voted for Uncertainty pending a psychiatric exam to determine if she was potentially curable. So did Hud. Jenny and Maggie voted for Hell. So we had another caucus.

Maggie said, "You first, Jack."

"I may not get as good a read as you and Jenny, but she seems to have a touch of remorse, perhaps as much as one could expect from a woman who is mentally unbalanced and a borderline in terms of intelligence. I erred on her side because she may be salvageable."

Hud added, "I feel about the same as Jack, but wish I could see her childhood more clearly. It's murky to me."

"That's at least in part a function of her intelligence level," Maggie said. "Jenny?"

"I voted Hell because of the fact that she allowed it to happen with no apparent protest. I don't see much mental illness."

Maggie said, "I'm going to bring her back and we'll read her again. Bring her back."

The young woman came back. She was crying and embarrassed by her nudity and simply collapsed between the two angel guards.

Maggie said, "Hilda, a chair for her, please."

They got her a chair and got her seated and she managed to calm down a little. I relaxed and tried to get deeper into her mind. I finally did and picked up on child abuse by her father and two brothers. It reinforced my decision for Uncertainty. Again Maggie had her removed and we talked.

I asked Maggie, "Did you pick up the child abuse on the first read?"

"Just a hint. I should have pursued it further. I switch to Uncertainty and take it as a lesson learned. Jenny."

"Agreed."

"Hilda, bring her in, please."

She was practically a basket case by the time they got her in the chair again.

Maggie said, "You are guilty as charged. Now, I have two choices: one is to end your life and send you to Hell and the other is to send you still alive to Uncertainty where you can attempt to rehabilitate yourself. For various reasons, I have decided to give you one chance, and send you on to Uncertainty."

The woman sobbed, "Thank you, Ma'am. I'll try hard."

"Good. Hilda, send her on."

Finally number 12, the last of the three women came up. We seemed to have more trouble with the women. Number 12 was 43 year old, Debra M., the former owner of a child day-care center in Burlington, Vermont. She had been convicted of sexually molesting and physically abusing some of the children. This had occurred over a five year period, 1989 to1994. She had served two years and was released on probation .

She got out of prison and, incredibly, within six months had a license to open a foster home for children. She was arrested two months ago and accused of making child pornography and of sexual abuse of children, one just three years old. I read her to be guilty and not at all remorseful. In fact, what she was thinking was that this judgment process might give her the opportunity to get free and resume activities. I voted for Hell. There are no children in Hell. But Hud, Jenny, and Maggie were for the Terminus.

"Why just Hell, Jack?" Maggie asked.

"I don't know. She really has no remorse. I guess I got soft. I can't tell much about her in terms of mental illness and that's the main reason I voted Hell. She must be a complete loony."

"I see no real sign of mental problems," Maggie said. "Of course she is a deviant. I am going to override you on this one pending the psychiatric report.

"I don't feel strongly about it. I would like to point out, however, that if she had come to my court when I was alone, she would be on her way to Hell right now. I say this not to criticize but to point out that we're all going to make mistakes. Maybe we need more checks and balances at our level."

Maggie said, "I'm in sympathy with you on that, but we don't have twenty years to do this. If your sending her to Hell is out of step with the rest of us, at least you were out of step in the right direc-tion. It would be worse, for example, if you had recommended the young woman, Becky, from Tennessee for Terminus instead of Hell.

But we do have a check on that as all soul destruct cases must come through me."

Jenny said, "That's true. And if you had made a mistake and this day-care woman had been sent to Hell and flunked out, there would still be time to send her to Terminus or the demons would give her a lobotomy."

By the time we finished with those 12, spending way too much time on them I thought, another group had arrived. We did another 10 together and it went very well. We agreed on nine of the ten. The disagreement was over Rafael F. from Mexico City. He was 18 and had just been sent to prison for murdering a tourist couple from Brazil. The angel judge reported no remorse.

He clearly had done it but his mind was a jumble of conflicting images about the incident. Apparently he had agreed to have sex with the woman while the man watched. The woman tied him up and then turned him over to the man for sex. He protested as violently as he could, bound as he was, to no avail. The man finished, and they left him tied and gagged while they went to a restaurant to eat. When they came back, he was loose and waiting with a kitchen knife. He killed them both. He felt, in his mind, that the murders were justified, so he showed no remorse.

I felt that he was partially justified and voted for a try at rehabilitation on Uncertainty. So did Hud. The ladies had voted for Hell.

Maggie said, "This is one of the hard ones for me. I vacillated all the way from Uncertainty to Terminus. I guess I voted for Hell because it was in the middle."

I said, "It hinged for me on whether it was premeditated or not. I decided that he had been frightened half to death and they were due back at any moment. He could have run but knew he might run right into them outside and figured they would overpower him. So he waited. The rest is so jumbled that I couldn't get a clear picture. Did he threaten them and try to leave or did he attack with no warning? Did he intend to kill them or simply lose control when they entered? Did he just plan to disable them and leave or was his intent to kill all along? He stabbed each of them once, the man in the stomach where it would not have been fatal if the main artery had been missed and the woman in the leg, again puncturing a major artery. Why didn't he go for the throat or heart?"

"Good questions, Jack," Jenny said. "I went through a similar process and finally decided that he should have run as soon as he was loose. We learned that Rafael did belong to a street gang involved in series of robberies and beatings of elderly citizens. I figured he just decided to get even with this couple."

Hud said, "My vote was based on my inability to get a clear read on what happened. He was certainly justified in defending himself but not in deciding to kill them for revenge. But I really couldn't tell, so I erred on his side because the stab wounds were, in my opinion, designed to disable not kill."

Maggie mused a few moments and said, "I decided based on my read that he had enough time to think it through and leave. I didn't vote Terminus because of the abuse he endured prior to the incident. But maybe I missed something. Let's deep read him again and question him a little bit. Hilda, bring him back please."

They brought him in and stood him in front of the bench. We all took another read and mine was more jumbled than before. He was so afraid he was shaking. Maggie called for a chair for him.

Then Maggie said, "Lourdes, please translate."

"Are you comfortable, Rafael?"

"Si, Senora.

"Rafael, I'm going to ask you some pointed questions about the incident at the Dos Amigos apartments. You will, of course, answer truthfully. I can tell if you don't, so be careful."

"Si, Senora. I will tell the truth."

"Good. After the couple left, how long did it take for you to get loose?"

"I'm not sure but maybe an hour."

"When did you expect them to return?"

"The woman, she said they would be back in an hour and then we would really have some fun. She had a whip she rubbed me with and laughed."

"How long were you loose before they returned?"

"Two or three minutes, I think. I run to the kitchen to get the knife so I would have it when I left. Just when I get back to the living room, I hear the key in the door. I am scared, so I quick hide behind the door."

"Did you try to kill them or did you just mean to disable them so you could run away?"

He paused for a moment and said, "I don't remember. I was so scared. All I remember is jumping at the man first."

"What is the next thing you remember?"

"Running. I was running down the street and had the knife with me. I threw it in a ditch. I was scared that he could follow me."

Maggie turned to us and asked if we had questions.

I said, "Rafael. Tell me about the gang you joined."

"I quit before they arrested me for the other murders. I went into a vocational tech school learning about computers and supporting myself by sleeping with the rich tourist ladies. When I found out what the gang did, I quit."

There were no other questions, so Maggie sent him out.

"He told the truth as he believes it to be, with one exception," Maggie said. "In his subconscious, it shows him actually waiting nearly half an hour for them to return, not three minutes like he said. I guess fear could cause you to become disoriented and confused."

Jenny said, "I think I want to change to Uncertainty. He seems worth salvaging."

Maggie agreed, "I think I would like to see what our shrinks have to say, but I agree. Hilda, take him for a psych exam."

A little later the results came back.

Maggie looked at it and said, "They seem to think he will respond to counseling and recommend trying. I'll switch to Uncertainty, too. Hilda, bring him in."

She told him he was going to Uncertainty and not Hell.

fifty-six

We split up after those ten, because there was a backlog of new arrivals. We agreed that any cases where we had serious questions between Hell and Uncertainty would be delayed until we could have a second reading. The rest of the day I had a steady procession of prisoners and judges. Most prisoners and judges were clearcut candidates for, at least, Hell; and I recommended nearly half for Terminus. Heavy duty.

The media waited all day to get in but to no avail. Maggie was busy and preoccupied with the new process, and really didn't want to deal with interviews and questions when she still had so many questions herself. When we all finally quit at 6:00, we had managed to process only about 7000 total cases. We would have to do a hell of a lot better than that. We were shooting for a group-read maximum of 100 every 10 minutes for eight hours or about 5000 per day for each of us. For Hud, Jenny, and I that would make 15,000 per day. Most days would not have anywhere near that number to deal with, we hoped, once we caught up with the backlog. Maggie would spend most of her day on our Terminus recommendations plus those that the district courts had recommended for Terminus. We were going to be busy.

As we prepared to leave, Gilbert, the office manager ran up and said to Maggie, "I have a real problem with the media and don't know what to tell them. There are more than 100 still here. It's a mess."

Maggie looked at her watch and said, "Tell them I'll be on the front steps in 5 minutes. And I'll give them 10 minutes today."

She turned and said to us, "I have a couple of ideas to slow the media down a little. Come to the door and listen."

Maggie opened the door and stepped into the glare. Immediately, the reporters began to scream out questions. Maggie held up one hand and managed to restore order.

"Let me make a statement," she said. "I'm far too busy to spend much time in press conferences at the present time. I know you all want to get in and see what is happening, but the truth is, we just don't have room for all of you.

"So here are the rules. Each day, starting next Monday, you must select three pool reporters, one from radio and TV, one from print media, and one from the internet and other media. One cameraman and two still photographers will also be allowed. You can change them daily if you wish. Those selected will be required to have passed through the Judgment Line prior to being approved to enter. This is easy for us to detect since you will have had the injection to make you glow red.

"You will be welcome anywhere in the complex, but you must remain silent observers. We have nothing to hide, but video and pictures will not be permitted of those being judged. Only the judges' break room will be strictly off limits, if it is occupied. You must not approach a judge unless they indicate that they have time to talk to you, so don't ask. When they have time, they will signal you, and then you may ask questions. The same is true for the psychiatric crew, the office crew, the household staff, and the security crews. These people are going to be very busy, and we can't handle distractions. In other words, no papparazzi!" She chuckled and broke the tension with the crowd.

"Finally, I know some of you already know Arthur. Come out here a minute, Arthur. He will be admitting your six reps each morning. There is one more rule. Arthur, what do you wear to work?"

"Nothing, Ma'am," Arthur replied.

"That's right. No one in Heaven or Hell or any place else in the Universe wears clothing but us. This court is an extension of Heaven and all business is conducted in the nude. Your team will be expected to comply. You may enter through this door, disrobe, and then signal Arthur on the house phone when all of you are ready." She indicated a door into the reporters' lounge area.

There was a loud buzz of conversation and laughing among the reporters. I heard one say that he was glad he had practiced at the Riviera last summer.

Maggie signaled for quiet and said, "One more thing. I know that the courts are taking only prisoners and judges now. I'll arrange for the Savannah court to take any reporters who show up so you can qualify to be on the team. Just have your credentials ready for them. Good night." I was amazed that there were no screamed questions from the crowd, just a couple of pleasant "Good nights". Maggie's authority must have impressed them.

She stepped back through the door and Arthur shut it behind her.

Maggie grinned and said, "That should give them something to think about. Today was fun, but I'm tired! Let's go."

We got home in time to catch our favorite anchorman, old Jim from CBS. He led off with a story about the opening of Reckoning that morning and shook his head sadly when he explained how the media had been shut out all day. He said he did have a report coming up from Diane, who had been on the scene all day. Then there was an ad about the best headache pill in the world, recommended by all the leading physicians and hospitals and movie stars and car mechanics and so on and so on. And a few more commercials that we muted until Jim returned.

"Now we have that report from Diane DePlene, who's standing at the entrance to Reckoning. What can you tell us, Diane?"

"Not a whole lot, I'm afraid. We were denied access all day long. Only about an hour ago we were able to meet with Miss Maggie, but she made her statements and then took no questions. It's very strange. In any event, she did make that statement and here is a tape of that."

We watched Maggie come in, deliver the message and leave.

Diane said, "You can see how strange this has become. Now I have to be nude to be a reporter!" And she gave a little laugh.

"Yes, well, Diane, if that's what it takes."

"Oh, I'll do it. I plan to be in Savannah for court at eight o'clock sharp Monday morning."

"Diane, how have you all decided which radio-TV reporter is first?"

"We drew numbers right after the briefing and I won. I get in Monday with an ABC cameraperson."

"Good. Well, thanks, Diane. See you, and I do mean see you, Monday." Old Jim chuckled to himself.

"Very funny, Jim. This is Diane DePlene. CBS News, Clarksboro, Georgia."

There were several other special reports on the judgment process. One was an interview with a prominent judge's wife from Colorado, who was concerned because her husband had been called to judgment but hadn't returned. She couldn't understand why not. She had called the police, but they were of no help to her because they really didn't know anything. I had a hunch he was not ever coming back, because those going to Uncertainty are allowed to communicate with their families on a limited basis before they are sent off. Of course, he may not have had an opportunity to call yet.

Another was a segment with a famous TV evangelist explaining what Heaven and Hell were really like. He didn't have a clue.

During dinner, Maggie and I answered endless questions for Mark and Laurie. They wanted to visit Reckoning and Maggie promised them they could as soon as things calmed down a little. I guess I was all hyped up over the day's events because when we went to bed, I couldn't sleep. I couldn't even lie down! Maggie couldn't either.

Finally she said, "I can't get that judge's wife out of my mind. It's cruel to leave family members uninformed. I'm going to tell Deena to get some angels assigned to each court who can call the next of kin of those who are detained or sent away."

"Good idea."

"And I'm going to try to be nicer to the media. They're just doing their job."

"Good idea."

"And I'm going to spend more time with the kids."

"Good idea"

She rolled over and punched me and said, "Is 'good idea' all you can say?"

"Ouch. I can say 'bad idea' too."

She grabbed me in a vital spot and said, "Let me try to relieve your tension."

"Very good idea!"

I finally got a couple of hours of sleep.

We spent a quiet weekend. Monday morning we REGENed over to Reckoning at about 8:00. I wanted to drive, but the reporters were like a swarm of mosquitoes. Chastity had come in to meet with Maggie and she looked good, as usual. She was having logistical problems of some sort but they quickly got them solved. She said she was on her way to China to sort out some sort of cultural breakdown.

As for me, my bailiff, Martha, took me upstairs to the group read room where about 80 people waited. I closed my eyes, took a deep breath, and concentrated on the group. When I opened my eyes, it was like seeing a game board with 80 lights. Each light was a measure of evil. If it was bright, then that person was very evil. There was a cutoff brightness level where if it was any brighter the person went to Terminus instead of Hell. In this group, 19 were bound for Terminus. Another 55 were clearly going to Hell. I unfroze the Terminus group and sent them out and then did the same with those destined for Hell. The six left were all problems. Three were between Terminus and Hell. I took a deeper read and assigned two to Terminus and one to Hell.

The other three were between Hell and Uncertainty. These conflicts usually arose when the person was mentally deficient or had experienced memory lapses when their crime occurred. It was hard for me to read either type yet, but Bishop had said Hud and I would quickly get better at it, so I didn't worry about needing extra time right now. Two resolved themselves fairly easily, but in the third case, I couldn't decide.

It involved a young woman named Cathee G. from Tipler, Alabama. She was in jail for murdering her stepfather one night after he had tried to sexually assault her. He had been doing this for several years and she apparently had decided not to put up with him any longer. Her mother and younger sister heard the shot and came to the bedroom and found her standing there with the pistol in her hand. She was in a dazed condition and seemed unaware of what had happened. At the trial, she admitted she had killed him and was given 12 years.

The only problem was I didn't read the evil or guilt that should have been there. The angel judge took this to mean that she had no remorse and should go to Hell. But I wasn't so sure.

"Martha, I want Maggie to read this young woman, and then I want the two of them to meet with me."

"OK, boss." Martha said. "There's a group of 58 more next door waiting for you."

And so it went for the rest of the morning. Right before lunch, Martha took me to Maggie, who was in my courtroom downstairs with the young woman, Cathee.

"What do you think?" I asked as I entered.

Maggie said, "Martha, please take her out for a moment." Then she said, "Jack, I think that she's innocent. But even with a deep read, I'm not positive. How did you tumble to it?"

"I don't know. Maybe I'm getting stronger. Anyway, the light wasn't bright enough for Hell. The angel concluded that since there was no apparent remorse and since she admitted guilt, that she should go to Hell."

"I know. Let's save her for Hud and Jenny to read and have a group meeting at 5:00 this afternoon."

"OK. I'll tell Martha to keep her in a holding cell."

The reporters had arrived about 1:00 that afternoon. I happened to have a few minutes and signaled them that I would take a few questions from them. They came into my courtroom and we introduced ourselves. There was Diane, who had passed through the Judgment line successfully. She was about 40 and in pretty good shape. She saw me glance at her and blushed all over.

I grinned at her and said, "You'll get used to it."

She grimaced and said, "Maybe, but I surely feel foolish."

The ABC cameraman assigned to Diane yesterday had not made it through the Judgment Line, so she had Marc Billings from Fox News instead. From the Pensacola Tribune were Eileen Harris, a 58-year-old veteran reporter and her assigned photographer, Linda Delano from a paper in New Orleans. Finally, there was Walt Korov from Newsweek with Marysue Ling, a photographer for Vogue Magazine.

Diane got the camera rolling and began.

"This is Diane DePlene of CBS News, your pool reporter for today at Reckoning. I apologize for the nudity which you are about to see, but it is the only way we can get in to bring you the news."

Marc panned down from a tight shot of her face to a full view of Diane and the others. I wondered if the networks would run it.

Diane continued, "Our first stop here is the courtroom of Jack Warner, one of the four judges God has chosen to run Reckoning. He also happens to be the husband of the now famous Maggie Warner. Mr. Warner, Jack. May I call you Jack?"

"Sure. We're pretty informal here, Diane."

"You definitely are. Now, Jack, tell us what exactly is happening here at Reckoning and how it is going."

"Well, Diane, as you know, Reckoning is the final stop for those who have chosen, and notice I say 'chosen', to cause harm to others. The people who arrive here have been passed through two levels of judgment, the local court and the district court. They have all been recommended for either Hell or Terminus. One of the three of us–Jenny or Hud Raines or I– confirm the Hell recommendations and can send the person back to Uncertainty immediately if we feel it's justified. This rarely happens, though, because the lower courts are doing a really superior job. Now, we can also advance a candidate from Hell to Terminus. This is more frequent. All candidates for Terminus must pass by Maggie, who is the final word. Of course, God could screen and intervene if She sees fit."

"You've met God, haven't you?"

"I surely have. Several times."

"What is She like? What does She look like?"

"Ruth–that's Her name by the way–looks like someone's grand-mother. She's very calm and gives me, at least, a feeling of inner peace and security."

Statements like this were about all we were supposed to make about God and Heaven. Diane seemed satisfied, however.

"Well, is the process working as planned?"

"So far, so good. We've processed about 16,000 as of noon today with no major glitches."

"Any advice for those still to be judged?"

"Just to remember that most of you have nothing to fear. We expect to see fewer than one-tenth of one percent of the population here at Reckoning. Remember, we are looking for those who caused major harm to others. For a simple example, Diane, did you ever start dating someone who you knew was actually going with some-one else at the time?"

"Well, yes. I suppose a lot of us have."

"How did the other girl react?"

"Well, I suppose she was very upset."

"Exactly. You caused a minor hurt for that girl. Yet this morning you passed judgment with no problem."

"Oh, I see. Well, thank you, Jack. We've just touched the tip of the iceberg, but I'm being told that this is all the time we have for today's report. This is Diane DePlene at Reckoning. Be sure to tune in tomorrow night for more exciting developments concerning the Judgment Line."

I answered some questions for the other reporters and went back to work.

I guess it was my day for unusual cases. About 3:30, I was read-ing a group of 64 and one of the 'lights' was burned out. I couldn't get anything but murkiness from this person. I held him back and tried again with no penetration at all. He was an elderly judge from Tibet. I was afraid to send him off with Martha alone, so I went with her to see Maggie. I signaled Hilda and told her to ask Maggie to join us before her next case.

About three minutes later she breezed in and said, "What's hap-pened, Jack?"

"Take a reading on this guy."

Maggie did, or at least, tried to. She said, "This one has managed to block his thoughts."

"I'm glad I haven't gone crazy."

"Where's he from?"

"Tibet."

"Hilda, get a Tibetan interpreter sent down from Noah II. Right away. Let's try again, Jack."

We both concentrated for several seconds and I got exactly zero. Maggie was a little more successful.

"I don't get too much, but I can see past the block a little. He's a holy man but, nevertheless, is radiating evil. He has used his powers for sexual and monetary gain. He is one of those rare people who has become at least partially aware of his powers."

"Can he read others?"

"I doubt it, other than major emotions like happiness or anger."

About then, Hilda came in with a young female angel from Tibet. When she saw our man, she recoiled, her face a mask of horror.

"What's the matter?" Maggie asked.

The young woman just stood there pale and shaken. Maggie gave her a quick read, then turned to the holy man and told him to stop. When that didn't happen, she turned on the power and sent him to his knees. She waited a minute and then really seared him. He went down and lay there twitching.

The young woman sagged to the floor and Hilda ran for the first aid kit. An ammonia capsule brought the angel back.

Maggie said to her, "Easy now. He won't bother you again." She turned to Hilda and said, "Get a security team and send this one to Terminus with a mandatory interview with Ruth prior to termination. Label him as 'extremely dangerous'. Only someone with above average powers may handle him. Make sure the security—no, wait. Have George report here at once."

"What in the hell is going on?" I asked.

"That young woman was terminated by this bastard as part of a sacrifice several years ago. She was 12 and he had been abusing her for 2 years prior to that. When she came in, he was quite surprised, and turned his power toward her. At that moment, I got a perfect read on him."

"That son of a bitch should have his balls cut off."

"We'll do better than that. Jack, send Martha to get Hud and Jenny. Fast."

I went out and told Martha and she left. George arrived moments later, and Maggie briefed him.

"I want you personally to escort him to Deena on Noah II. She herself is then to take him to Ruth for an interview. I've never seen such evil."

"Will do, Maggie. Is he able to stand?"

"Not a chance. Better get a wheelchair."

He was wheeled out just as Hud and Jenny arrived.

"What's up?" Jenny asked.

"I want you and Hud and Jack to read this asshole before I send him off. I seared him and his defenses are down, so you shouldn't have any trouble getting through."

We three all concentrated. Suddenly I was past the block and then just as quickly, I wished I weren't. Evil rose from within this man like nothing I've ever seen or even imagined. He had committed nearly every foul act that one could imagine under the guise of being a judge, a holy man, and a healer. This was exactly why Terminus was created.

Jenny staggered back and said, "Whew. That's a first class monster. It almost gags you."

Maggie agreed and said, "The main reason I wanted you to see him was that he has developed his powers to the point that he was actually blocking his thoughts to Jack and partially to me. Jack, fortunately, was alert enough to suspect a problem and called me in. Thanks, Jack. There are a few like him around, so we'll have to be careful."

Isn't the good news team always around when you wish they weren't? When we came out, there was Diane talking into a microphone on a video cam.

"We don't know exactly what took place but an elderly gentleman was taken from the courtroom in a wheelchair. He looked as if he were ill or something. The head of security accompanied him and they went directly to the REGEN room. Here are the judges now. Maybe one of them will bring us up to date."

She stood there looking expectantly at Maggie who started to blow her off. I reminded Maggie that she was going to be nicer to the press. She glared at me but signaled Diane to start.

Diane said, "Well, this is a bit of luck. Mrs. Warner has agreed to answer a few questions. Mrs. Warner, what just happened in there?"

"Please call me Maggie. We encountered an unusually evil person, so utterly evil that I wanted to give all of the judges an opportunity to read him."

"That nice looking elderly man who got sick in the room? What did he do that was so evil?"

"I don't have time to give you a complete list, but for starters, he sexually abused more than 200 girls and boys between the ages of 10 and 14 and then sacrificed all of them in the name of religion. He called himself a healer, a priest, and a holy man, among other things."

"My God! What will happen to him?"

I left about then for a group reading and missed the rest. Just as well. I was tired of thinking about the Tibetan.

I worked until 5:00 and then went to the group meeting. The girl, Cathee, was brought in for Hud and Jenny to read. In fact, we all four did.

Maggie said, "Got it that time. What do you all get?"

Hud said, "I believe she's completely innocent, but I can't verify."

Jenny agreed, "This is one who shouldn't be here but, like Hud, I can't tell why. I guess that's why they sent her to us."

"I finally managed to get it," Maggie said. "Right before this murder, Cathee actually fled into the bathroom. Someone on the outside opened the bedroom window and shot him. Then they threw the gun inside on the floor. Cathee heard the shots, came out, picked up the gun, and was standing there in shock when her mother and sister came in. They assumed that she did it and convinced her that she had. Unbelievable."

"What do we do with her?" I asked.

"She doesn't really belong on Uncertainty," Maggie said. "Let's send her to Noah II and let the resident shrinks work her over and send her home."

Everybody agreed.

Maggie turned to her and said, "Cathee, you have been living under a false impression. Sometimes our minds play tricks on us and we become confused. Do you understand that?"

"Am I going to be sent to Hell?"

"No, dear, I'm going to send you to a place where you can get some help sorting out your life's memories. I want to tell you right now, though, that you didn't kill your stepfather. Think back to that night. You were in the bathroom when he was shot. When you came out, your mother and sister came in and told you that you had done it. Do you remember?"

"Well, I think so. I remember seeing Mama at the window before I went to the bathroom. And then I remember that she was in the doorway with my sister, Ellen."

"Yes, dear. You remember now. The people I'm sending you to see will help you sort it all out. Hilda. Send her to Deena. I'll call Deena and tell her why."

Hud stretched and yawned and said, "Let's go home. I think I've had enough excitement for one day."

fifty-seven

We were all dying to see the news that night, so we gathered in the Raines' living room. Old Jim was there right on time, just like a good and loyal friend.

"Good evening. Topping the news this evening are the first pictures and interviews from inside Reckoning. Before I switch to Diane, let me warn you about the segments you will see. Mrs. Warner requires that any reporter who enters Reckoning be nude. Also she requires that a pool of three reporters and three camera operators be selected every day by the media corp to represent all the others. These upcoming segments contain full frontal nudity pictures of the six pool personnel and of the staff at Reckoning. We had planned to edit them but decided we would have nothing left. If nudity offends you, change your TV channel now.

"We were extremely fortunate that our on-the-scene reporter, Diane DePlene. was selected to represent the radio and TV media on this historic first day of the Judgment Line. Let's go live to her. Diane, can you hear me?"

"I can, Jim. As you know, it has been a hectic 24 hours. At 8:00 this morning, I was in Savannah for my own required judgment process, which I passed. I can tell you that I do emit a red glow to the judges, as proof that I passed. Some didn't, including the pool cameraman from ABC who had been selected to accompany me to Reckoning. We were fortunate to be able to replace him with a FOX representative. We finally got into Reckoning about lunch time, and just after lunch, I managed to get this interview with Judge Jack Warner."

The screen cut to her face as she introduced the segment. Then the camera panned down and there was the shot I didn't think they would show. She asked me the first question and then there I was in front of the world in the buff. I was used to it on Noah and in Hell and here at home but it was a little chilling to know the world was watching. I had a moment of kinship with Diane.

Jenny didn't help. She said, "Lucky you weren't in the shower, Jack. You might have put on a show in front of the whole world."

Everybody had a good laugh. Diane finished my segment and switched to Maggie's. This was followed with a segment on Diane's judgment process in Savannah which was really well done. It should help relieve some of the anxiety the average person was feeling before their own judgment. Diane said she had been afraid because she had done some things for which she was ashamed but they apparently weren't that bad after all. She then recapped briefly the episode with the Tibetan.

Jim came back on, and thanked Diane for her coverage. He was probably glad to see her 'uncoverage' too. He told Diane that he hoped she would be selected again the next day, and that in any event he would see her tomorrow with more in-depth coverage of Reckoning. He then switched to a report about the small South American country of Costa del Oro.

"The president of the small country of Costa del Oro announced today that his country has decided not to participate further in the Judgment Line. He is demanding the return of his brother, a judge who has not yet returned from his visit to the lower judgment court this morning."

We had a good laugh over that one. Jim finished the rest of the news and signed off. We went home to eat dinner with the kids, who were still completely hyper and bursting at the seams to talk about what they had seen on TV. We had a great conversation for almost two hours. They are amazingly savvy and both are eager to get involved in the judgment process in some capacity. I'll have to give that one a lot of thought.

The next several weeks went along pretty routinely. We got up to the anticipated speed in processing but really didn't have enough cases most days to force us to maximum levels. We had three more cases of people with powers, two of which involved people who were evil and one faith healer who actually could heal to some extent. We sent her to Deena to see if she wanted to try to recruit her.

Despite this enormous undertaking, we soon discovered that we loved and needed our new home, which became our sanity and our sanctuary at the end of each day. The kids were doing well. Laurie's powers had not blossomed in the past several weeks as we had feared they might, so maybe she could be normal for a while longer. I made Tom a partner in the construction business since he was really running everything anyhow. The only thing strange was going downtown and trying to do things we always did like eat at Burton's. The first free lunch period we had, Hud and I announced we were going to Burton's for lunch. We arrived with about 10 media vehicles, had old friends come and ask for autographs for their 'kids', and were carefully given what was considered the best table in the house. That outing wasn't a fun or relaxing experience, but we knew it would die down over time.

It was going to be a long three years.

fifty-eight

More than three years have come and gone now. It was April 6, 2018 when we finally could see the end of this Judgment Line. The last stragglers had been rounded up and were in the judgement queue. I was ready for the end as were all the others, but it wasn't boring. Not for one minute.

The three years had passed quickly and many things had changed. Let me bring you up to date. First the kids.

Laurie was 17 now and a junior at Clarksboro High. She was a cheerleader and an academic whiz. Her powers were beginning to emerge and Maggie has been working with her to set her on the right track. The last time she was around Bishop, he said she was now above the strongest, in terms of potential, that he had ever seen including Xerma, who is Ruth's superior, and Balzerch. It was sobering information.

Mark was 14 and in the eighth grade at Trenton Middle School. He was playing soccer and basketball, and was trying to convince me to let Charity give him the physical enhancement injections.

Jimmy and Wayne were 18 and 15, respectively. Jimmy would graduate this year and was headed to Georgia Tech to major in Electrical Engineering. Wayne was a freshman and was active in football and baseball. He had a great year in football and was going to be a fine quarterback. On top of that, he was an excellent student.

Bennie and Marie were fine. Their daughter was at the University of North Carolina studying Geology. Ruth occasionally talks Bennie into an off-earth assignment but only if She holds time. He loves his real estate work and has made so much money, I think he'll soon be subsidizing Her instead of the other way around. Sadly, Earl Ray died of lung cancer in August of 2016. I'm going to do a lot of fishing in his memory when next week is done.

Eloise and Bob have retired from the management of Uncertainty and built a lovely home on the bank of the river about a quarter mile from us. We see them almost daily. Bob went back to being an architect but only works from his home office. Eloise took up flying again but strictly as a hobby. She takes long walks on the property and I sometimes watch her from the balcony and regret not having made a pass at her. She is still smashing.

We heard last year that the Kosarkians had finally tried Balzerch and found him guilty. He was terminated and sent to Kosark's Hell. I wish they had destroyed his soul, though. Evil like that should be eradicated. That guy just might escape from Hell some day. Who knows what might happen then?

Deena and Chastity had petitioned Ruth for permission to live on Earth for a while after Judgment. It was granted and we made them a huge apartment out of the old mill on Arrowhead Creek, just about 200 yards from our house. They planned to move in week after next. I had really come to like Chastity and was still hoping Maggie wasn't reading what I had in mind the first chance I got.

Jenny's father died last year. She took it hard because they had been very close. There had been no chance to petition Ruth for a cure because he just keeled over with a heart attack. She would probably have refused to intervene anyway. I don't know what Maggie would have done in that case. We haven't talked about that, but will have to get around to it some day.

I had finally sold Tom the whole business and he was now specializing in restoration work in Savannah. Melissa had bought Hud's practice and was doing well. Diane DePlene, now the full-time news anchor for CBS, was on hand April 13 for the official closing of Reckoning as a full-time court. Maggie was to deliver a speech to the world that afternoon at 4:00. Diane had somehow charmed her way into being the pool reporter on this last day.

She bounced over to where I was standing that morning and said, "Jack, I remember that first day like it was yesterday. I had to come in nude and was embarrassed to death when you looked at me. Now I hate to wear clothes at all. Believe it or not, I've even joined a nudist resort for relaxation."

"I told you you'd get used to it. We never wear anything at home unless it's cold outside."

"I've never had a chance to visit your home, even though you've extended several invitations. I've got to do that soon. I'm going to take a long leave after this winds down, so maybe we can work something out."

"We'd love to have you. We've got a beautiful guest apartment above the garage that you can use. Just let us know."

"Thanks, Jack. I will."

I read her. She meant it.

We only had 100 cases to finish, so we were easily done before noon. About six billion people had been judged in three years and three months. I was so glad it was over.

The world was showing signs of being a better place. Nearly all militaries had been disbanded. Disbanded! People walked the streets and felt safe again. You could leave your keys in your car again. You could let your kids walk to a park.

It didn't, however, stop all crime. Drugs were still a problem but honest police and judges and politicians were working on the problem and would find solutions. There were still thieves and con men and embezzlers and forgers and so on. But the violent crimes against people were practically non-existent. It was a gentler world already. Maggie would be covering this in her speech later today.

At noon, Hud and I slipped off to Burton's to join Bob and Bennie for lunch. And we found that all was normal at Burton's again. We got just a run-of-the-mill table next to the kitchen, and the other diners had about quit staring at us and whispering and pointing. And thinking, I'm sure, about how we look naked. Bob and Bennie were into a joint venture to build an entire subdivision of Victorian-style homes between here and Savannah on a beautiful 70-acre wooded tract with a 25-acre lake in the middle of it. They had hoped to get Tom to do the construction work but he was swamped. So they asked me if I would do it. They didn't plan to start for about three months, so I agreed. But first I needed a vacation.

Bennie asked Hud what his plans were.

Hud said, "I'm giving up law, Bennie. Believe it or not, I'm going to open an antique shop with Jenny and Jack and Maggie's help, when they have time. I don't need money, so I should be successful!" We had a good laugh over that one.

"Sounds like fun," Bob said. "I've always loved antiques."

"We'll get you to furnish our model Victorian when we get it up," Bennie added.

"Glad to do it," Hud said. "That'd be great advertising for us."

We finished lunch. As we were leaving, I said, "Be sure to catch Maggie's speech at 4:00. It's going to be very interesting."

They said they were planning on it.

When we got back, Maggie and Jenny were in the judge's lounge talking to Deena and Chastity.

Maggie said, "Deena wants everyone to go on a real vacation when we get done here, and when she and Chastity finally get settled into the apartment. She wants to go to Vegas and then to the mountains, preferably that uninhabited meadow she visited three years ago."

"Sounds good. We'd better wait until late May on the mountain area though or it'll be too cold."

Deena said, "I hadn't thought of that, but there's no real hurry."

"What's the schedule around here for the afternoon?" I asked.

"Not one thing until 4:00," Maggie said. "So you boys can spend the afternoon watching the lady angels and chatting with the reporters."

"They've gotten really good at that," Jenny added. "Don't go into any dark closets with them, Chastity! You know what, gals? Why don't we check out those gorgeous new male angels Ruth sent over?"

" Very funny," Hud said. "Let's go someplace we're appreciated, Jack."

We left and went to talk to Diane and company.

I thought 4:00 would never get there, but sure enough, on the ten thousandth check of my watch, it finally said 3:48, time to go to Maggie's courtroom. The invited group was small, just our group and the select news people. We allowed an extra camera and sound crew to handle the live feed. A couple of minutes before 4:00, Maggie went to her bench. The lights were dim but the audience could plainly see her face. At precisely four, she began.

"Greetings. I am Maggie, assistant to Ruth, who is the first level God for our own Earth. Most of you have not met me and that is probably just as well. Most of those who did are no longer among us.

"Judgment is complete for the present. God is pleased. So pleased, in fact, that I have a surprise for you."

Maggie rose and moved off to the right of the seat in the center. She signaled Deena, the lights came up, and Ruth appeared! I had no idea! She hugged Maggie and sat down. The lights dimmed considerably, but there was still just enough light to make out Her face. She began to speak.

"Citizens of Earth. I am Ruth, your God. I am pleased to have this opportunity to address you. As you know, my assistant, Maggie Warner, and her associates have just completed the Judgment Line as I requested. And everything went quite well. It seems to be a huge success. Let us hope so.

"Earth is the youngest of my worlds and had been advancing quite rapidly. However, the situation had gotten out of control with respect to my rules. My number one rule, as you now know, is to conduct yourself in such a way that you cause no major harm to others. All of your various religions already include this provision. However, many people had chosen to ignore this, so that the rate of abuse of this particular rule was accelerating at an alarming pace. We have solved that problem with the Judgment Line. Those who broke the rule have, for the most part, been terminated.

"I hope you have learned from this process. I know that we haven't totally eliminated violent crimes, but you now know that you will pay a terrible price for going in that direction. So beware. Do not incur my wrath again. I, as your God, can reward you with

447

Heaven. I also can give you Hell or Terminus. Now that you are certain of this, be certain that you stay on the right path.

"I wish you good luck in the future. Maggie will remain on Earth as my representative. She will explain her post-judgment role and how you fit into it. And I'm sure she will have some ideas and changes of her own. I must leave now."

And She faded out.

The room was deathly still for a few moments and then Maggie retook the chair vacated by Ruth.

"She is right. Earth is now a friendlier, safer place to live. It is largely up to you, the remaining citizens of Earth, to see that it stays that way. The post-judgment process She mentioned will be very simple and direct. It has always been God's policy to judge people after they have died, but She felt that this system had failed here on Earth. The Judgment Line was set up in an attempt to bring Earth back into line.

"She wants to return to the policy of judging after death as soon as possible. So post-judgment is geared in that direction. Your specific legal systems will function as before with two important exceptions. First, any person accused of murder, rape, child or spouse abuse, or any action which caused major harm to other persons such as being a drug kingpin, will continue to be judged by my Judgment Line district courts for an initial five year period. At the time of arraignment, the prisoner will be transported by your police to the nearest district court for trial. If guilty, they go on to the next stage, which is either directly to Uncertainty or on to Reckoning for Hell or Terminus. We hope that by the end of five years we will have practically stopped such premeditated actions. We'll see.

"The second difference in your legal system is that for the first time in many years, almost 100% of the judges and lawyers are relatively honest. This should provide more equity and fairness. I will continue to monitor the judicial system at random to ensure that it will stay that way.

"That is all that we will do for now. If you have problems, you must solve them yourselves just as before. You can't pick up the phone and call Ruth or Her assistant for help. You have a distinct advantage that no other world has ever had because you have seen Her and heard Her speak, and you are now certain that there is a Heaven. Make the best of it. Change your lives while you can. I wish you good luck. I will be in contact with you as I continue to evaluate the Judgment Line process."

Maggie came down from the bench, signaled for the cameras and sound crew to stop and said, "That's all for now. Thank you for coming."

Everybody clapped. We all went to the reporters' lounge where Arthur had arranged to have hors d'oeuvres and drinks for the pool reporters and us. It was pre-agreed that we would give a final interview here and then disband. Maggie gave the interview while the rest of us partied, and after about a half an hour, we broke up and it really was all over. Diane promised to come back for a visit without cameras and recorders, and then went outside to give the evening newscast by remote. We went home to watch it. I'll have to admit it was kind of sad suddenly leaving Reckoning behind after the intense years we spent there.

When the news came on, we were still snacking. Deena and Chastity had come home with us to watch.

Diane came on and said, "Good evening. This is Diane DePlene, speaking to you live from our CBS remote unit with the day's news, the last day we will be coming to you from Reckoning and from the scene of the Judgment Line. Tonight we have an unprecedented event to recount for any of you who missed the live telecast at 4:00. Maggie Warner addressed the world on the closing of Reckoning and the end of the current Judgment Line. During her speech, God, whose name is Ruth, came on and made a brief statement. We are going to bring you both statements in their entirety and then follow with what is probably our final interview with Maggie Warner. Let's go right to that tape, please."

We watched Maggie and Ruth again. Then Diane switched to the interview.

"Maggie, that was quite a surprise when God joined you on the bench for a statement. Did you know in advance She was coming?"

"Well, yes, I was the only one to know, but She only gave me 15 minutes notice. Ruth doesn't plan things like that very far ahead. It depends on whether or not She can break free. It's difficult for Her."

"I imagine so. She seems to be charming."

"I've thought of how to describe Her many times, but 'charming' had not really crossed my mind." They both laughed. "She is a tremendous source of strength and hope for the future."

"What's in your future, Maggie?"

"For the next five years, I will continue to operate Reckoning on a part-time basis to process those who flow through the district courts. One day a week should be more than enough. And part of that day will be devoted to defining and refining some changes I am considering to the Judgement Line process. But I'm primarily planning to spend a lot of time with my family. My kids are on the verge of being grown, you know. And I'm going to work part-time, very part-time, in an antique business that my co-judge and neighbor, Hud Raines, plans to start. Finally, I'm going to vacation a lot more."

"How do you plan to work with the news media in the future?"

This was a set-up question. Diane had to agree to ask it to get Maggie to do the interview.

Maggie said, "At the present, I don't have any plans at all for the media, Diane. Right this moment I'm giving my last interview for at least five years. That goes for the other three judges from Reckoning as well. On the fifth anniversary of today, I will give my next interview."

"I guess I had better make the best of this one. Maggie, I have heard rumors from the angels at Reckoning that other worlds have conquered disease and sickness and have discovered long-life drugs. What can you tell us about that?"

This was also pre-planned. We planted this on Diane through William, the angel attendant we assigned to the reporters' lounge. Deena said God thought that if the Earth scientists knew these things were possible, they would work twice as hard finding them or, alternatively, at finding some way to reach these other worlds.

Maggie managed to look really pained and said, "Angels sometimes talk too much. I really have not visited any world except Hell and the Noah Stations, so I'm not positive what exists on other worlds. I couldn't really give justice to your qustion, Diane."

450

"What about on Hell and the Noah Stations? This angel claimed to be 2000 years old, which, if true, means there are such drugs out there somewhere."

Diane was really pretty quick. But so was Maggie.

"I am not authorized to talk about Hell and Noah, so I can't answer that question. That doesn't mean these things do or don't exist. It just means I am forbidden to tell you."

"Have you been to Heaven?"

"Yes, but only in the receiving chamber. It's like a big ball-room in a hotel on Earth. I know nothing else about Heaven first-hand and I can't tell you about any second-hand things I may have picked up."

"Do you think the REGEN machine technology will be made readily available to Earth?"

"No, I don't believe so. But the knowledge that it exists gives you two choices: develop your own or develop a way to reach a planet with the technology already for sale."

"Then there are such planets out there?"

"There are."

"Could you tell us about them?"

"I really can't."

"You have been to Hell?"

"Yes."

"What is it like there?"

"Keep living a good life and be kind to others. You don't want to find out. Let's just say it's a helluva place, Diane!"

"You're not going to tell me anything about off-earth places, are you?"

Maggie laughed. "You're right about that, Diane."

"Are you pleased with the outcome of the Judgment Line process?"

"I believe that 'pleased' would be a good term to use. I agonized the whole three plus years over the decisions we had to make con-cerning whether or not to send a person to Hell or to Terminus. But the world is definitely a better place without them. There's not any doubt about that. So, I'm pleased but I'm also relieved that this first

451

phase is over. Day after day of observing evil in all of its most vile forms takes its toll. It'll sure be nice to be relatively normal again!"

"Do you think you went deep enough? I mean the way I understand it, you only judged on major harm. For example, you send a drug kingpin to Hell and a drug street seller or user gets by unpunished."

"Not necessarily unpunished. They still must answer to society under society's established system of laws and punishments. This first Judgment Line, we looked only at the individuals committing major harms for two reasons. First, they are frequently the ones with money and power, and because of that, they had generally been able to beat the system. These were frequently found to be among the politicians, the military leaders, the wealthy business people, and judges and lawyers. Remember, we took them out first.

"The second reason was that not all levels of harm deserve termination and Hell or Terminus. We decided to go only for this capital punishment level and leave the other levels to your own individual judicial systems. We didn't want to completely dictate just how citizens in different countries live with each other. For example, a petty thief in some countries gets a hand cut off. In others they would be whipped publicly. In the U.S., they would get probation. If a particular society is happy with their legal system and forms of punishment, so be it. I also need to point out that this opens the door to allow each society to change the system or the punishments as they see fit."

Here's another example, Diane. Suppose two men are at a bar, both more than a little drunk, and they begin to fight over something. A woman, let's say. Suppose that one man is stronger and he breaks the jaw of the other. Now the former has caused harm to another. But he does not, in the opinion of most, deserve termination. Here's the problem: in some societies there are people who might be so opposed to fighting that they would vote to terminate both of them. And that's what makes it hard. What's that old saying? 'Everybody's strange but me and thee, and sometimes I worry about thee'. If you start pruning too deeply you might be the only one left!

"Our goal was to take out the ones who believed, based on their past experiences, that they were above the system, and also the ones who were truly evil in terms of harming others. We were quite successful in this.

"We also wanted the process to be completely open, transparent, to act as a deterrent to such activities in the future. I believe we succeeded in this, too. So far, everything looks very promising. I have to warn you, though, that Ruth's next Judgment Line might be deeper.

"What I'm trying to say is that we didn't want to change the flavor of life as we know it in various societies. The basic orneriness of the human animal is what makes us unique and interesting. Ruth doesn't care if you have two spouses, for example, as long as you are good to both of them. She doesn't care if you drink beer or liquor or take drugs as long as you don't harm others. She doesn't even mind a bit of cussing. Have fun and live but don't harm others. And the Judgment Line has made it possible for you to do that again. It had gotten to the point where a few were making life miserable for the rest. Ruth decided Earth could do without them.

"Finally, remember that Ruth did not give up Her right to judge you at death just because you were judged here. How you live the rest of your life will determine whether you go to Hell or not. And I can't tell you because I don't know what She will consider to be major. So be careful. Be kind."

Diane had been listening intently and momentarily seemed to forget she was doing an interview.

"Whew," she said. "I think I understand. God, this Ruth you talk about, wants us to live and enjoy our lives without being controlled by or threatened by people who want to cause us harm. She doesn't worry about the details we use to do it as long as we don't cause major harm to others. Is that right?"

"Yes."

"What about the Ten Commandments? If we break those, we're supposed to go to Hell."

"Remember this, Diane. Each religion has its own version of a 'Ten Commandments'. This does not mean Ruth uses them as part of Her judgment. Adultery, for example, is a sin for Christians but an accepted practice in societies where their religions allow polygamy. Remembering that no religion has a lock on Heaven, and carrying that thought further, it would seem that if you live the Ten Commandments, in whatever religion such a system exists and under whatever name it is called, then you would never cause harm to another and undoubtedly would go to Heaven. But when you get there the guy living next to you may have two wives and have just as much right to Heaven as you do."

"One final area. Your powers, Maggie. We know you can read minds. What else can you do?"

"What makes you think I can do anything else unusual?"

"Not just you, Maggie. For example, I saw Mr. Raines pick up and move a desk by himself, and I couldn't have lifted one end. I saw Miss Jenny zap a horsefly in court with just a glance. I saw you disappear from your courtroom when you thought you were alone and then a few minutes later, come out of the bathroom."

"You must be hallucinating," Maggie joked. "I know a good doctor, Diane!"

"That's another thing. None of you missed a day of work in over three years. You don't get sick."

"We've always been a healthy bunch. Let's just call it good clean living."

"I see in my notes here that Mr. and Mrs. Raines' son was diagnosed with leukemia about three years ago but is now a football star this year at the high school. How do you explain that?"

"It just proves the power of prayer. He went into remission."

"OK. I can take a hint. Anything else that you want to say?"

"No, I don't think so. At least not this time. Maybe we'll see each other in five years. Thank you, Diane."

The picture faded out and was replaced by the live Diane.

"There you have it. A remarkable woman. There's apparently a whole universe full of wonderful things awaiting us. We need to buckle down and work together and learn how to reach it.

"Now in these last few moments before I sign off, I have a special guest, Jim Marshall, retired anchor for CBS news. Jim was anchor when Maggie made her first speech nearly three and one-half years ago.

"Well, Jim. It's all over. There have been a lot of changes since that day when we all thought Maggie Warner was a hoax. What are your comments?"

"Good to see you again, Diane. I have thought about those early days a lot recently. I was confused like everyone else except for Professor Hamrich, who said it was the work of someone off-earth. I gradually began to accept what was happening and, I must admit, found myself liking what I saw. I have concluded that the world is a better place today and I, for one, am glad. Relieved, even. And so hopeful for my grandchildren. Tomorrow night's lead story will not likely be about a bomb blast killing 70 in some embassy or another or about a serial killer striking again. I feel some positive energy again, and some hope for the future."

"I know how you feel, Jim. Coming in to do the news has become a pleasure."

"I want to congratulate you, Diane, on the job you have done in covering this Judgment Line. It was truly excellent reporting, and you deserve all the credit you can get. Thank you for letting me join you on this one."

"Thank you, Jim. You're a major part of the reason for my success. This is Diane DePlene coming to you from CBS news in a kinder, friendlier, gentler world. Good night."

fifty-nine

There's not much more to tell. Over the next several months we did catch up on our rest. We took Deena and Chastity on vacation. We had a ball in Vegas and Maggie won, as usual. We didn't go to the Golden Swan this time, though. I didn't think Mr. Gonzales was still around anyway.

We went to Deena's mountain meadow for a week. We had our camping gear REGENed in, set up security boundaries, and had the place strictly to ourselves. It was here that I first got into Chastity's pants although come to think of it, she hadn't been wearing any. I hoped Maggie was right about Ruth's position on adultery or we six were in big trouble.

Maggie had been helping Laurie develop her powers, especially in the area of mind-reading. One afternoon a week, they were going to Reckoning to read the prisoners at the same time. Laurie's school wasn't too pleased but finally gave in and called it vocational training.

She is unbelievably strong. We had a quite a row about her trying to read around her father's block but I think I came out ahead. I hope so, anyhow. Hud got his antique business started and I was back in construction with a new crew headed by the Benson boy Tom had hired during the work on Arrowhead.

In early July, Ruth called Deena and Chastity back to work. Deena reported to us that the scientists had finally come up with a form of Wham that only lasted one hour and could be taken safely about twice a week. Ruth wanted them to introduce it on Earth on a small scale. She also set up a meeting with us for July 16. Deena didn't know why.

On July 16, we met Deena and Chastity on Noah and REGENed over to Heaven. Ruth was not there yet so we had coffee and loafed around until She came. She looked older and more frail than ever.

She said, "I've been planning to have you all here for some time but I have been so busy. I also am experiencing some increase in frequency of my blackouts although my memory and judgment seem to be holding their own. Nevertheless, the old clock is ticking along and I will have to retire soon. Maggie, I think you will be the one. What is your current thinking on the job?"

Maggie was quiet for a few minutes, then said, "You've surprised me a little. I wasn't ready to answer that yet. What's your best guess as to the time frame?"

"Within the next 30 years, I hope. But I do want to take some time off before I die."

"I understand. I won't say no right now but I will tell you that I'm leaning strongly in that direction. My main concern is that I'm not really sure I'm cut out for God duty."

"You would be fine, but your personality is such that you might not be happy doing it, so I respect your honesty. I do have an alternate in mind. You know her well. It's Laurie. But I really don't want to approach her until she's in her late twenties."

"I'm glad you want to wait. She needs to carve out a life of her own before worrying about the problems of the universe. She's so strong that I don't honestly know where she's headed. Right now, her personality is not at all like mine. She's the one with the godlike qualities, in my opinion."

"You may be right, Maggie. Now, the other reason for this meeting. Most of the angels in Heaven watched with interest the coverage of the Judgment Line. As a result, I have had two requests through Deena from residents to allow an exception to the 'no mortal visits' rule. One is from your father, Jack. I believe he died when you were about 20 years old. The other was from Jenny's father who died three years ago. The rest of your parents are still living, correct?"

We all nodded agreement.

"If you want to do this, I'm inclined to grant the requests. I owe all of you a lot and I want to reward you in any way that I can. And this is something I can do easily. So why don't you come up early Saturday and bring your kids? Plan to stay over until Sunday. Deena can take the Warners to the Warner residence in Heaven, and Chastity will accompany the Raines. It will be an interesting two days for all of you. Be sure to brief the kids on the need for absolute secrecy when they return."

I was overwhelmed. Heaven is very private, and I knew that mortals rarely, if ever, get to visit. I know it is on an earth-like planet in another solar system in our galaxy and is much larger than earth. I have been there many times, you recall, but only in God's receiving room. I had thought about my father a lot and had kept my eyes open during the Judgment Line in the hope that he would be one of the angels chosen to work on Earth. But if he was there, I hadn't seen him.

I said, "Thank you, Ma'am. I'd love to visit my father. We'll be here."

Jenny echoed my statement.

The next week trudged along in slow motion. I spent a lot of time with the kids telling them about their grandfather. He died well before they were born, so of course they had no memory of him. My mother had remarried before the kids were born and her new husband had always been and would continue to be 'Grandpa'. But they were old enough to understand what was happening. Another grandparent would not change anything.

On Saturday morning, we REGENed up to Noah and went with Deena to Heaven. The Raines left with Chastity. Deena explained before we left that in Heaven, a resident could create whatever setting for living that they desired. My father had chosen to have a farm. Deena said we would REGEN in to the end of the lane and walk in from there. When we got there it was very familiar. In fact, it was the same lane I had walked to and from the school bus stop and to get the mail for many years as a boy. It was about a third of a mile long and went past my uncle's house on the left, a big white Ohio farm house. It then curved around and passed my grandparents' similarly big white farm house with its impressive bank barn, also on the left. The lane ended at our house, the house I grew up in, another big farmhouse on the left with two large barns laid neatly in behind it. A large creek cut through the farm and ran behind our barns.

As we walked slowly in, Deena said it was an exact reproduction of our old farm and was actually in production. Heaven needed a lot of food, and angel farmers supplied much of it. Though there was no requirement for an angel to work, most chose to anyway. When we passed my uncle's place, Deena said he was away on assignment so we wouldn't see him or his wife. We walked slowly on and as we approached my grandfather's house, I saw a man in the field driving a team of huge gray horses pulling a wagon full of what looked like hay. As we got closer, he pulled up and stopped. It was my grandfather. He had died when I was about 13, but I remembered him well. He was a tall man, bald but with a fringe of white hair around the edges. He had held his age at about 50.

He walked forward and extended his hand and said, "Welcome home, Jack. It's been a while."

I took his hand and said, "Hello, Grandpa. It's been too long. This is my wife Maggie, and our kids, Laurie and Mark. Maggie, kids, this is my father's father, Mark Warner."

Maggie took his hand and said, "Hello, Grandpa. It's nice to meet you at last. Children, your great-grandfather Warner."

He solemnly shook hands with both of them.

He said to Mark, "I believe you carry my name, young man. That makes me proud."

"Me, too," Mark answered.

"Why don't you all go to the house while I park this wagon and put the horses in the barn?"

"Can we ride with you, Great-grandpa?" Laurie asked.

"Sure. Jump on up here." To us he said, "Go on in. Your grandma and father are there waiting for you."

The enormity of the situation began to sink in, and I felt, well, I don't know how to explain it. Maybe 'otherworldly'. Maybe 'surreal'. Maybe just plain overwhelmed. My heart was beating out of my chest, and I was breathless.

Deena, Maggie and I walked slowly up to the house. It gave me some time to regain my composure. As we walked up on the back porch, I saw my grandma busy at the sink. When we got to the screen door, she turned and saw us.

She said, "Lord, John. Look who's here! It's Jack and Maggie. Come in, folks. Come in!"

We went in and I gave my grandma a big hug. So did Maggie. Maggie knew her because she hadn't died until after we were married. She did die before Laurie was born, though. I looked over toward the table and the man just getting up was my father, John Warner.

He walked over, extended his hand and said, "It's good to see you, Jack." And we exchanged a quick intense hug. "This must be Maggie?"

"That's right, Dad. This is Maggie."

Maggie gave him a hug and said, "I'm happy to finally get an opportunity to meet you."

Deena was hanging back and I said, "Have you two met Deena?"

Grandma said, "Oh my, yes, she was here last week. Hello, dear."

Deena greeted them both.

"Where are the kids?" Grandma asked.

"They're riding in on the wagon with Grandpa," I said.

"Good. I'm just working on lunch. Why don't you all sit right down at the table and visit? There's some cold lemonade there. Help yourselves."

Deena said she had to leave, but would return tomorrow evening at 6:00 to get us.

Maggie walked over to the sink to see what Grandma was fixing. I sat down at the table and poured myself some lemonade. It was the real thing, made with real lemons and real sugar. Not a trace of chemicals or artificial sweetener.

Dad said, "You've done well, Jack. I've kept track of your life since I had to leave and I've got to tell you, I'm proud of you. I can't wait to meet the kids. And to get to know Maggie."

461

"It was a shock when you died, Dad. It took me a long time to accept it. It's hard when you really would like to believe in a heaven but at the same time wonder what kind of God would let a man of 40 die so young."

"I understand. How's your mother?"

"She's fine, Dad. You know, of course, that she remarried. She's happy. He's a good man and they've done well over the years."

"I'm glad she remarried. She was too young to be widowed."

"She was, she was. Listen, Dad, I'm kind of new to this heaven business." I needed to change the subject. "You're going to have to bring me up to speed. I'm surprised to find the family farm recreated and families still together."

"You have lots of choices when you get to Heaven. First, nothing is required of you. You can have free food, shelter and recreation if you desire. You can loaf on a beach for all eternity if you want to. You can marry or not, be with your family or not, almost anything goes as long as you don't harm another. Of course if you have a history of harming others, you don't get here in the first place, so that's not really a problem. Most of us sooner or later get bored with loafing and gravitate into some sort of occupation or interesting hobby. Farmers, like your grandfather and I, just naturally took up our old work here because farming is what we enjoy. Movie-theater owners tend to open movie theaters, store owners stay store owners, and so on. But if you always wanted to be a train engineer, then they'll round up a train for you to run. Heavens draw on the resources of thousands of planets. Our Heaven is subsidized by taxes from other worlds since Earth is still unaware of the universe. We will, of course, have to contribute in the future when we eventually mature.

"Of course, what we and other farmers produce contributes to the overall economy of Heaven. In our case, we keep what we want for ourselves and give the rest to Central for distribution. There is no money here nor is there barter. Not needed. Everything is free. If you want it, and it's there, you can have it. If it's not there, you can petition for it to be secured. It's an interesting system."

"It surely is. I noticed Grandpa using a team of horses. Is Heaven that backward in the use of technology ? It seems really inefficient."

"Technology is whatever level you choose. I can take you to a neighboring farm where even plowing is automated. Your grandfather chooses to use 1950's technology. And I liked that choice for him, too. Seems comfortable and, well, right in his case. He prefers horses and I like the old tractors, but we still are on the same wavelength. Maybe it's not efficient but we aren't under any pressure to produce efficiently. It's much more productive, however, than it was before on earth since there aren't any diseases or harmful insects. And most of all, as you can see, we are happy."

He was interrupted by a cheery voice from the porch. "Hello! Anybody home?"

A striking dark-haired beauty of about 40 came through the screen door and set a package on the sink counter. She said, "You must be Maggie. I've been looking forward to meeting you. I'm Debra, John's wife."

I almost fell out of my chair. I don't know why, but I never even considered that the old man would have remarried. There was every reason why he should have, but I was still surprised.

She bounced over to me and said, "And you are Jack. It's good to see you."

I said, "Good to meet you, too."

Dad said, "Debra grew up in Indiana on a farm and got to Heaven about when I did. Breast cancer did her in. She was trying to decide what to do when we met at the house of a mutual friend. I finally convinced her that the farm life was for her."

Debra laughed and said "I'm not at all fond of farming, but fortunately I don't actually have to participate! I spend a lot of time working at the museum in town."

I said, "If I ever get here, and Maggie says there's some doubt of that, I don't plan to do much farming, either."

"You'll probably run a casino," Maggie threw in.

Everybody had a laugh and then Grandpa and the kids arrived. Each of the kids was holding a kitten. Grandpa said, "These kids will make good farmers some day. They like horses. And kittens!"

Dad said, "Later on we'll saddle up a couple of mares and they can ride. You two young'uns, come over here and meet your grandfather."

I introduced them to everyone and there were hugs all around. The kids were a little overwhelmed but overall did fine considering the circumstances. Laurie had probably read them all and knew exactly which buttons to push to get her way.

We had a big lunch of fried chicken, potato salad, sliced tomatoes, butter beans and corn, all from their farm. And several loaves of warm homemade bread with real butter and grandma's strawberry jam. It's been a long time since I had food that actually tasted good. Maybe "real" is a more appropriate description. And I was careful not to say that out loud, either! Don't want to upset the wife, who is a fine cook! Apple pie, just-churned ice cream, and soft homemade chocolate chip cookies followed. After lunch, we waddled on down to our house. Dad took Maggie, the kids and me on a walking tour of the farm. Debra had to go back to the museum for a couple of hours.

I particularly wanted to see the creek. It was a large one, flowing lazily to the west. There was a large bend just below the barns near where they had made a tractor and horse crossing. In that bend, a pool formed that was about five feet deep in the center. This had always been our swimming hole. I used to carry soap and a towel on the tractor and stop for a bath at the end of a hot day.

When the kids saw it, they wanted to swim. Dad told them to go ahead, it was clean. They did. It was a hot afternoon so I decided to join them.

"Come on, Maggie. Let's go in," I said.

"Hmm, I don't know. Looks cold to me," she said.

"Let's wade in a little bit and see."

We waded in towards the kids, which was a mistake for Maggie because they had her in and under before she knew what had happened. We did have a good time and when we got out, we just walked in the sun a while to dry. No clothes to worry about, of course.

Later in the afternoon the kids rode the horses and even Maggie tried one. All in all, it was a really pleasant afternoon. Almost too perfect.

When we finally got back to the house, Debra had returned from town and was working on dinner. She had a roast in the oven that smelled just marvelous. We all took showers, then Maggie went in and helped with dinner. Dad and I settled in the living room.

We talked a while about the Judgment Line. He had been asked to be a judge but had declined.

"If Earth was in such a shape that a judgment was necessary, then I didn't want to see it," he said.

"It was bad. In some ways, it still is, but it's improved a lot since the judgment."

"I'll bet it has," he said laughing. "How did you all wind up in charge?"

"It was really Maggie who God wanted. She has extraordinary powers."

"I know. I tried to read her and hit a blank wall. Come to think of it, I hit a blank wall with you, too."

"I've gotten stronger in the past few years. You must be pretty good if they asked you to judge."

"I suppose I'm above average, but powers are not of much use here. I get anything I want free anyway."

"How do you handle relationships here? I mean, suppose you and Debra have a falling out. What happens?"

"Even if it's serious enough to split us up, nothing happens. One of us walks. That's it. If I want two wives, and both agree, there's no problem."

"What about mother? What if she comes up and wants to be with you again?"

"Hmm. That's a tough one, son. I don't know. Never thought about it. I don't have an answer for that one. I think Debra would accept a second wife but your mother wouldn't have any part of it. Also, she's got the new guy to consider. Let's just say I'm not looking forward to that happening." He chuckled a bit. I could tell he wanted to change the subject.

About that time, Maggie called us to dinner. The roast was as good as it had smelled.

After dinner the kids went out for a walk, then went to their rooms to talk and read. The four of us settled down again in the living room.

"Dad and I were talking earlier about Heaven and relationships between people," I said. "But what I really want to know is, what it's all about? On Earth we are told that if we live a good life we will be rewarded with Heaven. Who benefits from this process and why does it take place?"

"That's another hard one to answer, son," Dad said frowning. "And I'm not sure I'm the best one to handle it. As you say, Heaven is a reward for living the way Ruth wants us to, but I am not sure myself why She wants it or what Her motive is in all this. Some say that Heaven is just another step in a long process of life. In other words, some of us will go to another level, others won't. However, if anyone has been called to go on since I hit Heaven, I'm not aware of it."

Debra said, "Another popular theory is that Ruth is a super being from another universe, accumulating a large force of humans for some unknown future purpose in that other universe. Time means nothing to Her, of course, and what is an eternity to us may only be a few seconds to Her."

Maggie said, "Unless She lied to me, She is a mortal taking long life drugs, and is about 8000 years old. She expects to die just like us, in the next 2000 or so years."

"You know more about Ruth than we do," Dad responded.

"I probably shouldn't talk about Her, but She didn't say not to. Now, She does claim to report to a higher entity, and that one is over all the Gods in our universe. Ruth is just one of many, in other words."

"That's curious," Debra said. "I wonder how many levels there are?"

Maggie said, "I got no hint of that. In fact, I don't have any information at all about the levels above Ruth. Not yet, that is."

"Well, all I know is that Heaven is several notches above the tchadbe farms of Hell," I said.

We chewed on the same theme for another hour or so and then went to bed. Maggie was unusually quiet, and after we got in bed, I asked her what was bothering her.

"Jack, I get the feeling that this visit was orchestrated for our benefit. I don't mean it's not real. I believe this is Heaven and your father and Debra exist and really live this way. But something's wrong. Let's stretch our minds to their bedroom and listen."

We did. I was surprised to hear Debra sobbing and Dad trying to comfort her. I couldn't make out what the problem was and it felt very weird reading them anyway.

"What do you think is wrong?" I asked.

"I'm not sure. But it's something to do with us. He's saying something about telling us tomorrow morning. I guess we'll have to wait and see. I just can't get a handle on it without a deep read, Jack, and I'm really uncomfortable doing that."

Next morning, I woke up to the smell of bacon frying. I shook Maggie awake to go to breakfast. We got downstairs and found Dad and Debra cooking.

"Good morning," Debra said. "I hope you slept well."

"Very well," I said. "Breakfast sure smells good."

"Ready in five minutes," Dad said. "There's juice on the counter over there if you like."

We got our juice, and sat down at the table. Pretty soon eggs, bacon, toast, grits, and a huge bowl of fried potatoes were sitting in front of us. Oh, and homemade cinnamon rolls. Here comes another five pounds!

"We need to tell you all something that we're not supposed to talk about," Dad said. "The angel, Deena, came here last week to tell us about your upcoming visit. We were requested to have everything in tip-top order. In other words, to give you the impression that Heaven was in fine shape and that all was well. In fact, that is not the case at all. Heaven has been severely neglected. The place is literally falling apart. Supplies don't arrive on time, new arrivals have no place to live, the infrastructure is wearing out and not being replaced, and the head angel in charge of Heaven, whose name is Conner, says he can't make the necessary changes because God has failed to give him the required support. Debra and I are not the simple farmers that we appear to be. We were asked to portray that while you were here. In fact, Debra is second in command to Conner in Heaven's hierarchy and can confirm that he has tried his very best. Something is wrong. And we need to find out what it is so that we can fix it."

Silence for a minute while we tried to absorb their bombshell.

Debra picked it up.

"Things were going downhill here before the Judgment Line began, but have been deteriorating really rapidly in the past year or two. We tried to talk to Ruth but She was always busy or would assure us She would take action. Then nothing would happen. Out of sheer frustration, I went and looked up Deena.

"As you know, Deena is head angel for off-Heaven affairs. Problems on Earth, Hell, other parts of the galaxy, these are her responsibility. But I thought she might have some insight into what was causing the inaction on Ruth's part. Deena was kind and sympathetic. She confessed to having some problems of a similar nature over the past several years. She promised to stay in touch and keep us updated on anything new. That was six months ago. She did talk to us several times but without much new information. Then last week she showed up and told us about your request to visit with us. She said ——."

Maggie interrupted, "Wait a minute. Something's wrong. Ruth said that you all requested an exception to the mortal rule and wanted us to visit."

Dad said, "Deena very distinctly said the request originated with Jack. What do you suppose this means?"

Maggie said, "Deena is definitely up to something. I'm not sure what."

I said, "It looks to me like she has been working both ends to some purpose. She made Ruth and us think the request came from you, and made you all think it came from us. Apparently, neither of us made a request."

"Curious," Dad said. "Do you all trust her?"

"With our lives," Maggie said. "We literally have trusted Deena with our lives. Several times."

"Just a minute," I said. "What exactly were her instructions?"

Debra concentrated a minute and said, "Two things. First, She said that God had requested that this visit be kept quiet so that other residents of Heaven wouldn't think this was a new perk. She also said that Deena couldn't take you anywhere but this farm."

I said, "My guess is that Ruth did tell her to say that. But I think what Deena had in mind was exposing Maggie to the real situation in Heaven. Ruth's instructions precluded her doing this exposing personally so she left us with you, Dad and Debra, and hoped you would bring it up and show us around. Remember, She said God forbade Deena herself from taking us off the farm. Of course, God will chew her ass for leaving us here alone, but Deena's no virgin as far as that goes."

"I think you've got it, Jack," Maggie said. "That's the only explanation for maneuvering us into this position. Clever."

"I still don't understand," Debra said. "What good is it to expose you and Maggie to the problem?"

I looked at Maggie. She gave a little affirmative nod so I said, "Maggie is the leading candidate to replace Ruth when She retires a few years from now."

Nobody knew what to say. Finally, Dad cleared his throat and said, "Well, congratulations, Maggie. This is truly astounding news. I, for one, can only see positive changes for the future."

"Thanks," Maggie said. "But don't get the cart before the horse. What Jack didn't say is that I haven't decided for sure that I want the job."

Debra said, "I can understand why. Multiply the problems with the Earth and its Heaven and Hell by several hundred and it adds up to one big headache."

"That's certainly part of it, but it's also my basic nature. I'm lazy and don't want to make the effort! In any event, it's pretty clear that Deena wants us to get a feel for Heaven, so I guess we'd better go to town or someplace off the farm. Then we'll shake her down at 6:00 when she returns."

Debra walked over to the phone and said, "I'll call and see if Grandpa and Grandma are awake and can come entertain the kids. I hope they got the damn phones working again."

They worked, and Debra said they were on their way. My bet was they were up and ready to come over before the sun even came up.

sixty

We went out to the barn and Dad slid open the big doors. Sitting inside was a red 1955 Ford Crown Victoria that looked like it had just come off the assembly line. I just stared.

Dad laughed and said, "I've always been partial to the '55 so I get a new one nearly every year. You can drive 'er, Jack."

We loaded up and started down the lane.

Debra said, "Take a left at the hard road and we'll go through the village on our way to town. It won't take long to show you what we're talking about."

It didn't. The paved road was rougher than the lane. It was full of potholes. When we reached the village, the single gas station was closed, with a sign saying "NO GAS". We stopped at the village store and went inside. There was some food on maybe half the shelves. The meat counter had a sign posted that read "LIMIT 2 LBS. CHICKEN". I heard a man ask for sugar. He was told they were out until at least Tuesday. Dad said if it got much worse they would have to use the food machines at the Central in the city. So far the Central had been able to keep them operating.

We got back in the car and headed for the city. On the outskirts we found an open gas station, and Dad told me to pull in.

An attendant ambled out and said, "Fill'er up?"

"Might as well," Dad said. "Next time I stop you may not have any."

"You got that right," the attendant said. "We may have to close at the end of the month if them rumors are true."

"What rumors?"

"Word is gas is unnecessary since we got them atomic powered cars. Supposed to be much easier and cheaper to just plug 'em in once a week. Gas'll be phased out and people like you and me will have to park our old cars so they can turn to rust."

"That'll be the day. Where did you hear this bullshit?"

"Mr. Parks, the boss, heard it at the Central yesterday."

The attendant finished and I thanked him. We pulled out and headed into the town center.

Dad said, "See what I mean? They're after my old cars and tractors now. Things are a mess."

"They sure seem to be," I agreed. "What is this Central?"

Debra said, "It's the local branch of the administration section of the Government of Heaven. I keep my office there, not at a museum, and move about by REGEN. It's partly recreational since anyone can go at any time and have drinks, use the food machines, dance, even gamble for fun. If you want something you can't find, you can petition for it right there on the spot. Until the last couple of years, it was automatic that your petition would be approved. Now you're lucky if the volunteer even shows up to take your petition."

Maggie asked, "How are the residents of Heaven reacting. I mean, I know they're not pleased, but have they gone beyond that? What choices do they have?"

"They're beyond displeased, I think," Debra answered. "As to choices, it's tough. We exist at the pleasure of Ruth and have few choices except to complain. Our REGEN machines are restricted to this planet. The only exception is when they are used to bring supplies to the surface from ships. But they are programmed to work only with a down-shipment, so they couldn't help us anyhow. You can't rebel against the administration because we're all volunteers. Our only recourse is to complain directly to Ruth and hope She responds. You are the first outside ears I've ever had."

"I just don't understand why She is letting things slide. She can't lack resources," I said. "I believe you said Heaven occupies only 12 percent of the usable surface of this planet. So space isn't the problem. Has She simply lost interest? Is it a test? Is it a punishment?"

"We simply don't know," Dad said. "When Conner and Debra meet with Ruth, She always seems to be genuinely concerned and promises to help. But nothing, and I mean nothing, happens. So we don't know which way to turn."

Debra said, "The Central is just ahead on the right. Pull in and I'll show it to you."

I wheeled the Crown Vic into the parking lot and found a space with no problem. We climbed out and headed to the front entrance. It was a large older building that Debra said was a replica of the county courthouse that had burned before I was born. We walked to Debra's office, went in, and found someone seated at her desk.

Debra said, "Conner. What a surprise. I thought you were meeting with Ruth this morning?"

"I did. Just got back. She moved the meeting up to 7:00 and it didn't take long to do what I had to do. I was just leaving you a note."

"What happened? Did you get any better idea today of what's wrong?"

"Not much and no. I was given firm assurances that reforms were starting right away. The same line we've gotten the last umpteen times we've met with Her. There was one new development, though."

"What's that?" Debra asked.

"You are the new Head Angel. I resigned on the spot."

Debra was clearly shocked and concerned. She stammered, "But you and I agreed to fight this out to the finish. You can't just abandon me in the middle!"

"I have to, Debra. No patience left. I'm going to go home and sit for a few years."

Debra just stood there dumbfounded. She finally looked around, and seeing Maggie and me standing there, said "I'm sorry. Conner. This is John's son, Jack, and his wife, Maggie."

"I'm pleased to meet you," Conner said extending his hand. "I hope you all can help somehow, maybe come up with some solution."

"We'll try," Maggie said.

Debra said, "Conner, please! We have to talk. I don't want this job!"

He laughed and said, "Neither did I. Remember? You told me it was my duty. Now it's your turn."

"I'll be over to see you first thing tomorrow morning. We need to talk this over some more. Please, please Conner." Real desperation in her voice.

"OK, but I won't be changing my mind, Debra. I can turn the files over to you then. You also have a meeting with Ruth tomorrow afternoon at 3:00. See you in the morning. Nice to meet you all."

And with that, he left. Debra sighed deeply and looked at Dad who shrugged his shoulders and grinned.

"Don't grin at me," Debra said. "If I take this job, you're in it up to your ears."

"You'll be great," Dad said.

"Bullshit," Debra said.

We toured around the Central a little bit but anyone could read that Debra's heart wasn't in it. I suggested we go back to the farm. It was lunch time and Dad said that first he had a surprise for us. We drove across town and suddenly, there it was, just as I remembered it: Archer's Burger Shack, home of the best burger in the Midwest. And it had long been the local high school hangout. It was a fifties-style restaurant, but when I was in high school in the late 80's, we didn't know the difference.

I pulled the Ford into the lot and we went in. The place hadn't changed a bit. There was an open booth and a waitress with red hair walked us over to it. Too bad Hud wasn't here. He would have appreciated this one.

Dad said, "I never really came here while you were still at home but I thought you'd enjoy it one more time."

"I am at peace. There is nothing like an Archer Burger Supreme Basket for lunch. Supplemented, of course, with a huge chocolate malt."

"It doesn't take much to make you happy," Maggie said.

"I may open one of these in Clarksboro when we get back. The local kids need this experience."

The waitress arrived and we all ordered. There was a jukebox on the wall and I played a few 50's songs. We chatted a bit about Debra's promotion and then the food arrived. Of course, I had ordered twice as much as I could eat, but I tried anyway, and wound up so full I could hardly get up, but I managed to roll into the Ford. We left and headed back to the farm.

We took a different route back but saw about the same problems as before. We passed a shopping center with just one tenant, a small nail salon. We saw a new car lot with virtually no inventory. Many service stations displayed "NO GAS" signs. This was depressing.

When we finally arrived back at the farm, it was nearly 4:30. We went inside, greeted Grandma and Grandpa and asked them to stay for dinner. Deena was due at 6:00 so we'd have plenty of time to eat before we left. The kids were excited after an afternoon of swimming and horseback riding. I promised to get horses for them at Arrowhead. Weak moment, I think. Horses are a hell of a lot of work.

Dad, Grandpa and I went to the living room to talk while dinner was being prepared. We briefed Grandpa and chewed the problem over some more but came to no firm conclusion. Turns out, we didn't even know what the question was.

Deena arrived at 6:00 and agreed to stay for dinner. Debra and Maggie briefed her on the two days. She feigned surprise and concern over our having left the farm but I know our Deena. She knew what was going to happen. Had planned it, even.

We had a great dinner. Coupled with lunch, it caused me to gain about 5 pounds that day. I always thought of myself as too thin, so I wasn't too worried.

Goodbyes were sad, but we knew we had to go. We promised to try to figure out what was going on, and to help all we could with Heaven's problems.

When we got back to Noah we sent the kids to the recreation room and met with Deena in the briefing room.

Maggie said, "You're going to catch hell for letting us go to town in Heaven. What's going on there?"

"You know I've caught hell before, guys, so I'm not too worried about that. I've still got my job, don't I? Ruth already knows about your little adventure, and wants to see all of us tomorrow at noon. As to what's going on, in spite of Her assurances to the contrary, I think She has lost it. Her condition is worse than She will admit. She hasn't stabilized at all."

"What can we do?" I asked. "Really, what can we do?"

Deena shook her head and said, "I don't know except to confront Her, gently of course, and see what happens."

About then Chastity and the Raines arrived. They had also had a good visit, and Chastity had made sure they, too, saw the deplorable condition of Heaven while they were there. We talked a while and then went to Arrowhead.

Next morning about 11:00, we REGENed up and met Deena and Chastity. They took us over to Heaven and to Ruth's receiving room. She came in about 12:15 and ordered lunch for us all. Then She sat quietly and read us all but Maggie.

She sighed deeply and said, "So I see you are all unsure about me?" She looked at Maggie and said, "Do you go along with the others?"

Maggie said, "I don't think 'unsure' is exactly how we feel, Ruth. We have seen evidence that something is wrong at Heaven and want to know why. It's reasonable to suspect that your illness has progressed further than you led us to believe."

Ruth bent forward and put Her hands over Her face. Then She sat up and said, "I've tried so hard to maintain the illusion that all is well. I even fooled myself, I guess. But I'm sick, not demented. I realize that you six are reasonable people and wouldn't carry these thoughts without cause. What do you think I should do?"

She paused. We waited for Her since nobody had an answer for that one. Then a voice and a bright light appeared above Ruth's head.

"Ruth, this is Xerma. I'm going to intervene."

We looked at each other in amazement. Even Deena and Chastity had never met Xerma before this. Chastity quietly explained to us that Xerma had 2nd tier powers, and was, in effect, Ruth's immediate superior. I knew then that Ruth's reign was over. This was extremely sad, and I feared what was to come next, for Her and for us. Xerma's strong voice boomed out again.

"Ruth, as of today, you are officially retired. I want you to come to Xemial and we'll arrange medical treatment on Yunal 6. Please ask your spouses to come with you. Go get ready to leave."

"I understand." And Ruth got up and walked away. Just like that. She was gone.

"Good. Now, Maggie. I want to formally offer you the job of God, which Ruth has held for many thousands of years. I know it's premature and that you haven't completely decided. I also know that you haven't really been briefed on the other worlds under Ruth's rule as God, but I'm willing to personally give you intense on-the-job training. I have another candidate, but I have been watching your progress for years, and you're the one I want. You and your team. I can give you one week to decide."

Maggie looked around as if she had been trapped. She said, "I am honored to be considered and I will decide within the week. But I must have the answers to several questions. And there are several conditions which must be met."

"Very well. Let's hear them." Still just the voice.

"First, about Heaven. How does the budget process work? Why was Ruth trying to save money from being spent on Heaven? Do I have to live within a budget?"

"There is a budget of sorts, Maggie. I wouldn't want to spend half of my resources on Earth's Heaven, for example. But most worlds in our universe, some not governed by Ruth, are very wealthy and you will never be strained to provide for your own personal worlds. What has happened in Heaven is the result of an unfortunate communication error. It will be your job to correct that error with no real budget constraint. You see, Ruth misunderstood a casual comment I once made about some of my Gods taking more than their fair share of my resources. She took it to heart and thought I was criticizing her."

"All right. How many worlds will I have to watch over?"

"I am reorganizing and reducing the numbers per God as we speak. You will have 53 where Ruth had 217. That will be much easier. I might increase your load a little after you learn the ropes."

"Is living on Earth going to be a problem?"

"Not at all. I should think you would like to use these offices and facilities during working hours but that's up to you. We can set up the special REGENs that the Gods use at your home if you like. Some of your staff will about have to stay here, though."

"Why don't you appear to us?"

"If you want me to, I will. I'm not like you, however. I am human and mortal, but very different from you because I'm from a different world."

"Please do. I find it somewhat intimidating speaking to just a voice."

The light moved down to the chair and then began to dim. A figure began to emerge. Xerma wasn't kidding. She was different. First of all, She was large. She was sitting in Ruth's chair but I would have put Xerma at about seven feet tall and 220 pounds. Her skin was a reddish color, much like Mesarch's had been. Her hair was a deep mahogany red color and was long and flowing. Her facial features were very different from ours. She had a large protruding forehead, a wide nose, and a normal looking mouth. Her chin was wide and prominent, giving Her face a caved-in look. Not unattractive, but different. Xerma stood up and made a 360 for us. She appeared to be much like us from the neck down. She had large breasts and very large buttocks. Her genitals appeared to be similar to ours and were covered in red hair. I later learned that She had two openings, one for recreational sex and one for conceiving children. Her feet were huge, probably men's size 15 or 16. She had six toes on each foot and six fingers on each hand.

"What do you think?" She asked.

"I'd hate to wrestle with you," Maggie said.

Xerma laughed and said, "We're a little larger than your type of earthling, but I'm actually small for my world."

"Where are you from?"

"From the planet Xemial, star system Ytera in the Uberrith Galaxy, two over from your Milky Way. I am responsible for six galaxies in all."

"How many inhabited worlds do you yourself have?"

"About 2200. There are many more, however, that we don't choose to work with. Some are just too primitive. Earth was an exception even though it is still primitive. Others have matured into worlds that no longer need our services. These two categories include many more thousands of worlds. Others lost their star and are gone, while others are in the very initial stages of evolution. It is very complex. Maggie, I know you have a million questions about the other worlds, but I have briefing materials for that. Also, you can visit any world at anytime you choose. Just let me know and I'll arrange it."

"All right. I do have one more question, though. What's this all about? I mean, why are there different levels of Gods, and what purpose does Heaven serve? Who gains and loses? What purpose will I serve if I choose to replace Ruth?"

Xerma chuckled. "That sounds like several questions, but let me try. The universe is quite old, older than you can imagine. Ruth is 8000 years old and that's not even a few seconds compared to the age of the universe. Back in the early days, worlds were constantly at war with each other. They had developed faster-than-light space travel but had not discovered the long-life drugs. So in spite of being able to travel to the stars, their lives were fairly short. No one knew what happened when one died. No one was giving the idea of an afterlife much thought. You died, you were gone.

"But eventually, death became an obsession and much study was devoted to it. Finally, a breakthrough occurred when a gentleman from another universe with exceptional mind powers died and managed to return as a spirit, for want of a better term. That is, his soul returned. He reported to his family and friends that all persons who had died were just 'out there' somewhere in a kind of limbo, without purpose or direction. He then said that he had a plan to organize these souls, and promised that he would return later to explain it to them.

"He went back to that limbo area, found a star system with empty planets, and started the first Heaven and Hell for his home planet. He called together all the souls from his home planet and, along with several recruits from among them, announced a judgment process. We believe that this was where the doctrine of 'not harming others' originated, by the way. This man then used his powers, particularly his ability to control minds, to send the souls to Heaven or to Hell. Those in Heaven he choose to call angels, and those in Hell were known as demons. His name, by the way, was Jeremiah Godde.

"His home planet and the people on it were very much like your Earth. So Jeremiah returned, announced the existence of Heaven and Hell, and warned the people that they would be judged at the time of their death. He then left to return to Heaven and vowed not to reappear to them again. The people, of course, thought it was a hoax and most paid no attention to what he had said. But there was a hard core group who believed him. Thus, modern religion was born. It was essentially a very simple plan, laid out in black and white for anyone who cared to look.

"The word about Jeremiah's Heaven spread through the souls of other worlds and they searched him out to learn about having their own Heaven and Hell. Part of the problem, you see, was that those souls which really belonged in a Hell were still, after death, able to cause harm to the souls which should have been in a Heaven. The key to Jeremiah's early success with the solution to this problem was partly luck. On the planet he picked for his Hell, he discovered a huge deposit of an extremely rare element known as SLKR-276, which was critical to space travel. This discovery allowed him to finance his Heaven and make it a true reward for those who went there.

"He put a team of scientist souls on a research project involving how to put the soul back into a body, and they eventually succeeded. First, he gave bodies to the residents of Hell and used them to mine the SLKR-276. He gave bodies to his angels and let them do whatever they wished on Heaven. Soon, the souls from other worlds wanted this opulent lifestyle, too. Since he had almost unlimited resources, he added new worlds to his empire by creating Heavens

480

and Hells for their people. When it got too big for him to handle, he recruited other Gods to take over part of the worlds. He decided that the new Gods should be mortal since he had long ago lost touch with the feelings and ways of his subjects.

"Jeremiah is still living in Heaven at his home world but is no longer active. I personally have never had any contact with him. That, in brief, is about all I know. The gainers in the process are those who go to a Heaven because they are separated from their tormentors, who are sent to Hell. What purpose will you serve, Maggie? The answer, simply put, is that you will continue this winnowing process and the system of punishments and rewards for your worlds.

"Your final question was that you want to know 'what's it all about'? Maggie, I don't know the answer to that myself. We know Jeremiah started the God structure. But who created Jeremiah and the others he sent to Heaven and Hell? Who decided that after death the souls would survive? Who created the universes? I don't know. We don't know. Perhaps there is an ultimate God out there watching over everything. There has to be something but I haven't a clue. And I myself have unanswered questions."

Xerma leaned back and looked at us. Nobody said anything for a few moments.

Finally Maggie said, "How long have you had your position?"

"A little more than 5000 years."

"We four have known about Heaven for about five years. If you don't have a clue, Xerma, you can imagine how we feel. But your answers helped a lot. I hadn't thought through the implications of there not being a Hell, and of the continued dominance of those who are evil. Set up the way you describe it, putting people into Heaven has that as one of its rewards. While I still have questions I haven't resolved yet, I do feel better about the whole situation. Thank you, Xerma."

"Take your week, Maggie, and discuss it with your loved ones. Please don't any of you mention this conversation to anyone outside of this room. I'll see you here one week from today. If you have more questions, pass them up through Deena."

And with that, Xerma was gone.

Deena broke the silence. "I've never heard that history of Gods before. I doubt that Ruth had either. I'm sorry She wasn't here to listen. It's apparent that they have big plans for you, Maggie. That's why they're pushing you to make a quick decision."

"Why do you say that?" Maggie asked.

"Think about it. Who was selected above all others to conduct the Judgment Line? Who was the first mortal to visit Heaven? Who was the first mortal or angel to hear this history of Gods? Who has just been offered the job of God with virtually no strings attached? Who, with only five years experience, is being courted by people thousands of years old with enormous experience in being a God?"

"It does seem rather strange when you put it that way," Maggie conceded. "But how am I supposed to decide? Can Xerma be trusted? Is there some dark, deep plot none of us know about?"

"I don't know," Deena countered. "She seems to be OK to me, but remember, I'm also the one who hired Carmen."

"I get the feeling that they are desperate to have a God from Earth for some reason," said Hud. "And right now. Remember, Ruth kept saying that a lot of important things came from the primitives, and Earth was a created primitive. Maybe Maggie is one of the things they hoped to get."

"Hud may have hit the nail on the head," I said. "Something is still wrong and they think they need Maggie to solve or cure the problem in this one apparently small section of the whole, what is it?– organization. We can't just limit our thinking to our one little universe any more because there's so much more out there, as it was described to us. But it does seem to be set up in a sort of regimented pattern, like a gigantic multi-layered pyramid, doesn't it? Maggie, I'll bet you move up rapidly in the hierarchy."

"I still may turn this down. I've just got to internalize this mass of information and see if I can resolve some doubts I have, There were some situations at the Judgment Line that I can't get my mind around. Some unfinished issues." Maggie said.

"I know you can think this through, Maggie," Jenny said. "While it's you they want right now, on their time scale, what's a few years' wait to get Laurie or one of her children? I think they want a primitive and Maggie is the first one they've ever found who fits the job description."

Nobody said anything for a while. Then Maggie said, "I've got a lot to think about. Let's go home."

On our way home, Jenny talked excitedly about the visit with her father. He had remarried and was very happy. We all shared some of our experiences and concluded that even though it wasn't completely aboveboard, it was overall a worthwhile trip. We finally arrived at Arrowhead about 5:00 that afternoon. It was hot so we all took a dip in the pool. I can't tell you how good it felt to be home.

The next week passed quickly. We were all busy and Maggie spent much of her free time in seclusion focusing on her decision. We had a group session Saturday night in our common room. Maggie started us off by saying that she had just about decided to take the job but wanted one last talk with us.

"I believe I'm going to accept, although I am still not 100% sure," she said. "I can clearly see the pros and cons from my standpoint. But I keep thinking about Dad Warner and Debra and their problems and about those who we sent to Hell and Terminus who really deserved it. It is helping me see that in my new position, I can do a lot more."

"What about the unanswered question of 'why me'?" Jenny asked. "It still strikes me as strange."

"Me, too. And I'm going to ask for a real answer before I accept."

"What about the time constraints, and the pressure?" Hud asked.

"I am going to stick to an 8 or 9 hour day and finish raising my kids no matter what happens. I'm sure that there will be times when it isn't going to be easy. As to the pressure, we'll see. I can always resign, you know, and unlike Ruth, I don't intend to agree to find a successor first."

Maggie continued, "What I really wanted to talk about is you three. Ruth needed lots of angels to assist Her, and I will, too. I'll keep Deena and Chastity and undoubtedly Debra. But they can't make the same decisions mortals make. I need the three of you to help judge and to generally represent me on other worlds. I don't know how Xerma will react to this, but they, whoever 'they' are, either want me or they don't. If you all would promise an average of two 8-hour days per week each, I believe I can reduce my time needs and the pressure at the same time. And remember that you have been selected just like I have."

I looked at Hud and Jenny and both nodded yes. I said, "You've got that and probably more if you really need it."

"Good. I knew you would all agree. We'll see what Xerma says on Monday."

sixty-one

We left for Heaven early on Monday, July 23, and loafed around Noah with Deena and Chastity until we had to leave. Xerma had specifically excluded Deena and Chastity from joining us today.

Deena said, "I guess She regards this as mortal business, and She's right. Maggie, are you going to take the job?"

Maggie said, "Yes, I probably will, if Xerma agrees to my conditions and answers the one remaining question."

"I think She will. And I suspect that's why Chastity and I aren't invited."

We REGENed over about 12:00 and found lunch waiting. We had just begun to eat when Xerma appeared, Or materialized. She was just suddenly there.

"Please go ahead and continue eating while we talk. Have you thought about the job some more, Maggie?"

"I have, but I still need answers to a few more questions."

"I thought you would."

"First, I would like to request that my three spouses be appointed as my assistants and have the power to represent me in in the judgment process except for Terminus decisions. They would also represent me in the other Heavens when needed."

Xerma was quiet for a few moments and finally said, "I don't see why there would be any objection. They are mortal and experienced and have powers. It's never been done but that doesn't make it wrong. All right. It's approved. You three must continue to work with Bishop, however, improving your powers."

"Secondly, I want to be considered a short-timer. If my daughter is your next choice, she will probably be ready in 30 to 40 years. I may want to quit then. If she doesn't want the job, I still reserve the right to quit without finding my own successor."

"Agreed. What else?"

"I want to know exactly why you and Ruth and apparently others out there are so anxious to select a woman of my age and experience to be a God. I want the whole story."

Xerma was quiet for so long, I was afraid Maggie had seriously offended Her. She finally got up and paced for a few minutes and then went to a communication device and spoke to someone at length. Then She turned back to us.

"I told those fools that you wouldn't play without the story but they didn't believe me. They were afraid you wouldn't take the position if you knew. But they have just agreed to let me relate the story to you.

"First, let me explain who "they" are. I report to a person with third tier powers. His name is D'Lorn, and He is in charge of all Gods in our universe. D'Lorn sits on a council made up of all the third-tier Gods from other universes. The top person in charge of it all was handpicked by Jeremiah Godde to replace him several thousand years ago. This person is Vandora. She has fourth-tier powers, and the buck stops with Her, to use one of your phrases. Vandora is, among other things, chairperson of this council.

"Several thousand years ago, a crisis arose in the administration of the Heavens and Hells. It started about the time Jeremiah stepped down. It wasn't Vandora's fault. She was doing Her best and She was the best the entire system had to offer. The crisis wasn't immediately obvious and everything seemed OK. Then reports began to filter in. The quality of life on the Heavens was deteriorating in spite of almost unlimited resources. Output and productivity on the Hells was declining. So Vandora sent word out to get things corrected. Immediately. Everyone did their job, and for a while, things were back to normal. Vandora kept up the pressure but the deterioration eventually returned with renewed vigor.

"They tried to coax Jeremiah out of retirement but He had lost interest. The immortals have their problems, too, and one of them is boredom. Jeremiah had a terminal case with respect to administering the Heavens and Hells.

"Then someone observed that the problem hadn't really begun until the long-life drugs allowed gods at all levels to rule for thousands of years instead of hundreds. But no connection could be proven so the information was set aside and largely ignored. They did have the foresight, however, to seed the Earth in order to create a new primitive. As you know, we have gotten some remarkable things from the primitives over time. Anyway, when intelligent humans finally began to emerge on Earth, Ruth was instructed to watch and report anything unusual. You, Maggie, were the subject of the most encouraging report. Your emergence and your exceptional mental powers were not entirely unexpected. You see, Earth was seeded in part with sperm from Jeremiah Godde. He is the direct ancestor of all of you.

"Now, what you don't know is that with the exception of Jeremiah Godde, no one developed much in the way of mental abilities until the long-life drugs gave them the time to really work on their powers. Even then, they weren't anywhere close to yours. I worked 2000 years to get to my level, and Maggie, at age 40, you are stronger than I am now. You are exactly what we had hoped would emerge. A young God with great powers. All the Gods hired in the last several thousand years have been at least 2000 years old and therefore had spent years on the long-life drugs."

Xerma leaned back and sighed and said, "And that's the history in a nutshell. Any questions?"

Maggie asked, "What do the long-life drugs actually do?"

"While they do have a positive side, the negative side-effect is that they eventually seem to repress the desire and ability to focus on a job for long periods. We don't exactly know how or when this occurs. The pattern is that after some specified time period, the person stops caring at all about their task and lets things slide. It goes on undetected for some time before it's discovered, and by then, things have gotten bad. Ruth hit that point 50 or 60 years ago, and you know the condition Hell and the Earth were in when you joined up. Heaven's a mess, too. With you, it should be many years before any problem exists and by then, maybe we'll have a solution for the drug's side effects."

"What do you think that I, one person in one little piece of one universe, can do to rectify this?"

"Well, we all have the same optimistic opinion with regard to you. We all do read your concerns and your doubts and your questions, but all of us also read unbelievable concern and tremendous ability in you. And we suspect there is no real limit to your powers. They are still developing, you know. Now, our plan is for you to take my job in 20 to 25 years, and then move up to the next tier, D'Lorn's position, and within 75 to 100 years, that buck will stop with you. If you so choose, we'll substitute Laurie, if she agrees. Also, others on Earth will undoubtedly start emerging over time. We have some other primitives potentially underway but they are at least 1000 years away."

"I'm overwhelmed," Maggie said. "I thought that all I'd have to worry about was stepping into Ruth's shoes, but now I have to wrap my head around so much more that I'm spinning."

"It's you, Maggie. We've been waiting for thousands of years for you to arrive. And right now it's time for a decision."

There was a pause.

"Maggie," I said, "do you understand this better than I do? Are you aware of the implications?"

"Yes, Jack, and I'm ready. This hierarchy is crystal clear to me now, and all of a sudden, I can see where I'm going and what my place is in all this." There was a confidence in Maggie's voice that I had never heard before. She's really going to do this!

Suddenly, a bright light appeared and two more figures emerged. One was a Mrs. Angelo-type, but somewhat older. She walked over to Maggie and stopped in front of her. The other figure, a tall thin male, greeted Xerma warmly.

"How are you, Xerma?"

"Quite well, thank you, D'Lorn. I'm delighted you could join us for this event. I'd like you to meet Maggie."

"I've heard all about you, Maggie. Very nice to finally meet you."

"Yes, I've heard about you, too. My pleasure."

"So, this is the one?" said the female, placing a hand on Maggie's shoulder.

Xerma said, "Yes, this is Maggie and her spouses Jack, Jenny and Hud. I'd like you to meet Vandora."

Hud and I leaped to our feet. I felt a rush, a pit in my stomach, a breathlessness I couldn't explain. Anxiety. Thrill. Maggie said, "I'm pleased to meet you, Vandora," and held out her hand. Vandora shook her hand and then shook hands with the rest of us. She said to Maggie, "I believe you have decided to join us."

"Yes, I believe I can do it. And I need to do it. There is so much unfinished business."

"Good. You start out on the first tier, in Ruth's job. That will be your learning phase. But we do want you in my job as soon as possible."

"I hope I can progress rapidly."

"You'll be fine. If you need me, ask Xerma. I must go now."

She turned to Xerma and said, "Please keep D'Lorn and me informed of Maggie's progress."

And with that, both D'Lorn and Vandora vanished.

AFTERWORD

Up until now, you have heard the story of the Judgment Line through the voice of my husband Jack, so you have primarily his point of view. But I need to leave you today with some thoughts of my own, thoughts that until now have not been made public.

I took the position they offered me, of course. And I have been able to spend uninterrupted and focused time on the problems I have seen and the changes I am considering. While the original Judgment Line as a whole was valid and was a good beginning, it was far too simplistic and not really well thought out, so there still remain some potentially disturbing portions. Omissions. Confusion. Some real puzzles. And it is these problems that I intend to research and to solve before we have another Judgment Line. Yes, I said another.

I must give credit at this point to Diane. She confided her concerns about some of the Judgment Line details to me privately after our last interview aired. Neither of us made them public, of course, but I assured her that I had the same concerns myself. And that conversation gave me the impetus to get the ball rolling. I now have sufficient power and influence to begin the process.

I know you are more than curious about what the future holds. For the present, suffice it to say that the phrase "harm to others", which was the basic premise for the original judgment, will be undergoing some significant modifications. And when I do decide to clarify and expand on the words "harm" and "others," I will do so in sufficient time to allow for you to alter your life style. I will also go back to the Customs and clear up the word "being".

But for now, just keep living a good life. We'll see you at the next Judgment Line.